TRUST NO ONE

Alex Walters was educated in Nottingham and at Cambridge University. After leaving university, he worked in management roles in the oil industry, broadcasting and banking, before moving into management consultancy. Having worked for various global practices, he now runs his own specialist consultancy company, working in the UK and abroad. His consultancy work in recent years has specialized in various aspects of the criminal justice sector, including police, prisons and probation, as well as various public bodies including the UK parliament. He lives in Manchester with his three sons.

ALEX WALTERS

Trust No One

AVON

This novel is entirely a work of fiction.
The names, characters and incidents portrayed in it are
the work of the author's imagination. Any resemblance to
actual persons, living or dead, events or localities is
entirely coincidental.

AVON

A division of HarperCollins*Publishers*
77–85 Fulham Palace Road,
London W6 8JB

www.harpercollins.co.uk

A Paperback Original 2011

1

First published in Great Britain by
HarperCollins*Publishers* 2011

A catalogue record for this book is
available from the British Library

ISBN-13: 978-1-84756-285-2

Set in Minion by Palimpsest Book Production Limited,
Falkirk, Stirlingshire

Printed and bound in Great Britain by
Clays Ltd, St Ives plc

MIX
Paper from
responsible sources
FSC www.fsc.org **FSC® C007454**

Of course, this has to be dedicated to Christine, with thanks for everything. And to James, Adam and Jonny for their continuing love and support.

I'd also like to thank all those, necessarily nameless, who gave me advice and information about various aspects of undercover work. And thanks to Sammia Rafique, my excellent editor at Avon, and to Peter Buckman, as always a wonderful agent and an astute critic.

This has to be for Christine, of course.
For everything.
Au revoir, love, wherever you are.

Prologue

The last time she saw Jake, Marie found herself awake, sometime after midnight, staring into the darkness. She told herself it was because they'd eaten late, because she'd drunk too much wine. Because tonight, after their conversation in the restaurant, after what had been said and not said, their lovemaking had left her restless rather than relaxed. All that was true, but she couldn't fool herself that it was the whole story.

She rolled over in the bed. Jake was asleep, on his back, snoring softly. She was tempted to wake him, caress him, hope that more sex would calm her tense nerves. The logic of the addict. A second impulse, maybe more rational, was simply to slip away, now, in the small hours. Put an end to all this before it was too late.

Jake deserved better. This was her mess, not his. Whatever she did, she had to do right by Jake. She'd sit down and talk to him properly. Tell him what she could. Not the whole truth. Probably not much of the truth. But something. Enough. Enough so he'd understand. One day soon.

She pushed back the duvet and sat up, for a moment enjoying the small-hours chill of the bedroom on her naked body. Beside her, Jake stirred, rolled over, but didn't wake. She eased herself out of bed and reached for the old dressing gown that Jake had loaned her. It was too small to have been Jake's, and she assumed that it had belonged to some past girlfriend. Fair enough. Jake's business.

Moving quietly across the room, she paused to gather up her handbag and the clothes she'd left neatly piled on the chair by the door. There was no point in staying in bed. She'd only toss and turn till she woke Jake, and despite her earlier impulse, that wasn't really what she wanted. She'd do what she often ended up doing these days, here and in her own flat. She'd make herself a hot drink, read a mindless magazine or watch some content-free television, or just sit out on Jake's balcony, listening to the distant ripple of the water and the sounds of the night. Calm herself to the point where she could sleep again.

And if that failed, she told herself, she'd wake Jake and give sex another shot after all.

With a kettle boiling in the kitchen, she dressed quickly, more conscious of the cold now. They'd had a quiet evening – a few drinks in the pub, an Italian, a bottle of wine between them – and her outfit was practical rather than decorative. Jeans, a sweater, smart boots.

She'd never doubted that she'd stay over again tonight. It had been inevitable long before she'd knocked back her first large red. But, as usual, she'd brought no change of clothes, reasoning that she'd have time in the morning to get back to the flat, to shower and change, before she needed to get to the shop. She told herself that it was because she wanted nothing taken for granted – but whether by herself or by Jake, she didn't know.

She made herself a decaff coffee and wandered back through to Jake's neat living room. It was like the man himself – unostentatious, slightly chaotic, primarily functional, but occasionally intriguing. The walls were bare except for two small but expensive-looking pieces of figurative art, sitting incongruously alongside a large signed photograph of the 1974 Leeds United team. Jake was a man with some obvious shallows and many hidden depths, only a few of which she'd so far managed to plumb.

She hovered by the television for a moment, then picked up her leather jacket from Jake's sofa. Returning to the kitchen, she turned off the light, then did the same in the hallway and the living room, plunging the flat back into darkness. Satisfied, she pulled open the large picture window that gave on to the balcony. It was one of the joys of Jake's quayside flat. Her own building looked out over the city, with a distant view of the Pennines and on a sunny day she could glimpse the grey-green hills between the buildings, giving an unexpected sense of space and distance amid the cluttered office blocks. But this was something different again, the kind of view that estate agents measured in the millions – a direct outlook over the heart of the quays and the old ship canal. Off to the right were the modernist lines and angles of the Lowry complex, and over the water the bewitching jumble of the Imperial War Museum. In the foreground to the left, glowing crimson, the imposing monolith of Old Trafford. Beyond all that, there was the mess of industrial buildings that formed Trafford Park. In the daylight, it felt like the ultimate urban landscape, a bustling blend of the old and the new, commerce and leisure. But at night, when the football crowds and concert-goers had disappeared, it was almost peaceful, with the gentle brush of the water against the quayside, the rippling lights across the face of the canal.

She closed the window behind her, and zipping up her jacket, lowered herself on to one of the chairs, adjusting the back so that she could stare up into the starlit sky. The constant glare of Manchester dimmed the spectacle, but it was a clear night and she could make out the scattered patterns of constellations. Beginning to relax for the first time since she'd woken, she closed her eyes, enjoying the moment of peace, imagining herself drifting away on the cool night air. Trying not to think.

Without realizing, she nodded into sleep and when she woke what might have been minutes or hours later, she had a sense that something – some noise, some movement – had invaded her consciousness. She sat up, trying to work out what had disturbed her. It was a half-familiar sensation – as if someone had been hammering at the door or pressing on the bell in the moments before she'd woken.

She glanced at her watch. She'd been asleep only for a few minutes. But something had changed. A light reflected off her watch. She twisted and saw that the hallway was illuminated. Probably Jake had got up to use the bathroom.

She climbed to her feet, preparing to go back inside. Then she stopped.

It took her a moment to work out what she was seeing. Through the picture window, past the living room, in the hallway. The front door half-open. A man standing in the hall, leaning on the frame of the bedroom door. Not Jake. Someone she didn't recognize at all.

There was something about the man's movements, his body language. It wasn't the posture of a house-breaker – not furtive, cautious, on edge. This was different.

The man was a pro. Somehow, even from this distance, with his back half-turned towards her, she had no doubt. A hitman. Fucking wet work. And Jake was the bloody target.

It wasn't entirely a surprise. She knew what Jake had done. She knew the kinds of enemies he must have made. And she knew that, in part, she was responsible.

Her first instinct was to try to intervene. But even as she

was considering her options, the scene changed. The man pushed himself away from the doorframe and stood back. Two more figures appeared, dragging Jake, still naked, between them. Jake was half-resisting, half-falling. He'd been hit already, blood pouring from a cut in his temple, streaming down his pale face.

She moved back slowly, pressing herself against the balcony railing, keeping out of their line of sight as they manhandled Jake into the living room. Three of them. All pros. She could tell. She'd met people in that line of work. They were a type. Cold, calm, methodical to the point of compulsion. Psychopaths who'd found their vocation.

Her handbag, with her mobile inside, was on the floor by the patio chair. She eased herself forwards, moving as silently as possible. Inside the room, the men had thrown Jake on to the couch. He lay, crumpled, his hands clutched to his groin, blood now smeared across his chest. He looked semi-conscious.

She reached the handbag, pulled it to her, and began to fumble inside for her phone.

At that moment, the balcony was flooded with light.

She looked up, startled, momentarily dazzled. The balcony floodlights were operated from a panel of switches alongside the interior lights. One of the men had hit the lights for the living room and inadvertently turned on the external lamps at the same time.

She stood, caught in the high beam, conscious that at any moment one of the men might look in her direction. There was no time.

She backed to the balcony railing. It was only the second floor. She paused, trying to envisage the layout of the apartment block. There was another identical balcony immediately below. If she could reach that, it ought to be feasible to lower herself further and drop to the ground below. It was possible, she thought. She hoped.

Throwing the handbag around her neck, she hoisted herself up on to the railing. As she did so, one of the men looked up, his attention caught by her movement in his peripheral vision. She heard him shout something, but didn't wait to find out what.

She hung for a moment on the outside of the railing, then began to slide down, her feet desperately flailing for the top of the railing below. A drainpipe running down between the two floors gave another half-handhold, but she could barely cling on. Above, she could hear the window being dragged back.

She found her footing on the lower railing, paused for a breath, and then, clinging helplessly to the drainpipe, half-dropped, half-slid down again, her hands clutching for the top of the railing where her feet had been resting a moment before. She grasped it, and her fingers sliding agonizingly down the metal rails, lowered herself to the bottom of the lower balcony. From above, she could hear whispering voices, but could make out no words.

Hanging from the lower balcony, she twisted her neck to look down. Her feet were perhaps four or five feet above the ground. She realized with relief that she was hanging above one of the decorative flower beds that surrounded the building; a softer landing than the concrete that stretched away elsewhere.

She released her grip and dropped, landing and slipping awkwardly on the soft earth. She was momentarily winded, but was up and running almost immediately. Her car was parked on the street at the rear of the building. Even if the men had set off immediately, she should reach it before they could.

She pounded hard along the pathway, thanking Christ that she was wearing her low winter boots. Even so, she almost lost her footing on the slick paved surface as she turned the corner.

Her little Toyota was a hundred yards or so ahead, tucked into a row of other parked cars. She had her handbag open as she ran, struggling to find her keys. She glanced over her shoulder. The main doors of the apartment block were open. One of the men was peering out, maybe three or four hundred yards behind her.

She reached the car and pulled out the keys at more or less the same moment, thumbing open the central locking. Then she was in and starting the engine.

She looked in the rear-view mirror as the engine roared into life. As she pulled out into the road, she could see the man, still a long way behind. He'd halted in the doorway, aware that there was no point now in trying to pursue her.

She kept her foot down as she headed along the quays, the roads empty at this time of the night, passing between the lines of silent shops, restaurants, hotels, offices. The lights out on to Trafford Road were on red, but she didn't slow, hoping to Christ that no late-night patrol car was lurking nearby. Moments later, still with no other traffic around, she reached the roundabout and took a sharp left, her foot hard to the floor.

Once she was on the motorway, she finally relaxed enough to look in the mirror. There were no cars behind her. Breathing more slowly now, she pulled off at the next junction, taking a right and following the road round until she saw the massive complex of Salford Royal Hospital on her right. A good place to stop, she thought. In a hospital, people would be coming and going at all hours of the night. Her car wouldn't be conspicuous.

She took another right and entered the hospital grounds, following the signs to one of the visitors' car parks, pulling in among a small scattering of other cars. She paused for a moment to gather her wits, the panic finally subsiding, then dug out her mobile. She couldn't use the formal channels, couldn't reveal that she'd been in Jake's flat. She dialled 999 and gave a false name, reporting a break-in and serious assault at Jake's address. Her number was withheld, so there'd be no clue to her identity showing up on the operator's caller ID. She answered the questions as briefly as she could, trying to give nothing away. No, she didn't know what was happening, she was just a passer-by, didn't want to get involved. Then, feeling guilty at her own impotence, she ended the call.

It was all she could have done, but she felt no confidence that her call had been taken seriously. Then somewhere behind, in the heart of the city, she heard the rising wail of a police siren. Maybe they were already answering the call. Maybe.

She could feel her training kicking in, leading her through the ramifications of all this. Someone had taken out a contract on Jake. She could easily guess why and probably even who. But the real question was how. How had they known? And where did that leave her?

She tracked back through her movements of the previous evening, working out whether she'd left any sign of her presence, anything that would allow her to be identified. She'd taken her clothes, her bag, her mobile. There was nothing else, other than her DNA. No one was likely to make the link, unless she'd already been compromised.

The other question was whether the man had seen her car registration. She thought not. It was dark, she was pulling out from between parked cars, he was a long way away. But she couldn't be sure. If he had, she was a dead woman already.

Shit. The professional part of her mind was grinding through its dispassionate gears. But the other part of her brain was silently screaming. Jake. Jake lying naked, crouched at the feet of three professional fucking assassins. Jake with blood already pouring from him. Jake, her lover only hours before. Jake.

It was possible she'd frightened them off. They might have left the job unfinished. The police might have turned up in time. Any fucking thing might have happened.

But it wouldn't have. She knew that. They were pros. They always finished the job. They didn't leave witnesses. They got what they wanted.

And they'd got Jake.

PART ONE

Summer: Preparation

1

She was looking for her car when she noticed the moving van on the far side of the car park. Going too fast, Marie thought. Not just exceeding the notional speed limit – most drivers here did that – but hitting thirty, forty miles per hour. Open road speeds, in an unlit airport car park littered with jet-lagged arrivals from the long-haul red-eyes. Jesus.

Not her business, though. There'd been a time when she might have felt obliged to intervene, pull out her warrant card to deal with some loser getting his kicks scaring others. But not now.

God, she was tired. Tired and woozy. Not exactly jet lag. She hadn't got her sleep patterns together long enough for it to kick in, or at least that was how it felt. Two days in Washington had been a stupid idea. A knackering interruption to her training, not the relaxing jolly that had been sold to her. She could see why none of the others had wanted to go. She'd learned nothing, met no one of any value. Just a dreary round of mind-numbing presentations, tedious seminars, formal dinners, late-night sessions in the bar, fending off the advances of drunken marrieds who assumed, naturally, that their drawling American accents would be irresistible to any Brit.

It felt as if she'd had no sleep for days. She'd expected to be out cold on the return flight, but she'd slept fitfully, disturbed by the comings and goings of the flight attendants and the noisy family next to her.

She felt semi-conscious. She'd already alighted from the shuttle bus at the wrong stop and was having to trawl through the rows of vehicles, dragging her wheeled suitcase behind her, to wherever her own car was parked.

She'd planned to go back into work today, but that increasingly seemed like a bad idea. Everyone expected her to take the day off, anyway. All she wanted to do was head home and crawl into bed. Liam would be pleased, at least.

From somewhere close by, she heard the roar of an engine. That bloody van. It had reached the end of her row and was turning left, down towards where she was standing, its speed undiminished.

Instinctively, she stepped back, pulling her case with her, positioning herself between two parked cars. Joyriders, maybe, or some drunk. Either way, best avoided.

She moved back into the shadows, expecting the van to roar by. But just before it reached her, the driver braked hard. For a second, she thought the vehicle would skid, but the control was perfect. The van slammed to a halt just a few feet from her.

The driver's door opened slowly and a figure, little more than a silhouette, leaned out. 'In the back,' the man said quietly. It was a command, and the object in his hand suggested he had the means of enforcing it.

What the fuck? She looked frantically around her. Moments before, as she'd watched the van careering round the edge of the car park, there'd seemed to be numerous other people making their way back to their cars. Now, suddenly, the place was deserted. Somewhere, across at the far edge of the car park, she could hear the churning of a car ignition, but that was no help to her.

'In the back,' the voice said again.

She stepped forwards, as though to obey, leaving her case and handbag on the ground behind her. Then, as she drew close to the van, she raised her right foot and kicked the driver's door as hard as she could. It slammed shut, trapping the arm of the half-emerging figure.

'Shit—'

She was already running, her head down, expecting gunfire at any moment. Instead, she heard the revving of the van's engine and a squeak of tyres as it U-turned.

Where the hell was her car? In the half-light, all the vehicles looked similar, indistinguishable colours and shapes.

And then a further thought struck her.

Her keys. Her fucking keys. They were in her handbag.

She was running headlong now, with no idea what she was going to do. There was no point in trying to reach her car. Her only hope was that someone else would appear, someone who could help her.

She could hear the van's engine coming up behind her. No longer speeding, but moving slowly, taunting her, knowing she couldn't escape. There was nowhere to go. A high metal fence lined the car park perimeter. The entrance was half a mile away across the vast expanse of tarmac.

She stopped and turned, blinking in the van's headlights until it pulled in alongside her. A head peered out from the passenger seat, the face invisible. A different voice.

'Christ's sake. You're going nowhere. Just get in the back.'

She heard the sound of the driver's door being opened, footsteps. She stood silently, gasping for breath, as a silhouetted figure emerged from behind the vehicle. He gestured her to step forwards, a pistol steady in his other hand.

'Nice try. Hurt my bloody hand, though. Now don't open your mouth; just get in the back.'

After only a moment's hesitation, she obeyed both instructions.

'And you're sure you still want to go ahead?' Winsor had asked, two months before.

'Yes,' Marie had replied confidently. Then, after a pause, 'I think so, anyway. As best I can judge.'

He'd nodded approvingly and inscribed an ostentatious tick on the sheet in front of him. 'Exactly the right answer,' he said, a proud teacher commending a promising pupil. 'Confident, but realistic. Just what we need.'

Patronizing git, she thought. Par for the course down here. She could live with it from the operational types. They might have been promoted to pen-pushing and desk-jockeying, but most had been through it. They had some idea of the front line.

Winsor was a different matter. He was a sodding psychologist, for Christ's sake. Most of what he said was either blindingly obvious or plain wrong. Quite often both at once, remarkably. He was here on sufferance because they were supposed to give due consideration to the psychological well-being of officers. Winsor ticked a few boxes and showed that the Agency cared.

And yet here he was, passing judgement about her suitability for a job he probably couldn't even imagine. Assessing her psychological equilibrium, she'd been told. Seeing whether she was really up to it, whether she could handle the unique pressures. In truth, though she doubted Winsor's ability to assess her mental state, she knew the assessment was needed. This was a big deal. She wasn't sure, even now, whether she really appreciated quite how big.

'The main thing,' Winsor said, unexpectedly echoing her thoughts, 'is that you appreciate the magnitude of the challenge.'

Maybe he was better at this than she'd thought. 'I've spoken to people who've done the job,' she said. 'Hugh Salter, for example.'

'Ah, yes. Hugh.' He spoke the name as if experimenting with an unfamiliar word. 'Well, yes, Hugh was a great success in the role. For a long time.' He left the phrase hanging, suggesting that he could say more.

She knew that Hugh had been withdrawn from the field eventually, but that was standard. No one did this forever. There'd been rumours about Hugh, but there were rumours about everyone. It was that kind of place. Whatever the truth, Hugh was still around, still apparently trusted. If she got through this, he was likely to end up as her contact. Her buddy, in his words, though that wasn't how she'd ever describe him.

'What did Hugh tell you?' Winsor asked.

'He said it was a challenge. Hard work. That it required certain qualities.' She tried to recall exactly what Hugh had said. Nothing very coherent. She'd sought him out one evening when a group of them had been in the pub after work. Show willing, prepare for the selection process. But Hugh was already two or three pints ahead of her, and had mainly been interested in boosting his own ego. He was keen to let her know how difficult the job had been, how ill-suited she was likely to be to its rigours. Not because she was a woman, he'd been at pains to emphasize. That wasn't the problem. The problem, she'd gathered, was that, like almost everyone else in the world, she just wasn't Hugh Salter. Her loss.

'What sort of qualities?'

'Resilience,' she said, though Hugh had offered nothing so succinct. 'Attention to detail. Alertness.' She paused, recognizing that she was trotting out clichés. 'He said the main problem was the balancing act.' She paused, trying to translate her memory of Salter's semi-drunken ramble into something coherent. 'Not just the obvious tension between the under-cover work and your home life. But the balance between the day-to-day stuff and the real focus of the work.'

Winsor looked up, showing some interest for the first time. 'Go on.'

She paused, unsure how to render the phrase 'fucking balls-ache' in terminology acceptable to an occupational psychologist.

'Well, it strikes me that it's almost as if you're leading a triple life. You spend a lot of the time building up the legend, making yourself credible in the right environments. Just getting on with the fictitious job. The real stuff – the intelligence gathering, the surveillance, all that – is only a small part of the picture, time-wise. So you end up doing a lot of stuff which is very mundane, but you can't allow yourself to switch off, even for a moment.' It wasn't exactly – or even remotely – what Salter had actually said, but it was what she'd inferred from his beer-fuelled diatribe.

Winsor was nodding. 'Absolutely,' he said. 'That's what most applicants fail to appreciate.' He leaned forwards, as though sharing a treasured secret. 'That's one reason it's so difficult to find suitable candidates. It's not a question of ability. It's a question of temperament.' He waved his hand towards the open-plan office outside their small meeting room. 'Not surprising, really. It's a rare mix that we're looking for, and probably even rarer in a place like this. You lot want excite-ment, the adrenaline rush. That's why you all hate the form-filling.'

Winsor was wrong about that, she thought. It might be what attracted some of them in the first place, but the ones who stayed, the ones who progressed, were those who paid attention to the detail. That was what the job was about.

Gathering data, analyzing the intelligence. The fucking balls-ache. Most likely, Winsor was the one hankering after excitement.

'So what do you think the job needs?' she said.

He riffled aimlessly through her file, as if that might provide the answer to her question. 'As you say, a lot of it's very mundane. We set it up, provide the background. But it's up to the individual officer to make it work. And all the time you're waiting for the opportunities, the chances to gather intelligence.' He paused. 'Most good officers can handle the pressure. It's the boredom that does for them.'

She wondered whether he was talking about Salter. 'So what do you reckon?' she said, deciding she might as well cut to the chase. 'Have I got the temperament?'

He didn't answer immediately, but flicked again through the file, this time apparently searching for a particular document. She had no idea what was in the thick, buff-coloured folder. Her original application form. Annual performance appraisals. Results of her promotion boards. Perhaps other, more interesting material.

'I think you just might,' he said finally. 'Have a look at this.'

He pushed the file across the desk towards her, holding it open. It was a printed form, incomprehensible to her, covered with Winsor's own scrawlings.

'It's the results of the personality questionnaire you completed,' he explained. 'Each of these lines shows a continuum between the extremes of various personality traits. So, for example, whether you're inclined to follow prescribed rules or do your own thing.'

'Wouldn't that depend on the rules?'

'Yes, of course. And the context. But we've all got our preferences and inclinations. At the extremes, you get people who feel hidebound by any rules or direction, however reasonable, or people who feel uncomfortable breaking or bending a rule even when they recognize that it's necessary.'

'And where do I sit?'

He pointed at a pencil mark on one of the scales. 'In that respect – as in most aspects, actually – you're pretty well-balanced. Close to the middle of the scale, with just a small bias towards rule-breaking.' He smiled, suggesting that this was some kind of psychologist's in-joke.

'And is that good?'

He shrugged. 'As you say, it depends. But in this case, yes. That's the balance we're looking for. We don't want someone who's constantly in danger of going off-piste. But equally there'd be times when you'd need to improvise. We don't want someone who'll fall apart if they can't apply the rule book.'

She nodded, her eyes scanning down the sheet in front of her. She could see broadly how the scales worked, but the terminology was opaque to her. 'What about the rest of it?'

'We've got a full debrief scheduled for this afternoon,' he said. Marie decided that Winsor himself was probably rather closer to the compliant end of the spectrum. 'I'll go through it all in detail then. But on the whole it looks very satisfactory. You're a pretty balanced individual.' He picked up his pen and gestured down the column of scales. 'Here, for example. You're fairly affiliative, enjoy working with others. But equally you're comfortable operating on your own when you need to. This is a role that depends on effective networking, building relationships, but you will also really have to work in isolation. Not many people are comfortable with both.'

'No, I can see that.' She squinted more closely at the paper. 'What about these ones? Those look more extreme.'

Winsor leaned forwards, reading the form upside down. 'Ah, now, that's quite interesting. Those traits show how you deal with your emotions. Would you consider yourself an emotional person?'

She found herself slightly taken aback by the direct question. 'I don't know. Not particularly, I suppose. I suppose I'd see myself as – I don't know – pragmatic. I just get on with things.'

It was difficult for her to answer the question. None of her colleagues would see her as emotional, she thought. But that was a point of principle. Whatever they might say publicly, some of her colleagues still held largely unreconstructed views of female officers. When she'd first joined, she'd been determined not to allow her femininity to be perceived, however unfairly, as a weakness. Whatever crap had been thrown at her – and there'd been plenty in those early days – she'd been determined just to take it. If she had a bad day she never let it show. That was nothing more than simple professionalism. It was what you did. Whatever might be going on outside of work, you didn't bring it through the office door. It was a philosophy that many of her colleagues, male and female, failed to apply. She'd had a bellyful of supposedly macho senior officers who came in and simply unloaded the garbage that happened to be filling their own domestic lives.

But Marie found it hard to distinguish between this work persona and whatever reality might lie beneath. She never showed any strong emotions and, to be frank, she rarely seemed to feel them. Of course, like anyone else, she went through cycles of joy or gloom, she had good days and bad days. But these were variations around a relatively placid norm. When real adversity came around – when she and Liam had being going through a tough time, or when her parents had died, not entirely unexpectedly, within a few months of one another – she simply buckled down and got on with life. In other circumstances, she reflected, a psychologist like

Winsor might see that as unhealthy. Now, he seemed positively enthused by the assessment.

'If we look at these scales, you see, you come across as someone who keeps their emotions carefully in check. You're very conscious of the image you project to others. Your inclination is to subordinate your own feelings to the job at hand.'

He was beginning to sound like a tabloid horoscope, she thought. 'Those don't necessarily sound like positive qualities.'

'Well, again, it depends on the context. And if your responses were at the very extreme end of the scale, I'd have a concern. It might suggest an inability to cope with emotional issues. But this indicates simply a preference for control. Which in this role is important. It's a very isolating job. If you're faced with emotional issues, you have to be able to cope with them yourself. Of course, we keep an eye on agents out in the field, assess their well-being periodically. But we can't provide too much support from the centre without risking compromising the operation.'

'And you think I'd be up to it?' She gestured towards the assessment form. 'On the basis of that, I mean?'

'Well, it's impossible to be sure.' He reached across and picked up the file. 'It's a fairly blunt instrument, this. And it can't give us a definitive insight into the "real" Marie Donovan, whoever that might be. What it really tells us is how you see yourself and how you think others see you. But, for all that, I think, yes, that overall it does indicate that you're likely to be suited to the job.'

Well, that was something, she thought. A fairly lukewarm endorsement, but an endorsement nonetheless. One hurdle climbed.

Winsor was still leafing aimlessly through her file. Finally, he paused and ran his finger carefully down one of the documents.

'You're unmarried?'

She nodded. 'So far.' This had been typical of Winsor's style. Off-the-cuff, apparently random questions, but each one with a little hidden barb.

'But you have a partner?'

She knew he already had the answer. When she'd joined the Agency, Liam's background had been checked out as thoroughly as hers. A clause in her employment contract obliged her to inform her superiors if her domestic circumstances were to change. The way things were going with Liam, that clause might become relevant before long.

'I live with my boyfriend,' she said, 'if that's what you mean.'

'And how does he feel about you applying for this role?'

That was the question, of course. How did Liam feel?

'Well, he's got concerns, of course. But he's fully behind my career. If it's what I want to do, he'll support it.' Which was all true as far as it went.

'And your boyfriend,' Winsor said conversationally, 'what does he do? His job, I mean.'

'He paints. He's an artist.'

'Ah.' Winsor managed to invest a wealth of meaning into the single syllable. 'Would I recognize his name?'

She smiled. 'I don't think so. Not yet.'

'Well, perhaps one day.' Winsor looked at his watch, as if he were already losing interest. 'And what about you?'

'Me?' She wondered momentarily whether he was enquiring about her own artistic prospects.

'Yes.' Winsor was beginning to pack up his papers. 'Why do you want the job? What made you apply for it?'

Another good question. She'd had an answer all prepared – opportunity for career development, new challenges, a desire to step outside her own comfort zone, all that kind of nonsense. But Winsor's nonchalant query had, presumably as intended, caught her off guard and she found herself blurting out something closer to the truth.

'I don't know. I suppose I feel in a bit of a rut. A bit passive. Time's getting on. The big three-oh next year. I just want something new. I want to take more control.'

He was barely looking at her, struggling to fit the stack of files into his briefcase. 'At work or at home? The rut, I mean?'

She paused, aware now that she was saying more than she'd intended. 'Work, I suppose. I've spent the last year doing intelligence analysis. Crunching data. Spotting patterns. It's important work and I'm pretty good at it, though I say so myself. But I don't think it's making the most of my talents. I want a bit more control over what's going on. I want to make things happen.'

He finally snapped shut his briefcase and looked up, his expression suggesting that he'd taken in nothing of what she'd been saying.

'Well, yes,' he said. 'Always good to take control. That's very interesting. As I said at the start, this session isn't really part of the formal interview process. I just like to have an informal discussion with candidates before I put together the detailed feedback on the psychometrics. Gives me a bit of context.'

And if you believe that, you'll believe anything, Marie told herself. Winsor had protested just a little too much about the unimportance of their conversation. She hoped she'd struck the right balance – alert enough not to let anything slip, but not so tense that she seemed phony.

The whole thing had been like that. Two days of interviews and exercises. A traditional selection panel with four stern-faced senior officers asking a series of apparently random questions. A series of role-playing exercises, supposedly with other candidates, that had left her feeling slightly wrong-footed. She'd suspected from the start that not all the participants were genuine candidates. Some of them would be plants, there to observe or to throw additional spokes into the wheel. Or perhaps that was just paranoia. Either way, it felt like appropriate preparation for whatever this job might throw at her.

'As I say, I'll be giving you some formal feedback on the psychometrics this afternoon. After that, you're free to leave. And we'll be getting our heads together to make the decision. We should be able to let you know tomorrow.'

'But you really think I'm in with a chance?'

Winsor looked momentarily embarrassed. 'Well, I'm not in a position to say for sure. Obviously, it'll be a collective decision. But, yes, on the basis of what I've seen, I think you've a very good chance.'

There was an expression in his eyes that she couldn't read. As if, she thought, he couldn't be sure whether or not he was giving her good news.

There was a bright light shining in her eyes, and she could make out no more than the outline of the man sitting opposite. So they weren't afraid of clichés, she thought. An interrogation scene from an old war movie. We have ways of making you talk, Britisher.

It had been a surreal experience. At the airport, with the pistol held against her, she'd climbed into the back of the van. It had clearly been prepared to accommodate passengers, although the rear compartment was enclosed and windowless. There was a row of seats bolted to the chassis, and an interior light. All the home comforts you'd need if you were being kidnapped at the crack of dawn by a bunch of apparent lunatics. Behind her, she'd heard the sound of the rear doors being locked.

Her initial, instinctive reaction had been panic. That was

why she'd tried to run, unthinking, her mind still fogged by lack of sleep. It was only when she'd seen the pistol pointing unwaveringly at her that she'd realized the truth.

It was a test, of course. A fucking exercise. Part of the training. If she'd been more awake, she might have expected it. Even the trip to Washington had probably been part of it. She'd seen it as an odd intrusion into her supposedly sacrosanct training schedule, and wondered why they'd been so keen for her to attend. The conference itself was genuine enough, of course. In fact, that was just bloody typical. The Yanks were keen to have a Brit there and had apparently funded her travel and expenses. The Agency had been its usual opportunistic self, killing two birds with one bloody great transatlantic rock.

The aim had been to destabilize her, presumably. She'd spent the last two months in character, preparing in a controlled environment for the experience of going undercover. They were giving her an identify, a legend, that would enable her to blend unobtrusively into the local business community, building on the reputation established by her predecessor in the area. Their key targets were themselves local businessmen, running criminal networks in the shadow of apparently legitimate commercial operations. The plan was for her to work in the same shadowy hinterland.

She had become Marie Donovan, businesswoman, and had been coming to grips with the financial and legal implications of the mundane printing and reprographics franchise that she'd be taking over. She'd had dealings with the bank, with the solicitors, with the franchise owners. The ground had been prepared for her, but then she'd been on her own, a new starter still finding her feet. The business people she was dealing with no doubt thought she was an idiot, a would-be entrepreneur without a clue. But, from their responses, she guessed that they'd encountered such characters many times before: deluded halfwits who wanted to stick their life savings or redundancy pay in some ridiculous business fantasy. It was no real skin off their nose whether she succeeded or failed, so long as she had the necessary funding today.

But after the first stumbles, it hadn't been too bad. She'd been surprised how quickly she got into character. She'd also been surprised at how quickly she'd begun to enjoy it. It was a new challenge, a new way of thinking. A whole new life.

That was why she'd been annoyed and bemused when they'd dragged her out of her preparations to attend that bloody conference. A last chance to be yourself, they'd said. Enjoy it. Right.

And now, after two days of being herself, they'd sprung this on her. She didn't even know what game she was supposed to be playing. Presumably she was back in character, back to being Marie Donovan, tinpot entrepreneur. But if so, who were these jokers supposed to be?

'We know who you are, Donovan,' the figure behind the light said softly. 'We know what you are.'

She knew she had to behave just like the fictional Marie Donovan would behave in these circumstances. Except of course that the fictional Marie Donovan, if she were real, would never find herself in these circumstances.

But how would she respond? Fear, of course, and bewilderment. But also anger. Donovan – the businesswoman Donovan – was as feisty as the real one, accustomed to battling her way through a man's world. Even with a pistol being waved at her, she wouldn't take any crap.

'What the hell is this?' she snapped. 'Who are you people? You can't just drag people off the street—'

'We know what you are,' the voice said again. 'We know what your game is.'

'I don't know what the bloody hell you're talking about. How do you know my name?' She allowed a small tremble to creep into her voice during the last sentence. Donovan might be feisty, but she'd still be terrified in this scenario, however much she might try to hide it.

The man behind the light was leafing through a sheaf of documents. She leaned forwards, peering, trying to see what he was doing, who he was. They'd blindfolded her when they'd taken her out of the van, and she'd seen nothing till the light had been shone into her face. She wondered whether she might recognize the voice. A colleague? Someone from the training team? She estimated that the van had driven for maybe fifteen or twenty minutes, but she had no idea where they were, and she'd seen nothing that would give her any clues.

'Just moving into the area,' the man said. 'Taking over a print franchise. Making your way in the world. What's the story, then, love? Getting over a messy break-up, want a new start?'

'Something like that,' she said. 'Though I don't know what business it is of yours, or why you've been snooping into my private life. Who the fuck are you?'

This was more or less the legend that had been established for her. She'd split up with a partner down south, pretty acrimoniously, and was trying to start afresh up here.

'Never mind me, love. More to the point, who the fuck are you? Who is Marie fucking Donovan?'

'I haven't a clue what you're talking about.'

'Haven't you, love? Where've you been for the last couple of days?'

She hesitated, working through the implications of this. She'd been given no brief about how to play the American trip in relation to her supposed cover story. She hadn't envisaged any overlap between the two. So the smart bastards were putting her on the spot. They'd set her up beautifully to trip over her own feet.

'What business is it of yours?'

'Just got back on the 7.05 arrival from Washington DC,' the man said. 'We watched you walk into the arrivals hall. Nice luggage.' He made the last phrase sound mildly salacious.

'You've been fucking following me?'

'Question is,' the man went on, 'what were you doing taking time out, right in the middle of setting up this new business of yours? And why Washington?'

'Who the hell are you?' she said. 'The provisional wing of the local enterprise agency? What's this all about?'

'Thing is,' the man said, 'we're not sure you're what you seem to be. We're not sure your little story hangs together.'

'What little story?'

'This little tale of splitting up with your partner, making a clean break. All that bollocks.'

She began to rise to her feet. 'I don't know what you want. But you can't just keep me here.'

'We can do what we like, love, until we find out a bit more about you. We get nervous about people coming into our territory, you see.'

'Your territory?' she said. 'What is this? The Wild fucking West? I'm buying a printing franchise, for Christ's sake.'

'So you say. It's just that we've got an interest in that business of yours. It has a bit of history.'

She felt a sudden unease. The print franchise was an established business, used by a previous officer operating in the same area. She'd queried whether this was good practice, whether there was any risk that her predecessor had been compromised. She'd been told that, on the contrary, it made life easier. Simpler to take over an established business than to build one from scratch. And, far from being compromised, her predecessor had credibility as a wheeler-dealer who could supply goods – vehicles, people, documents – that others couldn't. He'd been withdrawn from the field only because he was suffering from health problems. A recently-diagnosed heart condition, she'd been told. She was beginning to understand why that might be a problem in this line of work.

The story they'd put about was that he was taking early retirement, and that Marie was an associate in the same line of illegal business. That she was buying into more than just the print shop. All it needed was for her predecessor to effect a few introductions to the right people and she'd be off and running.

Shit, she thought. Maybe this wasn't an exercise after all. Maybe it was for real.

If so, she couldn't imagine that this was just their way of making the introductions, short-circuiting the usual social niceties by bundling her into the back of a sodding van. If this was for real, they'd already sussed out who she was. And that meant that she wasn't likely to leave this place alive.

Jesus, what was she thinking? Of course it was just an exercise. She was allowing them to play with her head. This was another of Winsor's fucking tests. Physical assault, threat, psychological torture. Let's see how she copes with that little lot.

'What history?' she said. 'What are you talking about?'

The man suddenly leaned forward, his features finally becoming visible to her. He was no one she recognized.

'Don't you understand, love? We know who you are. We know who you work for. Do you get it now, bitch?'

There was a venom in the final word that shocked her. Christ, she thought. I was right. It's not a fucking exercise. She began to push herself to her feet, her mind racing.

'I don't—'

The man pushed the table violently against her, knocking her back into the seat. 'Sit down.' He leaned towards her, the pistol back in his hand. He was tapping the barrel gently against the tabletop as if he didn't quite know what to do with the weapon. 'You're going nowhere. You're going to tell me all about your undercover work. You're going to tell me who else is undercover. You're going to tell me who's a grass. You're going to tell me every fucking thing I want to know.'

'Look, I really don't—'

'Know what I'm talking about. Change the record, love.'

She took a deep breath. She would say nothing. She thought – she hoped – that she'd have said nothing even if she believed that it might help secure her release. But these people weren't going to release her. Not if they believed she was an undercover officer. Not now she'd seen this man's face. She could feel herself on the verge of breaking down, but she wasn't going to give them the satisfaction of seeing that.

'I don't know who you think I am,' she said, struggling to keep her voice steady. 'But you've got the wrong woman. I haven't a clue what you're talking about.'

The man smiled and shook his head. 'You've got bottle, I'll give you that, darling. But you'll talk in the end. You'd be surprised how persuasive we can be when we put our minds to it.'

As he spoke, she silently eased her chair back a few inches, giving herself room to move her legs. Then, suddenly, she thrust the chair back further and kicked out with both feet at the edge of the table, driving it back into the man's groin. Immediately, she was on her feet, trying to force her way past him to the door.

It almost worked. Her aim had been perfect. The man doubled forwards in pain, momentarily losing his grip on the

31

gun. She'd been unsure if there was anyone else standing behind him in the darkness, but there were only the two of them in the room. She was past him and already reaching for the door when he grabbed her wrist, pulling her savagely back round towards him.

'Stop it, you stupid bitch.' He grabbed her throat and forced her back hard against the wall. She was reaching for his face, trying desperately to claw at his eyes.

Behind them, she heard the sound of the door opening, and she knew that any chance she might have had was gone.

'OK, Josh. That's enough. I think we've seen what we needed to see.'

The man – Josh – loosened his grip, and she stared, baffled, at the figure standing in the doorway.

'Not bad, sis. You did good.'

'What the fuck, Hugh?'

Salter. Hugh fucking Salter. Grinning at the terror on her face and Josh's testicular agonies. Not that she was wasting any sympathy on Josh, whoever the hell he might turn out to be. From the look on Josh's face, the feeling was largely mutual.

'Thought you'd got us sussed at first, sis. Thought you'd rumbled it was just a training exercise.'

'I had. But your friend Josh there was just too convincing as a macho sexist bastard.'

'Ah, well,' Salter said. 'He's bloody good is our Josh. Mind you, he'll need to keep his balls on ice for a few days. That's quite a kick you've got there.'

Josh was still glaring at her. 'Just fuck right off,' he said. She assumed, perhaps over-charitably, that the words were aimed at Salter.

'Bit of risk goes with the territory, mate,' Salter said, still beaming. 'Especially when you tangle with Marie Donovan, undercover officer.'

It was the closest Salter would ever come to acknowledging her success. But it was close enough for her.

'What's this all about, Hugh?' she said.

'Training exercise, like I say. Which you came through with flying colours. Sorry if Josh went a bit over the top, but we had to get to the point where you'd start to think it might be real. Up to that point – well, it was useful, because at least it showed us you could stay in character . . .'

'Even at the crack of dawn after two days of just being myself?'

'Quite so. And you did it well, but there was no real pressure. Not till Josh managed to get you questioning whether it might be real after all. Then we saw what you were made of. Josh in particular, I think.'

'Christ, you don't do things by halves, do you?'

'Can't afford to, sis. Look, this is what it's going to be like. I mean, not like this – let's hope not, anyway. But having to keep up the act even if you're being challenged, even if you're scared out of your wits. Having to improvise when things don't go to plan. Having to remember which lies you've told and to whom.'

'Jesus, Hugh, anyone suggested you get a job in sales?'

'They like people who tell the truth, do they? But you'll be all right, sis. If you can get through this lot, you'll cope with anything the job can throw at you.'

'I hope you're right, Hugh. Because it doesn't feel that way just at the moment.'

'You did good, girl,' Salter said again.

'Well, thank you, Hugh.' She turned and nodded to Josh. 'And thank you, too, I suppose. You make a very convincing total bastard.'

She moved towards the door, wanting now just to be out

of there, to be heading home. To be sleeping. The adrenaline had melted away, and she felt as exhausted as she had back at the airport. As she pulled open the door, she paused to look back at Salter.

'In fact, you both do,' she said. 'You both make very convincing total bastards.'

Liam waved the bottle in her direction. 'Want any more?'

'No. You finish it. I've had enough.' She drained the last dregs of the red wine, and climbed slowly to her feet. 'I'm knackered,' she said. 'Think I'll turn in.'

He poured the last of the wine into his own glass. 'What time you off in the morning?'

'Not too early. About eight, probably.'

'We can have breakfast together before you go, then.'

'If you're up.' She immediately regretted the response, which sounded more sarcastic than she'd intended.

'I'll be up,' he said. 'Want to see you before you go. One last time.'

'It's not forever, Liam. A month. Then I'm back.'

'For a weekend. Then you're off again. And so on. Maybe forever.'

She bit back her exasperation. 'We've been through this, Liam. Dozens of times. It's what I want to do. It's a new challenge. It's terrific experience.'

'I know. I know it's what you want. I'm not trying to stop you. I don't have to like it, though.'

'No, well, you've made it very clear that you don't.'

'You've said yourself, Marie. It's risky. We're having to live apart. You can't expect me to like that. Or pretend to like it.'

She nodded. 'OK. It's not going to be easy. But we'll get through it. They won't let me stay out in the field for too long. No one does. A year. Eighteen months, max.'

'Almost there already, then,' he said. The tone was ironic, but he was smiling now at least.

'Come to bed,' she said. 'It's our last night. We ought to make it worthwhile.'

'OK,' he said. 'Five minutes. I'll just finish the wine.'

'Don't drink too much. I don't want you incapable,' she half-joked. 'How are you feeling now, anyway?'

He shrugged. 'Not so bad. Tired. Aching a bit. But I've been feeling better lately. Not so difficult walking.'

She looked at him, wondering what was going on in his mind. Whether he was really feeling better or just trying to make the best of things. Since he'd received the diagnosis, he'd become harder to read, more withdrawn. When she tried to talk about it, he just shrugged it off. There was nothing to say, he insisted. Maybe it would be all right, maybe it wouldn't. All he could do was take each day as it came.

'OK,' she said. 'But you don't want me falling asleep on you.'

'Certainly don't.' He raised the wine glass in her direction. 'Here's to you, Marie. Here's to us. Here's to the future.'

He sounded very slightly drunk, she thought. And there was no way to tell whether he was being sincere. 'Yeah,' she said. 'To me. To us. To the future.'

PART TWO

Winter: Operational

2

They'd thrown open the large picture windows and a chill wind was gusting off the canal through the apartment, but the stench of blood was unavoidable. The young officer, Hodder, stood hesitantly in the kitchen doorway, trying to catch Salter's eye. He looked faintly bilious.

After a moment, Salter thumbed off the mobile phone and looked up. 'All OK, son?' There was only a few years' difference in their ages, but Salter categorized most colleagues as 'son', 'mate' or 'guv', depending on their relative rank. He was a tall angular man, his head shaved, his eyes staring disapprovingly at the world through narrow steel-rimmed glasses.

'Didn't want to interrupt,' Hodder said. He gestured towards the phone. 'Your sister?'

Salter stared at him, uncomprehending, then laughed. 'No, just my little joke. One of our esteemed colleagues, Marie Donovan.'

'Don't know her.'

'You wouldn't,' Salter said. 'Covert. Deep cover.'

Hodder shook his head. 'Don't know how they do it,' he said. 'Months on end. Leading a double life. Must drive you bananas.'

Salter smiled. 'It does, son. Take it from one who knows.'

Hodder blinked, suspecting he'd made a gaffe. 'No offence. Didn't realize you'd done it.'

'Years of it. And, yes, it can leave you pretty messed up.' He gazed impassively back at Hodder, as if daring him to take the conversation further. 'How are things through there?'

'They're nearly done with the crime scene stuff. Just finishing up.'

'About bloody time,' Salter said. 'Sooner we can all get out of this place the better.'

'It's a mess in there,' the young man said. 'Though they've taken the body out now.' His expression suggested that this was a relief.

'Thank Christ for that. This is a nasty one.' Salter peered quizzically around, as if his words might apply equally to the compact kitchen in which they were standing. 'Will hit the resale value, too. That living room'll need completely stripping back.' He laughed mirthlessly. 'No consideration, those buggers. Still, Morton won't care any more.'

He straightened as the scene of crime officer poked his head around the door, his eyes blinking under his protective headgear. Like a bloody tortoise waking from hibernation, Salter thought.

'All done, Hugh,' he said. 'Yours to mess up.'

'Beyond even my talents to mess this place up any further, mate,' Salter said. 'Anyway, I leave the detecting to you people these days.'

'I was told you lot had commandeered the place. Ordered us plods to keep our size elevens out till you'd done the serious stuff. Imagine that went down well with the boss. No skin off my nose either way.'

'That right?' Salter shrugged. 'Nothing to do with me, mate. You know me, always happy to help out the local coppers.'

'And up yours as well, former DI Salter,' the other man said cheerily. 'You deserve this fucking lot.'

'No one deserves this lot,' Salter said. 'Not even me.'

He followed the SOCO back into the living room. The smell of blood had been strong in the kitchen. Here, despite the open windows, it was almost overwhelming.

'Jesus.' Salter looked around. There was a large congealing pool of blood in front of the white leather sofa, further smears and splatters around the walls, across the furniture. Everywhere. Another officer was crouched by the door, carefully packing away the remaining equipment. 'What've you found?'

'Plenty of DNA,' the SOCO said. 'Most of it's the victim's, though, and I imagine you already know who he is.' There was an unmistakable undertone of irony.

'Don't worry, we'll share the good news with you in due course, I'm sure. Anything else?'

'Reckon there was a woman here, too. In the bed.'

'You can tell that from the DNA already? That's impressive.' Salter was peering vaguely around the room, giving a convincing impression of disinterest.

'No. Smell of perfume on the sheets. Unless your man was into Versace or whatever it is.'

'Anything's possible, mate.' Salter looked up, as if he'd only just realized he was engaged in a dialogue. 'A woman, eh? Lucky sod.' He gazed back at the bloodstains on the sofa. 'Well, not so lucky, I suppose. What do we think happened to her? Was she part of this?'

'Like you say, Hugh, anything's possible. Or maybe she'd buggered off before all this happened. Maybe he'd already got what he paid for.'

'Jesus, you like to think the worst of people, don't you?'

'Goes with the territory.' The SOCO was losing interest,

recognizing that Salter had no intention of sharing any information. 'Anyway, we've plenty of stuff, but it'll take some work to sort it all out.' He paused, before making one last effort. 'Strikes me as a professional job.'

Salter was peering at the pool of blood. 'Messy one if so,' he said, non-committal.

'That's your trouble,' the SOCO said. 'Once you start talking, there's no stopping you.'

Salter smiled and then raised his eyebrows as the shrill note of the front doorbell sounded through the flat. 'Saved by the bell,' he said. 'Sounds like the big guns have arrived to take over from us minions.' His tone suggested that he included himself in the last group only as a matter of courtesy.

The two SOCOs took the hint and picked up their cases. Salter followed them out into the hallway. Hodder was already opening the front door.

'Gentlemen.' The man on the doorstep was a squat, rumpled-looking figure, probably in his early fifties, his grey hair swept back in an ineffectual attempt to hide an increasing baldness. Despite his dishevelled appearance, he carried an air of confident authority.

'Guv,' Salter acknowledged. By contrast, his own brand of cocky superiority suddenly appeared slightly gauche.

The older man peered at the two SOCOs, his expression suggesting that, though he hadn't met them before, he would remember them in future.

'Keith Welsby,' he said. He gestured towards Salter. 'From the Agency, like my colleague here.' Somehow he succeeded in conveying the relative seniority of his own role compared with Salter's. 'All done?'

The lead SOCO nodded. 'On our side, sir.'

'Thanks very much, then. We'll be in touch in due course.' He was still holding open the front door, and the tone of dismissal was unmistakable. The SOCOs needed no further prompting.

Welsby closed the front door behind them, and then turned slowly back to Salter and Hodder. 'Right, lads,' he said, his face expressionless. 'So what the fucking fuck's been going on here, then?'

3

Her head aching, her mind still in some other place, Marie
Donovan sat at her large wooden desk, trying to smile at
the young man opposite. She hadn't chosen the office furniture
herself and it was all too imposing for her taste. Perched in
the leather swivel chair, the young man looked like a mouse
caught in a boxing glove.

'It's still not right, is it, Darren?' she said at last, knowing
that she had to go on with all this, despite everything. She
glanced down again at the document. She was trying to find
the right words. With Darren, she was always trying to find
right words. Simple ones, that he could follow.

'Darren?' she prompted.

He blinked. 'Miss?'

'It's Marie,' she said. 'You can call me Marie.' Christ, she
thought, it's as if he's never left school. She imagined he'd
been the same there – meek, compliant, fundamentally useless.
'I was saying that we still haven't got the printing right here,
have we?'

'I did my best, miss.'

'Marie,' she repeated. 'I'm sure you did, Darren. But you
need to concentrate. Let's have a look at this, shall we?' She
held up the printed document. 'What's wrong with it?'

Darren gazed at the handful of sheets, a brief shadow of

44

panic crossing his face in response to the direct question. He leaned forwards and squinted. 'It's a bit blurred,' he offered finally.

She nodded. 'It's very blurred. You let the original move while it was printing. OK, what else?'

Darren looked dismayed that the inquisition was not yet finished. 'Um. It's a bit, well, wonky.'

'It's very wonky,' she agreed. 'You didn't square up the originals. Anything else?'

He gazed silently at the document, then back up at her. The look of panic had returned. 'Miss?'

She leaned forwards and picked up the paper again. 'It's printed on both sides of an A3 sheet, right?' She paused. 'A big sheet.' She stretched it out to show him exactly what a big sheet looked like when it was stretched out. 'And each side is divided into two halves?'

Darren was staring at her now with an expression of abject misery. She'd lost him at the first mention of paper size.

'OK,' she went on, 'so it's a big sheet that's supposed to be folded in half to make a four-page A4 – that's a littler sheet – booklet.' She carefully folded the sheet to demonstrate. 'Like that, see?'

Darren made no response. Knackered as she was, she was momentarily tempted to lean over the desk and give him a violent shake. She had a fear that she might actually hear what passed for a brain rattling around in his skull.

'So that means,' she persisted, 'that both sides need to be printed the same way up. Right?' She was determined not to be deflected now. 'Otherwise some of the pages will be printed upside down. Right?'

A glimmer of light shone in Darren's eyes. 'Right,' he said. 'You don't want pages to be upside down.'

She unfolded the sheet and spread it carefully in front of

him. 'OK,' she said slowly, 'so, now turn that sheet over and tell me what's wrong with it.'

She had expected him to turn the sheet over left to right, or possibly right to left. Instead, he grasped the sheet carefully between his finger and thumb and turned it over top to bottom. He stared at the upright print in front of him, and then looked up at her, his eyes bright with welling tears. 'I'm sorry, miss,' he said at last. 'I can't see anything wrong with it.'

She could think of nothing to say. She peered over Darren's shoulder through the glass partition that separated her office from the rest of the print room. Her assistant Joe was busily working at the large reprographic machine, his eyes determinedly fixed away from their direction.

'Tell you what, Darren,' she said. 'Why don't you speak to Joe? Get him to show you how it should be done.'

Darren nodded, his face brightening at the prospect of escape. 'Thanks, miss. I will.' He rose, almost falling over the chair in his eagerness to leave the office.

'Marie,' she said through gritted teeth, as the office door closed behind him. 'It's Marie. Fucking Marie.'

She shouldn't drag it out. She should sack him now before it was too late, before he'd been working there long enough to have employment protection. She should sack him before she was tempted to kill him. She wasn't a social worker. She was a businesswoman.

Except, of course, that she wasn't. That was the whole trouble. She was only pretending to be a businesswoman. Doing a pretty good job of it, some would say, managing to expand the business in the face of a recession. But still only playing.

And if she was only playing, she might as well help out someone like Darren along the way. She knew Darren's type from her early days as a policewoman. Disadvantaged. In Darren's case, disadvantaged in virtually every possible way – socially, parentally, intellectually, physically. Without even the gumption to get himself into trouble. But that wouldn't stop someone else getting him into it. Someone a bit smarter, more confident, more streetwise. Which narrowed it down to almost anyone else in the world. Someone would take advantage of Darren, exploit him for their own purposes, set him up, and leave him swinging gently in the wind when things went wrong.

Maybe she could delay all that by a year or two if she kept him employed here. The only risk was that she might end up murdering him herself in the meantime. Particularly on a day like today. After everything that had happened.

She was distracted by the buzz of her mobile phone on the desk. A text, apparently a routine domestic message: Running a bit late. See you 6.30. Just to remind her, in case she might have forgotten, today of all days, that all this – the business, the print shop, Darren and the rest – wasn't really what it was all about.

She rose casually and fumbled in her jacket pocket for the other mobile phone. Not the one she'd used hours before, in her hopeless call to the emergency services. The customized one that was left switched off until she needed it. She switched it on now.

She dialled the familiar number and then, with the usual mild embarrassment, went through the authorization process – another anodyne code phrase. Salter's voice, at the end of the line, gave the appropriate coded response.

'Good to hear your voice, sis.' Salter's little joke. They were supposed to converse as if in some non-intimate relationship. At some point, Salter had decided that he was going to be her brother. Somehow, even as cover, that felt intrusive, but there was little she could do about it now.

'Hello there, Hugh,' she said. Strictly speaking, she wasn't supposed to use his real forename, but she'd done so as soon as he'd started to call her 'sis'. With any luck, it would help the other side track the bugger down more easily.

'Afraid it's bad news, sis.'

She felt an empty feeling in the pit of her stomach. Up to now, she'd been living on hope, clutching at the pitifully thin straws she'd tried to conjure up in the dark hours of the morning. Waiting on a miracle. She hadn't dared return to Jake's flat, or even try his phone line. Partly because now she couldn't risk being linked to whatever might have happened there. But mainly because she knew, in her heart, that there would be no reply.

'We've had a death in the family,' Salter went on. 'Thought you ought to know.'

'A death?' She held her breath for a moment, trying to keep her voice steady. 'Whose death?'

'It's J, I'm afraid,' Salter said. She could read nothing into his tone. 'Out of the blue.'

Quite suddenly, she'd run out of words. She held the phone away from her face, breathing deeply, trying to hold herself together. 'I don't understand, Hugh,' she said finally. 'What do you mean?'

'What I say, sis. Poor old J's dead. Dead as the proverbial fucking doornail, I'm afraid.'

She bit back her first response, feeling bile at the back of her throat. There was a note in his voice she'd never heard before, something that leaked through the veneer of cynicism. *He's pissed off, of course,* she thought, *that's part of it.* But there was something more.

She spoke slowly, trying to keep her voice steady. 'Oh, for fuck's sake, Hugh, stop playing games. What's happened?'

'What I say, sis. J's dead. Taken in the night. Unexpectedly.

Not an easy death, from what I understand. He suffered before the end.'

She lowered herself slowly back down on her office chair, not entirely trusting her legs to support her. Her mind suddenly felt clear, as if she'd been dragged somewhere beyond emotion. 'Suffered?'

'Yeah, it's a bastard. A real bastard. Even that bugger didn't deserve it.'

She could feel herself clamming up, just wanting to get away from all this. This conversation. This job. This fucking life.

'Yeah, it's a bastard, Hugh. So is there anything you want me to do about it?'

There was another pause. 'He was one of yours, wasn't he, sis?'

She held her breath again, concentrating, trying to ensure that she gave nothing away. 'I put his name forward, Hugh, that's all. Nobody forced him to be an informant.'

'No, suppose not, sis. Sad to see him go.' There was no obvious sincerity in his tone. 'Leaves us in a bloody hole as well. Anything you can do to help will be much appreciated, I'm sure.'

'I'll bear that in mind, Hugh.' She cut off the call, aware she was in danger of losing control. She didn't know what her next reaction would have been – grief at Jake's death, at the fucking manner of his demise. Tears at her own guilt and impotence. Blind fury at Salter's smug irony. Whichever, it wouldn't have been pretty. Now, she sat in silence, staring through the glass partition to where Joe was still patiently taking Darren through the intricacies of the reprographics machine.

It wasn't her fault. Yes, she'd been the one who'd suggested Jake as a possible informant. But, like she'd said, no one had compelled him to go along with it. He'd had his own reasons.

She knew he'd wanted out, that he was sick of the endless brown-nosing to Kerridge and Boyle and their crowd. That was the saddest thing – that Jake probably really thought he was doing a public duty by grassing up Boyle.

She'd known that. She'd judged it just right, known that when they came along with the offer he'd be ripe for the picking. That was what the job was about: spotting the talent. And it didn't always go right. Sometimes there were casualties.

And sometimes the casualties were lovers.

She knew that at any moment Joe or Darren would glance in this direction and that, when they did, she had to appear normal. A businesswoman struggling with nothing more traumatic than keeping this bloody enterprise afloat in the face of a howling recession.

Calmer now, her mind focused on the image she wanted to project, she opened the office door. Joe nodded and walked across to her, leaving Darren fumbling, apparently aimlessly, with the controls of the machine.

'Kid's bloody useless,' he murmured under his breath. 'You know that, don't you? We should cut our losses and sack him before it's too late.'

'He's just a boy, Joe. Give him a chance.'

Joe shrugged. 'You're the boss. But you can be too soft, you know?'

'Take it from me, Joe,' she said, 'that's not one of my failings.'

4

From somewhere in the next room, Marie could hear the shrill sound of her mobile.

She eased her body down into the hot water and tried to ignore the insistent tone. She contemplated, just for a moment, allowing her head to dip below the surface to enjoy the underwater silence. She fought the temptation to stay down there, hold her breath, let the silence become permanent – though the truth was she could think of worse ways to end it all.

It was a strange bloody paradox, this. Here she was, supposedly out on her own, cut off from all contacts. And she still couldn't get any peace and quiet.

She closed her eyes and breathed out as the phone finally fell silent. It was a temporary respite, she knew. The call would have gone to voicemail. Liam would leave a message. And then the voicemail would begin its automatic callback, another three bloody blasts of that impossible-to-ignore sodding ringtone.

That was Liam as well, that bloody ringtone. He'd set it up as a supposed joke, a couple of months back during one of her weekends at home. Some pop hit that she hadn't recognized. She'd no idea what it was and hadn't taken the trouble to find out, but she assumed – based on previous experience – that it represented some private joke at her expense. Her more knowledgeable work colleagues – possibly even Darren in this instance – no doubt amused themselves whenever her phone rang.

Liam knew he wasn't supposed to call her on this number. That it wasn't secure and that his calls could compromise her position. But of course it had been Liam calling. It was always Liam at this time of the evening, and that was another problem.

Every evening, she shut the shop at six, spent half an hour or so catching up with the paperwork, or perhaps redoing whatever task had been allocated to Darren that afternoon. Then she headed back to her flat, getting in at around seven or so. Whatever else she might have planned for the evening – and that was generally work of one sort or another – she tried to create some space for herself, an hour or so without commitments.

Very often, as tonight, that involved running herself a very hot bath, pouring herself a large glass of red wine and digging out some not-too-demanding book or magazine in which she could briefly lose herself. And almost equally often, again as tonight, as soon as she lowered herself into the scalding, scented water, she heard the insistent sound of the mobile from the next room.

She closed her eyes as the ringtone sounded once more. Tonight, of all nights, Liam was the last person she wanted to speak to. She wanted to cut herself off, put the real world on hold. Forget what she was doing, what she was involved in.

What she had done to Jake.

She kept telling herself that Jake had known exactly what risks he was taking. And that, last night, she'd done what she could. If she'd tried to do more, she'd be dead herself.

Even so, as she'd told Salter, it didn't feel good. Just at the moment, it felt fucking awful. It wasn't even that she was overwhelmed with grief. She kept expecting that it would hit her – the real emotion, the full sense of loss. But it hadn't, not really. She felt horror at what must have happened to Jake. She felt fury at those who had done it, and even more, at those who had paid for it to be done. She felt anxiety about her own possible exposure.

But there was a numbness, a dead spot, at the heart of her response. When it came to Jake himself, when it came to the simple fact that Jake was gone, she felt – what? Sorrow. Regret. Loss. But nothing like the depth or strength of emotion she'd expected.

She knew all the emotional clichés. She could envisage exactly what Winsor or the counsellors back at the Agency would say if she were ever in a position to share her feelings. That she was in shock. That she hadn't yet accepted the reality of Jake's death. That she had to work through all the fucking stages of grieving. And maybe that was all true. But, for the moment, it didn't feel that way. It felt like Jake had been a good friend – good company, a good laugh, pretty good in bed – and that now he was gone. The world hadn't ended. But Jake had left town, and he wouldn't be coming back.

Christ, she didn't know what she felt. When she'd embarked on the affair, she knew she was putting both of them at risk. It had been a few months of madness. She'd have ended it soon, whatever happened. It had been a fling – fun, dangerous, exhilarating, doomed. Why should she be surprised that, in the end, such turbulent waters turned out to run shallow?

Beyond the door, the ringtone trilled on. Finally losing patience, she skimmed her magazine across the bathroom floor so that it crashed like a wounded bird against the white-tiled wall. Cursing Liam, she dragged herself out of the water and reached for a towel. Still naked, trying to dry her body as she hurried out of the bathroom into the living room, she picked up the phone. Inevitably, just as she touched it, it fell silent.

She threw the towel around her shoulders and looked at the display. Two missed calls. The first number, sure enough, was Liam's. The second, though, wasn't the voicemail service she'd expected, but another mobile number. The number wasn't one she recognized. If it was important, she thought, the caller would leave a message. Most likely, it would be a wrong number or a cold call. In any case, her instinct now was to let others do the running. If someone had a job, she could be found.

She was still holding the phone when it rang again. Liam's number. She thumbed on the phone and spoke before he could. 'I've told you not to use this number.'

'And a good evening to you,' Liam said. 'You're answering now, are you?'

'Yes, and I shouldn't be. I'll call you back.'

Before he could object, she disconnected and fumbled in her handbag for the other mobile. She ought to stop and put on some clothes, she thought. The bedroom was warm enough, but she preferred not to be at any disadvantage when talking to Liam. But if she delayed he'd just call back again on the original line.

It took her a moment to switch on the phone and dial Liam's number. She expected him to be irritated, but he sounded only resigned.

'On the right phone now, then?' he asked. 'Important to get these things straight.'

She paused, mentally counting to ten. 'It's not a game, Liam. I don't do these things for fun.'

54

'You can say that again,' he said. 'Though Christ knows why else you do them.'

'To make a bloody living, Liam,' she said patiently. Almost immediately, she regretted the words.

'Because I don't, you mean?'

'Oh, for Christ's sake, Liam . . .'

'How much have I made this month? Sold two pictures. Hundred quid each. Not bad. Just remind me how much the mortgage is again?'

'That's not the point. You know I've always been happy to support your painting. You've got real talent . . .'

'Maybe. Maybe not. And what happens when I can't paint?'

This was a topic she always tried to steer away from. It was unproductive, pointless. And the last thing she needed today. 'Don't be so bloody melodramatic, Liam.'

'I'm not being melodramatic. I'm being realistic. It's a degenerative disease. I'm going to degenerate. Maybe later, maybe sooner. But eventually.'

And in the meantime you can wallow in the prospect, she thought, though she knew how unfair she was being. They were very different people. Her instinct was to avoid trouble, not face it till she was compelled to. Liam's was to embrace it head-on. But she knew that he was pragmatic, not indulgent. And this was his trouble, not hers.

'You don't know that,' she responded feebly. 'You can't know that. And, anyway, eventually could mean decades . . .'

'Yeah, thanks for that,' he said. 'I feel much better now.'

'Oh, Jesus, Liam . . .' She'd lost it, she knew that. It was stupid even to be having this conversation. She took a breath and tried to start again. 'Anyway, how've you been?'

There was a hesitation which made her wonder what he wasn't saying. 'OK. Not so bad.'

55

'Are you all right?' she pushed him.

She could almost hear him mulling over his reply, wondering whether to make another semi-joking bid for martyrdom. 'Yeah, I'm all right. I'm fine. Really.'

'Have you been back to the doctor?'

'Not yet. I will.' He was beginning to sound tetchy.

'Liam, is it getting worse?'

'Christ, Marie, how do I know? No, it's not, not obviously. But it's never been bloody obvious, has it? Not yet.' For a moment, she thought he'd ended the call. 'I don't know,' he said finally. 'I imagine all kinds of things. But that's probably all it is. There's no way of knowing till it happens.'

'Go back to the doctor,' she said. 'See what she says.'

'You know what she'll say. Nothing. What can she say?'

It was true. They'd had the diagnosis, and that was unequivocal. Multiple sclerosis. He'd had the scan. They'd been shown the images, the lesions in his brain. Had it all carefully explained. There was no doubt. The only question was how far the disease had progressed. Was it still in the remitting stage, where the symptoms could still come and go? Or was it in the progressive phase, where the likelihood was an inexorable, if possibly slow, decline? The distinction, the neurologist had told them, was not always clear-cut, and Liam's condition seemed to be on the cusp. That was what she'd said, but Marie had suspected that her eyes, professionally expressionless, had intimated a different story.

'She'll give you a view. About whether it's getting worse.'

'I don't need a view. I'll know if it's getting worse.'

She couldn't tell whether the future tense was euphemistic. 'At least get it checked out.'

'If it keeps you happy.'

'It'll reassure me, anyway,' she said.

'Just as long as you care.' The tone was ambiguous.

'Anyway, you've got better things to do than talk to me. I'll let you go.'

She knew he didn't mean it, that he wanted to keep talking, but she could feel her self-control draining away. 'Look, I'll call you tomorrow. Same time?'

'Whenever you've got a moment.'

'Same time,' she confirmed. She began to mutter some half-hearted endearment, but he'd already ended the call. Dear God, why did she bother? They hadn't even made the effort to get married before they'd reached this state. She didn't know what she felt for Liam any more than she'd known what she felt for Jake. With Liam she really had believed, once, that it was love. Now, it just felt like an old habit, not quite abandoned, but increasingly buried under layers of semi-serious recrimination and bickering.

She shivered suddenly and realized that she was sitting with only a towel around her shoulders, her body still damp from the bath. The window blinds were open, and she'd probably brightened the day for some old man or pubescent teenager in the flats opposite. Either that, or traumatized some busy-body who'd be penning a shocked letter to the Residents' Association. The way things were going, she could guess which was more likely.

Welsby was out on the balcony, chain-smoking, watching the pale sun sinking over the quays and the industrial landscape of Trafford Park. He'd left Salter and Hodder inside, system-atically working through the flat. Salter had obviously expected him to lend a hand, but Welsby reckoned that was one of the privileges of rank. Not having to spend any more time than necessary breathing in the stench of stale blood.

'All right?' Salter said from behind him, the note of irony in his voice more or less concealed. 'Sir?'

'Not so bad,' Welsby acknowledged, without looking round. 'Getting a bit parky out here, though.' He gestured towards the dominant bulk of Old Trafford on the far side of the canal. 'And I could do without having to stare at the theatre of bloody dreams. Nearly finished?'

Salter sat himself down opposite Welsby. 'Getting there. I've left the youngster to finish off.'

'Aye, well, you deserve a break.' Welsby stretched out his legs and eased back against the chair. 'Mind you, your arse'll get numb if you spend too long out here.' He waved a packet of cigarettes towards Salter.

Salter shook his head. 'Giving up,' he explained.

'Again? Your bloody trouble, Hugh – no willpower. Some of us are properly committed.'

'Don't imagine my lapse will be too protracted,' Salter said. 'Not if I have to deal with many more fuck-ups like this one.'

Welsby nodded, his eyes fixed on the last gleaming dregs of the setting sun. 'That's the phrase I've been searching for,' he said. 'Fuck-up. Trust you to find the mot juste.'

'My literary background, sir. The real question, though, is who fucked up?'

'That's the question, right enough. Suggests we're not quite as watertight as we'd like to think.' Welsby dropped his cigarette butt and ground it under his heavy black shoe. 'Which is interesting.'

'One word for it,' Salter said.

'Ah, well. I lack your literary background. CSE in metalwork, that's my limit.'

'Very practical, guv. I don't like the idea that we're not secure, though.'

Welsby was lighting up another cigarette, hand cupped around the guttering flame with practised skill.

58

'Well, start getting used to it,' he said finally. 'Or, better still, start finding out who's leaking.'

'Not many of us knew about Morton,' Salter pointed out. 'Not officially, anyway.'

Welsby shrugged. 'Internally, we're a bloody sieve,' he said. 'I reckon nearly everyone had wind of this. Not necessarily the details. But the fact that we'd got a key bloody witness. Talk of the building.'

'You reckon?' Salter leaned forwards, his gangling limbs splayed awkwardly. 'Whoever did this had more than office gossip.'

'Too right they did.' Welsby took a deep final drag on his latest cigarette, then tossed it disdainfully in the approximate direction of the canal. 'We couldn't organize a nun-shoot in a bloody nunnery.'

'They knew what they were doing,' Salter mused. 'Morton wasn't short on security. They knew where the alarms were. Knew how to disable them. As for what they did to Morton – well, maximum pain for minimum effort, I'd say. Pros. Top of the range pros.'

'You get what you pay for,' Welsby observed. 'So who was paying them? And how did they find out Morton was our man?'

'Maybe Morton slipped up. Wouldn't be the first grass to have shot his mouth off inadvisably.'

'Can't really see it. Morton struck me as a degree or two smarter than the average grass. Still, it's a line we can peddle. Generate enough smoke to make sure our own arses are covered. But this is still fucking embarrassing.' He paused, and began to fumble painstakingly for another cigarette. Finally he looked up. 'How's it going, son?'

Salter looked over his shoulder, alerted by the change in tone. Hodder was hovering expectantly by the open windows.

'Just about done,' he said brightly. He'd tackled the task of searching a blood-drenched house with as much enthusiasm as an ambitious young officer could muster.

'Found anything?' Welsby scrutinized the young man with an expression that indicated a pre-emptive scepticism of anything he might be about to say.

'Not to speak of,' Hodder admitted. 'There's a laptop. Some official-looking papers, a notebook of some sort. And there's Morton's wallet.' He enumerated the list as if he had committed it carefully to memory. 'That's about it.'

'What about this mystery woman?'

'No signs. Certainly not anybody living in. Maybe somebody he picked up for the night. If so, it's possible she was in on it, I suppose. Gives a whole new dimension to the phrase "get lucky", doesn't it?'

'If you say so, son. You've been through the rooms thoroughly?' Welsby's question was addressed as much to Salter as Hodder.

Salter nodded. 'Proper job. Best we can with just the two of us, anyway.' He placed only the faintest emphasis on the number. 'I can't absolutely swear there's nothing in there, but if there is, Morton hid it bloody well.'

Welsby pulled himself slowly to his feet. 'You never know,' he said. 'Glass half-full, that's me. Might be something on that laptop.'

Salter rose awkwardly, straightening his long limbs with the air of a baby deer trying to walk for the first time. 'Morton was holding stuff back all right, but I reckon he was too smart to keep it here.'

Welsby stood, staring down at the grey waters of the canal, his crumpled face giving no clue to his thoughts. 'Probably. And even if there was something, that bunch will have got it out of him. You don't do that much damage to someone for fun.' He paused, taking one more look around him, and then began to make his way back into the flat. 'Well, not just for fun, anyway,' he added.

5

Marie was momentarily tempted to pull into one of the several unoccupied spaces reserved for disabled drivers, but decided against it. The last thing she needed was more guilt, let alone the risk of being clamped. Instead, she parked as close as she could to the entrance, and then sprinted across the car park, pulling her coat tight against the pounding rain. She reached the hotel with her head and upper body soaked, rain oozing coldly down her collar. *Jesus,* she thought, *and all those bloody disabled spaces standing empty.*

It was Liam she was thinking of really, of course. Liam who would be perfectly entitled to park in those spaces. Liam and his condition, and the unknown, unknowable prognosis. She had a superstitious half-belief, barely acknowledged even to herself, that if she didn't tempt fate, everything might be all right. Whatever all right might turn out to mean.

She stood in the reception, dripping rainwater gently on to the thick pile carpet. It was the usual sort of place; an anonymous, soulless business hotel, suitably mid range, conveniently positioned minutes from the M60. There were a dozen or more such venues, scattered around the city centre and the suburbs, catering to sales executives, visiting middle managers, off-site business meetings. Comfortable enough, with all the right facilities, but nothing too flash. They rotated the meetings around the various hotels, trying to ensure that they didn't become too familiar to the reception staff. It wasn't difficult. Most were transient youngsters, generally from Eastern Europe, here to make a few bucks before moving on or returning home. If she came back to the same venue six months later, the faces would all have changed. No one would remember who she was, or why she'd been there before.

'Ms Donovan,' she said to the bored-looking receptionist. 'Small meeting room.' She gave the company name. The receptionist smiled momentarily in a manner that suggested that she had, at least, received some instruction in how to greet customers, and began to thumb listlessly through a card index. Finally, as if in testament to her own considerable efforts, she triumphantly held up Marie's reservation. 'Meeting room for three,' she confirmed. 'Coffee at nine thirty and eleven. No lunch.' Her tone on the last words suggested disapproval of Marie's parsimony.

She collected the card key and made her way to the first floor. A small meeting room in this kind of place meant, in effect, a semi-converted bedroom – a fold-up bed disguised as a wardrobe, an imported table and office chairs. Coffee with a plateful of overpriced biscuits. Branded writing pads and pens. A bottle of water refilled from the tap.

She walked to the window. A view of the rear car park, a retail park, a cluster of trees half-concealing the M60 busy with the morning traffic. Anytown, UK.

As far as Joe and Darren were concerned, she was out seeing a client. She'd cultivated a routine of visiting the major clients at their offices. It was good business – they appreciated the personal touch. And it gave her the freedom she needed to pursue this double life.

She supposed she was being accorded some kind of privilege

here. Normal practice was that she maintained contact only with Salter. Salter was her liaison officer. Her buddy or minder, as he would say. They had a regular schedule of meetings, once a month in venues like this – to touch base, share information, chew the fat, make sure she wasn't losing her marbles.

Salter was her sole conduit back to the Agency. When operations were compromised, it wasn't usually because of smart counter-intelligence. It was generally because someone had screwed up or, even more likely, had been accidentally exposed – recognized as a face from way back, spotted somewhere they shouldn't be. She'd already had the experience herself, eyeballed by the sister of some small-time villain she'd put away years ago. She'd seen the woman staring at her, trying to work out if it really was Marie, gearing herself up for an altercation. Marie had passed swiftly on, eyes fixed on some window display, disappearing into the crowd before the woman could collar her.

So they kept the risks to a minimum. That was why today was unexpected. It was scheduled as one of her routine liaison meetings with Salter. Last night she'd had a call from Salter, through the usual channels, to say that Welsby would be joining them. Salter had been his usual semi-cryptic, game-playing self, but she'd gathered that the purpose was to discuss Jake Morton.

She wondered whether she should worry about that. But there was no reason why anyone should know about her and Jake, and every reason why Welsby might want to talk to her about the case. Morton had been a key witness in their intended prosecution of Pete Boyle.

Boyle was a pretty big deal. Their real target was Jeff Kerridge, the most influential player in organized crime in these parts. But Kerridge tended to keep his hands clean, and Boyle was his representative on earth. If they could make a case stick against Boyle, they'd be one step closer to nailing Kerridge. They'd arrested Boyle just a couple of weeks earlier, having finally mustered enough evidence to persuade the Prosecution Service that it was worth a punt. They'd charged him with drug trafficking, but they had a range of other charges, from conspiracy to money laundering, waiting in the wings. She'd no idea what would happen now. They had a wealth of documentary evidence, most of it supplied by Morton, but they'd struggle to secure the prosecution without Morton's own testimony to back it up.

There was a knock at the door. She glanced at her watch. She'd been early because she was supposedly the host. But Welsby and Salter were early, too. Welsby would be keen to get this over with, she supposed.

She pulled open the door. Salter had a beige raincoat wrapped around his skinny body and seemed his usual self – an unholy cross between Tigger and Eeyore. Welsby stood behind, conspicuously furtive in a battered anorak.

'Hi, sis,' Salter said. He peered round the room. 'Nice place you've got here.'

'Home from home,' she said, gesturing for them to follow her in. 'My flat's a soulless shoebox as well. Hi, Keith.'

Welsby nodded. 'Marie. Been a little while.'

She poured coffee and set the plate of biscuits between them, feeling the usual mild resentment that this role was, as always, allocated to her by default. Here, she was the notional host, but things would have been no different back at the office.

Still, she had some time for Keith Welsby – more than for Salter, at any rate. Salter was a smart-arse careerist, a former fast-track graduate now in his early thirties, probably not quite as bright or as capable as he imagined. Harmless enough, she thought, as long as you kept your distance, but his priority was always to protect his own backside. That didn't make her feel comfortable. In this job, she had no choice but to trust him, even if her first instinct was to play her cards close to her chest.

Welsby was different. Old school, a couple of years off retirement. His attitudes were, by the standards of the Agency, essentially prehistoric, but much of that was an act. He said what people expected to hear from an overweight, florid-faced old flatfoot. But there were no flies on Keith Welsby, and not just because most of his suits looked as old as he did. He was difficult to fathom. His attitude to her was avuncular and patronizing, littered with half-jokes about the shortcomings of women officers. But then he'd throw in a remark that suggested real respect for her ability. After a while, as she found herself striving to justify his good opinion, she'd concluded that this was just Welsby's distinctive approach to staff motivation.

They arranged themselves around the narrow table, Salter leaning forwards, apparently in charge. Welsby was stretched back, a little way from the table, his body language indicating that, despite his senior rank, this was not his show. Fair enough. She and Salter were the same job grade, but the convention was that the 'buddy' acted as supervisor for undercover officers. This would normally be a supervisory meeting, an opportunity for her to bounce issues or concerns off Salter and for Salter to check how she was doing.

'How are things, sis?'

She gazed at him for a moment. 'Fine, Hugh. So what's this all about?

'Morton, of course.'

Welsby leaned forwards in his chair. He was chewing gum, a substitute for his usual cigarettes. 'You knew him well, Marie?'

She took a breath and shrugged. 'I wouldn't say well. He was part of Kerridge's team. I know them all, more or less.'

'You suggested him as an informant?'

'I got to know him a bit. He's . . .' She stopped. 'He was the most approachable of Kerridge's bunch, so I used him as a route in. Worked pretty well, I thought.' It was worth reminding them that she'd got closer to Kerridge's circle than Salter or anyone else had managed. 'He seemed disenchanted with Kerridge. With the whole lifestyle, I thought. That's why I reckoned he might make a good target for us.'

You know all this, she thought. *It's all on file.* There was a long and bureaucratic process to get an intelligence source authorized, and everyone covered their backsides.

'You got it spot on,' Welsby said. 'Smart piece of work. We got a lot out of him. We'd have got more. We'd have brought down Boyle. Maybe even Kerridge eventually.'

She noted the past tense. 'You think this has ballsed up the Boyle case?'

'For the moment,' Welsby said. 'Can't see the CPS progressing with it unless we pull something else out of the shit.'

'Why we're here,' Salter said. 'We've been digging around in the excrement. See what we can find.'

She felt, at least at first, a surge of relief. Her second response was anger – that, for them, Morton's killing was simply an operational inconvenience.

'I'm privileged to be part of the excrement, then,' she said, keeping her voice steady. 'How did this happen, anyway? Surely Morton's security was top-level?' Given the hints Salter had dropped, she wasn't sure she wanted the full story. But Jake had given his life trying to help them nail Boyle and Kerridge. Whatever she might think or feel, she had an obligation to get involved.

Salter glanced at Welsby. 'Someone messed up,' he said. 'We don't know who or how – yet.'

'Someone exposed him?'

'Must have done. Either by accident or on purpose.'

'No one would be that careless, surely.'

Welsby shifted back in his chair. 'Easy to be careless, lass. One slip . . .' His voice was toneless. Marie looked across at him, wondering whether some response was expected of her.

'In any case,' Salter said, 'the alternative is worse.'

It occurred to her for the first time that there was a tension between the two men, things they weren't saying. Someone had exposed Jake, and no one knew who. If someone was leaking intelligence, they were all potentially compromised. And no one was more vulnerable than she was.

'So what happened?' she said.

'He had a visit,' Welsby said quietly. His mouth moved rhythmically around the gum. 'Middle of the night.'

'Jesus.' Marie pushed herself up from the table and strode over to the window, trying to repress the turmoil of emotion. More guilt. Loss. Fear. Above all, fear. She stood for a moment, staring at the half-empty car park, the blur of cars on the motorway, trying to find words that wouldn't leave her exposed. 'This was our one bloody chance,' she said finally. 'Our one chance to nail those bastards.'

'It's not over yet,' Salter said. 'Morton gave us a lot. Copies of paperwork, documents. Helped us get surveillance devices in there . . .'

She didn't want to be reminded how courageous Morton must have been in those last weeks. She still didn't know what had really motivated him. She'd known he wanted to cut his ties with Kerridge, but there seemed to be something stronger driving him.

They normally kept Chinese walls between informants and undercover operatives to minimize the risk of leakage, so she'd heard only secondhand reports. At first, they told her, he'd been like every other intelligence source, warily

68

feeding out titbits, constantly suspicious, scared of his own shadow at each meeting with his handler. But once he'd learned the ropes, found out who to trust, his attitude had changed. He seemed to have a mission to bring down the world he'd been part of. With no prompting, he'd offered himself as a prosecution witness in any case that they might bring, and had reinforced the offer by producing file after file of incriminating material.

She knew from Salter that Morton's behaviour had worried them at first. They thought he'd either lost the plot, or was playing some complicated double bluff. But after a while they'd concluded that he was serious. It could go on for only so long, but it gave them time to dig some real dirt. A month later, they arrested Pete Boyle, with Morton scheduled to be the key prosecution witness. Another day or two and they'd have taken him into witness protection. Another day or two. Just a question of getting the fucking paperwork in order.

She turned back from the window. 'These visitors. What did they do?'

Salter hesitated. 'They killed him. Eventually.'

'Christ.'

'What they did wasn't nice,' Salter said. 'Punishment. Pour encourager les autres.'

'As we used to say down the nick,' Welsby said. 'And we reckon they were trying to find out how much he'd told us.' He sat, chewing silently for a moment. 'And whether he knew anything he hadn't told us yet.'

Marie sat down and took a sip of her coffee. Cold and bitter. Appropriate enough. 'You think he did?'

'He'd more or less told us so,' Welsby said. 'Stuff he wouldn't hand over till nearer the trial.' He paused. 'He still didn't trust us. Not entirely.'

'Sounds like he was on the button,' Marie said tartly. 'As it turned out.'

Welsby leaned forwards and picked up one of the biscuits. He regarded it suspiciously, as if unsure of its provenance, then thrust it whole into his mouth. He chewed briefly before speaking, untroubled by the shower of crumbs across his shirt front.

'True enough,' he said. 'Whoever got to Morton knew what they were up to right enough.'

'You think Kerridge has someone on the inside?'

Welsby shrugged. 'It's possible. Or some poor bugger fell asleep at the wheel. Bastards like Kerridge hoover up every bit of intelligence out there, wherever it comes from.' He made a play of swallowing the last of the biscuit, then reached for another.

Salter had risen from the table and was busy, in a half-hearted manner, exploring the interior of the room, pulling open drawers, flicking absently through the bowl of coffee and sugar sachets on the hospitality tray, peering into the built-in wardrobe. It wasn't clear what, if anything, he was looking for. They all wanted to be out of this box-like room, Marie thought.

'Poor bastard should have just told us everything,' Salter muttered, his voice angry. 'He'd have been safer that way.'

'Not much,' Marie pointed out. 'But it would have made your life easier.'

'Yeah. Inconsiderate bastard.' He withdrew his head from the wardrobe. 'So what did he do with it? The other stuff, I mean.'

'You don't think they got it?' she said.

'Depends,' Salter said. 'I mean, in his shoes, I'd have spilled everything I fucking knew. But I don't know that Morton thought like that. What d'you reckon, sis?'

There was an edge to his voice, but she couldn't interpret it. She picked up the coffee pot and slowly poured herself a second cup, giving herself time to think. She made a point, this time, of not offering coffee to the others.

'Difficult for me to say,' she said finally. 'But you're probably right. Whatever else he was, he was a stubborn bugger.'

That was true enough. It was one of the things that had attracted her to him. He said what he thought, stuck to his guns. Miles away from the usual sycophants around Kerridge. It was one of the reasons Kerridge rated Morton. Kerridge lapped up the attention from the yes-men, but was smart enough not to be taken in by it.

'You knew him better than we did,' Welsby said. 'You knew what made him tick.'

Welsby's face was as uncommunicative as ever, his mouth contorted as he strove to extract some crumb of biscuit from his teeth.

She had the sense that she was being probed, or perhaps tested. Was it because they had some suspicions about her relationship with Jake? Did they think that Jake had shared his evidence with her?

'I only knew him in a work context, really,' she said. 'I saw him with Kerridge a few times. He didn't back down easily, let's put it that way.'

'So if he had something, he'd have kept hold of it?'

'Christ, how would I know?' she said. 'I never got the opportunity to see how he reacted to torture.' She took a long sip of her tepid coffee, waiting to recover her composure. 'Maybe. You've searched his place, presumably?'

'Yeah,' Salter said. 'Pretty thoroughly. Best we could before the plods took over, anyway. If there's anything there, it's well hidden.'

'Or it was found by whoever killed him.'

'Or it was found by whoever killed him,' Salter agreed. 'Which brings us back to the same question.'

'To which we don't have an answer,' she pointed out. 'I don't know what you're expecting me to say.' She could feel her emotions bubbling away and was having to concentrate on keeping control.

'You knew him better than most, sis.'

Salter's tone was studiedly neutral. She found herself losing patience with the game-playing.

'I'm not your fucking sister, Hugh,' she said quietly. 'Sometimes I'm not even sure we're the same fucking species.' She leaned back in her chair, regarding him coolly. 'What about Morton's handler? He'd be closer to Morton than anyone. He must have some insights. What does he say?'

She realized almost immediately that she'd struck a chord. Salter exchanged a glance with Welsby, a shadow of shared unease in their eyes. She watched Salter.

'Who was his handler?'

Salter shrugged. 'Me. I took it on.'

That was interesting. Not exactly against the rules. Salter had operated as an intelligence handler before he'd moved into undercover work, so he had the skills and experience to do the job. But, given the risk of exposure, it was unusual for an intelligence source to be handled from within the undercover team.

'Why you, Hugh?'

Salter glanced again at Welsby and shrugged. 'Sensitive one this, sis. We thought it best to keep it in the family. Keith's idea.'

Welsby was rocking back in his chair, eyes fixed on the ceiling as if he had spotted something noteworthy up there.

'You think there's a mole, then, Keith? Is that it?'

His eyes switched back to her, his expression suggesting that he had momentarily forgotten where he was. 'Some kind of zit, anyway,' he said.

'You think so, too, Hugh?'

'We've had stuff leak out. Morton was just the latest and the worst.' He paused. 'What we don't know is what else might have leaked. What else might be out there.'

'Jesus, Hugh. I'm out there.' The thought was frightening. There were always risks. But you had to start from the assumption that the foundations were secure. Now, suddenly, she didn't know who to trust.

Salter shook his head. 'You're as safe as you can be, sis. It's only a handful of people that know about your role. You know how it works.'

'I know how it's supposed to work. And I know how it was supposed to work with Morton. Doesn't fill me with confidence.'

'We can bring you back in,' Welsby said. 'If that's what you want.'

She looked at him. He was still swinging back on his chair, the metal legs looking as if they might buckle under his weight. She'd always liked Keith. She respected him. But she knew the way his mind worked.

'Not yet,' she said. 'If it looks as if I've been compromised – if you get a fucking inkling that I might be in trouble – then I want to know. But there's no point jumping the gun.'

'Good girl,' Welsby said.

He sounded sincere, and she didn't know whether she wanted to hug him or punch him.

'If there is a mole,' she said, 'any clues as to who it might be?'

Salter shook his head. 'Not enough to go on. Morton's the only biggie. The rest could be accidental.'

'We shouldn't have accidents,' she said. 'Not in this game.'

Salter smiled wearily, as if he too had once shared this utopian view of life. 'Yes, well, sis. We're all human, aren't we?' He paused, his smile broadening as if they were sharing some private joke. 'Even you.'

6

She'd first met Jake Morton at one of Jeff Kerridge's charity events. It had been during her first few months undercover, when she was working to build herself a network and some credibility, using all the contacts that Salter and her predecessor had passed on to her. It was hard work. She found herself parked endlessly on the phone, trying to set up meetings, pitch her wares, drum up some interest. In the end, she was little different from any other business start-up, struggling to get herself noticed in a market where everyone had a million better things to do than listen to her.

Slowly, though, she was making progress. Her persistence, along with a glowing recommendation from her predecessor, had secured her a meeting with Jeff Kerridge, supposedly to discuss his printing needs. Kerridge had ducked out at the last minute, presumably to demonstrate that he was far too busy for the likes of her. But she'd had a decent meeting with some not-too-junior underling and had come away with a trial print order and some heavy hints about other, less legitimate services that they might consider. More surprisingly, a week or so later, she'd received a lavishly printed invitation to a charity dinner that Kerridge was hosting at some country house hotel in deepest moneyed Cheshire.

'You better go for it, sis,' Salter had said. 'It'll be Kerridge's first test. If you're not generous enough towards his favoured bunch of disadvantaged kiddies, you can kiss any future orders goodbye. Just don't go donating too much if you're expecting to claim it on expenses.'

Even in less tense circumstances, this kind of event would have been her idea of hell in a posh frock. As it was, she was still finding her feet, working out where to pitch things. The first part of the evening was a charity auction, dominated by macho local businessmen trying to outdo each other to buy football shirts autographed by United or City players even Marie had vaguely heard of. Through a mix of boredom and embarrassment, she ended up bidding far too much for a designer dress donated by some local upmarket clothier. But no one seemed to mind, or even to notice much. By then the drink had been flowing freely and – as everyone kept reminding her – it was all in a good cause. The main good cause being, as far as she could make out, their own individual business interests.

At the formal dinner that followed, she was amused to find herself seated at the top table, just a few seats along from Kerridge himself. She had no illusions about why she'd been accorded this honour, or indeed why she'd been invited in the first place. In this world, unattached, semi-presentable women were always at a premium. She'd spent most of her time batting off half-hearted passes made by overweight businessmen whose wives were generally no more distant than the other side of the room.

'Why do we put ourselves through it, eh?' the man on her left said, as if echoing her thoughts. 'All this crap.'

'It's all in a good cause,' she said, echoing the mantra of the evening.

'Oh, right,' the man said. 'Nearly forgot that. Surprised nobody mentioned it earlier. Jake Morton, by the way.'

He wasn't exactly George Clooney, but he was an improvement on most of the men in the room. Trim with neat, slightly greying hair, an expression of amused tolerance on a slightly battered face. A former rugby player, from the look of it. A few years older than her, probably, but not enough to matter.

Jesus. She had to keep reminding herself that she wasn't single. It was one of the problems of this job. You threw yourself wholeheartedly into a fictitious life, and soon it seemed more real than the world you'd left behind.

'Marie Donovan,' she said.

He nodded. 'You bought the dress,' he said. 'Must have thought it was a bloody good cause to pay that much.' He leaned back in his chair and eyed her body appraisingly. 'Mind you, it'll look great on you.'

She thought that she ought to feel offended, but his tone was good-natured, perhaps even slightly satirical, rather than straightforwardly lecherous. More to the point, he was attractive enough for her to feel mildly flattered.

'At that price, I'd hope so,' she said. 'At that price, I'd expect it to look good on *you*.'

He laughed. Around them, bored-looking waitresses were serving the starter – some overdressed variant on a prawn cocktail.

'I get the impression this isn't your natural environment,' he said.

'Is it anybody's?'

'Oh, yes.' He gestured towards the rows of tables in front of them. 'Look at them. Enjoying every moment. Every mouthful of rubber chicken.'

'Rubber prawn,' she pointed out. 'Rubber chicken's next.' She was beginning to find herself intrigued by this man. 'So – why are you here?'

He pointed along the table. 'Work for Jeff. Three-line whip for his top team.'

That was interesting, she thought. She hadn't registered the name at first, but now she recalled her briefing notes, all the details that she'd painstakingly squirrelled away in her memory. James Morton. Apparently known as Jake. Director of finance for Kerridge's legitimate holding company. But rumoured also to be a significant player in the other, more clandestine parts of Kerridge's business. Definitely someone worth getting to know.

'He does a lot of this, does he? This is my first time.'

He shrugged. 'Well, that's Jeff for you. Likes to do his bit for the community.'

'Very commendable.'

'Especially his own community. Local councillors. Business types. People he wants to get onside. Customers. The big customers. And a few suppliers like yourself, if you're very good.'

She raised an eyebrow. 'You know who I am, then?'

'You're the print lady, aren't you? Came highly recommended, I understand.' There was an undertone to his words that was unmistakable.

'Glad to hear it,' she said. 'I hope I've lived up to expectations.' She'd already completed the trial order, ahead of schedule and at what she knew was a very competitive price.

'Done some good work so far, from what I hear. Printing, and all that.'

'And all that,' she agreed.

'Jeff appreciates a good supplier. So far I'm told you've done well.'

'Not the cheapest, but the best.'

'Something like that.' He smiled. 'Mind you, don't get me wrong. Jeff appreciates a cheap supplier as well.'

'I'll bear that in mind. And that you're the finance director.'

'Got me sussed too, then? Well, yes, that's my job.' He paused. 'For what it's worth.'

'Quite a bit, I'd have thought.'

'It pays well enough, if that's what you mean. Though maybe not enough to compensate for evenings like this.'

'And I was trying so hard to be sparkling,' she said.

He laughed. 'Funnily enough, the evening's rather brightened up in the last few minutes.'

'That'll be the prawn cocktail.'

He lifted his glass of white wine. 'Yeah, and the Chateau Toilet Duck. Cheers.'

'Cheers.'

That had been it, she thought. That trivial, jokey salutation. As they'd clinked their glasses, she'd felt as if something had passed between them. Some coded, inarticulate message. Some unspoken pact. Both knowing more than they were able to say. Not quite trust. Perhaps, at that point, nothing more than a balance of suspicion. But something.

That was where it had started.

That night, too, was the first time she really had an inkling of what she might be letting herself in for. It was the first opportunity she'd had to get anywhere close to her key targets – the smooth Jeff Kerridge and his much rougher number two, Pete Boyle. She already felt that she half-knew them from the files and reports that she'd worked her way through in preparation for the assignment, but meeting them in the flesh, after everything she'd read, was something else again. Everything she'd read indicated that, appearances aside, they were an unpleasant pair. Kerridge had built a business empire by ruthlessly jamming his hands into every pie he could find, legal or otherwise. He was what passed for the brains of the outfit, running a complex network of on- and off-shore companies that allowed him to funnel cash wherever he wanted for tax avoidance and laundering purposes. The forensic accounting team had tracked through some of those movements, but they didn't yet have enough to be confident that a case would stick.

Boyle was a different matter. A hard-case from Hulme who, by dint of being that bit brighter than his associates, had managed to claw his way up to near the top of the pile. The word was that Boyle looked after most of Kerridge's dirty work, and that some of that work could get very dirty indeed. Unlike Kerridge, who'd managed to stay squeaky-clean, Boyle did have a record, though it was mainly petty stuff from his youth. These days, he tended not to risk messing up his own Hugo Boss suit, if he could pay others to do the work for him. They were getting closer with Boyle. They'd picked up two or three of his associates over the last year or so on a variety of charges – GBH, demanding money with menaces, manslaughter in one case. No one had actually blown the whistle on Boyle, but they were gradually piecing together enough evidence to collar him. He'd left his metaphorical fingerprints in a few too many places.

At the dinner, true to form, Kerridge had been charm personified, chatting amiably with Marie during the earlier part of the evening. He had an old-fashioned manner which stayed just the right side of flirtatious. Probably just as well, Marie thought, eyeing Kerridge's fearsome-looking wife. 'Ah, Miss Donovan,' he'd said. 'The printer. I've heard some very good things about you. Your work comes highly recommended.'

'I'm glad to hear it,' she said. 'I hope I manage to live up to my reputation.'

'I'm sure you will.' He turned and waved in the general

direction of his wife, who was standing just a few inches behind him. 'My wife, Helen. This is Miss Donovan—'

'Marie.'

'Marie, who's handling some printing for us at the moment. You two should get together. I'm sure you'd have a lot to discuss.'

The two women gazed at each other with expressions that confirmed their obvious lack of any common ground. Helen Kerridge was a certain sort of Cheshire lady, Marie thought. Well-off, self-made, dismissive of those who thought their characters might be defined by something other than material possessions. Marie could imagine the older woman patrolling the upmarket clothes shops and restaurants of Wilmslow or Alderley Edge, killing days that had little other purpose.

'We could do lunch sometime,' she said, mischievously.

Helen Kerridge gazed at her for a long moment without speaking. 'Sometime,' she said finally, in a tone that suggested they should aim for one of the chillier days in hell.

Marie had seen Boyle only from the other side of the room. He was a broad muscular man, who clearly still devoted considerable time and energy to working out. He looked awkward in his undoubtedly expensive suit, a glass of fizzy wine in hand, with the air of a man who would much rather have been propping up some bar downing a pint of lager. Every now and then, his eyes scanned the room, his shaven head twisting on his thick neck, as if keeping watch for signs of trouble.

Marie's only real objective for the night had been to begin building her own profile, become acquainted with one or two of the right people, get her own face recognized. She'd wondered whether to approach Boyle, but couldn't find a reasonable opening. In the end, she'd been happy enough chatting to Jake Morton, who seemed the most promising route into the Kerridge empire.

Towards the end of the evening, when they'd finished eating and had moved on to brandy and liqueurs, Jake made his excuses and slipped away from the table. 'Got a three-line whip for a debrief with Jeff,' he'd said. 'He likes to make sure we've all done our bit.'

She'd found herself stuck with some pompous old fool who ran a haulage company in Macclesfield, nodding politely while he ranted on about fuel duty and VAT. After a while, while he'd gone off to secure himself another brandy, she'd slipped away from the table herself and made her way out into the hotel lobby.

She'd only ever been a social smoker and it was years since she'd had a cigarette at all. There were moments, though, when she could envy the little amicable groups congregating around the front doors of the hotel. She slipped past them and walked out into the car park, enjoying the cold of the night air after the alcoholic fug of the function room. It was a chilly night, but the sky was clear and full of stars. She paused for a moment, enjoying the relative silence. The hotel was in the hills, on the edge of the Pennines, and, as she crossed to the edge of the car park, she could see the lights of Manchester and the Mersey Basin spread out below.

She had been standing for a few moments staring at the view when she heard the sound of raised voices behind her. She turned, peering into the darkness. There was a small group of men standing twenty or thirty metres from her, clustered in the lee of a large 4x4 parked near the entrance to the car park. She could make out the flicker of cigarette ends, the sound of some sort of altercation.

Her curiosity piqued, she moved slowly and silently around

the edge of the car park, keeping close to the fence, trying to hear what was being said. None of her business, probably, but she shouldn't miss the opportunity to pick up anything that might be of value.

She stopped suddenly and held her breath. Now she was closer, she could make out Jake Morton's voice. She took another few steps then peered out from behind the row of parked cars.

It was Morton, no question. And next to him was the unmistakable bulky silhouette of Pete Boyle. There was another figure facing them, but she couldn't make out his face.

It was Boyle's slightly louder voice that she'd first heard. 'It's all right for you, desk monkey,' he was saying now. 'It's not you taking the risks.'

'From what I see, it's not you either, Pete,' Morton said. 'So don't come the martyr. I just say that we should play it cautious. If we go off half-cocked, we just risk drawing more attention.'

'Bugger caution. I've tried being cautious. That's why we're in the shit.'

'We're not in the shit, not yet. We just have to be careful, that's all.'

'We've had three people picked up in the last three months. Bail refused in every case. Somebody's grassing.' She could see Boyle drop his cigarette butt and crush it hard under his shoe. He looked as if he was envisaging performing the same action on some more animate object.

'We don't know that,' Morton said. 'Shit happens.'

'It's happening too often lately. We need to do something. Send a fucking signal.'

'We can't take somebody out just because you think he might be a grass—'

'Why the fuck not?' Boyle said. 'Even if we're wrong, we've sent a message.'

'We've sent a message that we're a bunch of fuckwits who don't know what we're doing.'

Marie had moved a step or two closer, listening hard. It was the kind of stuff they needed to get on surveillance, she thought. Which was presumably why Boyle and Morton were having this conversation out in the car park, in case they were bring tapped in their hotel rooms or cars.

'Come on, lads. Bit of teamwork. We're all pulling in the same direction.' It was the third figure who'd remained silent up to this point. Kerridge himself, she realized. He gently interposed himself between the two younger men with the air of a boxing referee who can see the bout slipping out of control. 'You've both got a point.'

There was nothing in what he was saying, she thought, but he had a natural, easy-going authority that had immediately reduced the other two men to silence. His own voice was unexpectedly soft, so that Marie had to strain to make out his words.

'Way I see it,' Kerridge went on, 'we've got some big deals coming up. Drugs, especially. That Rotterdam consignment's the biggest we've done to date. Can't afford for that one to go tits up.'

Marie made a mental note of the reference to Rotterdam. It was quite possible that her relevant colleagues were already on to it, but if not it would be another piece in the jigsaw.

'Too fucking right—' Boyle began. But Kerridge was continuing to speak, halting Boyle without raising his voice.

'But that's Jake's point. If we go stirring up trouble now, without knowing what we're about, that might be misinterpreted. We're moving into a different league with some of this new stuff. We don't want our suppliers to think we're a bunch of amateurs.'

'I don't—'

'I know you've got the best interests of the business at heart, Pete. And I'm not saying you're wrong.' He paused, in a way that seemed theatrical, though Marie could see that he was lighting a cigarette. 'But we need to get our ducks in a row. Do a bit of digging. If there is a grass, then, yeah, we dispose of him. Quick and clean. Take him out.' Another pause. 'I've no problem with that.'

Marie suddenly realized that she was wearing only her thin evening gown and its silly, largely decorative jacket to protect her from the cold. Even so, it wasn't the temperature that sent a chill down her spine. It was the clinical language. Dispose. Take him out. She was finally beginning to recognize the reality that she was dealing with.

She pulled her useless jacket more closely around her shoulders and moved another step or two, watching the three men. She was reminded, grotesquely, of a bunch of middle managers discussing a redundancy. Except that in this world, termination had a more literal meaning.

Up to now, though she hadn't realized it, this had felt like a game. Like another of Winsor's exercises. It was hard. It was a challenge. But there were no real consequences. If she failed, it might set her career back a notch or two. Maybe cause her a bit of feminist embarrassment.

But of course it was much more than that. She was dealing with people who, if they thought she was a threat, wouldn't hesitate to deal with her. Take her out. Dispose of her.

Jesus. For the first time, she began to wonder whether she was really up to this.

'What do you think, Jake?' she heard Kerridge say. 'You OK with that?'

Morton had taken a step or two backwards, she thought, as if he were trying to disassociate himself from the other two. Or maybe that was just wishful thinking on her part. She'd liked Jake, maybe even been attracted by him. She didn't want to think that he was really part of all this.

'It's the sensible way,' he said. 'We don't want any more screw-ups.'

And that was it. That was all he said, leaving her in the air. Not knowing whether he was really on board or just going through the motions. She knew what she wanted to believe, but she wasn't sure what she really did.

She heard no more of what the men said, because there was a sudden sweep of headlights from beyond the car park entrance. She glanced at the luminous face of her watch. Nearly midnight. This would be the first of the taxis arriving to ferry guests home.

She was about to slip back along the edge of the cars when the taxi pulled into the car park, turning to the left to arc round towards the hotel entrance. She was caught momentarily in the full blaze of its headlights, dazzled by the glare. She stopped, breathless, feeling like an unprepared actor gripped centre-stage by a spotlight. She was sure, in that moment, that everyone could see her. Kerridge and his cronies. The taxi driver. The clustered smokers.

Then the lights swept by and she was back in darkness. Kerridge, Boyle and Morton were tracking back towards the hotel now, apparently oblivious to her presence. Beyond the car park, lower on the hill, she could see the flicker of more cars arriving.

She paused by the car park fence, safe now in the night, waiting for her heart to stop pounding.

Shit, she thought. I'm really not cut out for this.

*

'Have you any real grounds to think so?' Salter had asked a few days later when she'd first brought up her thoughts about Morton. She remembered Salter slumped back in the hotel armchair, his feet propped up on the coffee table. It was impressive, she thought, the way he managed to sound simultaneously both scathing and uninterested. As if he couldn't quite be bothered to tell her what a stupid suggestion it was.

She shrugged, then made a show of pouring herself another cup of coffee, ignoring Salter's empty cup. 'Not really,' she said. 'Just a hunch.'

'Ah. A hunch.' Salter rolled the word round in his mouth, his expression suggesting that he might be about to spit it out physically. 'One of those.'

'Woman's intuition, Hugh. You know how it is. We're just better at that kind of stuff.' She smiled. 'You lot have parallel parking instead.'

'Well, I'll bear your suggestion in mind, sis.'

'That's all I'm asking, Hugh. Just keep him on your radar. There's something about him.'

'Good looking, is he?'

'Why? You jealous, Hugh? Don't worry, he's not in your league.' She shook her head, wondering why they had to go through all this crap. Just a bit of banter. Show that she was one of the lads. Or as close to being one of the lads as she was ever likely to get.

That had been her third liaison meeting with Salter. She made a point of using the word 'liaison', which was how it was described in the formal procedures they were both supposed to follow. Hugh preferred the more old-fashioned term, 'supervision', presumably because it made him feel more important. He might have been designated as her 'buddy' up here, but they were the same pay grade. She had every intention of reminding him of that if he showed signs of getting uppity.

The venue had been yet another anonymous business hotel, this one just off the M56 near the airport. The small meeting room was, as always, nothing more than a semi-converted bedroom. Not her ideal choice of location for a meeting with Hugh Salter, though so far he'd always been on what presumably passed for his best behaviour.

She didn't know quite why she'd mentioned Morton at all. It was partly because, at least to her own ears, her achievements to date had sounded pretty thin. OK, she'd got the business up and running, which was no mean feat for someone of her inexperience. And it had been a tough few weeks. She'd arrived at the print shop on her first day to find that Gordon, the supposedly ultra-reliable, long-serving, ever-willing assistant she'd inherited with the business, had decided that he was happy to turn his hand to anything except working for a woman. Her first task on her first day, therefore, had been to accept Gordon's resignation. Her second had been to call the Job Centre.

For the last couple of weeks, as well as the endless phone calls to drum up business, she'd found herself interviewing a steady stream of no-hopers, most of whom couldn't be bothered even to pretend they had an interest in printing. Fortunately, Gordon had grudgingly agreed to hang around for a couple of weeks to keep the show on the road through a stream of mildly sexist grumbling. And, a couple of days before, she'd finally managed to find a suitable candidate to succeed him, Joe Maybury, an experienced printer who'd just been made redundant from some print shop in Stockport. She was just waiting for the Agency to run the criminal records checks – even with the day-to-day stuff, as Salter kept reminding her, you couldn't be too careful

– before she offered him the job. So, as she told Salter, things were looking up.

But she was acutely conscious that all this was mundane stuff. Just laying the foundations. Getting her legend up to scratch. It was all necessary. You couldn't afford to cut corners at this stage. But by itself it was nothing. She had made only minimal progress in starting to build the relationships that would really matter – with the key players in the local underworld. Sure, she'd followed up all the introductions that had been provided to her, with some initial success. Some, like Kerridge, had agreed to see her. Some had made appropriately polite noises, and would probably be in touch if and when they needed her services. One or two had, to date, ignored her.

That was actually a decent strike rate, she told herself. She was particularly pleased to have made real progress with Kerridge, who was, after all, the biggest fish in this northern pond. Even there, though, a small voice whispered in her ear that all she had was the trial order for some legit business and the opportunity to hand over some money at a charity do.

It was that, probably, that made her mention Jake Morton. But what she'd said was true enough. She did have a feeling about him. And she knew from experience that her feelings in such matters were often right.

'I'm not saying we should approach him now,' she said. 'I'm just saying keep tabs on him.'

She suspected that Salter was more interested than he was letting on. If there was anything in what she was saying, it could turn out to be a big deal. And if there were any big deals in the offing, Salter wanted to be the one doing the dealing. He'd be careful to ensure his backside was covered, but he'd want to grab more than his fair share of any credit that was going.

Salter picked up the coffee jug, weighed it briefly in his hand, and then looked disapprovingly at Marie's recently filled cup.

'You really think he might be interested?'

'I really don't know, Hugh. Like I say, it's no more than a hunch. It was just something in the way he spoke—'

'What did he actually say?'

She thought back to her brief, inconsequential, mildly flirtatious conversation with Morton at the charity dinner. What had he actually said? Not much that she could put her finger on. Not much beyond polite small talk.

'It wasn't anything he said, Hugh. He's not an idiot. He's not going to start blethering on about Kerridge and Boyle and the whole shooting match to someone he's never met before, is he?'

'I wouldn't have thought so,' Salter agreed. 'So what makes you think he's pissed off?'

'Oh, God, Hugh. You know how it is. He makes a joke or two that sound like they're not quite jokes. His tone of voice. Things he doesn't say. I don't know.'

Salter was still toying with the coffee jug, as if he were hoping that it might magically refill itself or, more likely, that Marie might take the hint and order another round.

'It's always delicate, you know. If we get it wrong – if we even time it wrong – we've blown it for good.'

'I know that, Hugh. I'm not an idiot either.' She knew it very well, although unlike Salter she'd never worked as a front-line handler. Her intelligence role had involved collating data on potential intelligence sources – informants, grasses, whatever you wanted to call them. She knew how difficult it was to get the good ones on board, and how sensitive the seduction process had to be. Not the small fry – the ones who'd slip you some usually worthless titbit of information in exchange for fifty quid in untraceable fivers. But the ones who really mattered. The ones who could offer you real access to the people at the top.

There weren't many of them, but they were critical. In the end, these people were often the lynchpins of the Agency's painstaking efforts to build a watertight case against some target villain. They'd be major sources of evidence, maybe even key witnesses in the prosecution case. Success or failure might depend on what they were prepared to say or do, whether they were able to hold their nerve. They all knew the risks they were taking. Whatever steps the Agency might take to protect them – new faces, new identities, new lives – in the end they'd be left turning in the wind. Without friends. Without a past. Maybe without a future.

Christ knew why they did it. Sometimes it was for the money, which could be substantial, but rarely sufficient to justify the risk. More often, it was an insurance policy for those who thought their criminal days might be numbered. They seized on the promise that, when the proverbial did eventually hit the fan, they'd be looked after. If you already suspected that the ship might be heading for the rocks, then becoming a rat became a more attractive career option. Most often, though, from everything that Marie had seen, it was personal. Villains were remarkably persistent in holding a grudge, often for reasons that might be imperceptible or incomprehensible to the civilian world. Grassing someone up could be a highly satisfying form of revenge, at least for the few moments before you recognized the full consequences of what you'd done.

Occasionally, though, the reasons were more honourable. From time to time, a villain might genuinely see the light or get religion or simply realize that life didn't have to be that way. That was the hunch she'd had about Jake Morton. That, in his heart, this wasn't the life he'd chosen. That somehow, somewhere, he'd been suckered into it, drawn by the rewards it offered, and that now he was trapped because, quite simply, there was no way out. Once you'd stepped over that line, there was no easy way back. But, even on the basis of one half-flirtatious encounter, something had told her that that was what Morton had wanted. To be done with it all, to be normal, to rediscover the person he'd been before he'd sold his soul to Jeff Kerridge. Something told her that, if the time were right, if the approach were right, Morton could be persuaded to come over.

Salter had been watching her in silence for some seconds. 'If it's true,' he said, finally, 'he'd be one hell of a catch.' He gently placed the coffee jug back on the table and picked up a custard cream from the unappetizing bowl that had accompanied the coffee. 'I don't know quite where he sits in Kerridge's inner cabinet, but he's not small fry. I'm willing to bet he's got his financial thumbprints on most of the big deals that Kerridge is involved in.'

'I might be wrong,' she said.

'Yeah, of course you might. In fact, you probably are. But there's just a chance that you're not.'

It was funny, she thought. To succeed in this job, you needed to be able to conceal your emotions, maintain that poker face. And Salter, by all accounts, had been very successful. But just at this moment she could read his thoughts as easily as if he were articulating them out loud. This might be the chance they'd been looking for. This might be a chance to spear some of the big fish – Boyle, maybe even Kerridge himself. More to the point, this might be a chance to boost Salter's career.

'We can't rush it,' she said, suddenly nervous about what

Salter might do with what she'd told him. Jump right in there with his size elevens. 'Like you say, we only get one chance.'

He nodded, looking distracted, his mind already somewhere else. Planning his next upward move probably. 'Did you hit it off?' he said finally. 'With Morton, I mean.'

She blinked, surprised by the direct question. 'I suppose so. I mean, I only talked to him for an hour or so at this bloody dinner—'

'But you got on with him? Well enough to get a bit closer?'

'Well . . .'

'We need to keep on him,' he said. 'See if your instincts are right. Work out what might be the best way to get him on board. Do you reckon you might be able to do that?'

She shook her head and swallowed the last mouthful of tepid coffee. 'Christ, Hugh, I don't know. I've only met him once. I mean, we seemed to get on OK, but . . .'

'Give it a go, then. Even if you're not right about this, he's likely to be one of our best routes into Kerridge and his mob.'

She gazed at him for a moment as if she were about to refuse. Then she nodded. 'OK, Hugh. I'll give it a go.'

'Good girl,' he said, in a tone that made her want to punch him hard in the face. 'It could be a big one, this.'

Yes, I know, Hugh, she'd said to herself at the time. *That was why I brought it to you.* In reality, though, she had known that this was the best she could have hoped for. Of course, Salter would be able to shift, without missing a beat, from his initial sneering scepticism to snaffling the idea as his own. He was destined for the top, scrambling his way up on the backs of more scrupulous colleagues.

It didn't matter. As always, he'd got what he wanted. But

93

as they finished the meeting, she'd been left with a feeling that, almost without recognizing it, she'd achieved an objective of her own. She'd been given a reason to see Jake Morton again. Up to that point, she hadn't even known that she'd wanted to.

7

After her debrief with Salter and Welsby, Marie arrived back at the print shop to find the place in a familiar mild chaos. Joe was berating Darren about some new technical faux pas. Darren was giving every sign of paying full attention short of actually listening. She thought Joe was warming to Darren. It wasn't that Darren's performance had improved to any significant – or, for that matter, insignificant – extent. It was more that Joe, recognizing that Marie wasn't planning to dismiss Darren in the immediate future, had adjusted his expectations. Probably to somewhere below ground level.

There were times when Marie suspected that Joe Maybury – a tall, genial, undemonstrative man in his early thirties – might have a crush on her. There were other times when she was convinced that he was gay. Both, she supposed, might possibly be true. Or neither. Joe seemed disinclined to give anything away. She got on with him well, trusted him implicitly in deputizing for her on business matters, even went for a pint with him from time to time, but she had discovered nothing of any significance about his private life. Not that she had particularly tried. She was keen to protect her own privacy, and Joe's taciturnity suited them both fine.

He glanced up as she entered, allowing Darren the opportunity to scuttle away. 'Useful morning?'

She shrugged. 'Bread on the waters stuff. We'll get an order eventually, but not today.'

'Never is, though, is it?' Joe said. 'Don't know how you do it. Keep plugging away. Works in the end, I suppose.'

'One of my virtues,' she said. 'Patience.'

Joe looked meaningfully across at Darren. 'So I've noticed,' he said, 'though I don't know if "virtue" is quite the word.'

She laughed. 'What excitement did I miss this morning, then?'

'Nothing much. Post on your desk. Took a few messages. Nothing urgent. Darren printed off a thousand copies when I'd asked for a hundred. Usual stuff.'

She stopped at the door to her office. 'Anything interesting in the post?'

'Mostly crap,' Joe said. 'Couple of confirmation orders, but only what we knew about. There's a parcel of some sort – marked Personal and Confidential so I didn't touch it.'

She smiled at him. She had no problems with Joe handling the incoming mail. Most of it was, as he said, crap. Most of the rest was just dull. A very small proportion – bank statements, stuff about the business finances – was theoretically sensitive, but she had nothing to hide from Joe. Nothing about the business, anyway. The operation was well capitalized, because the Agency had ensured it would be. And it was doing pretty well so far. Even if the business had been struggling, Joe would have a right to know. Funny, she thought. She felt she trusted Joe more than most people – more than Salter, certainly, probably more than Liam, probably even more than she'd trusted Jake – even though she knew next to nothing about him.

She sat down behind her desk and began to flick through the stack of mail. It was mostly advertising bumf, glossy nonsense that poured in by the bucket load. Some uninformative VAT leaflet from the Revenue. And, as Joe had said, something else. A neatly sealed Jiffy bag, with her name and address handwritten in block capitals on the front.

She remained still for a moment, staring at the writing. Then she glanced up, for some reason half-expecting that Joe would be staring at her through the glass partition. But he was busy on the far side of the room, his attention fixed on one of the machines.

Jake.

It was Jake's handwriting. There was no question. She hadn't seen it often, but she'd seen it enough. Now, it was like seeing a ghost.

She picked up the envelope and peered at it, as if she might be able to discern its contents through the brown wrapping. Then, with a further glance towards Joe, she tore open the package and gazed inside.

She wasn't sure what she'd been hoping for. A letter? Some informal last will and testament? A word of goodbye? But the bag was empty, except for a small plastic data stick. She tipped it into her palm.

An insurance policy, maybe. Something that Jake had arranged to be sent if anything should happen to him. But why her? Or, more to the point, why now? If Jake had wanted her to have it, why hadn't he given it to her before?

She felt a chill run along her spine. The obvious answer was that he'd already known or guessed who she was. He hadn't given it to her before because he'd assumed, probably rightly, that she'd feel obliged to hand it over to her colleagues. And, as Welsby and Salter had intimated, Jake didn't trust her colleagues, not completely. But if anything happened to him, he might well see her as the only person he could trust.

It was all too possible. Jake was no fool. He'd been approached and recruited as an informant after meeting

Marie. They'd allowed a decent interval to pass before any approach was made, and taken every precaution to ensure that there was no traceable link. But that might not have prevented Jake from having his own suspicions.

She looked up to see Joe gazing at her through the glass wall of the office. For a moment, she thought he was watching her, but then she realized that he was just standing over one of the machines, engrossed in the smooth action of the printing. His eyes were turned towards her, but his gaze was fixed blankly in the middle distance, watching nothing more than his own reflection in the glass.

Christ, she thought. She was really beginning to lose it.

'Fancy a beer?'

Her mind was still elsewhere, her expression that of a diver surfacing back into fresh air.

'Sorry, Joe. Miles away. What did you say?'

The company accounts were open on her computer screen, but all her thoughts had been on Jake. Jake and the data stick. Jake and those last few minutes of his life.

Joe was leaning at the open door, glancing at his watch. 'I'm just about through. Wondered if you fancied a beer.'

It was Wednesday, she realized. In her first months in this job, that had been the dead point of the week. The furthest from her weekends back with Liam. The point in the week that she'd felt most alone, most exposed.

Looking back, her relationship with Jake had been a midweek affair, one more way of filling those lonely nights. It had made her realize that she couldn't allow herself to get too close to anyone. Even ordinary friendships were risky. It was too easy to make a slip, reveal some detail that didn't quite square with the woman she was supposed to be.

But she felt an unexpected ease in Joe's presence, a sense that neither expected anything of the other beyond companionable small talk. If Joe had a private life, he'd shown no signs of sharing it with her, and he seemed to have no interest in enquiring about hers. Their conversation remained resolutely superficial, and they had similar taste in films, undemanding crime novels, music. Marie had half-expected that Joe might eventually invite her out to a film or a concert – plenty of other men had done so on a much less secure foundation of shared interests – but the idea never seemed to occur to him.

She glanced at her watch. 'Jesus, that the time?'

'Seems to be,' Joe said. 'You OK? You look a bit tired.'

Typical of Joe, she thought. He gave little away, but he didn't miss much. He'd already detected that she was distracted, and he was giving her a ready-made excuse.

'Yeah, a bit. Didn't sleep too well last night for some reason.' She tapped aimlessly at her keyboard. 'Do you mind if we give it a miss tonight, Joe? I ought to get the VAT sorted, and then all I'll be fit for's falling asleep.'

'Your call, boss,' he said. 'Long as you don't get out of the habit completely.'

'This is alcohol we're talking about, right?'

'You're OK, though?' This time there was a note of real concern in his voice.

Christ, did she really look that bad? 'Why'd you ask?'

'Dunno. Didn't seem quite yourself this afternoon. Wondered if there was some problem.'

'No more than usual.' She gestured vaguely towards the computer screen. 'Just the standard balls-ache. Tax. VAT. Chasing up the customers who think it's a bit abrupt of us to demand payment in less than six months.'

He smiled. 'Definitely your territory, not mine. Even Darren's easier than that. OK, but you won't wriggle out of a beer next week.'

'Drag me there kicking and screaming,' she said.

'If you insist.' He pushed himself away from the doorframe and turned to walk away. Then he looked back. 'By the way, did you find that package?'

She looked up, her throat suddenly dry. 'Package?'

'Thing in today's post. Jiffy bag. Personal and Confidential. Didn't want it to get lost under the other bumf.' He waved his hand towards her paper-strewn desk.

He'd stepped back from the doorway into the darkened workshop. She couldn't read his expression.

'Thanks,' she said. 'Yes, I found it. Nothing important.' She wondered whether to offer more explanation, but anything would sound forced. 'But thanks anyway.'

'No problem,' he said. 'See you in the morning, then.'

He turned and walked away across the workshop. A moment later, she heard the slamming of the main door.

She sat for a moment, watching the doorway, acutely conscious now of the data stick sitting in her handbag beside her.

Typical Joe. Giving little away. Missing nothing.

8

'Guv?'

Salter paused in the doorway. Welsby was at the far end of the office, his chair close to the window. Despite the pouring rain, the window was wide open. Some of the papers from Welsby's desk – those not pinned in place by an array of empty coffee mugs – had already been scattered across the room by the icy draught.

Anyone unfamiliar with Welsby's tastes might have assumed that he had a love of fresh air. In fact, Welsby wasn't keen on any air untainted by nicotine. He'd viewed the national ban on indoor smoking initially as a personal affront and then – when it became clear that the ban wouldn't be rescinded in his undoubtedly shortened lifetime – as a personal challenge. He'd engaged in numerous spats with pub landlords, pointing out in answer to their threats that he *was* the fucking police, even though this was no longer strictly true. In the office, after a few unproductive run-ins with his superiors, he'd established a compromise that allowed all parties to save face. The only problem was that, in the depths of winter, his office was just slightly warmer than the average fridge. But even that had its upside. It meant that people disturbed him only when they really needed to.

'Guv?' Salter said again.

Welsby twisted awkwardly on his seat. His right hand remained dangling out of the open window. 'Morning, Hugh. Lovely day.'

'Glorious.' Salter perched himself on the seat opposite Welsby's desk. He moved the chair slightly to retain eye contact as Welsby ducked his head out of the window to take another drag. The impressive thing was not so much that the lit cigarette never entered the room, as that Welsby maintained his usual authority in the process.

The cigarette was only half-finished, but Welsby flicked it nonchalantly away, no doubt surprising some passer-by in the street outside.

'How's it looking?'

'Not good. I've been back through every possible compromise over the last couple of years. Most of them are something and nothing. Stuff that we've logged in case they suggest a pattern. Most probably just coincidence. Someone under observation who changes his plans at the last minute. Someone who stumbles across one of our surveillance devices. Shit happens. Buggers out there don't play by the rules.'

'But?' Welsby picked up the coffee mug and stared into it, as if expecting that it would have miraculously refilled.

'One or two incidents suggest something more.'

'Like what?'

'We've had one major operation screwed because the parties changed their plans at the last minute. In fact, reading that report, it looks to me like we were fed misinformation from the start. Then there were a couple of promising-looking enquiries that died on their arses because someone had got wind of our interest.'

'Doesn't sound a lot,' Welsby said. 'Like you say, shit happens. And the other side usually get ahead of the game with no help from us.'

'Maybe so. Nothing that couldn't be explained by bad luck and circumstance. But there's a lot of it, right up to Morton.'

Welsby nodded unhappily. 'Ah, yes, our friend Morton. Well, we should've been smarter with Morton. Got him into witness protection straightaway.'

'Meaning I should have?' Salter said. 'Don't remember anyone offering me any bright ideas at the time. All I seem to remember's a load of paperwork and endless questions about whose budget it was going against.'

'Nobody blames you, Hugh,' Welsby said, in a tone suggesting that, now it had been raised, it might be worth giving the idea some consideration. 'We've all learned some-thing. I'm just suggesting that it might be as much cock-up as conspiracy.'

'If you say so.' Salter pushed back his chair, as if preparing to leave. 'Though there's another consideration.'

'Which is what?' Welsby already had another cigarette between his fingers.

'Those incidents I mentioned. They're more interesting when you look at them all together.'

'How so?' Welsby's head was outside the window, wreathed in billows of smoke.

'There was one link between them. Different types of job. Different people involved. But if you track up the food-chain, it's the same party in the frame every time.'

Welsby spoke around his cigarette, neck twisted to peer back into the office. 'The suspense is fucking killing me.'

'Kerridge,' Salter said. 'Every time. The party was Jeff Kerridge.' He paused. 'Now maybe that's something we ought to talk about, guv.'

There was a curse from beyond the window. It took Salter a moment to register that Welsby had fumbled his cigarette so that it had fallen back into the room. Welsby swore again and stamped his foot down on the office carpet. He stared ruefully down at the scorch mark and then back up at Salter.

'Now look what you've done,' he said. 'You'll get me bollocked by Health and fucking Safety as well as by fucking Facilities.'

9

By the time Marie left the shop, it was already dark, the early evening gloom intensified by the unyielding rain. Jesus, this was a miserable time of year. Winter hanging on, no sign of any green fucking shoots. She made her way down the side of the building to the car park. It was a dreary place, a down-at-heel industrial estate on the outer fringes of Trafford Park. The car park was nothing more than a square patch of concrete sandwiched between the two parallel rows of factory units, lit by a single street lamp on the corner of the access road. Hers was the only car left, parked in one of the three spaces reserved for the print shop.

She thumbed open the car's remote locking, pulled open the door and flung herself inside, immediately securing the doors behind her. She realized that she'd involuntarily glanced into the back seat, her mind subconsciously reliving the horror film cliché of the killer appearing in the rear-view mirror. Get a grip, woman.

As she was about to turn the ignition, she was startled by a sudden explosion of sound. It took her the moment before her heart started beating again to realize that it was nothing more than her mobile phone. Liam's fucking ringtone.

She fumbled for the phone, expecting another perfectly mistimed call from Liam himself. But the number wasn't Liam's. It wasn't a number she knew, but it was naggingly familiar. As she pressed the call button, she realized that it was the unknown caller from the previous evening.

'Hello?'

There was an intake of breath, as if someone was preparing to speak. Then silence.

'Hello?'

She glanced at the phone's screen, wondering whether she had lost the signal, but the line still seemed to be open.

'Anybody there?'

Impatiently, she ended the call. She contemplated calling back, but concluded that, if it was anything important, they'd call again.

She started the engine, feeling calmer and back in control as she reversed out of the parking space. As she slipped out of reverse, she reached to flick on the headlights.

The silhouetted figure caught in the beam nearly stopped her heart again.

She slammed her foot on the brake and peered through the windscreen. Then she lowered the side window and thrust her head out into the chilly air.

'Christ, Joe, you scared the shit out of me.'

Joe shuffled embarrassedly forwards, hands thrust in the pockets of his donkey jacket. 'Sorry. Wasn't expecting you to pull out like that.'

'I thought you'd gone.'

'Changed my mind. Decided to go for a quick one on my own. A quick two, actually.' He gestured vaguely back towards the print shop building. 'Think I left my phone in the shop. Hope so, anyway. Either that or I've lost it.' He leaned forwards, hands on the car door, rain dripping off his hair, pressing his face into the open window.

She couldn't recall ever seeing Joe use his mobile in the shop. 'Did you look in the pub?'

106

'Yeah. Thought it must have fallen out of my pocket. But there was no sign. So I'm hoping it fell out in the shop somewhere. It should be switched on, so I can use the office phone to call it if I need to.'

'Good luck, then.'

'Thanks. Did you manage to get the VAT stuff finished?' She'd almost forgotten her excuse for staying behind. 'I was feeling pretty knackered, tell you the truth. Thought I'd just mess it up if I carried on. I'll finish it in the morning.'

'Good decision. There's still time for another quick one if you want to wait while I track down my phone.'

'Not tonight, Joe, thanks all the same. Really am tired. I wouldn't be great company.'

'OK. Next week, then.'

'Yeah. Next week. Promise.'

He smiled and straightened up, his face wet from the rain. 'See you in the morning.'

She raised the window, feeling increasingly uncomfortable. She should wait and offer him a lift home, in weather like this. His flat was only a short bus ride away, but it wasn't a night to be waiting at bus stops.

Her hand hovered again over the window control. Then she put it back on the steering wheel and shifted the car into first gear. As she accelerated down the access road back out towards the M56, she glanced into the rear-view mirror and saw Joe still standing in the rain, gazing after her.

She should have given him a lift. She could even have made the effort to go back to the shop and help him track down his bloody mobile. But something had stopped her.

She was turning out on to the main road before she realized what it had been.

He'd gone to the pub for a quick one. He'd had two quick

ones, he'd said. At least two halves. In Joe's case, more likely two pints. Bitter, his preferred drink. Two pints of bitter.

But, as far as she could tell, there'd been no trace of alcohol on his breath.

Her mind was still churning as she turned off the motorway and took the filter lane back in towards the city centre. She couldn't start building paranoid fantasies about Joe Maybury, of all people. And on the flimsiest of pretexts. It had been raining and windy, for Christ's sake. Joe could have swallowed a packet of mints before leaving the pub. It was hardly grounds for suspecting him to be . . . well, what, anyway? What exactly was she afraid of?

If her position had been compromised – if Kerridge or anyone else was on to her – she was potentially in some danger. But even Kerridge would think twice or three times before taking action against someone who was, to all intents and purposes, a police officer. Killing Jake was one thing. He was one of their own, a potential key witness, and his death would be a warning to others. But there was no mileage in stirring up the kind of shitstorm that would result from the death of an undercover officer. The smart move would be to frighten her off his patch, make enough trouble to ensure she was taken out of the field. Undermine her credibility as a possible witness. Which might be exactly what he was doing.

She came into the city centre along Deansgate, and then turned off left towards Salford. She was still getting to grips with Manchester and its bloody one-way systems. Even now, she constantly found herself trying to take what appeared to be the most obvious route to some destination, only to discover that her path was blocked by the sudden sweep of the tramlines or some jumble of filter lanes that allowed her to drive in any direction except where she wanted. But at least now she could navigate back from the print shop to her flat without getting lost.

She pulled off the main road into the network of side streets that led to the apartment block and the entrance to its underground car park. It probably wasn't where, given a choice, she'd have opted to live. She'd have preferred to be out of the city, maybe somewhere down in leafy Cheshire. But it was pleasant enough, she supposed, in its own way. The flat was spacious and nicely furnished. The block was located on the edge of the city centre, and she had a partial view of the higher landmarks – the new Hilton, the CIS Tower, almost compensating for the fact that most of her windows overlooked neighbouring apartments. And – above all, given her current frame of mind – the place felt secure, built for the kind of residents who had a little more money than had been usual in this part of the city.

She waved her electronic pass through the car window at the entrance barrier and drove into the car park. There was even a reserved space allocated to her flat, just a few yards from the lift. For someone in an advanced state of paranoia, the place was usefully reassuring.

She parked up, grabbed her handbag, locked the car and, with only a single glance over her shoulder at the brightly lit underground space, she pressed the call button on the lift.

As she watched the descending indicator lights, she felt the vibration of the phone in her pocket followed by the shrill buzz of Liam's ringtone. This time, she calmly pulled the phone from her pocket. Not Liam – she assumed he'd time his call for some far less convenient moment – but the same number as before. She pressed the call button and held the phone to her ear.

'Yes?'

She half-expected another silence. Instead, a voice said,

in what sounded like a stage whisper, 'You're on your own now?'

Just what she needed. A perv. 'Tell you what,' she responded amiably, 'why don't you just go right off and fuck yourself?'

She was about to end the call when the voice said, 'I'm calling about Jake.'

She paused, her finger resting on the button. 'Who is this?' She glanced back behind her at the deserted expanse of the car park, feeling suddenly uneasy. She had taken the opening question as some loser's half-arsed attempt at intimidation. Now she recalled that the first call had been terminated at the moment that Joe had appeared unexpectedly by her car.

'We need to talk,' the voice said, still semi-whispering. 'Tonight.'

'I don't think so,' she said, keeping her voice even.

There was another silence. 'I was an associate of Jake's. You don't know me.'

'So give me one good reason to trust you.'

'Jake sent you something.'

She hesitated before replying. Too long, she thought. 'Tell me who you are.'

'We need to meet.'

'If you've got something to tell me, just say it.'

'Somewhere public, then. The place you used to go with Jake on Saturday mornings.'

'If you say so.'

'Nine thirty, tomorrow morning. I'll know you.'

She opened her mouth to find some response, but the line was already dead. She thumbed back to the 'last call' number and pressed the send button. There was a moment's silence, then the repeated mantra: 'Call failed' in her ear. She tried again with the same result. The number was unobtainable.

She could ask Salter to try to track down the number. But

she knew already that it would not be registered, or would be registered to some party unconnected with her mysterious caller. A pirated SIM, discarded after use. That might mean something or not much. Jake had always mixed with people who put a high premium on being untraceable.

But this was someone with an interest in Jake. And who now, for whatever reason, seemed to have an interest in her. In her current state of mind, that was disturbing, though she couldn't decide whether that made her more or less inclined to accept his invitation.

That decision could wait till the morning, she thought, as the lift doors opened. She entered, waved her entry card at the electronic sensor and then pressed the button for the third floor. As the lift rose, she glanced at the CCTV camera that stared unblinking above the doors.

The corridor was as silent as ever. There were three flats on the floor and all were occupied – she'd even met her neighbours once or twice, waiting for the lifts. But most of the time there was little sign of life. It was the kind of place that attracted bored businessmen, living away from home during the week, working late at the office for lack of anything better to do. Just like her. Maybe she should have responded more positively to the overweight man who'd made a half-hearted pass at her as they waited by the lift a few weeks back. Perhaps they had more in common than she'd thought.

She slid the entry pass into the slot in the door and waited for the click and green light that signalled the door was unlocked. But nothing happened. She cursed, and inserted the card again, wondering quite how this system was better than a simple key. Still nothing.

It wasn't the first time. Usually, it was because she'd allowed the card to rest too close to her mobile phone, or so Kev the caretaker had told her. It was a pain in the backside, because the only option was to seek out Kev himself, who spent most of his time sitting around in his tiny flat, but was reliably elusive when actually needed. She swore again, louder this time and, in frustration, jammed hard down on the door handle, as if she might break in through brute force.

To her surprise, the handle dropped and the door opened.

She gently pushed back the door, her unease returning. She could see nothing unusual, no sign that anything had changed while she had been away. She paused, holding her breath, listening hard.

Nothing.

She stepped into the hall. Still nothing but the usual sounds of the flat – the flat click of the central heating thermostat followed by the distant rumble of the boiler firing up. The gentle rhythmic ticking of the warming radiators. The dripping tap that was waiting for a new washer.

She opened the first door on her left, her bedroom, and turned on the light. Empty, and as far as she could see, undisturbed. She moved quietly, opening each door in turn – the en-suite bathroom, the second bedroom, the small kitchen. No one and nothing.

Finally, she pushed open the door at the end of the hallway. The main living room. Empty, of course. She waited a moment before switching on the lamp, watching lights from the surrounding buildings, the distant glow of the city centre.

She wasn't sure how much longer she could keep this up. It was one thing to walk this tightrope when things were under control. But nothing seemed under control now. Maybe she was losing the plot, but it was beginning to seem that nobody else had much idea now what the plot should be anyway.

She moved into the kitchen, her mind already fixed on the bottle of Rioja waiting for her.

Then she stopped and looked back into the living room, her finger frozen on the light switch.

She didn't know at first what had caused her to hesitate. The room was apparently undisturbed. There was a sofa, two armchairs, a desk facing the window that she used when working at home. On the desk was a scattering of papers relating to the business, bits and pieces of office paraphernalia – stapler, hole punch – and her laptop.

Her laptop.

That was it. She always left her laptop open. Liam chided her about it, because it allowed the screen and the keyboard to become dusty. But it was a habit, just one of those things she always did.

Except that today she hadn't. The laptop sat closed on the desk. She walked forwards slowly and peered at it, trying to recall her actions that morning. She'd showered, eaten some toast in the kitchen, come in here to finish her coffee while watching the news headlines on TV. It was two days since Jake's death, and there'd still been no mention on the news, national or local. She'd collected some papers from the desk before leaving. Nothing unusual. She hadn't even looked at the laptop. She'd have noticed if it were closed, surely.

Crazy. Of course, she could easily have closed it without thinking, maybe last night, when she was tired, when she was still annoyed with Liam, when she'd had a couple of glasses of wine.

She looked more closely at the laptop, then, without touching anything, at the papers that surrounded it. Slowly, she moved across the room and looked carefully at the rows of books on the shelves behind the television. Crime thrillers, most of them, paperbacks thrust back on to the shelf in no particular order. Or, at least, in no order that would mean much to anyone other than Marie. They were, for the most part, in the order that she'd read them – sometimes scattergun, sometimes splurges of a single favoured author. She leaned forwards and ran her eyes across the spines.

She straightened and looked around, racking her brain. The rack of CDs. The cupboard against the far wall where she kept various personal documents and files – utility bills, bank statements, various domestic detritus.

In the end, she made her way carefully around the room, peering intently at the edges of the carpet, occasionally bending to touch the skirting board, running her nail carefully between the wood and the plaster.

Finally, she walked back into the hallway and returned to the front door. She crouched in front of it, her face inches from the entry mechanism. Her finger gently reached out and touched a mark on the wood.

'Shit,' she said.

10

She was back in the underground car park, away from the lift. Through the metal railings, she could taste the damp night air, hear the rustle of wind through the surrounding trees. The car park was half-full, rows of expensive-looking family saloons and the odd little sporty hatchback, like hers.

'Shit, come on, Hugh.' He always took an age to answer the secure line, keeping her waiting on purpose since there was only ever one possible caller.

'Sis?' He was fumbling with the phone. Somewhere in the background there was the thud of music, voices chattering. 'You know what time it is?'

She didn't, in all honesty. She glanced at her watch, and realized she would be unsurprised by whatever it showed. It felt like hours since she'd left the office.

'It's only eight fifteen, Hugh. Some of us are still working.'

'You think I'm not?' He'd moved the phone away from his face and momentarily the music grew louder. 'This is where the real work gets done. You know that.'

'Yeah. Boys' work, Hugh.' She was in no mood for the usual badinage. 'I've got a few problems, as it happens.'

'What's the trouble, sis? Tell Uncle Hugh.' He sounded pissed, she thought. Not very, but enough. Though, knowing Salter, it could be just an act, another way of throwing her off guard.

'Someone's broken into my flat, Hugh. Or at least it looks that way.'

'Looks what way?' He sounded genuinely puzzled. Third or fourth pint, she thought. Chewing the fat with Welsby and his mates.

'Professionals, Hugh. People who knew what they were doing.'

'You sure, sis?' He sounded more sober suddenly.

'Not absolutely, no. Professionals. That's the point.' She briefly recounted what had happened with the entry system, then with the laptop. And the other things she'd spotted.

'It doesn't sound much. Sure you're not imagining things?'

'No, Hugh, I'm not fucking sure. That's why I wanted to talk to you about it. Maybe I shouldn't have wasted my fucking time.'

'All I'm trying to say is—'

'Look, Hugh. We both know how this game is played. We both know there are people out there who can do this in their sleep. There are probably one or two of them in the pub with you right now. The only surprise is that I spotted anything at all.'

'Assuming you have spotted something.'

'Yes, Hugh,' she said patiently. 'Assuming I have spotted anything. That's the thing with professionals, you see. They make it hard to be sure. Thought I'd made that point.'

'So what do you think, then? Kerridge's people?'

'Well, that's one possibility, isn't it?' she said. She allowed the silence to build, giving Salter time to contemplate the alternative.

'You think it's us?' he said, when it was clear she wasn't going to continue.

'You tell me, Hugh.'

'Jesus, Marie. If it is, nobody's told me.'

He sounded sincere for once, if only because he'd actually used her bloody name.

'But it's possible,' she prompted.

'Anything's bloody possible,' he said. 'What do you think, that we're checking up on you?'

'Like you say, Hugh, anything's possible. You and Keith seemed to think that Morton might've had something he'd not shared. You also seemed to think that I might know something about it, Christ knows why. So no, I wouldn't put it past you to be doing some checking up on me.'

'Not me, sis,' Salter said. 'Not my style.'

Like hell it isn't, she thought. *All you mean is that it's not you this time.*

But she'd noted the first person singular. 'What about Keith? You think it's his style?'

'Can't see it. But it's a bit of a madhouse here at the moment, truth be told. I'm not sure what to think.'

'Shit,' she said. 'I must really be in trouble if I come running to you, mustn't I?'

'It's what I'm here for, dear sister. Your buddy and mentor.'

'Thanks for that, Hugh. I feel so much better.'

'Hang on in there.'

She cut the call, feeling the cold of the windswept car park. Where had that got her? All she'd done was expose another sliver of vulnerability to Salter. And discovered that, yes, it was quite possible that it was her own lot who'd broken into the flat.

She walked over and stood by her car. Her instinct was to get in and drive. Just drive. Not to any particular destination. Certainly not home, if that's what it still was. Not to Liam.

It was the first time she'd consciously acknowledged that thought. There had been a time, not too long ago, when she would have seen Liam as her refuge. Whatever else might go wrong, she had known she could go back there.

And suddenly she didn't want to. Had she fallen out of love? Or was it even simpler than that? Was it just that, before too long, she might be the one doing the looking after? That Liam might turn out to be not a refuge, but a burden? Was she really that shallow?

Shallow, or just out of her depth. Miles out of her fucking depth.

There was a flash of angled light across the far wall of the car park. Headlights, turning into the entrance. Another resident returning after a night out or an overlong day at work.

She walked back over to the lift, not wanting to be caught down here on her own. The long drive could wait. One day – one day soon – she'd do just that. She'd get in the car and drive, keep driving, maybe through the Tunnel south into Europe, or maybe a ferry north. One day.

The lift doors opened and she stepped in. One day. But not today, and not tomorrow. Tomorrow she had an appointment to keep.

She slept badly. She'd downed the remaining Rioja across the evening, in the vain hope that it would help her relax. It hadn't, of course. She'd become increasingly anxious, unable to concentrate even on some inane reality show on TV. She'd spent a good half-hour, earlier in the evening, running through the supposed evidence of a break-in, more and more convinced now that she'd been mistaken after all. Before she'd phoned Salter, she'd felt certain that the books and CDs on her shelves had been reordered. But maybe she'd moved them herself. She remembered pulling some of the books out looking for one she'd offered to lend to Joe. Had she put them back in the same order? Probably. Maybe.

And the laptop? Was she really that much a creature of habit? Why had she been so sure?

The more she looked, the less certain she became. She'd thought that part of the carpet had been raised, but when she examined it again, she wondered whether it had just been poorly laid in the first place. She'd even thought that the skirting board had been prised from the wall in one place. Perhaps it had. But if so, it had been replaced very skilfully.

But that was the thing about these people, whether Kerridge's or her own. They were experts. They knew exactly how to come into a place like this, do what they had to do, and then leave without a trace. And that raised another question. If they were so skilled, why leave the front door unlocked? Because there was no way to enable the electronic lock again before leaving? Because they wanted to leave just one sign that they'd been, enough to stir her unease?

Or maybe because the lock was just faulty and the break-in had never taken place.

Sometime later, with the wine bottle nearly empty, she realized that she'd forgotten about the data stick. Bloody typical. Only a few hours earlier, it had been the one thing on her mind. Then, in a few minutes, all this had knocked it clear out of her head. And she was supposed to be a professional herself.

Pouring the last of the wine, she turned on the laptop. She'd checked it earlier for any signs of intrusion, but the computer was no more revealing than anything else she'd checked. The machine was highly secured, but in any case she kept nothing on there that might be of interest to any third party, legitimate or otherwise. As far as her inexpert eye could judge, there was no sign that anyone had attempted to access the machine. But she knew that her inexpert eye was incapable of judging very far.

She slipped the data stick into one of the USB ports and waited, her brain mildly fogged by the wine, to see what might be revealed. Almost immediately, she was disappointed. The data stick was password-protected, and she had no idea what password Jake might have chosen. She tried a few obvious ideas – Jake's and then her own middle name, the name of the street where Jake had lived – but with no success.

Why would Jake send her this unless he thought she had a reasonable chance of guessing the password? Which meant that the password must be something obvious. But the harder she thought, the foggier her mind became. More sensible to try again in the morning when she was fully sober.

The perfect end to the perfect evening. Jake had sent her something that might be of vital importance, and she was too stupid even to work out how to read it.

She slipped the data stick back into her purse, stuck it safely under her pillow, and went off to bed, accompanied by a pint glass of water, already steeling herself for the hangover she'd face in the morning.

It was only as she was getting into bed that she remembered that the front door was still unlocked.

It probably didn't matter. If someone had broken in earlier, the electronic lock hadn't prevented them. No one else was likely to turn up tonight. But she felt exposed enough already. She stumbled back into the living room, grabbed a wooden chair, and jammed it under the door handle. Not elegant, but probably a damn sight better at keeping out intruders than that electronic bollocks.

With the chair in place, she felt more secure, but as it turned out, that didn't help her sleep. At some point in the night she found herself awake, staring into the darkness, listening to the unceasing sounds of the night – the buzz of a car on the main road, a distant drunken singing, somewhere a faint sound of machinery.

That was it, she thought. One of her sources of unease. If

it had been her own people who had broken in – if they had suspicions about her behaviour, or if they thought she was holding something back – they'd have done more than just search the flat.

It was what they did. They had people who were experts at that – breaking into houses, planting intercept devices, slipping away with no trace that they'd been there. It was why, almost instinctively, she'd made her call to Salter from out in the car park. Because now she had to work on the assumption that she might be under surveillance.

She lay in the darkness, dry-mouthed, already faintly hungover, thinking about the implications, wondering whether there really was a tape machine in here somewhere or maybe even cameras, sound or movement activated, slipping softly into action as she entered the flat, spoke on the phone. Tracking her every move around the apartment.

Well, more fool them, if so. Whoever they were, they wouldn't get much out of observing her flat, in either information or entertainment value. But the thought of being watched by some pervert, officially sanctioned or otherwise, didn't do much for her comfort. And already they could have watched her unthinkingly insert the data stick into her laptop. Instinctively, she rolled over in bed and felt under the pillow for her purse.

Jesus, she thought, *I can't go on like this.*

It felt as if she'd fallen asleep only minutes before the alarm woke her at seven. She felt like death, a dull ache at the back of her head, her mind still dulled by the aftereffects of the wine. In the last moments before she'd fallen asleep, her brain had been running repeatedly through possibilities for the data stick's password, the options growing increasingly surreal as sleep crept over her. There'd been a point, just before she lost

121

consciousness, when she'd been sure she'd cracked it – the solution had sprung into her mind as clearly as if Jake had whispered it into her ear. But now, in the pale morning light, she had no idea what that brilliant insight might have been.

She dragged herself out of bed, showered, and rapidly downed two pints of water, a black coffee and half a slice of toast. Feeling at least marginally more human, she began to consider what to do next.

She knew now that she was going to keep the rendezvous with her mysterious caller. She'd harboured some vague idea that whatever was on the data stick might clarify things. But with that option now closed, at least for the moment, she felt she had to pursue every lead, however tenuous. The caller might turn out to be some irrelevant crazy, but there was no risk in meeting him in a public place.

She had little doubt where the caller had meant. *Place you and Jake used to go on Saturday mornings.* Every once in a while, they'd go at weekends for a coffee and breakfast in a café bar up on the edge of the Northern Quarter. Sometimes they met there, sometimes they'd already been together all night. The place was nothing special – one of half a dozen places selling Italian-style coffees and pastries where you could find a quiet corner to chat, read the papers, relax. They'd chosen it because it wasn't one of the chains and because, at that time in the morning, it was less busy than most, tucked away in a back street.

She felt uneasy going back there, anxious that the memories might prove too much. She knew she still hadn't fully come to grips with Jake's death. Perhaps this would bring it home, one way or another.

She grabbed her coat and car keys, remembering, as she saw the propped chair against the front door, that she still had to deal with the entry system. For the moment, there wasn't much she could do. As she waited for the lift, she called Kev the caretaker. He wasn't there, predictably enough, but she left a message on his voicemail. Sometime, maybe in the next six months or so, he'd get around to calling her back. Sometime beyond then, ideally within the next decade, he might organize a repair. In the meantime, she was just grateful that she had no possessions of any great value.

It was a fine day, she realized, as she headed back into the city centre. She hadn't been able to face opening the curtains in the flat, and the sudden glare of the sunshine surprised her. The first signs of spring, maybe, at long last. It was still early, but the traffic was already backing up on the main roads, endless streams of commuters heading into work. She was used to driving against the flow and was surprised by the weight of traffic. She was already running late.

She followed the inner ring road round past the arena and Victoria Station, the 1960s monolith of the CIS Tower on her right, before turning off towards the Arndale Centre car park. It was the easiest place to park at this time of the day, and still relatively empty as she drove in. She parked and made her way down the grimy concrete stairs into the upper floor of the shopping mall. Like the car park, the Centre was largely deserted, many of the shops not yet open.

She'd been conscious, driving into the car park, of another car following her up the ramps, twenty or thirty feet behind. She'd parked as soon as she reached a floor with plenty of space, and had assumed that the car behind her would do the same. Instead the driver had continued past.

She'd noted the car at the time, alert for any sign that she might be followed. A dark grey Mondeo, though the rear registration plate was too grimy for her to make out in the gloom of the car park.

Now, walking through the empty mall, a feeling of unease

overtook her. She'd registered the car before it had followed her into the car park. It had been behind her for some distance, three or four cars behind on the ring road. Perhaps coincidence, perhaps not.

As she took the escalator down to the ground floor, she glanced back over her shoulder. The upper concourse was deserted, apart from a bored-looking security guard staring vacantly into the window of the Apple Store. Then, at the opposite side of the mall, she caught sight of another figure, someone in a long black coat, collar turned up, who had just emerged from the entrance to the car park. She observed him for a moment, wondering whether to wait at the bottom of the escalator to see whether he followed her down. See how he reacted, see if she recognized the face.

But the man – she assumed it was a man, though it was impossible to be sure from this distance – had also paused. He had a hand to his ear, and she realized that he was talking on a mobile phone. She waited another moment, but he showed no sign of ending his call. He had turned his back, staring blankly into one of the store windows, apparently unaware of her presence.

Finally, she made her way through the ground-floor concourse and out on to Market Street. Suddenly she wanted to be out in the open air, among the early morning commuters, the crowd streaming down from Piccadilly Station into the heart of the city. She turned left and hurried up towards Piccadilly Gardens, where people were stopping to enjoy the morning sunshine, cardboard cups of coffee clutched in their hands, grabbing a few restful moments before heading to work.

She turned left into Oldham Street and hurried through into the network of back streets that comprised the city's Northern Quarter, a bustling mix of fashionable shops, bars and cafés. The place she was going to was tucked away in a secluded courtyard, part of a converted warehouse building, down one of the side streets running parallel with Piccadilly.

She pushed open the door, enjoying the welcoming warmth, the rich scent of coffee and baking. She could see no one who might be her mystery caller. There was a young woman in a smart suit studiously thumbing some extended message into a BlackBerry. A couple of older women chatting over coffee and croissants. One young man in the queue ahead of her, dressed in a garish cycling outfit, helmet in his hand, clearly just getting a coffee to take out.

She glanced at her watch. Just gone nine thirty. Maybe her caller wasn't here yet. Or maybe he wasn't coming.

She ordered a latte and a pastry, and carried them carefully to a table at the rear of the room. The café had a rack of newspapers, so she took one of the tabloids, positioning herself facing the door. How long should she wait? Thirty minutes, maybe. As long as would be reasonable for someone killing a little time before an appointment. Not enough to make her conspicuous.

She'd dressed in a simple but smart business suit, slightly less expensive than it appeared – the look she adopted when meeting a client, rather than the more pragmatic jeans and jumper outfits she usually wore in the print shop. She wasn't sure why she'd bothered dressing up. Something about looking inconspicuous – another businesswoman running a little early for an appointment. But also about wanting to feel in control.

'Ms Donovan?' the voice said from behind her.

She turned, as calmly as she could, and gazed up at the short, plump man hovering a few feet from her table. Where the bloody hell had he sprung from?

'Sorry if I startled you,' he said, as if reading her thoughts. He gestured behind him. 'I was out having a smoke. They've a shelter out there to accommodate the addicts.'

She noticed now, looking past him, that the door which she'd thought led only to the lavatories also led out to the rear of the building.

She did know him after all, she realized, or at least she'd met him before. It was the faint Welsh accent that had reminded her. Somebody Jones. Morgan Jones. A low-rent associate of Kerridge's, one of the hangers-on who picked up bits and pieces of dirty work. The kind of person they'd call on when they wanted something low-risk done on the cheap. She'd seen him a few times at meetings with Kerridge's people, hanging about in the background like a bad smell.

He was still hovering above her table, looking awkward. 'You OK for a drink? I'm getting myself another one.'

'I'm fine. You go ahead.'

She watched him as he queued, wondering what this was all about. Jones didn't look relaxed exactly – his manner was too uncomfortable for that – but he seemed a different figure from anything she'd imagined from the previous night's call. He had the air of an unsuccessful businessman – which she supposed was pretty much what he was – in his cheap, ill-fitting suit.

He returned bearing a tray with a mug of tea and two croissants. 'Thought you might like some breakfast,' he said, lowering himself into the seat opposite her.

She shook her head. 'Morgan, isn't it?'

'I'm impressed. People don't usually find me that memorable.' He paused. 'Sometimes helpful in our line of work.'

She ignored the implied collusion. 'What's this about, Morgan? Why'd you call me?'

He picked up one of the croissants and took a large bite, showering crumbs. 'Sad news about Jake.'

'Very,' she said. 'Why'd you call me, Morgan?'

'Always took you for the straightforward type,' he said. He made the adjective sound pejorative. 'No messing about.'

'More than I can say for you. I'm thirty seconds from buggering off, unless you've something to tell me.'

'You heard what happened to Jake?'

'I heard rumours,' she said. 'Nobody's saying much.'

'No, well. You heard he was a grass?'

'That's one of the things I heard. I don't know if it's true.'

'It's true,' Jones said sadly. 'They'd got him down as a witness.'

She took a swallow of her coffee. More bitter than usual, she thought. 'They didn't look after him very well, then. According to the rumours.'

'What do you expect? No one likes a grass.'

She picked up her briefcase, as if preparing to leave. 'We just here to exchange philosophies, Morgan, or do you have some reason for wasting my time?'

'Nasty what happened to Jake at the end. You'll have heard the rumours about that, too?'

'I've heard something,' she said. 'Like you say, no one likes a grass.'

'You were close to Jake?'

None of your fucking business, she thought. 'Not really,' she said calmly. 'I liked him. He was a laugh.' She shrugged. 'Just goes to show.' She was watching Jones closely now.

'Word is,' Jones went on, 'that they thought Jake was just the tip of the iceberg. That, before they killed him, they tried to get him to spill the beans on who else might be involved.'

'Oh, yes?'

'Word is,' Jones said, 'that your name was mentioned.'

'That right? Always nice to be in people's thoughts.'

'No one likes a grass.'

'Oh, just fuck off, Jones. Don't try the hardman act. It fits you as well as that fucking suit.'

'I'm just saying . . .'

She had started to rise from the table. 'For what it's worth, Jonesy – and Christ knows why I'm even bothering to talk to you – Morton and I were friends, but that's it. I thought he was OK, God help me. If he was a grass, it's nothing to do with me.'

She was turning to leave the table when Jones said quietly, 'Morton named me as well.'

'What?'

'Told them I was a grass.'

Something in his tone made her hesitate. 'And are you?'

He didn't respond. His head was down, his eyes fixed on his now empty mug.

'Jesus, Morgan.' She sat herself back down.

'I'm not a grass,' he said quietly. 'I mean, I never meant . . .'

They never did. They never intended it to end up that way. That was one of the skills of the handlers. They identified the right people. They played on their weaknesses, insecurities. Their aspirations and desires. They did it slowly, slowly, step by step, each a tiny increment on what had gone before. So there was never an identifiable moment when it happened. Never a point where the informant could say, 'I used to be that, and now I'm this.'

'Do you want to talk, Morgan?'

He looked up at her, and she thought perhaps she'd taken a step too far. His expression was blank, as if he'd used up his last hope and was resigned to whatever the fates might throw at him.

'I'll get you another tea,' she said. 'Something hot and sweet.'

How English, she thought. *How do you respond to a crisis, except by offering a cup of tea?* But she wanted to give Jones a few moments to think, reflect on his options. Ease him gently in her direction.

Jesus, here Jones was, apparently on the point of mental

collapse, and all she could think of was how to take advantage of it. How to play him along. It was what she was good at. It was her job.

She queued behind some office-type getting a tray of hot drinks to take out. Occasionally, she glanced over at Jones, who was still sitting, head bowed, looking as if he just received some devastating news.

The woman in front finally finished her order, picked up the cardboard tray and departed. 'Hot drinks?' the young man behind the counter said, in a tone that sounded like an instruction.

She ordered a tea and another small caffè latte, fumbling in her purse for change. As the young man busied himself with the espresso machine, she glanced back towards Jones.

The table was empty. In the few seconds since she'd looked away, Jones had upped and gone, presumably through the same rear exit he'd used earlier. For a moment, she wondered whether to pursue him. But Jones was nothing more than a joker, a lightweight. Most likely, all this was bullshit, Jones chasing some half-arsed agenda of his own.

The only certainty was that she hadn't a clue what to do next. For a moment, she felt detached, weightless, light-headed. One of those dreams where nothing is solid, where everything changes in a moment.

'Cancel the tea,' she called to the young man. 'And I'll take the coffee to go.'

11

Liam was propped against the metal rail, staring at the open sea. 'Look, if you like, we can just stop now.'

Some acid response was in her mouth, but she bit back the words. It wasn't the moment. She was too tired. And, anyway, she didn't know what he meant. Stop what? Stop walking? Stop everything?

Christ, this had been a mistake. In the end, she'd decided to come back home for the weekend. She'd hesitated initially, wondering if there was a risk that she might be followed. But she knew, rationally, that it was unlikely. It was one thing to follow someone for a few miles across a city centre. It was quite another to remain undetected across two hundred miles or more, particularly if your target knew you might be there. Even so, she'd driven cautiously, taking a convoluted route out to the motorway. stopping repeatedly at service stations on the way down. She'd taken the M25 round to the east, over the Dartford bridge, and entered London from the south-west, again choosing an extended route to confuse any pursuer. If anyone had managed to keep up with her through all that, well, good luck to them.

In any case, she thought ruefully as she turned into the narrow streets that surrounded their home, if there really was a mole back at the ranch, there'd be much easier ways of identifying her. It struck her now, as she pulled up in front of the familiar front door, that there was really nothing she could rely on. Nowhere that was safe.

Still, she'd been glad to come back here. It would give her some space, she thought, provide an opportunity to think. And if something was about to kick off, if there was any truth in what Jones had claimed, this took her out of the immediate firing line. Only for a day or two, but maybe enough to get her head straight.

But it hadn't worked. She shouldn't have been surprised. Coming back here had been a strain for months now. It was partly the sense that she was drifting away from all this, that real life was elsewhere. But it was also that she and Liam were both trying too hard to overcome the suspicion that the best was past.

There'd been a familiar emotional pattern to these weekends. She arrived late Friday night, and they spent a tense evening, each taking umbrage at whatever the other said, spoiling for a fight. Usually they went to the pub for a pint or two. Sometimes that helped. More often it didn't.

By Saturday morning, they'd be at each other's throats. They'd have a blazing row, releasing all the tensions that had built up over the last two or three weeks. After that, things improved till, by Sunday evening, they'd recaptured something of the old warmth. And then it was time for her to go back.

That had been the way even during the best times. It went with the job. She knew that. If you spent a long time apart, it took a while to get back together again.

After she met Jake, the weekend pattern became more intense. It was her own guilt, and her resentment about feeling guilty. It was the sense that she ought to be able to have things both ways, that this shouldn't be a big deal, and the knowledge that of course it was. It was the awareness that she didn't know what she wanted, and that she didn't see why she should have to decide anyway.

But, mostly, it was Liam's fault. It was Liam making unreasonable demands, even when he said nothing. Especially when he said nothing. She had work to do, real work, while Liam just sat down here, disapproving of whatever she did. Playing the victim, indulging the hobby he called a job, sponging off her.

None of that was fair or true, of course, and her rational mind knew it. But it was a convenient mindset to fall into on a miserable Saturday when she was feeling knackered, tense and depressed by everything the world kept throwing at her.

Even so, they'd managed to come through. Even the worst of the weekends usually ended with the realization that the sparse time was slipping away, that they did want and need each other, that – once the dust had settled – they still enjoyed each other's company. Even in the last few months, she had warm memories of Sunday morning lovemaking, lunch in some country pub, a walk along the coast if the weather was half-decent.

But this weekend it wasn't working. It was her own anxiety, the fears she couldn't begin to share with Liam – or with anyone. But Liam was changing, too, she thought. He seemed distracted, a shadow of the lively fun-loving man she'd once fallen in love with. He'd always been prone to bouts of depression, sometimes intense, usually short-lived, and she could see signs of that now. It was the illness, obviously. But it was also his work, the dreams still not close to fulfilment, everything now in the balance.

And it was her. Her job, her absence, her refusal or inability to provide the emotional support he needed.

She wasn't sure if his condition had deteriorated since she'd last seen him. It came and went – relapsing and remitting, they called it. Most days he was more or less fine. Some days he could barely walk.

Today, he seemed OK, just a little below his best. He walked slowly, leaning on a stick, with a barely discernible limp. Occasionally a grimace crossed his face, so briefly that she wasn't sure whether she was imagining it. She suspected that he was learning to conceal the worst of his condition, and that he was feeling more pain, or at least more physical stress, than he was letting on.

Whatever the cause, they'd both been in a foul temper all weekend. Sunday morning had brought no lifting of the cloud, just further sniping and irritation. In an attempt to dissipate the fog of their mutual ill-feeling, they'd opted for a drive down to the south coast, some lunch overlooking the sea, a walk along the promenade. It was just another seaside town, reasonably accessible from their South London home, perhaps a bit more upmarket than most, but it had been one of their favourite places. Early in their relationship, before they'd moved in together, they'd spent regular weekends down here, getting to know each other, feeling their way around each other's hearts, minds, bodies, creating memories that sustained them through the difficult later months.

Today hadn't destroyed those memories, but they seemed increasingly distant. They'd had a mediocre lunch in an over-priced seafront restaurant where the waitress had seemed even more pissed off than they were. The town seemed stale and dull, and she struggled to remember why she'd ever liked the place, with its endless tacky souvenir shops and uninviting cafés. Even the walk along the promenade felt like a chore, Liam dragging slowly along, drizzle and cold winds pounding in from the leaden Channel.

Now Liam was hunched over the metal railing, staring out

to sea as if contemplating a watery suicide, telling her that he just wanted to stop. Well, who could blame him?

She moved up behind him and tucked her arm in his. At first, he made no response, then, after a moment, he slid his arm around her waist.

'Is this it, do you think?' he said finally. 'Are we finished?'

'Christ, Liam, I've been a complete bitch,' she said.

'True enough,' he agreed. 'On the other hand, I've been a total arsehole.'

She laughed. The first time she'd laughed that weekend. 'I won't challenge that incisive piece of self-evaluation.'

'What's making us like this? Maybe we really do need to give it up now.'

She turned to look him in the face. 'You keep saying that,' she said. 'I'm beginning to think you might mean it.'

'Don't know what I mean. Don't know what to think any more.' He waved his stick vaguely in the air. 'Not easy to get your mind around this. Makes it difficult to think about anything.'

She couldn't argue with that. It was the worst thing about his illness – the absence of any clear prognosis. Years more of this, or something much worse. And that raised another question. About whether she was strong enough to cope with whatever the illness might throw at them. Whether, if it came to it, she was strong enough to be Liam's carer.

'You need to talk to the doctor again,' she said, knowing that she was just trotting out the same meaningless mantra.

He turned and looked at her, then shook his head. 'It's not been a great day so far, but it won't be improved if we get into that old argument again. You know there's nothing she can say to me. I'll go back when I need to, but I'm not clutching at straws.'

Again, she couldn't argue. There were those who, faced with

Liam's condition, would pursue every possible solution. Second opinions, alternative remedies, any available form of quackery. There were those, too, who went into denial, pretended it wasn't really happening to them.

Liam's approach was different. Like most things in his life, he'd taken the diagnosis in his stride, simply accepting its reality. She remembered what he'd been like that first evening after his appointment with the neurologist. Shaken, and quieter than usual, but with the air of someone who'd perhaps received a larger-than-expected credit card bill or whose car had been damaged in some minor shunt. Not someone who'd just been given a potentially life-changing piece of news.

She'd felt guilty that day, too, because she'd allowed him to attend the appointment on his own. Her only excuse was that, typically, Liam had given her no real inkling of what was going on. He'd told her the full story only that evening. Hadn't wanted to worry her unnecessarily, until he was sure. She suspected that, with feelings caught between shock, anger and guilt, she'd reacted less calmly than Liam himself had.

It wasn't that Liam had been untroubled. In the weeks afterwards, he'd devoted himself to learning whatever he could about this baffling illness – borrowing books from the library, scouring the internet, sending off for leaflets from the MS Society. Mostly, he said, this mass of material just confirmed how little anyone knew – about the cause, the potential treatments, the likely prognosis. He'd confirmed to his own satisfaction that the limited medication he'd been prescribed was appropriate, and that, at least within the boundaries of conventional medicine, there was little else available. Liam had no time for alternative treatments. So that, as far as he was concerned, was largely that.

He was, or seemed to be, unfazed by the threat posed by the illness, but equally he harboured no false hopes. Maybe his condition would stabilize or even improve. Maybe it would continue to decline. Either way, other than the steps he was already taking, there wasn't much he could do about it.

'OK,' she said now, moving herself closer beside him. 'Your choice.'

'My choice,' he agreed. 'You reckon we can still make this work?'

'Probably,' she said. 'So long as we don't expect it to be easy.'

'It could be easier.'

'If I gave up my job, you mean?' The sea looked dark and threatening under the thunderous sky. The narrow beach was deserted, an occasional seagull shrieking in to gather some discarded remnant.

'It's not all or nothing. You could do something less demanding.'

'Like what? Waitressing? Teaching? Prostitution?' She was already pulling away from him.

'No, for Christ's sake, Marie, I'm not saying give up the job. I'm just saying you don't have to be doing what you're doing now. You've said yourself how demanding it is, that officers can burn out—'

'You mean I can't cope?'

'Oh, for fuck's sake, stop this and listen. I'm not saying anything like that.'

She had turned away and was staring fixedly out to sea, but she knew that, if only for once, he was right.

'What are you saying, then?'

'I'm not trying to stop you doing anything. If this is what you want to do, fine by me. It's not ideal but we can make it work. But you know you can't do this forever. Even if you want to carry on, they'll want to bring you back in from the field eventually.'

'Before I go native?'

'If you like. Christ, Marie, you're the one who's told me all this. I don't know how it works. You do.'

She did. However good she might be at this job – and at times she didn't know if she was any good at all – at some point, for whatever reason, they'd bring her back in. Quite probably that was what they were already planning. And quite possibly, if she took Morgan Jones seriously, it was what she needed.

'Shit, Liam, I don't know.'

'Neither do I, and it's not something we need to decide now. I'm just saying that things won't be like this forever.'

'So what are you saying?'

'I'm saying we run with it for a bit.' He laughed. 'Let's just try to be a bit less uptight, OK? Enjoy the time we do get together.'

She said nothing for a moment, her eyes fixed on the barely discernible horizon. *Oh, I do like to be beside the seaside*, she thought. She could remember a time when all this seemed to bring her to life, when she'd thought maybe they could come and live down here, find a way to make ends meet while Liam tried to make a go of his painting. She loved the tang of salt and ozone. The bite of the sea wind. The sense of being at the edge of things, with a world of possibilities out there.

'You're right,' she said. 'This was never going to be easy. We have to work with it for a while . . .'

She wasn't sure what happened next. She was turning back towards Liam and he was moving closer to her when his legs slipped from under him. He toppled sideways, his face ashen, his mouth shaped to utter some words he never spoke. His wooden stick clattered under the metal railing, falling silently down to the sands below. And then Liam was falling, too, his head striking one of the iron posts, his body sliding awkwardly into the rails as he lost his footing.

137

She reached out instinctively and grabbed his thick woollen coat. His weight was too much for her and he dropped forwards, his head striking the post again.

She could see blood on his scalp, mingling with his wet hair, dripping down his forehead.

Her mind was already running through the possibilities, her eyes scanning the deserted promenade. She crouched over him, sheltering his head from the rain, fumbling for her mobile phone.

Christ, she thought, what had they done now?

12

'Anything's possible. But it's nothing to do with me.'

'You'd have been informed, though, guv, surely.'

Welsby shrugged. 'In theory, but these days . . .' He jerked a thumb in the direction of some unspecified authority. 'Any one of those bastards might have authorized it. Wouldn't necessarily keep me in the picture. Might be an oversight. Might be deliberate.'

'Paranoia,' Salter agreed.

'Aye. Fucking paranoia. And when that takes hold, nobody gets spared. Even the pure in heart like you, Hughie.'

'Or you, sir,' Salter added dutifully.

'Yes, son. Even me.' He took a deep swallow of his pint and gazed thoughtfully around them. They were sitting under the smokers' shelter outside what was apparently one of Welsby's favourite pubs. Salter hadn't been surprised that Welsby had suggested meeting in a pub, but he'd expected somewhere different from this. Some down-at-heel back-street local with curled sandwiches and pickled eggs, not an upmarket gastro place. But Welsby always liked to keep people on their toes.

More practically, it wasn't the kind of place where anyone was likely to recognize either of them. Out on the edge of the Pennines, too far out of town, too middle class. A few of the upper echelons, on either side, might pop out here from time to time, but they'd be with their own families and equally keen not to be spotted.

It wasn't really Salter's kind of place. He wasn't a great drinker except for networking purposes – too much risk of losing control – and, if he was going out to eat, he preferred somewhere quieter, more discreet. Even on a Sunday night, this place was buzzing, full of families and couples at the restaurant tables, clusters of young men drinking by the bar. Most were eating. Pretentious pub grub, Salter thought. He'd followed Welsby to the bar, and eyeing the impressive array of real ales, ordered a pint of Carling on principle. Welsby had ordered something dark and rustic-looking which he held up as though inspecting a fine wine.

Salter had been wondering where they'd find a quiet corner to talk in this place, but that question had been quickly and predictably answered when Welsby had led them immediately out the back door into a rear courtyard. Unsurprisingly, they were the only drinkers who'd braved the damp night air to take advantage of the tables under the canvas awning. In the darkness behind them, the land fell away into the wind-blown emptiness of the Goyt Valley.

'So what did she say exactly?' Welsby said. He'd lit up a cigarette, making no very obvious effort to direct the smoke away from Salter.

'She was worried that her flat might have been broken into.'

'She wasn't sure?'

'That was the point. She thought it might be a pro job.'

'Officially sanctioned, you mean?'

'Maybe. She'd also thought of Kerridge.'

Welsby blew more smoke into the air. 'Like I say, anything's possible. No one tells me anything. Not losing her marbles, is she?'

'Wouldn't have said so, but you never know in this game, do you?'

'Too right,' Welsby said. 'Look at you. Bloody Carling.'

'I don't know,' Salter went on. 'She sounded rattled. But that's not surprising. If we are leaking, she's pretty exposed out there. In her shoes, I'd be rattled.'

'Why would Kerridge break into her flat, though? Bit subtle for him.' Welsby gazed impassively at the younger man, as if daring him to challenge this judgement.

Salter shrugged. 'You know him better than me, guv. But Kerridge must be getting jittery himself. If the case against Boyle sticks, it's getting bloody close to home. He's taken out our key witness, but he doesn't know what other dirt's out there. He may just want to know what Donovan's got before he resorts to scare tactics.'

'All a bit complicated for a simple plod like me,' Welsby said. 'But we can't take risks. If Kerridge is on to Donovan, we need to pull her out PDQ.'

'This is all guesswork . . .' Salter paused. 'But even if he is, maybe we should think about timing.'

'Secret of good comedy, so I'm told. OK, then, make me laugh.'

'We need Kerridge to make a mistake. Without Morton, we've barely got a case against Boyle. We don't know if Morton had anything more, and if so, whether it's out there somewhere . . .'

'Not even raised a fucking smile so far,' Welsby said.

'Our best chance is if Kerridge starts to get shaky. He doesn't know what other dirt we might have.'

'He'll know what we've got when it comes to court,' Welsby pointed out. 'It'll all be disclosable then. And he'll need his sides stitching back together when he's finished laughing at how little there is. There you go. Timing.'

'But he doesn't know that now. And neither do we. What if Donovan really does have something? Something she's not even sharing with her friends.'

'I hope this is going somewhere.' Welsby stared morosely into the bottom of his empty glass. 'I'm getting thirsty.'

'I'm just thinking that, if Kerridge is thinking that way, there might be some benefit to us in leaving her out there, just for a little while.'

Welsby looked up and gazed steadily into Salter's eyes for a moment, as if thinking through the implications of what the younger man had just said. 'Bait, you mean. You should be careful, Hugh. Some people might think you were a bit of a bastard.'

'I'm not suggesting we take any risks. We can reel her back any time we need to. All I'm saying is, let it run a little bit further.'

'We don't even know if Kerridge has rumbled Donovan. What about her other theory? That it was our lot?' Welsby paused. 'If it was authorized at our end, it was somewhere well up the chain. But, like I say, anything's possible.'

'If there is a leak,' Salter mused, 'it must be at a senior level. There weren't many people in the know about Morton. But if it was a pro job, they'd have needed Tech Support. If someone mobilized that bunch, we can find out who, presumably.'

'In the grand spirit of interdepartmental co-operation? Maybe. Wouldn't bank on it, though. Even at the best of times, it's harder to screw information from those bastards than it is to get it from the other side. If they've been told from on high to keep a lid on it, they'll keep a lid on it.'

'With what justification?' Salter said. 'The Boyle case is a major fucking deal. If someone's playing silly buggers around it, Tech Support would still need to keep us in the loop.'

'Depends what they've been told. Depends who's doing the telling. Might have invoked Professional Standards. Kicked off an internal investigation.'

'Against who?'

'Against you or me, maybe. Think about it. If you were one of the bigwigs, maybe in Kerridge's pocket, and you wanted a smokescreen, then getting Standards to dig about down below's a pretty smart move. It confuses the issue, throws a lot of crap about, and gives whoever it is the opportunity to dig up more dirt with all the Agency's resources on their side.'

'Shit. You mean on top of everything else we might be being investigated by Standards? Not exactly career enhancing.'

Welsby shrugged. 'For some of us, the future's already gone. But it's just an idea. Thinking out loud.' He leaned forwards, his eyes fixed on Salter. 'That's what you like to do, isn't it, Hughie? Explore all the angles.'

'I'm just shooting the breeze, boss. Truth is, we know nothing. Maybe it is just that Donovan's slipping slowly off her trolley.'

'I wouldn't entirely blame her, would you? Got a lot on her plate. At home as well, by all accounts.'

Salter raised an eyebrow. His buddying role with Marie was supposed to include an element of pastoral care, but he made a point of not getting too close. If she'd got problems she wanted to share, he'd be prepared to listen, but he wasn't encouraging her to unload. Like most people in this business, he preferred to keep his private life private, and he was happy for others to do the same. Welsby, though, somehow always managed to have his finger on what was going on.

'Boyfriend trouble?' Salter asked.

'Boyfriend not well is what I hear,' Welsby said. 'Maybe something serious.'

'Perhaps she'll be wanting out herself, then.'

'She's single-minded, that one. When she wants to be.' Welsby paused, taking his time over lighting another cigarette, his expression thoughtful. 'You're probably right, though. We should leave her out there, just for the moment. That single-mindedness could be just what we need. If she stirs some shit, we can all see what rises to the surface.' He took a first drag on the cigarette and blew out a steady stream of smoke, more or less in Salter's direction. 'Now, Hughie boy, it's good to talk and all that, but are you going to get me that pint, or do I keel over from fucking dehydration?'

13

The second time she'd met Jake, it had been unexpected. She'd spent the previous few days trying to think of a decent-sounding excuse for getting back in touch with him. She'd known after her meeting with Salter that she wanted to see Jake again. She tried to tell herself that her reasons were simply professional. He was an important contact, the most direct route she was likely to find into Kerridge's inner circle. If she wanted to make a success of this job, if she wanted to prove to the likes of Salter and Welsby that she really could hack it, this was her best chance. Even if it did mean making use of what Welsby would no doubt call her feminine wiles.

In her heart, though, she knew that her motives were no longer quite so pure. She was attracted by Jake. She hadn't quite registered it at first, or at least had been aware of it only as the vaguest inkling, the kind of half-stirring you might feel for some passing acquaintance. After all, they'd had a pleasant enough evening at Kerridge's charity do, chatting easily, knocking back a few glasses of wine. As the evening ended, and they made their way to the pre-booked taxis, she'd expected he might try it on, or at least ask her out. But he'd simply wished her a polite goodnight, and headed back for some sort of debrief with Kerridge. Looking back, the sensation she'd felt had been less than disappointment, but it had still been discernible.

Then, as the days passed, she could tell that it was growing into something stronger. Not so much a physical attraction, she thought, though she couldn't deny that there was that, too. It was a longing for friendship, for humour, for the warmth they'd briefly shared on that mildly boozy evening. The kind of relationship she had with Liam, she thought, and then caught herself wondering whether that was still the case. Perhaps that was why, suddenly, she felt so attracted to Jake Morton. Because he offered her something that she hadn't even realized she'd lost.

She was tempted just to pick up the phone and call him, but she didn't want to seem too eager. Like some teenager playing hard to get, she laughingly told herself. But she hadn't quite lost sight of her professional objective. She had to tread warily here. Whatever she might think about Jake at a personal level, he was still on Kerridge's team. She couldn't afford to give him any reason to be suspicious of her motives, even if she wasn't entirely clear about them herself.

She spent a few more days struggling to concoct a good business reason to call him, always hoping that, against the odds, Jake might decide to call her first. With every day that passed, it was feeling increasingly like an unrequited adolescent crush. Then one morning, just when she'd decided that she might as well take the plunge, she received a phone message from Ken Anstey. According to the records, Anstey was another of Kerridge's associates, once or twice removed, but with no link to Kerridge's legit operations. Anstey described his business as import-export, but most of it was import and all of it was dodgy. Small-time stuff for the most part – alcohol, cigarettes, occasionally drugs or serious porn. Most was sold into Kerridge's networks, and as always, Kerridge creamed off a decent slice for himself.

The authorities weren't that interested in Anstey himself. They were keeping tabs on pretty much everything he brought in, and he would be picked up eventually. For the moment, though, they were only too happy for him to keep doing his bits of business. Step by step, they were tracing Anstey's networks, following where the goods went, seeing who was selling and who was buying at each end. Anstey and his cronies got their hands dirty, but the real interest was in those who kept their hands clean.

'You don't know me,' Anstey began laughably. From what she'd heard, every officer up here knew Anstey, if only by name and half-cocked reputation. 'But I might have a bit of business to put your way. Give me a call when you can. Next day or two.'

Anstey left his name and a mobile number. She knew there was no point in leaving it more than the stated day or two. The number would be a pirated SIM card, operational for a few days then discarded.

She phoned Anstey back and did the deal. It was one of her first pieces of under-the-counter business, but straightforward enough. He wanted documentation, legitimate-looking shipping notices that indicated that duty had already been paid. A fallback in case they were picked up by customs. Easy enough to get produced, though unlikely to be effective if customs hadn't already been briefed not to detain Mr Anstey. Marie didn't tell Anstey that, though. She just quoted him a price and a delivery date.

Anstey never said so, but Marie knew she'd have been recommended by Kerridge's people. When she moved up here, the Agency had pulled the strings to spread the word among the right people. They'd have had her checked out, but everything would have seemed kosher. She'd built a good reputation in her previous patch – she was known as a fixer, someone who got you what you needed, even when others couldn't. Not difficult, when you had the resources and protection of the Agency behind you. But it made her look good. She delivered.

It had taken a month or two for the word to spread, but finally the business was starting to come in. She had the contacts. She could get you people, she could get you equipment. She could get you vehicles – untraceable, available when needed, then gone again. She could get you documentation, though behind the scenes that needed authorization in triplicate and there were limits as to what was permissible. The ability to produce fake passports would have given them a neat advantage in tracking movements across national boundaries, but that was a definite no-no.

The other thing she didn't deal – couldn't deal – was firearms. But it seemed easier for her to hold that line than it had been for her predecessor. In this skewed world, it was what they expected a woman to do. Women just had higher standards. The men didn't understand it, but they respected it. No one ever thought to question why she'd chosen to draw the line just there. If anything, coming from a woman, it was the kind of thing the pond life around Kerridge tended to respect, God help them.

Anstey was based in Bury, and she'd arranged to meet him at Birch Services on the M62. It was an anonymous place, a small service station located a mile or two off the junction with the M60, where the motorway was beginning to climb up into the Pennines. Up ahead was the bleak expanse of Saddleworth Moor. Behind, the drop towards the Mersey Basin and the Cheshire Plain. No one's idea of a destination. Just a place to pass through.

She'd had the documents prepared without difficulty. Decent forgeries that would fool a layperson without unduly challenging an experienced customs detection officer. Ten minutes in the service station car park, a handover of envelopes. Job done. Anyone who saw them would assume they were sales reps going about their business.

She arrived a few minutes early and bought a newspaper and a takeaway coffee from the Italian-style concession. It was mid-morning, the place relatively quiet – a few people like herself sitting in their cars, killing time before business appointments or stopping to make phone calls.

Anstey was late. Not a great surprise. From what she'd heard, Anstey was usually late. He liked to give the impression that he was a busy man – lots of important irons in the fire, only just time to squeeze in a meeting with the likes of her.

A car pulled in, swept round the car park and pulled in a few spaces along the row from her. She glimpsed the driver's face momentarily as the car passed. Not Anstey, but a face she knew. Not a coincidence, surely.

Kerridge's usual policy was to keep people like Anstey at a lot more than arm's length, so what was one of his inner circle doing butting into this meeting?

She watched as Jake climbed out of the car – a small Polo, not his usual style, she suspected – and strolled casually towards her. She could already feel her body tense, her heart beating faster, as she tried to read his expression. Maybe she'd been rumbled, after all. Or maybe for once the fates had just decided to give her a helping hand.

She waited just long enough to make him pause, then lowered the window.

'Morning, Jake. This your usual stamping ground?'

He looked around him, as if he'd not previously registered where he was. 'Not if I can help it. How you doing?'

'I'm doing OK,' she said. 'We have to stop meeting like this.'

'Probably. Mind if I join you for a second?'

'I'm waiting to meet someone.'

'Yeah, I know. Why I'm here. Won't take a minute.' Without waiting for a response, he walked around the car and pulled open the passenger door.

She waited till he'd lowered himself into the seat. 'What's this all about, Jake?'

'Ken Anstey, right?'

'Any of your business?'

'Yeah, my business. Pretty literally so, as it happens. Afraid Anstey's not available.'

'That right?' She was watching his face, still trying to work out what he was thinking.

'Picked up by the police, a couple of days ago. Various charges. Smuggling class A drugs. Tax evasion. Double-parking, probably.'

'Shame,' she said. Inwardly, she was cursing. Maybe some customs officer had just become overeager, or – probably more likely – Anstey himself had done something so inept they couldn't turn a blind eye. Or maybe someone had deliberately grassed him up to the local plods who wouldn't necessarily have been briefed on Anstey's status. 'Are you on messenger duties now, then?'

'Don't know if you knew, but Anstey did bits and pieces of work for us; one of our suppliers.'

'Just like me.'

'Yes, just like you.' He smiled for the first time. She had the sense he was doing this under sufferance. 'No, actually, Marie, not much like you.'

'Possibly the most backhanded compliment I've ever been paid. But go on.'

'Ah, well, Kenneth has caused us a more than a little embarrassment over the last day or two. Trying to wriggle his way off the hook by impaling others on it. Throwing dirt in all kinds of directions.'

'Including yours?'

'Including ours. Nothing we can't handle, of course. Anstey was never on the team.'

'Just a supplier.'

'Just a supplier. And, unlike some people, not a particularly reliable one. Generally more trouble than he was worth. Anyway, that's why I'm here. Apart from giving us a few headaches, he's also left rather a lot of loose ends. Things that just might come back to haunt us.'

'And you're the Boy Scout,' she said. 'Tying up the loose ends into fancy knots.'

'Something like that.' He was gazing flatly out of the windscreen, not looking in her direction. Ahead of them, a harassed-looking mother was struggling in the rear door of her car, trying to load a crying baby into a child seat.

It struck her suddenly that there was a potentially sinister undertone to his words. 'So I'm a loose end?'

'No, not really. Not you personally, anyway. But I've been sent to check. We know Anstey was doing some business with you, but we don't know exactly what. I just need to make sure it's not something that's likely to cause us any problems.'

He was smart. Just the right garnish of implied threat, then back to smiles and business. She gazed back at him, as if wondering whether she should trust him, then she shrugged.

'Can't see why it would,' she said. 'He asked me to get him some documents.' She tossed the padded envelope into his lap. 'Take a look, if you want.'

He tore open the package and flicked briskly through the pages. 'Shipping notices?'

'Yeah. Duty paid.'

'These fool customs, you reckon?'

151

'It depends. They're bloody good fakes, though I say so myself. If you got an officer who was really on the ball, they might get challenged, but they'd get you through the average inspection.'

Jake took another look through the papers, and for a moment she wondered whether she'd oversold the quality of the forgeries. Then he nodded and smiled.

'Maybe another service you could provide for us directly. These look good quality.'

'Tried the rest, now try the best,' she intoned. 'Everything's a marketing opportunity.'

'So I believe.' He stuffed the papers back in the envelope and handed them back.

'Two hundred,' she said.

'What?'

'Two hundred quid. I'm out of pocket.'

'Teach you to do business with the likes of Ken Anstey,' he said. 'A walking bad debt.'

'Unlike Jeff Kerridge.'

He said nothing for a second. 'I'll make sure you're not out of pocket. There'll be work for you.'

'Marketing opportunity, then.'

'Marketing opportunity; exactly. Marie . . .'

'Yes?'

'Look, this isn't the time or place. But I wondered if you fancied coming out for a drink sometime?'

She made no immediate response, but sat toying with the envelope, as though trying to compose an answer. Finally she said, 'Christ, Jake, I thought you'd never ask.'

Afterwards, when he'd driven off, she sat in her car for a while, wondering whether she knew what she was doing. She was only following Salter's instructions, she told herself. And even if her own instincts about Jake were off the mark, it was still the smart thing to do. Take the opportunity, find a way into the inner circle, get closer to Kerridge.

But she couldn't fully fathom her own motives. She was attracted to Jake, of course. She couldn't deny that. And not just to Jake himself, but to what he might be able to offer. Warmth, friendship, company, fun. And maybe sex, she added quietly to herself, as if that was nothing more than a half-joke, an afterthought. But, above all, something straightforward. No strings. No expectations. No ties.

And that was where things became tangled in her head. Because she felt, in her heart, that this wasn't going to be simple. Again today, she'd had the sense that he was going through the motions, reluctantly doing Kerridge's dirty work. Quite how dirty that work might get, she didn't like to think. But her instincts still told her that Jake wasn't happy, that he was looking for something different.

And maybe she could help him find it. But she knew that, if she did, nothing would ever be simple again.

That second meeting with Jake had been just before another, very different weekend that she'd spent at home with Liam. It had been her first weekend back. She'd deliberately avoided going home too frequently during those early weeks, much to Liam's irritation. Of course, he'd read the worst into her decision, but really it was just that she wanted to allow herself time to get into the swing of her new life. She had known that it would be difficult, juggling these two identities, establishing a new reality for herself in Manchester. She'd been advised, by Salter and others, that the first couple of months would be critical. 'It's like driving a car,' Salter had said during one of their preparatory meetings, his tone suggesting that this might be a concept unfamiliar to a woman. 'When you first start, you have to think about everything. How to steer. When to change gear. How much rev to give it . . .'

'I know what's involved in driving a car, Hugh.'

He'd nodded sceptically, then continued. 'It's hard work because you have to concentrate all the time. But after a while you stop thinking about it. It becomes second nature. It's the same with this business.'

It was a trite analogy, she'd thought at the time. But he'd been right. Those first few weeks she'd felt exhausted every night. It was partly because she was learning a new business, a new trade. Not just the printing, but everything involved in running the shop. Payroll. Tax. VAT. Bookkeeping. Invoicing. Taking orders. Preparing tenders. Costing up a job so they could actually make a profit on it. Cold-calling and following up prospects. Chasing the slow payers. A new world that she'd vaguely known existed, but had never had reason to explore.

All that was tiring enough. But the really hard part was the concentration needed to sustain her new identity. As Salter had implied, it wasn't a difficult task in itself. After all, like all the best lies, her legend had been designed to be as close as possible to the truth. She'd stuck with her own name – it had been known for officers to answer to the wrong one – and most of the details of her past had been left broadly unchanged. She knew that, back at the ranch, they'd spent a lot of time carefully checking online to make sure that she'd wouldn't be exposed by some out-of-date Facebook page or Google reference. The aim, from the start, had been to make her new life as effortless as possible.

That was the theory. But she was acutely aware of the mistakes she'd made during training, infrequent as they'd been. The odd passing reference to Liam or to some real-life work colleague. Some comment that didn't quite square with who or what she was meant to be. Most had been trivial, and probably wouldn't have been noticed by a casual listener. But she'd watched herself on the video replays and realized how easy it was to make an error. And, as the trainers had repeatedly emphasized, even one error could be one too many.

So she spent those first weeks thinking carefully about every word she spoke, hesitating before she opened her mouth. Constantly reminding herself that 'Marie Donovan' up here was, in some critical ways, a different person from the Marie Donovan back home. At the end of the day, she just wanted to hide herself away, safe inside her flat where there was no danger of saying or doing the wrong thing.

She'd been advised that the best approach for the first month or so was simply to immerse herself in it. She had to become the new Marie Donovan to the point where she no longer had to think about it. Unconscious competence, Winsor the psych had called it, as he talked her through a more sophisticated version of Salter's driving analogy.

She'd decided therefore that she couldn't afford to interrupt her immersion by paying repeated visits back home. That would just make the whole process even harder. Liam hadn't been pleased – well, of course he hadn't, she acknowledged now – but she'd pointed out that once she'd got through this initial acclimatization she'd be able to establish a routine of regular visits home.

He'd grudgingly accepted that, but set a deadline of a month for her first trip back. She'd planned to leave Friday lunchtime, telling Joe that she was visiting her elderly parents back in London. Almost inevitably, things hadn't gone smoothly. They'd had to redo a large print job because of some technical fault with the machine, and she'd finally got away later than she'd intended. She had taken the train from Piccadilly rather than facing the Friday night traffic on the M6, and though it wasn't quite peak time, the carriages were already tightly packed. With no reservation, she'd eventually found a seat next to an overweight man who made no great secret of his resentment at having to move his bag from the spare seat beside him. She'd reached Euston at the tail end of rush hour only to find that the Northern Line was up the creek, the trains sporadic and full.

It was gone seven thirty when she finally arrived at their South Wimbledon house, at least a couple of hours later than she'd expected. She'd been updating Liam periodically throughout the journey, but still he'd seemed to treat her late arrival as a personal affront.

'I was going to book us a table somewhere,' he said, looking pointedly at his watch.

'You still can,' she pointed out. 'What about the Italian?'

'They'll be booked up by now,' he said. 'Friday night, after all.'

She considered some sarcastic rejoinder, then decided just to go with the flow. He was only pissed off because he'd wanted her back earlier, she told herself.

'Let's just do the pub, then,' she said. 'We can grab a bite there. Better than ringing around the other places trying to find a table.'

He looked for a moment as if he were about to argue, then smiled. 'Yeah, why not? It'll be more fun than some overpriced pasta, anyway.'

As it turned out, it was quite a lot more fun. She hadn't realized, until she arrived back here in her home environment, quite how tense and constrained she'd felt in Manchester. It was as if she'd thrown off some ill-fitting garment and was finally able to breathe properly. At another time, she might have expressed her tiredness by getting irritated with Liam, but tonight all that seemed to melt away. Liam played it just right for her mood, cheerfully pulling her back into the moment, not bothering her with questions about how it had all gone.

Home. That was what this was. Not just the poky little Edwardian terrace that was all they'd been able to afford in this part of London. But all of it: Liam; the Irish pub round the corner that, unlike virtually every other pub in London, really did feel like a local; the neighbours that she hardly knew but who nodded to her and Liam from the surrounding tables as they entered the bar.

She hadn't realized till that moment quite how isolated she'd felt for the past few weeks. It wasn't only that she was living alone in that anonymous apartment block. It wasn't that, apart from Salter and Joe in the print shop, there was no one up there that she'd even been able to call an acquaintance. In the end, it was the fact that she was living a lie. She'd become a person without a past, without a context, without, in the long run, a future even. She wasn't a great one for nights out with the girls, but down here there'd at least been a few female colleagues who she could join for a drink or two after work, some old college friends that she saw less often than she ought to. There was a life outside the job.

Up there, there was nothing. She couldn't afford to go out and make new friends, even if she'd wanted to. She couldn't take the risk of letting people too far into her fictitious life in case they spotted something that didn't fit or decided that they wanted to know more about her. Once or twice, Joe had suggested going for a pint after work, his manner suggesting that he was inviting her simply as a workmate, rather than with any other intention. She'd eventually taken him up on the offer, but only because she'd thought it would seem odd to keep refusing. That had been OK. Joe himself was hardly the most forthcoming of individuals. But she'd spent the evening on tenterhooks, nervous of saying the wrong thing or simply of saying too much. It had been OK, but nothing like this.

'Penny for them,' Liam said, raising his pint in a mock toast.

'Sorry,' she said. 'Still thinking about the job. Takes a while to shake it off.'

'I can imagine,' he said. 'Though probably nothing that a few drinks won't cure.'

She laughed. 'Worth a shot, anyway. Nothing to lose.'

The evening had gone on from there. She followed Liam's advice and had those few more drinks, and she'd found that, yes indeed, all the stresses and strains of the job had quite quickly evaporated. They ate some forgettable pub lasagne, which she found surprisingly enjoyable, if only because, unlike most other meals she'd eaten over the last month, it wasn't some ready meal she'd bought from the Tesco Metro around the corner. They chatted amiably about this and that, somehow managing to steer clear of anything that would have changed the mood, like Liam's illness or her career. And finally, not long before closing time, they'd staggered back to their small house, gone to bed and made tipsy love, falling asleep in the warmth of each other's bodies.

It was only in the small hours, suddenly awake with Liam breathing steadily beside her, that she suddenly thought about Jake Morton. He hadn't entered her mind all evening, almost as if she'd deliberately boxed him away in some far corner of her head.

She'd agreed to go out for a drink with him the following week. Well, so what? It was nothing to be ashamed or embarrassed about. It was part of the job, following Salter's instructions. Building her network, just as when she'd attended Kerridge's charity dinner.

But she'd told Liam about that. She'd presented it as the tiresome chore it had been, and afterwards they'd had a good laugh over the phone about the naffness of the charity auction, the aspirational pretensions of Cheshire business folk at play. She'd talked about the fat middle-aged men who'd kept trying to entice her on to the dance floor, and about her role as Kerridge's top-table eye candy. She'd told Jake about every over-ornate frock, every ill-fitting tuxedo.

But she hadn't mentioned Jake.

There had been no reason for her to, of course. He was just someone she'd happened to sit next to. A brief acquaintance with whom she'd shared some polite chit-chat. Someone she probably wouldn't see again.

But now she was going to see him again. Not just as a passing acquaintance or as a business contact. She was going to see him for what she was sure Jake himself would see as a date. And she knew that, whatever her supposed good intentions, whatever she might tell herself about this being part of the job, there was at least a small part of her that wanted to see it the same way.

She rolled over, pulling the duvet more tightly around her. Christ, why should she feel guilty about all this? She was just doing her job. OK, she felt some attraction to Jake. She was only human. Alone, a long way from home, struggling with a new life. No one could blame her for being tempted. But that was all it was. She wasn't going to do anything about it.

For a long while, she lay awake, her mind empty but stubbornly refusing to shut down. Outside, she could hear the occasional hum of a car along the High Street. Inside, there was nothing but Liam's rhythmic breath, the slow clicking of the cooling radiators. It was nearly dawn before she finally slept.

She awoke late. Liam was already up and she could hear him moving about downstairs, clattering dishes, whistling tunelessly along to some tune on the radio. She pulled on her dressing gown and made her way down the narrow stairs.

Liam was in the process of setting the table in what they rather grandly referred to as the dining room. In truth, the house was little more than an extended two-up two-down, part of a network of terraced streets built at the turn of the nineteenth century for workers at the local mill. Some previous owner had knocked through the two downstairs reception rooms to create a more spacious living-cum-dining room, and they'd set up their Ikea dining table in the rear space, with a view over the tiny garden.

'Breakfast,' Liam said. 'Full English. Well, bacon, egg and sausage. Upmarket sausage, though. None of your girly rubbish.'

'Blimey,' she said. 'Beats my usual takeaway skinny latte.'

'We can offer coffee, too, madam. Even a skinny latte, if you want it.' She'd bought him a moderately upscale espresso machine for his last birthday, when she'd been feeling mildly flush after her promotion.

'You're spoiling me.'

He paused, halfway into the kitchen, as if this thought hadn't previously occurred to him. 'Well, I haven't had the chance recently. Thought we should make the most of it.'

'Fine by me.' She sat herself at the table in the manner of one about to embark on a fine-dining experience and watched him as he brought in the food and coffees. He was looking a little better, she thought, although it was always difficult to be sure. The last time she'd seen him, a month or so before, she'd thought he was having more difficulty with his mobility. Now, he was moving about in a more sprightly way, although she could tell that he was stabilizing himself against the furniture and doorframes with practised skill. He looked more cheerful, too, as if he were simply pleased to see her. As if, she added to herself, she wouldn't be off again in another forty-eight hours.

The breakfast was fine, even if, as Liam kept pointing out apologetically, the eggs were overdone and the bacon on the cold side. The best thing, though, was the atmosphere, the sense of relaxation and calm between them. This was like it used to be, she thought. When they first met, when they'd first started living together. When they'd been content just to be in each other's company, not necessarily saying or doing anything much. She'd almost forgotten that it could be like this.

Once they'd eaten, she showered and dressed, and then followed Liam through into what had originally been the house's second bedroom, but which had long been adopted by Liam as his studio.

'Couple of new ones,' he said. 'Did them while you were away.'

She'd never doubted that Liam had real talent. She knew nothing much about art herself but she'd heard others, who knew what they were talking about, praising Liam's work to the skies. At least one of his lecturers at art college had been convinced that Liam would be the next big thing, and had done his utmost to promote his work. But, so far at least, it just hadn't happened. It wasn't so surprising, he kept telling her. Talent – even if he really did have it, which Liam himself seemed to doubt – was only part of the equation. The rest was a mix of luck, confidence and a knack for unabashed self-promotion. None of those qualities, she was forced to concede, had been noticeably evident in Liam's life to date.

For her own part, while she had no idea of the commercial value of Liam's work, she did think it was rather good. Once or twice, he tried to explain to her why he painted the way he did, who his influences were, but all that sailed immediately

161

over her head. What she liked was the semi-abstract quality, the sense that you could almost pin down what he was depicting, but then somehow it slipped away. You were left with a wonderful mélange of colours that always threatened to cohere into something recognizable before once again melting back into uncertainty.

The new paintings were, as far as she could judge, at least the equal of anything he'd painted previously. She could see no sign that his talents were waning or – perhaps more pertinently – that the illness was having any adverse effect on his abilities. Though that didn't necessarily mean very much. She had no idea how much effort it might have cost him to paint the new pictures, whether he was finding the task harder than before.

'Beautiful,' she said, gazing at the pictures. She had the sense that she ought to say something more profound. 'Really beautiful,' she added.

'They're OK,' he conceded. 'Not my best. But not bad. It's not quite gone yet.'

She had the sense that he was trying to provoke some response with the last comment, but was determined to resist the bait. 'I won't ask what they're about,' she said instead.

He shrugged. 'That one's about eighty centimetres by sixty. The other's a bit bigger.'

'Ho, ho. Are they finished?'

'More or less. Or at least I've got to the point where I should abandon them. I keep making minor tweaks, but I'll probably end up ruining them.'

'Leave them, then.'

She looked up and peered out of the window at the patch-work of narrow gardens that stretched between the two rows of terraces. It was a perfect autumn day – a clear blue sky, no wind. One of those days when South London could look almost enticing.

'Let's go out,' she suggested. 'Up to the Common, maybe.'

So they did. They drove Liam's adapted Corsa – one of the few benefits of his illness had been that he'd qualified for the mobility allowance that paid the monthly rental – and parked up on the edge of Wimbledon Common. They spent the morning walking among the trees, enjoying the dappled sunlight, kicking the piles of newly fallen leaves. Like it used to be, she thought again. With no need to speak, no reason to bicker. No sense of doing anything much, except enjoying the moment, sharing the day. Enjoying each other.

It had been a perfect day, she thought later. Liam had seemed almost his old self, not quite able to skip among the leaves, but certainly stomping amiably behind her, half-resting on his stick, looking pleased to be there. They'd thought about stopping for lunch at one of the pubs on the Common – The Hand in Hand or The Billet, maybe – but everywhere was packed on what might well be the last fine weekend of the year. So, instead, they drove back home, and then took a walk through into the Abbey Mills, a cluster of old shops and craft stalls tucked around the River Wandle just behind their house.

It could be a bit naff, Marie thought, but it was ideal for a day like today. They could wander around, gaze at assorted trinkets they were never likely to buy, grab a pint in the pub, have an early supper in one of the restaurants.

With the sun setting over the pylons and industrial estates to the west, they sat outside the pub, sipping their beers and watching the endless flow of the narrow Wandle.

'Been a good day,' she said.

He took a swallow of his pint and nodded. 'One of the best. For a while, anyway. Mind you, I'm knackered.'

She looked at him. Now he'd said it, he did look tired. Maybe she'd pushed him too far. She kept having to remind herself that he was ill, that he wasn't the person he'd once been.

Looking at him now, she could see that his hand was shaking, that he was struggling even to hold his glass steady.

'Are you OK?'

'Yeah, yeah. I'm fine. Just tired, that's all.'

'They're good, you know. Your new pictures.'

'My . . .' He looked baffled, suddenly, as if she'd raised an issue that was too complicated for his understanding. 'What?'

'You sure you're OK, Liam? We can head back now if you like.'

'I . . .'

The change had come over him abruptly, the smiles of a few moments earlier wiped from his face. Now, he looked frightened, as if he'd suddenly stepped into some unfamiliar territory. He peered down at his glass as if wondering what it was. Then he looked back up at her, blinking, his expression returning to something closer to his usual self.

'Christ, sorry. Just felt – I don't know – dizzy or something. No, not dizzy exactly. More a bit . . . well, lost . . .' His voice trailed off, as if he didn't quite know what he was saying. Or more, she thought, as if he didn't want to be saying it.

She hesitated, wanting to tell him yet again that he should go back and see the neurologist. But she knew that she'd just provoke another row, and that was the last thing she wanted at the end of a day like today. She felt already as if what had just happened – whatever it was – had cast an unexpected shadow.

'Shall we get home?' she said.

He took another swallow of his pint. 'Yes, let's do that,' he said. 'I must be more tired than I realized. Been having too much fun.'

Yes, that was it, she'd thought, as they'd made their slow way along the narrow riverside path that led back to their house. For once, they'd both been having too much fun.

Later that night, she'd lain awake again in bed, listening to

Liam's gentle snoring and the distant sounds of the night. Liam had collapsed into bed almost as soon as they'd got in, looking all in. She'd half-heartedly watched some Saturday night television, drunk another glass of wine, and then had followed him up. But sleep had proved elusive.

It was all like a dream, she thought. For a few moments, earlier that day, she thought they'd recaptured it, that perfection they'd had when they'd first been together. Briefly, everything had seemed right again, and she could imagine a future – here, with Liam, watching him paint, not worrying about her own career. Just getting by with each other. Now, it felt as if all that had just melted away, like a dream that you can scarcely remember on waking.

She didn't even know why. OK, so she'd been reminded yet again that Liam was ill. That his condition was worsening. That it would continue to deteriorate. That whatever future there was here was at best uncertain.

But she'd known all that. For a short period, she'd been able to put it aside, pretend that it didn't exist, or at least that it didn't matter. Now, everything had come flooding back. Liam's condition. Her own isolated life and work up north. The reality that she'd have to face again once this weekend was over.

And Jake. Jake who meant nothing to her, except as a potential target for her work. Jake who was firmly on the other side. Jake who could be her entry point into Jeff Kerridge's inner circle.

Jake who was taking her for a drink in just a few days' time.

Later, when she was back up north and everything was beginning to slip out of her control, she would look back at that weekend as perhaps the last time she'd felt genuinely happy, truly content. The last time she'd felt really close to Liam.

The last time things had been simple.

Before Jake.

14

'Are you OK? You look all in.'

She paused in the doorway, suddenly conscious of how exhausted she was feeling. 'Thanks, Joe. You know how to brighten a girl's spirits on a Monday morning.'

'It's my sole aim in life,' Joe said, slumping down into the seat opposite her. 'No, you look fabulous as always. But knackered.'

'Stop digging. You're already in well over your head.'

'Sorry. Just thought you've not been quite yourself lately. None of my business, of course, so tell me to bugger off. But if there's anything I can do . . .'

She regarded him for a moment. The staccato, nervous delivery of the words was characteristic, but the content less so. Even in the pub, Joe's conversations rarely veered into personal territory.

What with everything that had happened since, she'd almost forgotten her unsettling encounter with Joe a few evenings before. When she'd returned to the office after meeting Morgan Jones, her brief suspicions had melted away, insubstantial compared with the potential break-in and Jones' disturbing claims.

After the events of this last weekend, any anxiety about Joe had slipped even further into the background. She'd had a late night, little sleep, an early morning and a long drive, and was at the point where she could barely think straight. Prior to Joe entering the room, she'd been staring vacantly at the company's accounts, scarcely registering, let alone making any sense of, the figures in front of her.

'No, I'm fine, Joe. Just not sleeping well for some reason.' She gestured towards the empty mug on her desk. 'Need less of this stuff.'

'If you're sure . . .' Joe made as if to rise from the chair, then paused. 'I mean, I'm happy to hold the fort if you wanted to take the day off.'

'When did you know me to throw a sickie, Joe?' She felt, momentarily, her suspicions flooding back.

'Wasn't thinking of a sickie. Just a day's leave. Months since you took any time off. Not as if we're run off our feet.'

Maybe that was it, she thought. Perhaps he thought that the business was in trouble. If so, she could understand his concerns. The business was doing pretty well in fact – and still would have been even if its capital hadn't been underwritten by the Agency. But times were tough. Joe was skilled in his field, but the market wouldn't be awash with suitable vacancies. It was only a few months since he'd been made redundant from his last job. They'd had a quiet few weeks. Marie herself wasn't worried because she knew there was enough business in the pipeline and plenty of good opportunities emerging from her marketing efforts. But that wouldn't be obvious to Joe, whose sights focused on the next job at hand.

She also wondered, sometimes, if she was fooling herself. It was easy to be blasé when you knew it wasn't your real livelihood. Marie paid herself a salary out of the business for form's sake – the accounts had to be audited for real – but the money was offset against her Agency salary. She worked hard at the business, but it was all play-acting. And there was another question. If she decided to pull out of the field – or if the powers that be decided for her – something would have to happen to the business.

They'd arrange some cover story – that she was selling up, closing or liquidating the business. A lot would depend on timing. If time allowed the transition to be managed properly, as when she'd moved into the role, the business might be 'sold' on to another agent. If not – and the signs were that any withdrawal might happen at the shortest of notice – the options were more limited. They might come up with some story about her being taken ill or having to leave for some domestic reason. But that would mean the closure of the business, and Joe and Darren would be out of a job.

Another thing to feel guilty about. You come into this job with big ideals, and you find that all you're doing is dicking around with other people's lives.

'All the more reason not to be skiving,' she said. 'Need to be out drumming up business.' She picked up the papers on her desk and waved them towards Joe. 'We're doing OK, Joe. But we can't afford to be complacent.' *Christ,* she thought, *I sound like a spokesperson for the Institute of Directors.*

'If you're sure. But doesn't do any good if you work yourself into the ground.'

She smiled. 'It's sweet of you, Joe. But I'm fine. Really. Nothing wrong with me that a couple of early nights won't put right. And a beer with you on Wednesday.'

He pushed himself slowly to his feet, still looking unconvinced. 'I mean it. You want me to hold the fort, not a problem.'

'Thanks, Joe. I really appreciate that. And I'll take you up on it sometime. But not just yet.'

Nobody had told her quite how much acting ability this

job would take. If this went belly up, she could always think about trying a few auditions. Whatever she'd told Joe, she felt bloody awful. It was mainly just tiredness. They'd spent the previous evening in casualty, going through the endless queuing and waiting that seemed to attend any kind of medical treatment.

When Liam had collapsed on the seafront, she'd initially assumed the worst – even though she didn't really know what the worst might be. In those first few seconds on the rain-soaked promenade, she'd envisaged all kinds of terrors: that he'd been taken out by some lone sniper, secreted away in an upper floor of one of the hotels that overlooked the promenade, aiming for her. Or, more prosaically, that he'd suffered some major physical trauma – a heart attack or a stroke.

It seemed like forever before her rational mind kicked back in, though it could have been only a few seconds. But then she was bent over him, the rain falling harder, as she tried to see what was wrong.

There'd been no gunshot, no wound, no sniper. That was all just her overactive imagination. Blood was oozing down his forehead from where he'd caught his skull on the metal railings, but he looked better than she'd initially feared. His eyes flickered and opened, slightly glazed, looking past her rather than at her face.

'Jesus,' he said. 'What happened?'

Her mobile phone was already in her hand. 'You fell. I was just about to call an ambulance.'

His eyes opened wider. 'Don't do that, for God's sake. I'll look a total prick.'

'You're not feeling so bad, then?' she said. They were most likely both of them in shock. Probably not the best time for sarcasm.

He dragged himself upright, grimacing at the wet pavement under his hand. 'I'm fine. Well, not fine. But not in need of an ambulance.'

She gazed carefully at his face, at the set of his eyes. 'You don't look fine. We need to get you looked at.'

'Get my head examined, you mean?'

He reached out for the railings and slowly began to pull himself to his feet, Marie helping to lift him by one arm.

'If you like. You hit it quite badly. You might have been out cold for a second or two, I don't know. You might have concussion.' She pointed to the cut on his forehead which was still bleeding. 'And you might need stitches on that, if you don't want to ruin your good looks.'

He touched his forehead, then looked at his bloodstained fingers. 'Too late for that, I'd have said. But, yeah, OK. I can't deny that my head's hurting.' He paused, as though considering the matter. 'Hurting a fuck of a lot, now you come to mention it.'

They made it back to the car, and set off in search of the closest casualty department. Predictably, the nearest hospital, which Marie had noticed earlier as they'd driven into town, no longer had an accident and emergency unit, and they'd been redirected further out of town to some newly built monstrosity designed to service the whole county.

Even on a rainy Sunday, the place was heaving with patients – most apparently suffering from gardening or DIY injuries. After a brief triage session during which a nurse ascertained that Liam's condition was not immediately life-threatening, they settled down to nearly five hours of queuing and waiting. Liam was eventually seen by a doctor, who ordered an X-ray. So they waited for the scan, then waited for the result, and then waited for the doctor to pronounce on the result. Then they waited for a nurse to dress the wound, and finally they waited again for some prescribed painkillers to be prepared. By the time they emerged into the night air, it was nearly nine.

'Well, that was worthwhile,' Liam said, touching his forehead very gently. 'I got a bandage.'

'And confirmation that you're not concussed, and that you didn't need stitches.'

'And a five-hour wait,' he said. 'Glad you suggested it.'

'You're welcome.' She held his arm, as he limped across the road towards the hospital car park. He was limping a little more now than he had been earlier, she thought. 'So what happened?'

His eyes were fixed on the road ahead, concentrating on negotiating the kerbs. 'What do you mean, what happened? I fell over.'

'But why?' she persisted. 'You weren't even moving when it happened. You didn't trip or slip. You just . . . fell.'

He made no response, but continued moving forwards until he was level with her car. She helped him lower himself into the passenger seat. It was only as she was climbing into the driver's seat that he offered any answer.

'I don't know,' he said. 'I just couldn't keep upright. It was as if I'd lost control of my legs. Next thing I was on my back, staring up at your face. There are worse things to be doing, you know.'

'Has this happened before, Liam?'

There was a silence, and it was clear that he was considering some further light-hearted answer.

'Falling, you mean?'

'Yes, Liam, fucking falling. What else do you think I mean?'

Liam hesitated again. 'Once or twice, yes. At home mainly.'

She was staring straight ahead through the windscreen. 'What does "once or twice" mean?'

'Oh, Christ, I don't know, Marie. I haven't kept count. A few times.'

'Like today? Out of nowhere?'

'I suppose.'

'Why didn't you say anything?'

'I told you about some of them. I'm sure I did.'

'When I came back last time, you had a bruise on your arm. Quite a big bruise. You said you'd slipped on an icy pavement.'

'I did,' he said. 'It was in the snow after Christmas. Everyone was slipping. It was fucking lethal. People complained to the council about it.'

'What about the other falls?'

'I don't know. I'm not as . . . as steady as I used to be. What do you expect?'

'I don't know, Liam. That's the problem. I don't know what to expect.' She started the engine. 'I don't know where things are going. I don't know if it's safe to leave you. You could have hurt yourself badly today.'

'It was a tumble,' he said. 'People have them all the time.'

'Not the same people. Not all the time.'

She was seeing things now she hadn't noticed earlier. An increased shaking in his left hand. A hesitation in his speech, as if he was struggling for the right words. Her mind went back to that first weekend, when they'd been sitting outside the pub by the river. Liam saying he felt lost. He'd been tired, then, of course, and he was tired now. They were both tired. And she was putting him under pressure. But he looked different. Not the confident Liam she'd always known. He looked drawn, anxious, shaken. Not in control. As if he was glimpsing a future very different from anything they'd envisaged. Just as she was.

She put the car into gear and slowly reversed out of the

172

parking space. 'Let's get home,' she said. As she spoke, it occurred to her that she didn't really know where that was any more.

Now here she was, less than ten hours later, trying to readjust back into this alternative life. Joe was right. She was knackered. She and Liam had got back around nine thirty, cobbled together some food, collapsed into bed. She'd slept badly, been up again at four thirty, setting off in the frosty dawn for the long drive back up to Manchester, hoping to get past Birmingham before the worst of the traffic, stopping only to grab a black coffee at Hilton Park, her mind numbed by the endless carriageway, the drone of the engine.

She didn't know what she'd left behind, and she had no idea what was waiting for her when she arrived. Worst of all was the sense of isolation. She couldn't burden Liam with this, not now, and there was no one else up here she could talk to. Not Salter, not Welsby.

She'd forgotten to charge her mobile over the weekend, and it had been lying, dead and useless, in her handbag. Struggling to keep her mind focused, she plugged it into the charger on her desk. After a moment's hesitation, she switched on the phone.

There were a couple of messages. The first was just silence, a few seconds' breathing, number withheld. Maybe a wrong number or a marketing call.

Or maybe just the leaver of the second message plucking up the courage to speak. That wheedling intonation, the faint Welsh lilt. Morgan fucking Jones, though he didn't give his name.

'Sorry about the other day. Cold feet. Don't know who to trust. But we need to talk. I've got out of town. I'll text you the details. Come and see me. I won't be going out.' The last

173

sentence spoken with attempted irony, but he sounded like he was bricking it.

She checked the number Jones had called from, but it had been withheld. Then she looked at the texts. One new message. Two words, 'Mayfield' and 'Wilson', followed by a sequence of letters and numbers. A postcode. Presumably Jones being security conscious.

She sat down at her desk and opened up her internet browser, typing the postcode into Google Maps. A back street in Blackpool, fifty or so miles up the coast. Jesus. Jones expected her to drive up there?

She had no idea whether she could trust him, anyway. Put it another way, in other circumstances she'd trust Jones a lot less far than she could throw his chubby Welsh body. He was the sort who'd have a good idea of the market rate of his grandmother. The question was whether she could trust him now. He was shit-scared, no doubt about that. That might just push him in her direction, particularly if he thought they were in the same boat. Or it might do the opposite. He might try to use her as collateral to talk his way out of trouble with Kerridge.

Making up her mind, she went out into the shop. Joe had his head down, adjusting the large reprographic machine. He looked up as she approached, his expression quizzical.

'OK, so you were right, smart-arse,' she said. 'As always. I'm dead on my feet. If you resist saying I told you so, I'll let you hold the fort for the rest of the day.'

His face showed no surprise at her change of heart. 'No problem. Any particular instructions?'

'Just keep Darren from destroying the place.' She glanced over to where the young man was engaged in sorting some reams of paper – a task with no real purpose except to keep him safely occupied.

'There are limits to my talents,' Joe said. 'But I'll do my best. You go and get some rest.' He moved away and began to tinker with the machine again, but looked up as she moved towards the door. 'And Marie – take care, OK?'

She turned, surprised. 'I always do, Joe. You know me.'

His face was unexpectedly earnest. 'Yes,' he said. 'I know you.' And he sounded, one way or another, as if he really meant it.

15

'You're sure about this?'

Salter was staring out at the quays below them, watching the cars and the trams and the scattering of ant-like pedestrians. It was a bright, chilly day, nearly lunchtime, and office workers were scurrying out to grab a sandwich or get a breath of air. He turned back and gazed at Hodder for a moment, his blue eyes blank behind his steel-framed glasses.

'Questioning my judgement, son?'

Hodder blinked and swallowed, as though struggling to come up with the right response. Salter didn't blame him.

'No. Of course not. I'm just—'

'Covering your own arse. Quite right. I'd do the same.'

'It's not exactly—'

Salter leaned back against the car park railing and smiled at the young officer. 'You're smart enough,' he said. 'You'll go far if you get the breaks. And, yeah, if you make sure your arse is always covered. Otherwise, you'll get shafted by cynical buggers like me.'

Hodder had no immediate answer to this. He moved to stand next to Salter, following his gaze. For some reason, Salter had chosen to park on the roof of the Lowry car park, the gallery itself immediately ahead of them with its distinctive silver cylinder. Beyond that, across the water, there were the angular lines of the Imperial War Museum, and then the industrial skyline of Trafford Park. Further to their left, there were the quays themselves, Old Trafford and the hazy rooftops of suburban Manchester.

'I'm just not really sure what this is all about,' Hodder tried again.

Salter smiled. He took a deep breath, as if enjoying the fresh morning air. 'Me neither, son. That's what I'm trying to find out.'

'But this isn't official?'

Salter's narrow eyes were fixed on the view below, his expression that of a not particularly benevolent god reviewing his creation. 'No, son. Not official.' He paused, the smile widening slightly, as if he was perhaps contemplating a thunderbolt. 'Just using our initiative. Always a good quality in an ambitious young officer.'

'And she's one of ours? Donovan.'

Salter glanced at the young man, momentarily surprised. 'Who told you that?'

'You did. You were talking to her on the phone when we were at Morton's flat. You said she was deep cover.'

Salter nodded, his eyebrows raised. 'Good memory, son. Useful quality in this business. Yes, she's one of ours.'

Hodder said nothing for a moment. 'So what's our objective?'

Salter swivelled so that his angular body was against the concrete wall. He brought his hands together in faint, ironic applause. 'Very good, son. Senior management material.'

Hodder shrugged embarrassedly; he had no clue what Salter was talking about.

'I'm assuming "What's our objective?" is management-speak for "What the fuck are you up to?"' Salter was still smiling mirthlessly. 'Good question, as well.'

177

'It's just that I don't really understand—'

'What the fuck I'm up to. No, well, that's fair enough. Not sure I do.' Salter fumbled in his pocket and brought out a cigarette packet. He proffered it vaguely towards Hodder who shook his head. 'Good lad. Me, I've given up. Till just now. Pressure of work and all that. Thought I'd follow Mr Welsby's good example.' He lit up, sheltering the cigarette from the buffeting wind. 'Right, son, let's try to answer your question. What the fuck am I up to?'

'I didn't mean—'

'It's the right question. See, I'm going out on a limb here. I'm putting some trust in you not to saw through the branch behind me. Not exactly my style.' The humourless smile returned. 'Mind you, I'm sure you know better than to shaft me.'

Hodder opened his mouth, but realized that no response was possible.

'So, to return to the question at hand, what the fuck am I up to?' It wasn't clear now whether Salter was talking to Hodder or to himself. 'I could spin you some bullshit about having Donovan's best interests at heart. And there'd be some truth in that. She's out there, twisting in the wind. We've a duty to keep an eye on her. But, then, one reason we've left her out there is that we don't know what she's up to. You know what I reckon?'

The last question was unexpectedly directed at Hodder. 'What's that?'

Salter nodded, satisfied that Hodder was still paying attention. 'I reckon she was a bit closer to Morton than she's letting on. Her business, of course. So long as she didn't get too close, if you get my drift. But I still think she might know some stuff she's not sharing. So that's another reason for keeping an eye on her.' He paused, as if wondering why he was telling

178

Hodder all this. 'Just filling you in on the mission, you understand? Just clarifying the *objective*.'

Hodder said nothing. Despite the morning sunshine and the scattering of iconic buildings, the quays looked a bleak, inhospitable place from this vantage point. Rows of soulless office buildings and apartment blocks. Anonymous hotels and chain restaurants. Acres of industrial buildings in the distance.

'But the real question,' Salter went on, 'the question that must be troubling you, is why I've not gone through official channels. Why I've not involved Mr Welsby. Why we're standing out here in the cold without any official mandate to cover our backsides.' He paused, apparently watching a suite of white clouds drifting slowly across the lower part of the sky. 'Thing is, son, I really don't know who to trust.' He moved his head to look Hodder in the eye. 'I'm trusting you. That's a big thing for me. But I don't kid myself that you wouldn't go running up the line if you thought I was going too far. In fact, I'd be disappointed if you weren't smart enough to do that. But for the moment, I'm putting my faith in your good nature and your – what's that word? – your integrity. That's why I'm telling you all this. There's some strange shit going on here. Someone's leaking. Donovan reckons someone might be bugging her flat.'

Hodder frowned, trying to work out the implications. 'You mean, that we might—'

'Christ knows. I don't, anyway. All I know is that I'm feeling jittery. I just want to know what's going on, that's all. I want to get some control of things. Make sure my own back's covered before I go any further.' He paused. 'So that's the objective. You up for it, son?'

'Guess so. If that's all we're talking about.'

'That's all I'm talking about. Keep an eye on her. See what's

179

going down. Then we can decide whether to take it up to Uncle Keith. Mr Welsby to you.'

'You don't think he's involved in this?' Hodder looked genuinely shocked.

Salter stared at the young man for a moment. 'Keith? Christ, no. One of life's line-toers. If I take this to him without knowing what's what, he'll be obliged to take it higher. That's what worries me. Don't know who to trust even up there where the air's thin. So this is just you and me for the moment. If you're in.'

'Yeah, I'm in.' Hodder smiled, momentarily revealing a different side to his personality. 'Besides, I like the challenge. Keeping tabs on one of ours. She'll know the tricks, what to look out for.'

'Too right she will. Don't underestimate Sister Marie. Test of your skills.'

'I'll do my best.'

'All you can do,' Salter said. 'So, any more questions before we kick off?'

Hodder looked around at the grim concrete interior of the car park. The place filled up on Saturdays and in the evenings, when people were visiting the outlet mall or attending a concert at the Lowry, but on a weekday morning the upper floors were largely deserted. 'Just one. Why'd we come up here?'

Salter pointed towards the quays below them. 'See that building there. Smart-looking place on the edge of the waterfront. You'll know that one. That's the place where we found Mr Morton's mutilated body. You'll remember that.' It wasn't a question.

Hodder peered downwards, wondering where this was going. 'Don't think I'm going to forget any time soon.'

Salter straightened and pointed towards the blurred jumble

of Manchester. 'And that block there. Square greyish place, just to the left of the Hilton. That's where she lives. Third floor. Decent little place, apparently.'

Hodder followed Salter's gesture, but all he could see was an indistinguishable jumble of buildings. 'OK.'

Finally, Salter waved his hand out towards the vast sprawl of Trafford Park. 'And that little estate over there, those rows of what I imagine are desirable industrial units . . .' He spoke the last three words as if they were somehow obscene. 'That's where our Marie works. Where she runs her print shop.' He swept his hand through the air as though drawing an invisible line between the three locations. 'From up here, you see, you've got a vantage point on her whole world.'

Hodder frowned, baffled. 'That's why we came up here?'

'Christ, no, son. We're not allowed to smoke in the sodding cars. We're not allowed to smoke in the sodding cafés. We're not even allowed to smoke in the sodding pubs.' He held out the stub of his still lit cigarette. 'Where the fuck else was I going to go to relapse?'

Hodder's eyes slid across to the large No Smoking sign that decorated the far wall. 'Strictly speaking, I don't think you're supposed to smoke in here either.'

'That right?' Salter tossed the stub over the metal railings. 'Well, sometimes, son, you've just got to break the rules.'

16

She'd never have admitted it, but Joe had been right. She was dead on her feet. All the stress of the past week, not to mention the weekend, had finally caught up with her.

She'd initially planned to head straight up to the coast, track down Morgan Jones, get all that – whatever it was – sorted. But after five minutes in the car, she'd realized that she was barely up to the drive, let alone whatever surprises Morgan might throw at her. She turned the opposite way, back into the city, and headed back to the place that perhaps she should learn to think of as home.

She had expected that the flat would still be unlocked, the door still jammed with the folded envelope she had wedged underneath to hold it closed. Now, she fumbled vainly with the catch and realized that the door was locked after all.

Kev the caretaker must have surpassed himself and actually got the work done over the weekend. Probably had taken great satisfaction in calling out an emergency locksmith so he could add the bill to her rent. She fumbled in her purse for the entry card, and then swiped it vainly through the mechanism three or four times. The light remained resolutely on red, and the door refused to open.

Shit. The entry system must have been reset. That meant tracking down Kev. Suddenly, she felt more tired than ever.

She wanted nothing more than simply to lie down here in front of her front door and fall asleep.

Sighing, she made her way back downstairs. Kev had a small office just off the main entrance, with his own flat tucked behind it. He was supposedly available 24/7. In practice, it was closer to two days in five, and there was a semi-permanent notice on his door saying: *Back in ten.*

For once, though, she was in luck. The door was open and Kev was sitting behind the desk, working his way painstakingly through that morning's copy of the *Sun*, a steaming cup of coffee and a half-eaten sandwich by his side. He looked up, his expression suggesting that he was accustomed to enjoying his break uninterrupted.

'Miss Donovan,' he said, peering at her over his reading glasses. He made the words sound vaguely salacious.

He cut a slightly disreputable figure, dressed like some faded dandy in a blue-and-white striped shirt and mustard-coloured cardigan. She didn't know if this was a misguided attempt at style, or if he'd just picked up the first clothes he'd found in some charity shop. The directness of his gaze suggested a quasi-sexual appraisal, though she'd seen him direct the same gaze at male residents, and had wondered vaguely about his sexual orientation. She suspected that his interest was generally voyeuristic rather than gender-specific. Behind his desk, there was a bank of CCTV screens linked to the security cameras covering the public areas of the building. It wasn't difficult to imagine that, somewhere in a back room, Kev might have an equivalent unofficial network covering the non-public areas. She could hardly bring herself to care. The more the merrier.

'How's the door?' he asked, fishing for recognition of his efficiency. 'Working OK now?'

'It's successfully keeping me out of my flat, if that's what you mean,' she said.

He nodded, contemplating the significance of this statement. 'Ah, yes. You'll need the card key resetting.'

She handed over the card. He gazed at it disapprovingly for a moment, as if either it was damaged beyond repair or simply the wrong card entirely. Then he pulled the machine out from beneath his desk and slotted the card into it, his expression now indicating that he was engaged in some highly complex technical operation.

'There, that should do it.'

'Thanks, Kev,' she said. 'And thanks for sorting the door so quickly. Sincerely.'

She was turning to leave when he said, 'Oh, Miss Donovan . . .'

'What is it, Kev?'

'It's just . . .' He was fumbling awkwardly in the top drawer of his desk. 'I think this is for you.' He held out a slim Manila envelope.

She glanced at the front. It was addressed to her, postmarked more than a week earlier.

Jake's handwriting.

She looked up at Kev, who was smiling smugly back at her, as if he'd just done her a good deed.

'How long have you had this?' she said.

He shrugged. 'A day or two.'

She blinked, trying to take this in. 'Why wasn't it in my post box?' There was a row of sealed pigeon holes in the lobby into which incoming post was delivered.

'It was delivered to the wrong flat.' His voice took on a defensive note. 'The address wasn't clear.'

She looked again at the envelope. The paper was rain damaged and the number of the flat had been smudged.

'Mr— the guy who received it must have sat on it for a few days,' Kev went on. 'I meant to put it in your box, but hadn't got around to it. I just thought about it when you came in. Is it important?'

She looked at Kev and then down at the envelope. 'Not really,' she said, then murmured to herself: 'Maybe just a matter of life and death.'

Back in the lobby, she hesitated. Her first thought had been to return to her flat to open the envelope. But if she was under surveillance there, she didn't want to let anyone know she'd received this, whatever it might be. She returned to the lift and made her way back down to the car park. Her tiredness had melted away, driven out by a surge of adrenaline.

In the middle of the day, the car park was deserted, only a few vehicles still remaining. She looked up at the grey concrete roof and spotted the cameras placed to give coverage across most of the parking area. She moved into a darker corner outside the range of the nearest camera, and carefully tore open the envelope. Inside was a single piece of paper, ripped from some reporter's-style notebook. In the centre of the sheet was an apparently meaningless jumble of numbers and letters.

For a moment, she was disappointed. Without consciously realizing it, she had already begun to build expectations about the contents of the envelope – that it would open some new door, offer some fresh insight into the circumstances of Jake's death.

It took her a moment to realize. It was the password, of course. She'd been wasting her time trying to come up with some word that might have had significance for Jake. He had done what the IT security-types always recommended and selected a strong password, nothing more than a random mix of characters. He had sent this and the data stick separately, one to the office, the other to her home, presumably on the basis that if either letter were intercepted, it would be worthless on its own. But he'd assumed that the two items would reach her at roughly the same time, and that she'd be smart enough to make the link.

She folded the paper carefully and clutched it in her hand, making sure that it was not visible to the cameras, as she made her way to the car.

Leaving the car park, she turned down on to the ring road then headed out to the M602. From time to time, she glanced in her rear-view mirror, wondering if she was being followed.

It was impossible to tell. The traffic was busy, and there was a steady stream of cars pulling on to the motorway behind her. The sun was low in her eyes, and it was difficult to concentrate on what might be behind her. When she reached the quieter M61, heading up north to join the M6, it might be easier to judge if anyone was sticking behind her.

A few miles further she reached the junction with the orbital M60, taking the northbound turning that took her across the East Lancs Road to join the M61. Soon she was out in the quieter Lancashire countryside, passing the Reebok Stadium and then the great sweep of Winter Hill ahead of her. There were a couple of cars close behind her, but she had no reason to assume there was anything sinister in their presence.

Nevertheless, when she reached Rivington Services, a mile or two further on, she pulled in, turning unexpectedly, earning a blast of the horn from the car immediately on her tail. She made her way into the car park, turned off the engine and watched other cars entering behind her. Some headed through to get fuel, others stopped. Businessmen making phone calls. Families stopping for a drink or a snack.

The adrenaline had worn off a little, and the tiredness was returning. She climbed out of the car, pulling her coat around her against the chill of the bright day, and retrieved her laptop from the boot. Slipping back into the driver's seat, she fumbled in her handbag for the data stick. When requested, she entered the password scribbled on the piece of paper.

As the window opened on the screen, she glanced up, feeling suddenly exposed. She was parked towards the end of the car park, away from the service buildings, and there were no other cars close by. There was no sign that anyone was interested in her presence.

There were several dozen files on the data stick, all with uninformative coded names. Some were Word files, but most were PDFs, images or copies of e-mails. She opened one of the image files at random. A series of photographs of Kerridge, taken with a long-distance lens, standing in what looked like one of the city centre car parks. There were other figures, mostly Kerridge's associates. But Marie recognized two other figures in the picture. Two Dutchmen – known players in money laundering. The Agency had been liaising with the Dutch police for a year or more about them. It was the usual story. The authorities on both sides of the North Sea knew exactly who they were and what they were up to. The difficulty was building a reliable case. So far, despite their surveillance efforts, they'd obtained nothing likely to stand up in court. Just as with Kerridge and Boyle.

The real trouble was money. These people operated 24/7, and did their business when other people were unlikely to be around. The cost of keeping tabs on them was enormous. Marie had seen major surveillance operations called off simply because the Agency's overtime budget had been spent.

She skimmed through the photographs in the file. They all showed the same scene, probably taken over a period of half an hour or so, as the group of men had talked, smoked, milled around. At one point, one of the Dutchmen appeared to be handing over a package to Kerridge. Probably nothing significant, she thought. These people wouldn't risk soiling their hands with actual merchandise. This would be a set-up meeting, agreeing the terms of the deal and the logistics of the delivery.

The photographs were hardly conclusive evidence, but they were important, showing a link between two sets of operators which the authorities had suspected, but had so far been unable to prove. They'd enable the investigators to draw another line between the countless dots that might one day produce a solid picture. A small step, but they were all small steps and every one constituted progress.

She closed the file and opened another. More pictures, this time showing Kerridge sitting in the sunshine outside an attractive-looking country pub. She recognized none of the figures other than Kerridge himself, but they would be familiar to some of her colleagues. More dots being joined.

She worked through several more files. There were copies of e-mail exchanges, some from Kerridge, some from other names she recognized, some that meant nothing to her. Again, nothing directly incriminating. But there was enough to help progress a case against Kerridge.

Much of it would be inadmissible as evidence given its uncertain provenance. But it was better than anything else they had, and would open other channels of enquiry. Shapes and details that made no sense in isolation would gain significance as part of a wider narrative.

Christ knew how Jake had pieced all this stuff together. At first, she'd assumed that Jake had turned informant just because he'd had enough, that he wanted out. But she knew from experience that most informants just go through the motions. They give up what they know, but don't go out of their way to dig more. Why would they? You don't expect them to take more risks than necessary. It was one of the key skills of the handler, to put enough pressure on the sources to come up with the goods without pushing them too far.

But she'd sensed that Jake was different. The more he'd talked, during their time together, the more she'd felt that something was driving him. Something more than just weariness at the lifestyle, dislike of his associates. He wanted to do something proactive. To bring down the house of cards.

She couldn't imagine how much risk had been involved. She didn't even know whether Jake had acted alone. But it was an extraordinary collection of material. He'd gone to the limits in exploiting his proximity to Kerridge and Boyle – copying documents, taking photographs, scanning material.

She opened a third file – more images. Photographs of documents taken with a digital camera or mobile phone. Slightly blurred in some cases, as if taken in a hurry. She squinted at the screen, trying to work out what she was looking at. Some were tickets. Ferry tickets for the Hull–Zeebrugge line. It was impossible to make out the details, but she suspected that the tickets were for trips made by Kerridge or one of his associates, probably under some assumed name. If the image were enhanced, it could help identify the alternative identities that Kerridge's people used for their overseas liaisons. They'd picked up one or two through surveillance, but the interaction with Kerridge's people was more frequent than anything they'd picked up so far.

There were more copies of tickets, and copies of invoices from transport and courier companies. They'd suspected, but been unable to prove, that Kerridge was involved in carousel fraud, a VAT scam involving the transfer of real or notional goods between different tax regimes. If they could track down the supposed transfers, they might start to disentangle the network of shadow companies involved.

Further into the file, she came across a series of images

taken from passports. An ID photograph she recognized as Kerridge, though his hair looked darker in the picture, as if dyed. The passport was in the name of Stuart Larson. There were more photographs of passports, some with images that she recognized. A driving licence with Kerridge's photograph, again in the name Stuart Larson. Two more passports with Kerridge's image and different names.

She flicked randomly through a few more files, convinced now that the material was dynamite. The key question was whether anyone, on either side, knew quite how much Jake had taken.

She suspected not. If anyone really knew what was on this data stick, they'd be making more serious efforts to recover it. Her impression was that everyone – Boyle, Kerridge, Welsby, Salter, Uncle fucking Tom Cobleigh and all – suspected that Jake had taken more than he was letting on, but no one knew what. The interesting thing was that most of this material related only to Kerridge, with few references to Boyle. It seemed that Jake had held back this side of his evidence – the other half of the picture – because he hadn't known who to trust.

She opened one more file, this one intriguingly labelled 'Stamps003'. To her surprise, it was a series of images showing just that – photographs of postage stamps. She skimmed through them, momentarily baffled. It looked like a child's stamp collection. Some British, others clearly foreign. What was this doing in here?

It took her a few moments to understand. Money laundering again. She was no expert, but she'd attended a few lectures on emerging trends. One of the trends was investment in high-value, low-volume commodities. They didn't come much lower volume than rare postage stamps. You might even make a profit on your dirty money.

There were further image files devoted to other commodities. Racks of wine, artwork, even rare books. All of these would open up more paths they could follow up, join yet more dots.

Her attention was caught by a movement in the corner of her eye. She realized she'd become engrossed in the material, forgetting where she was. She looked up, conscious now of the value of the evidence in her possession, her sense of vulnerability increasing.

She'd opened one of the car windows when she had pulled into the lay-by, but the interior had steamed up. She rubbed at the windscreen and peered out, then turned on the engine and heater.

She didn't know what had caught her attention. There were still few cars parked at this end of the car park. Several more had passed, but she'd become aware of something else, something she'd intuitively perceived as threatening.

It was only when the rear window had fully cleared that she spotted it. Just near the entrance to the car park, a few hundred metres behind her, sited directly in line with her, there was a parked car. A small anonymous grey saloon, almost unnoticeable from where Marie was sitting. At a conscious level, she couldn't be certain how long it had been there.

She was in no real doubt, though. The car's arrival had half-registered in her peripheral vision while she was engrossed in the material on the laptop.

She watched the car for another minute or two, hoping that the driver would decide to depart, having consulted his map, made his call, or completed whatever task he'd parked up to perform.

But the car remained motionless.

She made up her mind in an instant. Always assume the worst. That was a maxim that Keith Welsby had taught her.

He applied it as a general guide to life, but she'd adopted it only as an operational rule of thumb. As Welsby had often pointed out, at least it meant you wouldn't be disappointed.

The car engine was running. She checked in the rear-view mirror that there were no cars entering the car park behind her. Then she released the handbrake, put the car into gear, and floored the accelerator.

She'd picked this car partly for its performance. Deceptively nippy, the review had said. One way of putting it. She headed across the car park going far too fast, and then pulled out on to the perimeter road, by now getting close to sixty. A moment later, she was on the access road to the motorway, already well above seventy. She pulled out suddenly, cutting neatly between a lorry and a white van, then across into the outside lane. She was a trained high-speed driver, accustomed to velocities and circumstances more challenging than this. Even so, she could almost feel the animosity of the drivers she'd cut up.

She took a glance in the mirror, trying to see whether the grey car had pulled out in pursuit, but there was no sign of it. She kept up her speed, undercutting traffic in the outside lane, putting distance between herself and anyone who might be following her.

She didn't want to keep this up for too long. For all her skill, there was always the risk of coming up against some less accomplished driver. And if she got caught doing this speed, Salter wouldn't be pulling too many strings on her behalf.

There was a junction ahead. She contemplated turning off, but decided she needed to confuse things first. Give her pursuer – assuming there was a pursuer – some options to play with. She sped past the junction, waited for another.

Minutes went by with no sign of a turn-off. It was bloody typical. She should have seized the first opportunity.

Finally, she reached another junction, a link with the M65.

As far as she could remember, if she headed west she could do a loop round the end of the motorway and join the north-bound M6 at an earlier point than if she continued along the M61. If there was anyone behind her, it would help confuse things, open up more options about where she might be heading. She looked in the mirror. No sign of the grey car.

She hesitated briefly, then hit the brake and pulled the wheel to the left, cutting across all three lanes to the exit, momentarily startled by the appearance of a lorry bearing down on her in the inside lane. The driver flashed his lights in warning, but there was no real risk. She was already past, heading up the slip road, her speed undiminished.

There were a couple of cars following her up the exit, but none of them was grey. She pulled on to the M65, still keeping her speed up, then, when she was more confident that no one was behind her, she slowed down to the legal limit.

She realized she'd been holding her breath for some time. Gripping the wheel, she inhaled steadily, calming herself, the adrenaline slowly receding.

She could still see the startled expression on the lorry driver's face as she'd swept across in front of him. And she didn't need any great powers of deduction to know what he'd been thinking. *Women fucking drivers.*

17

Each time she'd met Jake over the preceding months, things seemed to have moved on. The first drink had turned out to be both less complicated and more successful than she'd really expected. They'd met in some upmarket bar-cum-restaurant just off Deansgate, shared a bottle of wine and eaten a pretentious sandwich. Jake had pitched it perfectly, she thought. Slightly more than just a drink, but nothing as significant as a dinner date. And Jake himself had been the perfect gentleman – almost disappointingly so, she'd thought later. She'd half-expected that he'd try it on at some point and had wondered how she'd react if he did. But the question never arose, not then at least. He'd organized her a taxi back to her flat and seen her off with an entirely decorous kiss on the cheek, but not before she'd agreed to another date.

He was a smooth operator, there was no question of that. Not remotely pushy, but with each step neatly judged. She had no problem with that. After all, her job was to get closer to Jake, in order to get closer in turn to Kerridge's operation. It looked like Jake intended to make the first part of her task relatively easy. The challenge was to make sure that her judgement remained as sound as Jake's.

On a personal level, she'd enjoyed the evening. Jake was good company – relaxed, personable, good humoured, an easy conversationalist but also a good listener. All the kinds of qualities, it struck her, that had first attracted her to Liam not so very long ago. She had pushed that thought from her mind. This was just work.

The second dinner felt somehow more significant, though, as if she were taking a step into a new territory. As if, at least in her own head, she'd already crossed a line and knew there was no going back. Once again, she'd had to admire Jake's perfect pitch. She'd somehow expected that he'd invite her to one of the swanky hotel restaurants adorned with the name of some celebrity chef. Instead, he took her to a small, French-style restaurant tucked away in some dark corner of the Northern Quarter, where the decor initially seemed a little rough and ready, but the atmosphere was relaxed and intimate. The food was unpretentious but excellent, and the wine flowed a little more freely than she'd intended. She still didn't feel that she was being actively wined and dined. This was nothing more than a pleasant supper between friends, Jake's manner suggested. But she recognized that the laidback ambiance probably would make her more susceptible to Jake's charms than if she'd had a starched waiter standing at either shoulder.

Nevertheless, she kept a careful watch on her tongue even as they moved on to a second bottle of wine. She was getting better at this now, chatting amiably about her fictitious life, steering clear of the danger areas. Even so, it required concentration. At one point, she almost found herself talking about one of Liam's paintings. She bit back the words, shifted the conversation on to safer ground, and felt a sharp stab of guilt at her silent disloyalty.

Jake, she suspected, was treading equally warily, though she could detect no obvious signs of caution in his relaxed demeanour. He talked cheerfully about his work in Kerridge's empire, but gave no hint that their activities were anything other than entirely legitimate.

'What's his main business, then?' she'd asked at one point, taking the risk of at least a gentle prod into the machinations of Jake's working life.

'Like I say, import-export stuff, mainly,' Jake said, pouring them both another inch or two of wine.

'All a mystery to me,' she said. 'What sort of import-export? I mean, what sort of goods?'

He shrugged. 'If there's a market for it, Jeff'll try to get his finger in the pie. He's the ultimate middleman, really. Does his bit to facilitate the trade, and creams off a nice slice for himself in the process.'

This sounded like a prepared line, she thought. Jake's skilful way of deflecting further enquiry.

'What sort of stuff is it, though? Typically, I mean,' she prompted.

He regarded her for a moment, as if even this kind of query might be too intrusive. Then he smiled.

'Oh, God knows. Anything and everything. Brings in a lot of cheap plastic crap from China. Stuff they give away at funfairs or that you see market traders trying to offload on an unsuspecting public. Can be surprisingly lucrative, that stuff. And then there's electrical goods – again, especially the stuff from China that can undercut the big brands . . .' He stopped and shook his head. 'Christ, Marie, I'm even beginning to bore myself now. Under Jeff's tutelage, I can talk about this stuff till the cows come home. But you really don't want to hear it.'

If only you knew, she'd thought at the time. But there was no way that she could convincingly protest that, no, she'd like nothing more than to hear every last detail of Kerridge's business. Instead, she was forced to change the subject.

'So what about you, then, Mr Morton? How come a fine figure of a man like you's still unattached?'

Even as she'd spoken the words, she'd half-regretted them. She didn't even know for sure that Jake really was unattached, though he'd certainly gone out of his way to give that impression. Mind you, she was acutely conscious that she'd done the same. And even if he really was, she wasn't sure that she'd really wanted to send out quite such an obvious signal. Not quite so soon, anyway.

Jake seemed unfazed by the question. 'Just the way it is,' he said. 'There've been a couple of serious relationships. One of them I'd really thought was – well, the one. But it wasn't. Just fizzled out. My fault, probably. Bit too ambitious in those days. Couldn't think of anything but work.'

'And now you're different?'

'Feels like it to me,' he said. 'But I'm not the one to judge.' He left the comment hanging in the air, suggesting that perhaps before long she might have the chance to decide for herself.

As it happened, that evening had ended innocently enough as well. An early finish for a school night, and separate taxis home for the two of them. Another chaste kiss on the cheek, perhaps lingering just a little longer this time. She found herself feeling both relieved and yet disappointed. She wanted to keep this just as it was, she told herself. A friendship with Morton, and no more. But she no longer knew whether that was true.

There was a third date, another dinner, this time just a little more upmarket, a restaurant named after a chef-proprietor whose name she was presumably supposed to recognize. Jake had been in a good mood. Kerridge had just paid all his senior managers a hefty bonus based on the previous year's business performance.

'Let's push the boat out,' Jake had said. 'Spend some of the old bugger's money. It's not often he gives much away.'

To Marie, the evening felt as if everything had been pushed up a notch or two. Not just in expense, but also in significance. Almost without her noticing, Jake had started to behave as if they were an item. That little bit closer. That little bit more intimate.

They'd duly indulged themselves. Cocktails, a better than usual bottle of wine, brandies. A meal with much greater ambitions than anything they'd enjoyed previously. Then, at the end of the evening, he'd invited her back to his flat for coffee. She'd almost laughed at the cliché, feeling that Jake ought to have been able to come up with something more original. But despite that – despite everything – she knew that she would say yes. And she knew that, from there, it was inevitable that she would stay the night.

She couldn't fool herself now that she was just doing her job. This was really stepping over the line. She was going well beyond anything the Agency – beyond anything even Welsby, for Christ's sake – would expect of her. It wasn't just that she was attracted to Jake. It wasn't even that she was looking for someone, something, different from Liam. As the weeks went by, her life with Liam was feeling increasingly remote, already slipping into history. Life up here, life with Jake, simply seemed more real.

A couple of weeks after she'd first spent the night with Jake, she'd had another of her regular liaison meetings with Salter. Salter had been his usual self – bumptious, cynical, clearly keen to get the meeting over and done with. But there had been something in his manner that told her he'd detected something, perhaps some change in her manner, some hesitation in the way she responded to his questions. She could feel him verbally prodding her, a covert bully searching for his victim's vulnerability.

'What about Morton?' he'd said. 'You getting anywhere?'

She tried to detect any edge in his tone, but there was no way to be sure.

'Maybe,' she said. She was standing by the window, staring out at the rainy morning, trying to avoid any need to catch Salter's eye. It was another anonymous suburban hotel, with a panoramic view of the M60 and a retail park beyond.

'Like you, does he?' This time, there was a definite leer in Salter's voice. But that was hardly unusual.

'I suppose so. We've been for a drink a couple of times.'

'Well done,' Salter said. 'Morton keen to . . . make your acquaintance, I imagine.'

She suspected that Salter had bitten back some lewder phrase. 'I wouldn't know, Hugh. I lack your masculine insight. He seems to enjoy my company.'

'And you his?'

She moved from the window and sat down opposite Salter, determined to look him directly in the eye. 'Well, it's probably more fun than this, Hugh. I'm just doing a job. Like you asked me to. Remember?'

It helped that, in fact, she was making some progress in that direction. As far as she could tell, Jake had no suspicions about her. He'd begun to acknowledge openly that she was in pretty much the same line of business as he was, running a legit front for a series of criminal services. Quite quickly, once his initial caution had faded, he'd begun to speak to her with surprising openness. It was as if, she thought, he'd been looking for some way of telling the truth, of coming clean about who he was and what he was doing. Well, she could empathize with that. More than once, as Jake had been talking to her, she'd found herself having actively to resist the temptation to respond in the same terms.

She knew that Jake's account of Kerridge's business was still

199

heavily sanitized, presumably because Jake thought he was protecting her own interests. He'd begun to talk openly about Kerridge's dodgy accounting practices – and his own complicity in them – and about the ways in which Kerridge fiddled duty and VAT. He'd even talked about Kerridge's smuggling operations – the apparently legitimate containers that came in through various British ports full of undeclared goods. But he hadn't yet touched on any of the seedier aspects of Kerridge's business. The drugs, the porn. The illegal immigrants. Maybe that was just as well, she'd thought, as she wrestled with her own conscience. She knew these things were part of Kerridge's business, and she couldn't believe that Jake wasn't aware of them. But as long as he said nothing, she could salve her own conscience by giving Jake the benefit of her limited doubt.

Even so, she'd already got some good material from Jake. Not evidence in itself, but at least material that confirmed some of their suspicions or provided them with other channels to explore. She'd passed whatever she had on to Salter, with more than a twinge of guilt. She wondered quite how, with all her good intentions, she'd managed to get herself into this position. Stuck in the middle. Betraying both sides.

Most importantly, as she spent more time with Jake, her initial suspicions were increasingly confirmed. It probably wasn't so surprising that he'd confided in her so readily. She could tell that he'd had enough. He'd had enough of Kerridge, of Boyle, of that whole world. He'd had enough of being the clean-up man, keeping things in order, maintaining the boundary between the legitimate business and everything that went on behind it.

She never heard him explicitly criticize Kerridge or Kerridge's business. It was all in his tone, an edge in the way he described his activities. And the way he talked about the future.

'I'm a chartered fucking accountant,' he said once, when talking about some delegated task that had particularly infuriated him. 'I don't need this. One day, I'll go off and do my own thing.'

They both knew why, for the moment, he didn't. He was well paid for his multiple roles – much better than he would be for an equivalent position in any legitimate small business. In any case, leaving Kerridge's employment wasn't that simple. Kerridge had a polarized view of the world. You were with him or you weren't. You didn't just hand in your notice and waltz over to the competition.

'So how'd you come to take the job in the first place?' she'd asked once, as they sat over dinner. They'd been back in the small bistro where they'd enjoyed one of their first evenings together. It felt right, she thought. Dark, discreet. Vaguely clandestine.

'Don't think I did. Not knowingly. Just answered an ad. Joined as finance manager, fresh from my accountancy qualifications. Looked like a good deal at the time. Well, it was a good deal. Much better than I could have got anywhere else.'

'But that was all legit?'

'Oh, yes. It was a while before I went over to the dark side. But Jeff realized I was a bright boy. Ambitious. Began to use me for all kinds of stuff. I didn't even know how dodgy some of it was. By the time I did, I was up to my neck in it.' He stopped and looked at her. 'What about you, then? How'd you end up doing this sort of stuff? Why not just stick to printing?'

It was first time he'd asked her that kind of question. Previously, he'd tended to maintain a gentlemanly silence about the more dubious aspects of her supposed business.

'Doesn't pay enough,' she said simply. 'Had a boyfriend who was into wheeling and dealing. He got me involved, and I discovered I was good at it. Better than he was, as it happened. I built up the contacts, and I've carried on from there. Why not?'

'Because one day you'll get caught,' he said. 'We're both riding our luck. Trick is to get out before it's too late.'

'Easier said than done,' she said.

He had paused, gazing into her eyes. 'Maybe we can do it together. Somehow.'

'Maybe. One day.'

She didn't know what to think. She was just doing her job. And she was having a good time with Jake; she felt alive. But she knew there was no future here. She had tried to get back to Liam at least every second weekend, so her time with Jake had been, for the most part, a midweek affair, snatched evenings and nights with the inevitability of work the next day. If she was honest, her relationship with Jake had felt like more play-acting, a neat adornment to a life that was ultimately fictitious. It was all a game, even if, increasingly, she was aware Jake hadn't seen it that way.

It was around this time that she'd formally recommended Jake as a potential informant. A Covert Human Intelligence Source, to use the jargon. She had felt uneasy, as if she were exploiting their relationship. But it was his choice, she told herself. All she was doing was opening a door. No one would compel him to walk through it. Salter had taken her recommendation back to the ranch and it had been processed officially, going through all the correct channels.

She had known how it would happen. The way that some skilled handler would make the approach to Jake. Subtle at first, delicate. Testing the ground. Checking whether Marie's hunch had been correct, without exposing too much. She'd done it herself and she'd been good at it. It was a form of seduction, she supposed. Raising the target's interest, highlighting all the positives, playing down the negatives. Assessing the target's motivation so that you could press just the right buttons. Taking it step by step, knowing when to go in harder and when to leave well alone. Slowly, slowly, reeling him in.

She was told officially when Jake had finally gone over. But she knew anyway. Something in his manner changed. He became more closed, a little more wary. He told her less about work, about Kerridge. Another barrier erected between them – translucent, paper-thin, but ultimately impermeable.

It was a painful irony. Both working on the same side, but never able to speak about it. Each, for different reasons, knowing that their relationship was unsustainable, but not knowing how to end it. Continually talking about a future that both knew would never happen.

'One day soon,' he'd said, as they finished that last meal, 'we can do something different. Get away from this.'

She'd sat for a while, her eyes fixed on the window beside their table, watching the eerily deserted streets of this part of the Northern Quarter. It was hard to believe that, barely a street away, there were bustling pubs and bars, a main road full of traffic.

For a second, it had been as if she hadn't heard him. Then she'd said, her face still blank, 'Yeah. One day, Jake. One day.'

18

'Panini and caffè latte,' Welsby intoned carefully. 'Do I look fucking Italian?' He sat down heavily at the table, making a play of dumping his cardboard-packed collation between the two of them. 'In any case, shouldn't it be a panino?'

Salter noted, as so often before, that Welsby's cultural ignorance was less all-embracing than he liked people to think. He peered at Welsby's lunch. 'Not really,' he said finally. 'You've got two.'

'Which just about equates to one half-decent meal,' Welsby pointed out. He peeled back the wrapping. 'Though man cannot live by bread alone. Even with mozzarella and fucking pancetta.' He looked up at the brightly lit space that surrounded them. 'How's it come to this? Coppers need chips and meat pies and full fry-ups. Not mixed-leaf fucking salads and vegetarian bakes. No wonder everyone's so irritable.'

'Must take the patience of a saint, guv.'

'Too right, Hugh, me old chum. Too fucking right.' He began to munch, with an enthusiasm that belied his previous words, on the warm sandwich, occasionally pausing to take a slurp of the milky coffee.

'Anything new on Morton?'

Welsby shrugged, then spoke around a mouthful of sand-wich. 'Not so's you'd notice. But our chums on the force aren't brimming over with information.'

'And after we'd been so forthcoming with them, as well,' Salter said.

'Yes, well. Need to know and all that. They've had the forensics back.'

'And?'

'Bugger all. Lots of DNA, but, as expected, most of it Morton's. Nothing that's on the database. Mind you, Morton's wasn't on the database either.'

'Professionals, then. But we knew that.'

'Well, they weren't after the DVD player,' Welsby agreed morosely.

'Anything else?'

'Not much. Mind you, I don't imagine this case is exactly top of their to-do list.'

'Nobody likes a grass,' Salter said. 'Even our lot think he had it coming.'

'Now, now, Hughie. That's not the attitude. Grasses are our bread and fucking butter.'

Salter nodded. 'Never been partial to bread and butter. Sticks in the throat. Even the Italian stuff.'

Welsby laughed. He'd already made short work of the second sandwich, and was tearing open a bag of exotically flavoured crisps. He pushed the opened bag towards Salter, who shook his head.

'Christ, Hugh. Have you got any vices?'

'Not ones I usually display in public,' Salter said.

He gazed around them. It was towards the end of most people's lunch hour, and the tables in the restaurant were starting to empty. He supposed it was a good thing, this replacement for the old canteen. Its new pastel walls and tasteful artwork provided an appropriate backdrop for the healthy, up-to-the-minute cuisine that wound up Welsby so successfully. A pleasant enough place to chill out for half an hour in the middle of the day. It was all a façade, though. The place was riddled with the same old vicious gossip and intrigue as in the days when overweight plods were knocking back the cholesterol pies.

'What about Sister Donovan?' he asked, as if the question was a natural corollary to his previous thoughts.

'Marie? What about her?'

'I was thinking about what you said. About her having trouble at home. This stuff about her flat being bugged. Maybe it's all bollocks. Maybe she really is just losing the plot.'

'Wouldn't be the first.' Welsby jammed a surprisingly large amount of crisps into his mouth. 'You'd know about that, Hughie.'

'What about her and Morton? You think there's anything in that?'

'Gossip and innuendo,' Welsby said mellifluously. 'Gossip and fucking innuendo. Which doesn't necessarily mean it isn't true, of course.' He paused. 'Dunno. We never actually caught them at it, so to speak. But then Marie's no fool.'

'Would have been pretty foolish if she'd got involved with Morton,' Salter pointed out.

'Ah, but we're all fools for love. Even you, I don't doubt.'

'Exception that proves the rule. You think it could have been love, then?'

'Love or lust. Pretty much amount to the same thing in my experience.'

'Ever the romantic, guv. Whichever, if she and Morton were some sort of item, do you reckon she really did get something from him?'

'Evidence, you mean, rather than chlamydia? Can't see it. Like I say, she's no fool. We gave her enough opportunity the other day. If she had anything, she'd have told us.'

'Assuming she trusts us.'

Welsby nodded. 'Well, there is that. But if she can't trust us, she can't trust anybody.'

'That's pretty much what I was thinking, guv.'

Welsby screwed up the empty crisp packet and tossed it in the approximate direction of the bin behind Salter's chair. It bounced off the side and fell forlornly to the floor.

'Why do I get the feeling that you're fishing for something, Hughie?'

'Don't know what you mean, guv. When I go fishing, I generally take a harpoon.'

Welsby pushed himself slowly to his feet. There was a sign on the wall immediately in front of him which politely requested customers to return their trays and utensils and to dispose of any litter in the receptacles provided. He gazed at the sign for a moment, with the air of one wrestling with an unfamiliar language. Then he turned, leaving the remains of his meal scattered across the table.

'We live in strange times, Hughie. All I can say is, if Marie Donovan's on the point of losing her marbles, you'd better be fucking sure you hold on to yours.'

19

She parked in an anonymous shoppers' car park, a half-acre of reclaimed space between a down-at-heel supermarket and a row of charity shops. There was little more depressing, she thought, than a holiday resort out of season. And, whatever its publicity might say, this place was hardly at the cutting edge of the leisure industry even in the height of summer.

It had been a fine day when she left Manchester, but as she'd driven along the M55 past Preston she'd seen the first dark clouds coming in from the west. Now, heavy rain was pouring down from a leaden grey sky. A few pedestrians scurried past, shoppers hurrying for shelter, elderly ladies apparently oblivious to the weather. A group of inappropriately dressed young men were stumbling along in the direction of the next pub, jackets pulled half-heartedly over their heads. A stag-do, clearly, but it was difficult to tell whether they were recovering from the night before or preparing for the night to come.

Marie pulled her own coat more tightly around her, fumbling with her umbrella, and began to make her way along the back streets behind the North Promenade.

It had taken her a while to work out what Jones' two texted words, 'Mayfield' and 'Wilson', might mean. She had thought it likely that 'Mayfield' might be the name of some hotel or bed and breakfast. A few minutes' online searching had confirmed that – there was a Mayfield Hotel with the postcode that Jones had sent. On that basis, she decided that Wilson must be the name Jones was using.

The Mayfield Hotel was easy enough to find, one of a series of small establishments on a back street running parallel to the seafront. The sea itself was hidden behind the endless rows of Victorian and Edwardian terraces, though she'd briefly glimpsed its grey expanse as she'd made her way from the car park.

The area, like the town in general, had seen better days, a legacy from the times when the North of England used to decamp to the seaside to celebrate its high days and holidays. These days, most of that population would board cheap flights to the Mediterranean or further afield instead, and few would come here for more than a day or two. The town survived on day trips when the weather was decent, drunken stag and hen nights, a scattering of the middle classes on weekend breaks with the kids at the Imperial or the Hilton. She didn't know who stayed in these back-street hotels. Young people or families on benefits, maybe, who might otherwise be homeless.

Most of the hotels – the word flattered the establishments – looked run-down, paint peeling, letters missing from their signs, front gardens overgrown. There were optimistic 'Vacancies' signs in some windows. Others had surrendered to economic realities and closed, boarded windows staring blankly at the deserted street.

The Mayfield looked better than average. It had been redecorated within living memory, and its entrance was kept tidy. It stood at the end of the street, its location within touching distance of the more salubrious residential district beyond. Not exactly luxurious, but respectable.

She pushed open the entrance and stepped into the gloomy lobby. It was a narrow hallway, decorated with a garish wallpaper from a different decade. There was an unoccupied reception desk to the left, a rack of tourist leaflets, a pervasive smell of fried food. On the reception was a neatly printed sign: Ring bell for service. She waited a moment, wondering whether anyone would appear, and then reached out to do so.

'Help you?' a voice said from the gloom at the far end of the passage. She squinted at a rounded silhouette framed in what she took to be the door to the kitchen. The figure shuffled forwards, and revealed itself to be a middle-aged man, dressed in a greasy blazer and tie. He had the air of a gone-to-seed army officer. Like everything else around here, he was well past his prime.

'I'm here to see one of your guests,' she said. 'A Mr Wilson?'

He took another few steps forwards and peered at her, in the manner of an immigration officer surveying a probably illegal alien. 'Mr Wilson?'

She hesitated, wondering whether she had misinterpreted Jones' text message. 'He asked me to meet him here.'

'That so?' The man's gaze was still fixed on her, his eyes now travelling over her besuited body with an all-too-familiar semi-sexual interest. It wasn't difficult to read his curiosity about what the likes of her had to do with the likes of the supposed Mr Wilson.

'Can you let him know I'm here?' she said.

The man said nothing, but made his way slowly around behind the reception desk. He lowered himself cautiously down on to a stool that creaked beneath his weight, then shook his head.

'You're used to more upmarket establishments than this, love. No phones in our rooms. You'll have to go and track him down yourself.' He smiled salaciously, as if the thought of a woman visiting a man's room was intrinsically erotic. In his life it quite possibly was.

'What room?' she said.

'Four,' he said. 'First floor. Up the stairs. Turn right.'

She was gratified to sense that her stare made him uncomfortable. 'You're quite right,' she said finally. 'I am used to more upmarket places. But you can't beat a small hotel for service.'

She strode past him up the stairs. His instructions were accurate enough, at least, and she found Room 4 without difficulty.

She knocked and waited. There was a lengthy pause, and then a muffled voice said, 'Who is it?'

'Marie Donovan,' she called back. She had the strong sense that the hotelier was listening from downstairs.

There was a fumbling with the lock. She wasn't sure what to expect. Jones' anxiety at their previous meeting and his caution in setting up this assignation led her to expect a cowed figure, trembling behind a locked door. Instead, he threw it open and stood before her, looking calm enough. He was dressed casually, in chain-store jeans and a neatly patterned sweater. He looked like an off-duty sales executive.

'You worked out the message, then?' he said.

'It wasn't difficult,' she said, finding herself troubled by his coolness. 'Hope nobody else found it as easy.'

He said nothing for a moment. 'Come in. We need to talk.'

'You sure you want to talk here?' She glanced over her shoulder. 'I don't know that Basil Fawlty approves of you having strange women in your room.'

He held up his hands. 'I'm not going to try anything.'

'Too fucking right you're not,' she said. 'Not if you want to keep the use of those arms.'

He laughed nervously and ushered her in. It was a bleak place – a single bed, a battered dressing table that Jones was using as a desk, a couple of chairs. There was a sink in the corner, so presumably no en-suite bathroom. Jones' old suitcase lay open on the floor. It looked as if it had been packed in a hurry.

She pulled one of the chairs round and sat down. 'What's this about, Morgan? It's a long bloody way up here.'

He nodded. 'I thought I should get away for a bit. Get my head straight.'

'You'll need to go a long way if that's what you want to do,' she said. 'Why'd you run out on me?'

'Lost my nerve.' He sat down opposite her. 'Thought someone was watching.'

'In the café?'

'Probably just being paranoid,' he said. 'Some guy at the far end. Reading a paper. Got the idea into my head that he was keeping an eye on us.'

She thought back, but couldn't remember anyone. Given her own state of mind, that surprised her. If there'd been anyone acting suspicious, she'd have been the first to notice it.

'So you just legged it?'

'I'm here now.'

'Rejoice and be merry,' she said. 'So what do you want?'

He stared down at his knees for a moment, then looked up at her. 'I didn't tell the whole truth the other day.'

'That right, Morgan? How will I live with my shattered illusions?'

'I said I'd heard about Jake Morton's death. That wasn't quite true.'

'Go on.'

It was clear that he was struggling to find the right words.

He was looking down again, and she had to listen hard to make out what he said.

'I was part of it. Part of the team that killed him.'

She acted without thinking. She hooked her foot around the leg of his chair and jerked it savagely to the left. Caught by surprise, he toppled sideways, falling awkwardly on to the worn carpeting. She was on her feet in a moment, her shoe pressed against Jones' throat.

'What the fuck are you talking about? Is this one of your stupid games, Morgan?'

It was only afterwards that she realized quite how angry she'd been. All the emotions of the past few weeks – all the fear, loss, resentment and paranoia – had found a release in the fury and revulsion she felt towards Jones' cowering form. It was fortunate, she thought later, that she'd been wearing low heels rather than stilettos.

She never knew what she might have done. There was a sudden sharp knocking at the door, and from outside the hotel owner was shouting, 'Everything all right in there?'

She lifted her shoe from Jones' neck and strode over to open the door. She stared at the elderly man, who was clearly startled that she, rather than Jones, had responded to his shout.

'Everything's fine,' she said. 'Sorry about the noise.' She gestured over her shoulder. 'Mr Wilson had a bit of a tumble, but he's OK now.'

The hotel owner peered past her. Jones was climbing slowly to his feet, looking nothing worse than dishevelled.

The man hesitated, seeking some excuse to continue his intrusion. 'If you're sure . . .' He looked her up and down, though his gaze was possibly admiring rather than voyeuristic now.

'I'll let you know if we need anything. Thanks for checking.'

She stood resolutely at the doorway until the man had backed away down the stairs.

When she was satisfied that he was gone, she closed the door and turned back towards Jones.

'Same question, Morgan,' she said. 'What the fuck are you talking about? Don't try to kid me you were involved in Morton's death.' She sat down again, indicating Jones to follow suit.

Jones opened his mouth and closed it again. 'I was there,' he said, finally. 'I mean, I wasn't involved in . . . all that. Not my style. You know that.'

'Don't know what I know, Morgan. But you're not the sort to get your hands dirty if you can help it.'

'I was driving,' Jones said. 'They'd asked me to sort the car for them, and then drive them. I waited down the street.' He stopped, struggling for breath. 'I thought they just wanted to put some pressure on Morton . . .'

She stared at him, offering no response or respite. His story made sense. That was Jones' level – stealing cars, petty stuff. She'd heard that one of Jones' few assets was that, through some miracle, he'd never actually managed to acquire a criminal record. His DNA and prints weren't on file. So he'd been able to make a living doing bits and pieces with no risk that they'd be traced back to him. It was a saleable commodity, even if Jones had little else going for him.

The professionals who'd done the hit were in the same position, of course, though by design rather than happy accident. The value of a professional hitman lay largely in untraceability. Yes, they brought a certain expertise to the party, but their major skill was in melting into the background afterwards. She didn't know who'd organized the hit or who'd involved Jones, but she knew Jones would have no clue who his colleagues had been. Jones was disposable. If anything had gone wrong

214

with the operation, he was there to carry the can. Probably why they'd recruited him in the first place.

'So who was it, Morgan?' she said anyway. 'Who organized it?'

'I don't know,' he said pleadingly. 'You know how these things happen. I was contacted, given the details of what to do. But I don't know who was at the end of the chain.'

'But you can guess?'

He looked up at her, meeting her eyes at last. 'Well, so can you. It must have been Boyle or Kerridge. Who else would have a reason to kill Morton?'

'So why are you telling me this, Morgan? This your idea of a good anecdote?'

Another thought had struck her. Whether Jones had seen her leaving Morton's apartment, seen her driving away.

'Like I said, I didn't expect them to do . . . what they did. I thought they were trying to get information. I didn't think it would go that far.'

'Don't come to me looking for absolution, Morgan. You can burn in the fires of hell for all I care.' She leaned forwards and jabbed a finger in his chest. 'What do you want? Why bring me all the way out here to tell me about your chauffeuring experience?'

'Because I heard what they said. In the car afterwards.'

She looked closely at his bloodshot eyes and trembling mouth, wondering if he was telling the truth. If they were pros, they wouldn't shoot their mouths off in Jones' hearing. Unless of course they'd wanted Jones to hear.

It was possible. They knew they'd been seen, that she'd been in the flat. That was an unknown quantity for them. So they'd scare the living daylights out of Jones, make sure he kept quiet. And maybe make sure he got the word out to others. A warning.

In any case, this was about territory. Yes, Boyle would have known that Morton's death removed their key witness. And he'd have wanted to get whatever information he could out of Morton. But ultimately this was about showing he was still in charge. Boyle might be behind bars, at least for the moment, but he was demonstrating, loud and clear, that this was no time for anyone to fuck with him.

'What did they say, Morgan? What did they tell you?'

He swallowed. 'They told me what they'd done to Morton. Told me they had to apply a few . . . measures.'

'Did they?' Marie had not sought to discover any more details about Jake's death. The hints dropped by Salter had been more than enough. She certainly had no desire to hear it from Jones.

'They said that he'd become more . . . forthcoming. That was when he mentioned me. Said I was a grass. He couldn't have known that, though. Not for sure.'

Maybe not for sure, she agreed, but it wouldn't have been a difficult guess. Jones was just the kind who became a low-level informant – self-centred, eager for approbation, weak-willed, in need of a few quid. No conscience about selling his mates down the river. The only problem with the likes of Jones was that, in the end, you got bugger all out of them. Nobody trusted them, so they had nothing of value to sell.

Jake had probably just been trying to buy time, give them some titbits in the hope of getting them off his back. Morgan Jones would have been one of the first names to spring to mind. Jake had presumably had no idea that the same Morgan Jones was sitting in the car outside.

'Like to have been a fly on the wall when your name came up, eh, Morgan?'

'Jesus,' Jones said. 'When they told me – Christ . . .' He

shook his head. 'They laughed about it in the car. Didn't take it seriously.'

She leaned forwards. 'Oh, they'd have taken it seriously. They were playing with you, Morgan. You won't trouble them, a small-timer like you. But one day, when you're not expecting it . . .'

Keep him on edge, she thought. He's more likely to tell the truth if he's scared.

He was looking back at her now, though, a different expression on his face.

'But they mentioned other names Morton had come up with. Names they seemed to take a lot more seriously.' There was a note of bravado in his voice now, as if he'd rehearsed this part. 'Yours, for example.'

She laughed. 'You're not very good at being menacing, are you, Morgan? I don't care what Morton might or might not have said. I imagine he'd say anything if he thought it might save his skin.'

His eyes were fixed on her, defiant. 'I know about you and Morton,' he said.

She held her breath for a moment, wondering again whether Jones had seen her that night. 'There's nothing to know about me and Morton,' she said. The lie felt almost corrosive. If she'd been the religious type, she might have thought of asking God to forgive her. 'You're a slippery old sod, Morgan. I don't know what to make of you. The other day you looked so shit-scared you almost got me feeling sorry for you. Now it sounds like you're trying to threaten me.' She looked around the shabby hotel room. 'And you're so sure of yourself that you're hiding away in this rat trap.'

'I'm scared all right,' he said. 'I know Boyle. You don't cross him. You don't even let him think you might cross him. If he thinks he can't trust me . . .'

Suddenly tired of all this, she rose and walked over to the bedroom window. She wasn't expecting a sea view. The room looked out over a small overgrown garden. There was a clothes line with an array of what she took to be table napkins. The rain was still falling and the napkins looked greyer than the heavy sky.

'You know what he'll do, Morgan. So where do I fit into this picture?'

'I could make life difficult for you,' he said. 'They told me what Morton said about you. He reckoned you were the real deal, a serious grass. Seemed to me they were taking it seriously. You're a pretty big fish in their eyes. Not small fry like me.'

'Glad to see you've got life in perspective, Morgan.' She was staring out the window still, ignoring the whining figure behind her. But she was also conscious of a growing unease.

'They're checking you out,' he said. 'You're probably right about me. If I get on the wrong side of them, I'll disappear one dark night. But you're different. You know Kerridge and Boyle. They've trusted you to deliver. You're like Morton, close to the inner circle.'

'I'm very flattered,' she said, without turning. 'But you're talking bollocks.'

'I don't think so.' He was sounding more confident now. 'I think there's something in it.' There was an edge in his voice that made her turn around. He was holding a mobile phone, some smart new model with a large screen. 'Have a look.'

She threw him a look of disdain, and then stepped forwards to peer at the screen. She was half-expecting some photograph of her scurrying away from Jake's flat on the night of his death. But it was a different scene, one she recognized immediately. It was one of the string of charmless hotels where she'd held a liaison meeting with Salter a month or two back.

The image showed her emerging from her car, though she doubted that anyone else could have identified her with confidence.

'If you're thinking of taking up photography, I'd stick to the day job,' she said. 'Assuming you've got a day job, that is. Why are you wasting my time with this crap, Morgan?'

'What about this one, then?' Jones switched to the next image. The same hotel car park. Another car. Salter, this time. Where in Christ's name had Jones got these pictures?

'You aiming for the portrait market, Morgan? You need to get a bit closer.'

'Got it on good authority that he's filth,' Jones said.

'I'll take your word for it,' she said. 'Why are you wasting my time with this crap?'

There was nothing particularly incriminating in the pictures themselves. It would be hard enough to confirm her identity in the previous shot, although her car might be more recognizable. And even if Salter could be clearly identified, their arrival might have been coincidental. Though the receptionist might remember that they'd met.

The really interesting questions, though, were who'd taken the photographs and how they'd come into Jones' possession. She presumed that he hadn't got them from Kerridge or Boyle. More likely, they'd been obtained by whoever was responsible for the leaking. She'd need time to absorb the implications of that.

'I'm just thinking,' Jones said, 'that these images will be of interest to certain parties.'

'You reckon?' she said. 'Well, you'd better go and talk to them, hadn't you? I've had enough of this, Morgan. You've dragged me all the way up here with some cock and bull story about Morton. And now you're boring me with your photo collection. What is this? Come up and see my etchings?'

He'd obviously expected a different reaction. The whine had returned to his voice. 'I thought we could do a deal,' he said. 'Don't want to get you into any trouble, Marie. I could give you these pictures or destroy them. For a price.'

'I don't know what you think those pictures are, Morgan, or why you think I'm interested.' She made a move towards the door. He reached out and grabbed her arm.

'Christ, can't you see I'm scared?' he said. 'You're right about Kerridge and Boyle. Shit, if they think I've crossed them . . .' He stopped. 'I thought maybe I could buy their goodwill with these.' He waved the phone at her. 'But Christ knows what that would be worth.'

'Bugger all, I'd say. Don't think "goodwill" is a term they're familiar with.'

'I need to get away, that's all. I've barely got a penny. Not enough to get right away from here. I could go to London, lose myself there. But I wouldn't be able to get a job. I should maybe go overseas. But that costs money.'

She was already turning away. 'I can't think of one good reason why I should help you. You've told me that you were involved in the murder of someone I thought of as a friend. You've tried some witless attempt at blackmail. You've wasted my fucking time. Just go fuck yourself, OK, Morgan?'

Her hand was on the door when she heard him say, 'What about this, then? Does this change anything?'

She turned. He was holding a gun, some battered handgun. Christ knew where he'd picked it up. His hand was shaking, but he was pointing it approximately in her direction. Close enough at this range, anyway.

'Oh, for Christ's sake, Morgan. Don't be more of an idiot than you need to be. Put that fucking gun down before you hurt yourself.' She stood motionless at the door, trying to keep her voice calm.

'You're all I've got left,' he said. He sounded much less calm than she did. His eyes kept flicking down towards the gun, as if he couldn't believe that he was holding it. 'I know you've got money. You can help me.'

She shook her head. 'I don't think so, Morgan. Put the gun down.'

'Help me.'

'What do you think I'm going to do? Pull two grand out of my handbag?'

He blinked, suddenly confused, as if he hadn't considered the logistics beyond pulling the gun.

'We'll go to a cash machine,' he offered finally.

'And get out a couple of hundred quid? Where will that get you, Morgan? A train ticket to London?'

She didn't believe he had any serious intention of using the gun – that was well beyond Jones' pay grade. But he might do anything by accident.

'Put the gun down,' she said again. 'Let's talk about it. See what we can do.'

She'd left it too late. He didn't believe her. She watched his trembling hand as he took a step towards her. His sweating finger was tensing on the trigger. The poor bastard didn't know what he was doing.

It was over in a second. She allowed him another step, then reached and grabbed his wrist, twisting it painfully, making sure that the gun barrel was pointed away from them both.

The gun could easily have gone off then, if Jones' finger had gripped the trigger. The bullet would have missed them, but who knew what the ricochet might have done in a room this size. At the very least, they'd have had an interesting time explaining it to Basil Fawlty.

As it was, Jones reacted as she'd hoped, his already tremulous grip loosening on the gun. She caught it smartly as he dropped it, snapped on the safety catch, and tossed it calmly into the far corner of the room. The benefits of firearms training. She should probably relieve him of the bloody thing, but she'd no desire to be saddled with an illegal weapon. Instead, she gave Jones' wrist another painful twist, and reaching for his throat, she thrust him back hard against the wall.

'Don't ever try anything like that again, eh, Morgan? Other people won't be as tolerant as me.'

He mumbled something she didn't catch. She thought she might as well take the opportunity while he was terrified out of his wits. 'Those photographs, Morgan. Where'd you get them? Just out of interest.'

She loosened her grip on his throat. 'Sent them,' he grunted. 'Someone sent them. Texted them. Don't know who. No number.'

She opened her hand further. 'Someone sent them to you? Why you, Morgan?'

'Don't know,' he said. 'There was a message. Said they'd be of interest to you.'

'Just shows how wrong people can be,' she said. 'So who knows you've met me, Morgan?'

He shook his head. 'Nobody. Haven't told anyone.'

'You sure?' She tightened her grip threateningly. 'You're not lying to me?'

His head-shaking grew more vehement. 'No. Really. I've not seen anybody.'

She remembered the man who might have been following her through the Arndale Centre before her first meeting with Jones. Anything was possible. She was inclined to believe Jones' protests, if only because he looked too shit-scared to be lying.

She pulled him around and tossed his shaking body towards the bed. He fell, half on the mattress, half on the floor.

'Take care of yourself, Morgan. Get away if you can.'

She made her way downstairs. Basil Fawlty was sitting behind the reception desk, fiddling unconvincingly with a computer keyboard. He looked up with undisguised curiosity as she passed.

'Nice place,' she said. 'But you need a better class of clientele.'

Before he could respond, she'd stepped outside into the damp air. Ahead of her, the skeletal framework of Blackpool Tower loomed above the grey rooftops. Ignoring the drizzle, she strode confidently off down the dreary street, back towards the town centre.

It was only when she reached the car that she realized that her hands were still shaking.

PART THREE

Winter: Outside

20

The last time she'd seen Jake, it had just been another midweek evening. He'd called her up late in the afternoon and suggested they meet for a few drinks, maybe a pizza afterwards. Perhaps go to one of the bars on the quays, as it had been a half-decent day for the time of year.

She'd had an exhausting day in the shop. Joe had been off delivering some completed work to one of their bigger clients, and she'd been left to deal with Darren by herself.

'Yeah,' she'd said to Jake, 'a few drinks sounds good. A lot of drinks sounds even better.'

They met in an old-fashioned real-ale pub round the back of the Bridgewater Hall. The pub was one of Jake's favourite haunts, on the nights when they fancied nothing more complicated than a few beers. It was a warren of cluttered rooms linked by narrow corridors, not much to write home about in itself, but with a real buzz to it even on a quiet midweek night. Later in the week, it would be heaving, drinkers squeezed together in a fug of alcohol and noise. Tonight it was relatively peaceful, just a few groups of office workers enjoying a beer at the end of the day and a gaggle of students trying to work out whether they could afford another round.

Jake was edgier than usual, she thought. Things had been more difficult for a few weeks, ever since he'd finally committed himself as an informant. She'd sensed the change almost immediately. She realized that he was trying to protect her, keep her at arm's length from himself, from Kerridge and his business. If he was grassing on Kerridge, he didn't want her to end up as collateral damage. If he only knew. But there was no way that she could tell him.

She could sense a growing unease in their relationship. There'd always been a tension – Marie had been conscious of her own caginess in talking about her past, her private life. But now there was a growing gulf. Two people who wanted to share everything, but couldn't even be honest about who they really were.

She'd been thinking seriously about ending it. She didn't want to. As time went by, she'd begun to feel that this relationship was more real, more important, than whatever she had with Liam. But it couldn't work. Whatever happened next – with Jake, with Kerridge, with Boyle – it would blow things apart, one way or another. She wanted to get out before that happened. Before he discovered who she really was. Before he realized the extent of her betrayal.

That night, she'd begun to wonder whether it might be Jake who'd act first. He was tense, withdrawn, almost losing his temper over some trivial half-joke she'd made about the beer. Not the usual laidback Jake at all. She had the sense he was building up to something.

An hour and several drinks later, they'd got a cab back to the quays, and were enjoying a pizza and a bottle of wine in some chain Italian. Jake's mood had lightened slightly, but he still seemed uncomfortable. *Christ, Jake*, she thought, *whatever you're going to say, just say it.*

'OK?' he said instead, gesturing towards her pizza.

'I've had worse.' She picked up her glass. 'Wine's good, though.'

'Hope you're not thinking of driving home?' Her flat wasn't far away, but far enough not to be walkable.

'That a proposition, Mr Morton?'

'Suppose so. If you're up for it.'

'More a question of whether you are, I'd have thought. You'd better pace the drinking.'

He smiled, silent for a moment. 'Been thinking,' he said.

'No good'll come of it. I'd stop now.' She was aware that her facetiousness masked an anxiety about what he might be about to say. She could think of some men who might invite her to bed as a preamble to dumping her, but she'd never put Jake in that category.

'About the future,' he said. 'About us.'

She looked at him warily. 'Go on.'

'It's just . . . well, I can't really explain. Not yet. But there are things happening. With Kerridge. With the whole set-up. Don't know where it'll leave me exactly. But it might be a way out.'

'Very cryptic,' she said. 'Kerridge about to go bust?'

'I can't tell you what's going on. I want to. But not yet. But it'll change things.'

'And what does that mean for us, then? What are you saying?'

'I don't know exactly. But it might give us the chance to do something different. Have a new start. Together.' He paused, swallowed. 'Get married even.'

Jesus, had he just proposed to her? She sat in silence for a moment, wondering how to respond. He seemed, just in that moment, different from the man who'd been with her for the rest of the evening; he was suddenly childlike, enthusiastic, as if he'd glimpsed a future that really might offer something new.

What could she say? That she couldn't be part of that future?

229

That she wasn't the person he thought she was? That she'd been lying to him all along?

That she already had a partner back home?

There was no answer she could give. Finally, when the moment had extended far too long, she said, 'That's great, Jake. We'll talk about it. When things become clearer. That's really great.'

It wasn't enough. She could tell from his face that her words had sounded like a rejection. That he knew now that her view of this relationship was different from his. That, one way or another, it was already all over.

She didn't even know whether that was what she wanted. Part of her wanted just to say yes. Wanted this to go on, for them to build some new future together. Why should that be so impossible?

Tomorrow, she'd thought. I'll think about it tomorrow. I'll think about what I want, and whether there's any way we could make this work. I'll think about what we can do.

They'd finished the bottle of wine, gone into one of the hotel bars for a last drink. They'd tried to talk, but the conversation suddenly felt stilted, as if both were conscious that the gulf was widening. Finally, too late, a little too drunk, they'd gone back to Jake's flat, gone to bed. Made love, and it was OK, but it had changed nothing. At last, they'd both slept.

And sometime after midnight, Marie had found herself awake, staring into the darkness.

That was the last time she saw Jake.

21

It was an old building; Victorian or Edwardian. A hotel, perhaps, or maybe a school. She should be able to tell just by looking inside one of the endless series of doors. At the beginning – or was it later? – she'd been given an entry card which was supposed to provide access, but each time she tried to use it the light remained fixed on red.

In any case, there was no time. She had to continue pacing down these endless corridors in search of Jake. She'd forgotten why that was necessary, or why Jake was there in the first place, but she knew it was important. A matter of life and death.

She turned corner after corner, expecting that she would find something to help her get her bearings. A sign, or some familiar landmark.

But the corridors just ran on, each as characterless as the last. Blank white walls, dark wooden doors. From time to time, she noticed CCTV cameras observing her, black lenses turning slowly to follow her as she passed.

At last, she rounded yet another corner and found that the corridor came to an abrupt end. There was one more door ahead, unrevealing as the rest. She fumbled for the entry card, knowing that this was her objective, that this time the card would fit. This was where she would find Jake.

231

As she fumbled in her pocket to extricate the card, her mobile phone began to ring somewhere else in her jacket. Struggling to find the phone, which she knew she'd had only minutes before, she looked up to see that the door was beginning slowly to open . . .

The ringing continued, shriller now but more distant. She opened her eyes. The dream was already fading, the details lost. She rolled over in the bed, squinting at the alarm clock. Not yet seven. Who the hell was calling at this hour?

She grabbed her dressing gown. The bell was pressed again, more insistent this time. Out in the hallway, she pressed the response button on the entryphone. It was a relatively sophisticated system, part of the security arrangements that had attracted her to this place, with a video screen linked to a CCTV camera in the lobby. She switched on the screen, expecting to see the postman or some other familiar early morning caller.

'Yes?'

It was someone she didn't recognize, a round-faced man with slightly overgrown hair. Two other men stood behind him. He was holding a wallet towards the camera. She couldn't make out the detail of the card it contained, but she didn't really need to. She had a similar one tucked away in a concealed side pocket in her handbag.

'Police, madam. Wonder if you could spare us a few moments. It is rather urgent.'

It was the exaggerated politeness that alerted her. She'd heard that tone before. Christ, she'd *used* that tone before. Usually in the phony war before you were in a position to read someone their rights. At least one of the men behind was uniformed, she thought, though it was difficult to be sure through the camera. Three of them, though. That wasn't casual.

She pressed the microphone. 'Sorry – you woke me up. Give me a second to get myself decent.'

She knew that she wouldn't have much more than that notional second. If she delayed, whatever suspicions they had would be confirmed and they'd be inside the place. In this job, though, you were always prepared. Like a fucking Boy Scout.

She grabbed the small case she always kept ready. She'd sometimes joked to Liam that it was like being pregnant, having your bag ready for the maternity ward. She wasn't sure he'd ever got the joke. She thrust the bag into the bathroom, then grabbed a set of clothes and dressed rapidly. Practical stuff. Jeans and a jumper. But she kept the jeans off for the moment, leaving her legs bare. She tossed the jeans, along with a pair of trainers, by the case in the bathroom, then emerged and closed the door behind her.

She pressed the entryphone. 'Sorry to keep you. Just getting presentable.' She fingered the buzzer and watched the three men push their way into the building.

She used the few seconds it took them to reach her flat to check her purse. Some cash, not enough. Credit cards. Those might not be much use, she thought.

She realized suddenly that she was already thinking of herself as a fugitive. Christ, she didn't even know what the police wanted yet. And even if, as her instincts were telling her, it was something serious, she knew she could extract herself from most things with a single call to Salter or Welsby. Assuming she could trust Salter or Welsby.

That was it, she thought. It was the sense she'd had for days, only half-acknowledged, that she'd already been cast adrift, that she was out here on her own. And it was the recognition that, somewhere deep inside, the idea wasn't entirely unwelcome.

There was a sharp knocking at her front door. She opened it, pulling the dressing gown more tightly around her so it wouldn't be evident that she was partially dressed underneath.

The round-faced man was still holding out his warrant card. 'Detective Inspector Blackwell,' he said. He made no effort to introduce the two men – one uniformed, one CID – behind him. 'Miss Donovan?'

She leaned forwards and made a play of examining his warrant. *Lone woman, vulnerable,* she thought. Encourage that thought.

'Ms,' she corrected pointedly. 'How can I help you?' Her face suggested blank incomprehension. Blackwell's was equally unrevealing.

'Do you mind if we sit down? It might take a few minutes. We need to check a few details.'

She glanced at her watch, allowing a look of mild impatience to cross her face. 'Yes, of course. Can I get you some coffee or something?'

'That won't be necessary.' In charge now, he led them without hesitation into Marie's sitting room. He looked around appraisingly, with the air of an estate agent surveying a new property. 'Decent view.'

'If you like office blocks, I suppose.' She moved past him to sit down, making sure she chose the armchair closest to the door. 'How can I help you?' she said again. 'I don't have much experience in – what's that phrase? – helping the police with their enquiries.'

Blackwell regarded her for a second with what might have been scepticism. Then he lowered himself on to the armchair opposite her, waving to the two other officers to take the sofa.

'Do you know a . . .' He paused and glanced at a notebook he'd pulled from his jacket pocket. 'A Morgan Jones?'

Christ, she thought, quit the play-acting, Blackwell. She'd

sat through too many interviews not to know all the tricks. The dramatic pauses, the quizzical looks, the silences. The unnecessary consultation of the probably blank notebook.

'Morgan Jones?' she repeated. 'Yes, I know him. Not well, but I know him.'

'Can I ask exactly how you're acquainted with him?'

'A sort of business acquaintance, I suppose.'

'A business acquaintance,' Blackwell echoed, his tone suggesting that this was an unfamiliar concept. 'What business are you in, Miss Donovan?'

'Printing,' she said. 'Reprographics.'

'And Mr Jones is in the same line of business, is he?'

She shrugged. 'I've no idea, to be honest. I got the feeling he had his finger in a few pies.'

'So how did you know him?'

She noted, with a slight chill, the past tense. She didn't know whether that had been a slip on Blackwell's part or a deliberate nudge. He seemed smart enough to know what he was doing.

'Can't remember where I first came across him,' she said. 'Friend of a friend thing, I think. But he gets in touch now and again. Tries to push bits of business my way.' Careful to stick to the present tense.

'Printing business?'

'That's what we do,' she said. 'If he comes across opportunities, he passes them on to us.' It was a lie, but the most innocuous one she could think of. And like all the best lies, not a million miles from the truth. Jones had put business her way. Just not usually printing.

'Very altruistic.'

'Not really. If it comes to anything – which it has once or twice – I pay him a commission. A lead's a lead, wherever it comes from.'

'And when did you last see Mr Jones?'

There was no point in lying. If the police were here, they already had some information about her and that could well include knowledge of her movements the previous day.

'Yesterday, actually,' she said. She stopped, as if the possible implications of their visit had only just struck her. 'What's this all about?'

'Why did you see him yesterday?'

'What's this all about?' she said again. 'Has something happened to Jones?'

'Why did you see him?' Blackwell's tone had changed slightly. She recognized that tone, too. Getting down to business. Cutting the crap.

She shrugged, acknowledging that her question wasn't going to be answered. 'Usual stuff,' she said. 'He'd contacted me about what he thought might be an opportunity for us. Some graphics work for an exhibition. Turned out not to be our sort of thing. Too specialist.'

'But you went up to see him? All the way to Blackpool. Long way to go for an opportunity . . .' His tone placed verbal quote marks around the last word.

'Maybe. I wasn't feeling too brilliant yesterday. Thought a breath of sea air might do me good. So I decided to kill two birds with one stone.'

It sounded feeble even to her, but Blackwell didn't seem inclined to question her account just yet.

'What time of day was this?'

'Late morning. I got there about eleven, I suppose. Stayed there about an hour.' She had little doubt that Basil Fawlty would remember precisely when she'd been on his premises.

She glanced across to where the junior CID officer was jotting down these points in his notepad. She tried again. 'What's this about? What's happened?'

Blackwell was gazing past her, staring at the view beyond the window, his expression suggesting that he had momentarily forgotten her presence. 'Jones is dead,' he said.

'What happened?' she said after a moment's silence. 'A heart attack?'

'His heart had stopped beating. But that might have been attributable to the bullet in his brain.'

She stared at him blankly, trying to conceal her shock. After a moment, she allowed her mouth to fall open, the expression of one who has just heard bad news of a not-very-close acquaintance.

'My God.'

Blackwell's steady gaze had returned to her. 'We think you were probably the last person to see him alive.' He paused just a beat too long. 'Apart from the killer, of course.'

'Are you treating me as a suspect?'

He smiled, with no evident trace of humour. 'We're not at that stage, Miss Donovan. We're just trying to ascertain the facts.'

'You're not saying no, then.'

The smile grew broader, if not noticeably warmer. 'Should I treat you as a suspect?'

'I don't know,' she said. 'You're the one with the information. How do you even know he was murdered? Bullet in the brain could mean suicide.' She paused, wondering if she was being too bold. 'Not what I'd have expected of Morgan. But it's not what you'd expect of anyone.'

Blackwell nodded, as though giving serious consideration to an idea that hadn't previously occurred to him. 'I think the forensics would enable us to discount the possibility of suicide,' he said after a time. 'If we hadn't already spotted that there was no gun in the room.'

She found herself growing tired of Blackwell's smart-arse

style. 'What do you want from me, then? I've told you everything I can.'

'I doubt it,' Blackwell said amiably. 'What about your meeting with Jones? Tell me about that.'

'What do you want to know?'

'You said he had some business to put your way.'

'There's not much to tell,' she said, conscious of the risks of taking her fabrication too far. 'It was the usual something and nothing. That was often the way with Jones.'

'But you still went all the way up there to see him?'

'I've told you,' she said. 'It was just a whim. In any case, Jones' leads have sometimes come good. The way things are at the moment, you don't ignore any possibility.'

Blackwell's interest seemed momentarily sparked. 'Business not so good?'

'We're doing all right,' she said. 'Better than most. But times are tough for everybody.'

'And you weren't surprised that Jones asked you to meet him at a hotel?'

'I don't know anything about his personal life. I've usually met him either at our offices or over a beer or a coffee. I don't even know if he lives locally.' She paused and then corrected herself. 'Lived, I mean. I don't know if he was married. I didn't know anything about him, and I didn't really want to. No offence, but he wasn't somebody I'd normally spend much time with.'

'But you weren't worried about going to his hotel room?'

'With Jones? No. I can look after myself if anyone tries it on.'

Blackwell watched her with the air of someone about to spring a trap. 'And did he?'

'What? Try it on?' She shook her head. 'What's your idea? That Jones made a pass at me and I shot him in the head?'

'There was no kind of altercation between you?'

She recalled, just in time, Basil Fawlty's brief intervention the previous day.

'No, Jones was sweetness and light. Fell off his chair once, though. Made me wonder if he'd been drinking. He was swinging back on one of those wooden chairs – you know, rocking on the two rear legs like kids do. Then it slipped from under him and he ended up on his back on the floor.'

'He hadn't been drinking,' Blackwell said. 'No sign of recent alcohol in his body. Perhaps you just made him nervous.'

'Perhaps he was just clumsy,' she said. 'But there was nothing else. He told me about his opportunity. We discussed it a bit, and I decided it was a non-starter for us.'

'Who was the opportunity with?'

'He didn't tell me the name. That was typical of Jones. Liked to be a bit cloak-and-dagger. He was probably worried that, if he spilled the beans too early, I might be tempted to cut out the middleman.'

'And would you?'

'No. You've got to have some integrity. If you go around shafting people, word gets about.'

'Did Jones do or say anything to suggest that he might be worried?'

'Worried?'

'For example, about the prospect that somebody might be about to put a bullet in his brain.'

'No more than usual. He was always the anxious type. But he didn't act like someone who thought he was in danger, if that's what you mean.'

'Did he say anything unexpected? Anything to suggest that things weren't business as usual?'

'I don't know what business as usual meant to Jones,' she said. 'He was one of life's wide boys. He did anything he could to make a bob or two. But there was nothing that seemed out of the ordinary.'

'But you wouldn't have been surprised if he'd got himself mixed up in something risky?'

'Probably not,' she said. 'But there was nothing that suggested it.' She had a sense that Blackwell was trying to steer her towards some conclusion. He was hard to read. Maybe not as clever as he thought, or perhaps just a little cleverer than she wanted to believe. 'I'm not sure there's much else I can tell you.'

Blackwell sat more comfortably back in his chair, his eyes fixed on her. 'Now I wonder whether that's true, Miss Donovan. I've an inkling there are some things you're not sharing with me.'

'Is that so?' she said. 'Funnily enough, that feeling's mutual. Perhaps we're both wrong.'

He drummed his fingers gently on the arm of the chair, as if his mind was elsewhere. 'Or both right. I did a little searching on "Holmes". I was surprised to find a cryptic reference to you.'

Her face was expressionless. 'You've lost me.'

'The police database. Quite a sophisticated beast, these days. You'd be surprised. Or perhaps not.'

'I've no idea what you're talking about. You're saying you found a reference to me on the police database?'

'Sort of.' He was looking almost cheerful now. 'Just your name. With a warning flag.'

'I'm sorry. I assume that means something to you because it means nothing to me. What sort of a warning flag?'

'I don't really know, to be honest,' he said. 'I'd never come across one before. Whatever it is, it's clearly not intended for the likes of me. Basically just told me to alert a higher authority.'

She shook her head. 'I don't know how sophisticated this beast of yours is, but it sounds to me like you've got the wrong person. I can't imagine that the MD of a back-street printing outfit will be of much interest to any higher authorities. I'm even up to date with my VAT returns.'

He frowned. She had the sense that he was disappointed that his great revelation hadn't produced some more dramatic response. Whatever Blackwell might know or suspect, it wasn't her job to confirm any of it. She could safely leave that to the judgement of those same higher authorities.

'Unless you're involved in something other than printing, Miss Donovan?'

He was off beam, she thought. He'd concluded that she was under some more serious investigation. Just as well for his career that she wasn't. The Agency wouldn't have taken kindly to his blowing the gaff on one of their targets.

'I really don't know what you're implying. That I'm some sort of super villain? By day, business cards. By night, bank heists. That sort of thing?'

For the first time, Blackwell looked mildly irritated. Possibly because he was in danger of appearing foolish in front of his subordinates. The smile was still hovering around his face, but it seemed increasingly ambiguous.

'Thing is, Miss Donovan, I'm not keen on being jerked around. And at the moment that's how this feels. I've got somebody murdered with what, as far as we can judge at the moment, was probably an illegal handgun. There's no evidence of any straightforward motive such as robbery. That suggests something a little out of the ordinary, though Jones doesn't seem to have had a criminal record. Then I discover that you've made a visit to Jones' hotel room for what sounds like the world's least convincing business meeting. And on top of all that I find a reference to you, on our records, telling me to alert the relevant authorities. Which I duly did. And got bugger all back. Now what would you suggest I should be thinking?'

It was the longest speech he'd made, and for a moment it looked as if the effort had taken something out of him.

'I haven't a clue,' she said. 'With respect, it sounds as if you might be letting your imagination run away with you.' As Blackwell had been speaking, she'd felt a growing unease. Something she'd overlooked. 'What time do you think Jones was shot?'

Blackwell stared at her, as if affronted by her impertinence. Finally, he said, 'We don't have an exact time yet. Yesterday evening sometime. No one heard anything. The hotel owner was out for the evening, and Jones was the only guest last night. Not exactly peak period.'

'How was the body found?' she said. 'If he was killed yesterday evening, it must have been discovered overnight. Who found it?'

As she had been speaking, a related thought had occurred to her. God, she was slow this morning. It always took a coffee or two to get her brain working.

'And how come you're here? I mean, where did you get my name? The hotelier would have told you that a woman visited, but he didn't know who I was. Even Jones didn't know my home address. How did you track me down so quickly?'

Blackwell remained silent for another few seconds, then pushed himself slowly to his feet. His body had the same rounded quality as his face. Not exactly fat, but tending to the plump. More comfortable sitting in a chair than climbing out of it. He made his way slowly across to the window and stared out at the jumble of buildings.

'You didn't expect us to track you down so quickly?' he said.

She opened her mouth to speak, but realized he was just

playing the same games. 'I didn't expect anything,' she said. 'Except that I'd be in the office by now. I'm also not expecting that you're going to tell me anything. But I don't understand how or why you've turned up on my doorstep so quickly.'

There was something he was keeping back. If they'd found Jones' body overnight, if they'd tracked her down so quickly, that had to mean they'd been tipped off.

She suddenly knew why she felt so uneasy, what else had been nagging at her mind. The gun. Jones' fucking gun. She'd taken it off him when he'd tried his half-arsed hardman act. She'd held it in her hand. Her fingerprints would be all over the gun that killed Morgan fucking Jones.

'It's a very interesting point you make, Miss Donovan,' she heard Blackwell say. 'I think it might be helpful if we were to carry on this discussion at the station. I think now's the time for us to put this on a more formal footing.'

Her mind was still working through the implications. She didn't even know if they'd actually found the gun. Blackwell had said that it wasn't in the room. He hadn't said it hadn't been found.

'Are you arresting me?'

'I think it's the phrase you used earlier: "Helping us with our enquiries",' Blackwell said. The smile had returned. 'Though that's often a euphemism, I think. But, no, at this stage I'd just like a witness statement.'

'And if I refuse to come?'

'I don't think you'll do that, Miss Donovan. You strike me as the co-operative type.'

She wondered whether to call his bluff. But it was too late to play games. She had only two choices. She could go along with Blackwell, get him to put a call in to Salter or Welsby, try to get all this sorted. But she was growing increasingly convinced that this wasn't just some tangle of coincidence.

That she'd been set up. Someone had tipped off the police about Jones' death. Someone had given them her name. And that could be someone in the Agency. Anyone in the Agency.

As for her fingerprints on Jones' gun, well, it was difficult to believe that Jones had tried to make her a suspect in his own death. But maybe Jones hadn't known that was the deal. Maybe he'd thought he was setting her up for something else. That would be just like Jones. Thought he'd done a deal, while all the time he was just setting himself up as the victim.

But with her fingerprints on the murder weapon, even her undercover status wouldn't give her automatic protection. Murder was murder, whoever had committed it. In time, she could no doubt talk her way out of this. The forensics should prove that she hadn't fired the gun that killed Jones, whatever her fingerprints might suggest.

But that was assuming that anyone would be prepared to listen to her. That someone out there had an interest in preventing her from taking the fall for this. She didn't know any more whether she could trust Salter or Welsby or, for that matter, anyone else.

She climbed slowly to her feet, pulling the dressing gown more tightly around her, hoping that Blackwell wouldn't spot the clothes underneath. When in doubt, follow your instinct.

'How long's this going to take?' she asked. 'I need to phone my assistant and let him know I'll be late in.'

'I think the timing will rather depend on you. You can call from the station.'

'OK.' She gestured down towards her dressing gown. 'Give me a few minutes to get showered and dressed. Help yourself to some coffee if you like. There's milk in the fridge.'

Blackwell looked for a moment as if he was about to deny this request. Then he nodded. 'OK. But be quick.'

'Don't worry,' she said. 'It's my time we're wasting as well as yours.'

She stepped into the bathroom and locked the door behind her. Moving as quickly and silently as she could, she discarded the dressing gown and pulled on the jeans and trainers. Then she stepped over to the window and pushed it open.

She'd checked out this escape route before she'd moved into the flat, never seriously expecting that she'd use it. It was one of those things that went with the job, a degree of caution and forward planning that coloured everything she did. However routine each day might seem to be, there was always the risk that something might go wrong. Since she'd taken up this role, she'd lived with the idea that, one dark night or one bright morning, someone might come looking for her. She'd never imagined it would be the police.

The window opened outwards, and was held by a pair of brackets designed, for security purposes, to prevent the panel opening more than a few inches. One of her first tasks after moving in had been to remove the screws that held the brackets in place and substitute a set of dummy screws that slotted only a quarter inch or so into their sockets. She took a metal nail file which she left on the window sill for that purpose, and prised out the four dummy screws, allowing the window to open fully.

Once the window was open, she moved back across the bathroom and turned on the shower, leaving the shower door open so the rushing water would be clearly heard from outside. The sound of the running shower could buy her an extra few minutes.

Finally, she picked up the overnight bag that she'd left tucked behind the wash basin. She lowered the cover of the lavatory, climbed on to it, and eased her way out of the window.

She dropped silently on to the metal landing of the external fire escape that ran along the rear of the building, then she turned and replaced the dummy screws back into the window brackets. With a little luck, they might waste a further few valuable minutes trying to work out how she'd effected her escape.

She hurried down the metal steps, pressing herself close against the wall so that there was no risk that Blackwell or one of his team might spot her from the window.

Within a few moments, she was skirting the perimeter of the building to the underground car park. The reality of what she was doing had begun to hit her, and for a moment she was tempted to give it up, return to the building and throw herself on what might pass for Blackwell's mercy.

This really was all or nothing. She didn't even have a plan. Just get away, buy herself some time. Work out who she could trust. Then, if she could find some help, she might be able to talk her way out of this.

It didn't sound much. Christ, it wasn't much. But it was all she had.

Within minutes, she'd reached her car and was opening the electronically controlled gates on to the main road. As she pulled away, she glanced in the rear-view mirror and saw the heavy gates closing behind her. She felt convinced, in that moment, that she would never pass back through them.

It felt as if part of her life had ended. She probably could live with that. The real problem was that, as yet, there was no sign that anything better was about to take its place.

22

As she reached the ring road, she began to think about what to do next. It was as if she'd been operating on automatic pilot, instinct overriding any rational thought. Now she had to make some decisions.

Her first thought was just to get away, to drive as far as possible. Maybe head back down to London. Lie low somewhere near the place she used to call home.

But that wouldn't work. Any minute now, they'd be kicking off a full-scale search for her. If she was a murder suspect – and if she wasn't before, she would be now – they'd want to stop her getting out of town. They'd check all the main routes. It wouldn't take them long to get her car registration. She would have only a few minutes' head start, and that wouldn't be enough.

The better option was to lose herself in the city. They'd track her down eventually, but she might buy herself some time. Then all she had to do was work out what to do with it.

She headed towards the city centre. It was still rush hour and the roads were busy with commuters heading into work. She glanced in her rear-view mirror, alert for any sign of pursuit, expecting at any moment to hear the wail of sirens, the pulsing of the blue lights.

She pulled off towards the main shopping area, heading

for the large multi-storey car park next to the Arndale. She found a parking space in a corner of one of the lower floors. While the higher floors emptied overnight, these lower floors remained fairly full. Her hope was that the car would stay unnoticed for a day or so until someone registered that it hadn't been moved.

Breathing deeply to steady her nerves, she turned off the engine and sat silently, contemplating her next move. After a moment, she reached into the back seat for her laptop. She booted it up and inserted her wireless mobile connection. After a tense few minutes, she was able to access the internet.

She had a narrow window in which to get things sorted. Her disappearance would trigger a chain of formal responses – not just the local police search, but also, in due course, a response from within the Agency. Whatever they might think about her motives or behaviour, their first action would be to put a lid on everything. They'd suspend her official bank accounts, stop her credit cards. They'd put a trace on her official mobile numbers and try to use them to track her movements. They might even shut down the business, though more likely they'd allow it to tick along until they found out what was going on, leaving poor old Joe to wonder what had happened to her.

That meant she had to move quickly. She logged into the business account, ran through the security procedures and transferred a substantial sum into her personal account, giving silent thanks that these days transfers were virtually instantaneous. She was breaking all the rules, but could see little alternative if she were to have enough cash to survive even for a few days.

Finally, the transfer completed, she logged out and shut down the laptop. She climbed out of the car, stuffed the computer back in its bag, threw the overnight case over her shoulder, and locked the car.

As she walked away, she felt another tremor of anxiety. It was as if, item by item, she was leaving the trappings of her life behind – first the flat, now the car – with no certainty that she'd ever reclaim them.

She made her way down through the mall into the street. She'd followed the same route the previous week before meeting Jones in the café. Involuntarily she glanced back, wondering again about the man she'd noticed then. This early in the morning, the centre was largely deserted, just as it had been before. This time, though, there were no suspicious figures, just a couple of security guards chatting with a woman opening up one of the stores.

Outside, the rain had passed, but the morning air still felt chill and damp. Nearly nine thirty; time for the banks to open.

They'd rebuilt all this area after the IRA bombing in the mid-1990s. Marie couldn't remember the city as it had been before, but most of the locals seemed to think that the Provisionals had done the place an inadvertent favour. The old Arndale Centre had been rebuilt, and they'd opened up the heart of the city from St Anne's Square up to the cathedral. There were new open spaces, fashionable-looking cafés and bars, striking buildings, with just a few remnants of the old city left standing as you approached Victoria Station. It was an attractive city, she thought, with its blend of modern aspiration and Victorian heritage, and it was much more approachable in scale and impact than London. She wondered now how well its optimism and vibrancy would withstand the impact of recession and cuts in public funding. Now that times were getting tough again, the money might melt away. You didn't have to go far from the city centre to find real poverty.

The likes of Kerridge and Boyle thrived on that. They might not get their own hands dirty, but their trade was anything but clean. Their people brought in drugs, firearms, exploited labour, porn, illegal booze and cigarettes. Anything they could sell for a profit. The end users were the flotsam and jetsam of the receding economic tide, poor bastards with nothing else to live for.

That was why she'd wanted to do this job in the first place. She loved the adrenaline rush, the sense of risk. But above all she wanted to make things happen, to have a real crack at people like Kerridge. The wealthy men floating above the misery they caused, casually creaming off the money, untouched by anyone – the police, the Revenue, immigration. The small fry went down, the big fish could afford the best advice. You never caught them in the act. You needed a different kind of policing – monitoring, gathering intelligence, building a case painstakingly step by step. That was what she'd wanted to do.

Now the rug had been pulled from under her. They'd finally got Boyle into custody, and what had happened? Their key witness was dead. The only loose cannon who'd been involved in that killing had been murdered himself. Her own position looked to be fatally compromised. Even if she somehow managed to talk her way out of the worst of this, it was difficult to see how she'd rebuild her position or credibility. She'd be out of the field, back behind a desk.

It was nine thirty-five now, and the first shoppers were beginning to appear. She pushed open the door of the bank and stepped into the warm interior.

This early, the place was empty. The sales desks were deserted – they were probably all out back receiving a pre-work pep talk from the sales manager. Even the cashiers were looking bored. Marie walked up to one of the cash desks and explained that she wanted to make a withdrawal.

She had half-expected some objection when she named the amount, but the cashier merely noted down the sum and said, without looking up, 'I'll need two ID. One photo.'

Marie pulled out her passport and driving licence, and slid them through to the cashier. The young woman glanced at them briefly and then looked up at Marie's face. Her eyes flicked back down to the two photographs on the documents, but there was no sign of suspicion.

'That's fine.' She pushed the documents back across to Marie, and began to tap on the keyboard in front of her.

Marie momentarily tensed again. Maybe they'd imposed some blockage on her account already. Maybe there'd be some warning on there: If you see this woman, press the panic button.

But it was unlikely. Even if the relevant wheels were already in motion – and experience told her that, for once, bureaucracy was likely to be her ally here – it would take them a little time to track down her personal account. But not long. A few phone calls would give them everything they needed. But then they'd need the relevant authorization. It would take a little while. Maybe an hour or two.

'How do you want it?' the cashier said. 'Fifties OK, or do you need something smaller?'

Marie almost laughed in relief. 'I could do with some twenties and tens. If you can do a couple of hundred in those, and the rest in fifties, that'd be great.'

The cashier noted down the request. 'I'll need to get it from the back. Just bear with me.'

It was an anxious few minutes for Marie. She was still half-expecting that this wouldn't work. They'd have insufficient cash. They'd want to know why she needed all this money. The manager would appear and murmur quietly, 'If you could just step this way, Ms Donovan . . .?'

But none of that happened. After a few moments, the cashier reappeared and carefully counted out the money.

'Is there anything else I can do for you today?' she asked finally. It was a routine question, part of the spiel they were trained to deliver. Marie was tempted to ask whether she had any tips on avoiding police manhunts.

Her relief lasted little longer than the few minutes it took to return to the open street. She'd overcome one hurdle. She was solvent, with enough cash to last her till – well, when exactly? Till all this was resolved, one way or another, she supposed. If things weren't sorted within a few days, they'd catch up with her anyway.

But almost immediately, she felt vulnerable again. As if everyone who passed was staring at her, as if they'd seen her picture or read her description. As if they knew exactly who she was and what she was supposed to have done. Down at the far end of the road, at the junction with Market Street, two police officers, a man and a woman, were standing chatting with a street-cleaner. It took all her willpower not to run. Instead, she forced herself to walk casually towards them, heading back towards the centre of town.

By the time she reached the corner, the police officers were already disappearing into St Anne's Square. She walked further along Corporation Street and then paused for a moment outside an upmarket-looking hairdressing salon, before pushing open the door. The receptionist looked up as she entered.

'Can I help you, madam?'

Marie looked past the receptionist into the interior of the salon. There was one customer having her hair washed. Two stylists were sitting drinking coffee and chatting about last night's television.

'I know it's short notice,' Marie said. 'I'm just in town on business for a couple of days. Wondered if there was any chance of fitting in an appointment today at all?'

The receptionist gave her a look that suggested the chances were somewhere between slim and zero, and pulled the appointments book towards her.

'We've just had a cancellation,' she said. 'Was supposed to be ten fifteen.' She glanced up at the clock over the desk. 'Might be able to fit you in now.' She called over her shoulder. 'Jo, can you fit this lady in now instead of Mrs Tremlett?'

Jo – one of the two chatting stylists – put down her coffee with a look of weariness. 'Yeah, that's fine. Just give me a minute or two.' She gestured for Marie to take a seat.

An hour later, Marie emerged from the salon feeling, externally at least, like a different person. The stylist had been slightly surprised by her request for a radical change, cropping her shoulder-length hair into something much shorter, colouring her hair darker.

'Do a lot of sports,' Marie explained. 'Get sick of it getting in my eyes.'

The stylist had expressed some scepticism about the change, but ultimately just shrugged. When the new style was complete, she'd shifted her position to claim full credit. 'Yeah, said it would suit you,' she said. 'Wouldn't work with everyone's face, but looks good with yours.' Marie decided to accept that as a compliment.

She stepped back out into the street and made her way up Market Street towards Piccadilly Gardens. It was approaching eleven fifteen. Her window of opportunity was rapidly closing. It might have been sensible to use her phone before getting her hair changed, but she felt much less conspicuous now. Her hope was that her phones would have been left operational for the moment, in the hope that she might make contact or even allow them to trace her movements.

She entered a chain coffee shop, bought a caffè latte and a sandwich, found a discreet corner, and switched on her secure phone.

As she'd expected, there was a string of messages. She listened to the most recent first. Salter's sharp voice, 'For fuck's sake, Marie, just call in.' She didn't bother with the rest.

She wanted to get a heads-up, find out what was happening. Her first thought was to call Salter, but instead she dialled Welsby's number. On balance she was inclined to trust him slightly more than Salter, if only because he was less likely to shaft her simply to advance his own career.

'Keith. It's Marie Donovan.'

There was a momentary pause, and she wondered whether Welsby was trying to have her location tracked. They'd have been waiting for her to make contact. She couldn't afford to talk for long.

'Christ, Marie. Where the hell are you?'

'In a bit of trouble, Keith. That's where I am.'

'Too fucking right you are. What the fuck's going on?'

'I've been set up, Keith.'

Another pause. 'That right, girl?' It was impossible to read his response.

'I didn't kill Morgan Jones. Why the hell would I want to do that?'

'You tell me,' Welsby said. 'Way I've heard it, your prints were all over Jones' room.'

'I know,' she said, keeping her voice low. 'I went to see Jones yesterday. He said he had some business for me. That was part of the set-up. And how did anyone know they were my prints? They turned up on my doorstep at seven this morning. They wouldn't have had time to trawl through the database. Someone tipped them off.'

'That doesn't make you innocent.'

'Christ, Keith, you don't think I did it?'

'Not looking good, girl. Even got your prints on the murder weapon.'

So Blackwell had been holding back that bit of information. Not really a surprise.

'They found the gun, then?'

'Dropped in a bin along the road. Didn't take a lot of finding.'

'Of course not, Keith. Do you think I'd be that bloody careless if I really had done it?'

'So how come your prints were on it? Jonesie asked you to fondle his weapon, did he?'

It didn't matter whether he really didn't believe her, or was simply protecting his own backside. Quite probably, there were others listening in. Either way, she was getting nowhere.

'He made a half-arsed attempt to threaten me. I grabbed the gun off him and threw it across the room. Maybe he did it to get my prints on there.'

'Frame you for his own murder? Even Jones wasn't that much of a fuckwit.'

'They misled Jones. He thought he was helping set me up. He just didn't know what he was setting me up for.'

'You need to work on your story, girl. When we catch up with you, you'll be telling it to more cynical buggers than me.' Another hesitation. 'Something else you ought to know. You asked why you'd have killed Jones. You might have had a motive.'

'What motive? I hardly knew him.'

'What I hear, looks like Jones was involved in Jake Morton's death.'

'Jones wouldn't have had the bottle,' she said. 'He wasn't a killer.'

'Maybe there to hold their coats. But looks like the gun

that killed Jones was the one that killed Morton. They found some traces of blood on Jones' clothing – the used clothes in his wardrobe, I mean. The ones he was wearing were liberally covered with his own. This stuff's different. We're getting it checked but it could be Morton's.'

'So what?' she said. 'I wasn't happy about Morton's death, but it's not turned me into a screaming vigilante.'

'That right? One more thing you should know, girl.'

'What's that?'

'Word is,' Welsby said, 'that you and Morton were close. Any truth in that rumour?'

'For Christ's sake, Keith. He was one of our major contacts, one of our best potential routes into Kerridge and Boyle. Of course I kept close to him. It was what I agreed with Hugh.'

'Maybe too close?'

'I'm a professional, Keith.' She could feel the lies dragging her further into the mire. How the hell did they know all this, anyway? Was it something else the phantom tipster had thrown into the pot? 'What are you trying to say?'

'I'm trying to say nothing, girl. Just letting you know what's being said. Ugly things, rumours.'

'Keith, it's all bollocks. I've not done anything.'

'Then get in here, lass, and let's sort it out.'

'I can't, Keith. I don't know who to trust.'

'You can trust me. Get yourself in here. You're only making things worse.'

She was almost tempted. Everything would become straightforward, one way or another. She simply had to keep telling her side of the story. Answer their questions. Point out the things that didn't make sense. Get forensics to prove she couldn't have fired Jones' handgun. Nice and simple.

Except that she didn't believe it would be. They'd got their claws into her now. The case was open and shut. Why would

256

the local police complicate things by ignoring what appeared to be the obvious? Could forensics even prove a negative? After returning from her meeting with Jones she'd showered, changed her clothes, and put most of the old set into the wash. After all that, there'd probably be no evidence of her firing the gun in any case.

'I can't come in, Keith. Not yet.'

'You don't trust me?'

'It's not like that, Keith. I wouldn't be able to deal with just you, would I? Somebody's set me up, and it's somebody pretty close to home.'

Before Welsby could reply, she cut the call. She turned off the phone, swallowed the dregs of her coffee, and made her way out of the coffee shop. In the street, she paused for a moment, took out the secure phone, opened the back and removed the SIM card. She dropped it to the pavement and ground it slowly under her heel. She repeated the process with the card from her own phone. Over the top, but she felt more comfortable with all links cut off.

She was conscious that, even in the limited time she'd been talking to Welsby, they might have got some sort of fix on her location. She hurried away from the Gardens up towards Piccadilly Station. She considered just jumping on the next train to anywhere that wasn't there. But they might have the station under surveillance. She was better off staying put.

Looking more confident than she felt, she made her way up the station approach, and then crossed through the glossy concourse, keeping her eyes peeled for any signs of police. There was a British Transport police officer hovering by the entrance to the platforms, but for the moment he was distracted by an elderly man asking for directions. She hurried out of his sight, down past the entrance to WH Smith, across to where the escalators led down to the taxi rank at the rear of the station. At that time of the morning, there were plenty of taxis, bored drivers chatting in the brightening sunshine. She approached the front of the rank and gave the driver the name of one of the large city centre hotels.

The hotel itself was less than half a mile away, but she felt disinclined to spend any more time out on the street. She was also conscious that she was about to arrive at a relatively upmarket hotel with no reservation, credit card or much in the way of luggage. Maybe the taxi would make her appear more credible.

The taxi driver was, fortunately, one of the taciturn types, and said nothing till they'd arrived outside the hotel. 'Up on business?' he said, as he counted out her change. She'd asked for a receipt for appearances' sake, though she couldn't imagine that Welsby would be too keen to reimburse this trip.

'Just for a day or two,' she said.

'Hope the weather improves for you.'

'Won't see much of it, anyway,' she said. 'Stuck inside most of the time.' That was true enough, anyway.

She made her way into the expansive lobby of the hotel. It was a new construction, another offshoot of the city centre regeneration, with a well-reviewed first-floor restaurant with views over the city. She'd met clients here a couple of times.

She'd selected it partly on the grounds that it was more upmarket than Welsby or Salter would expect her to use. More upmarket, that was, than the soulless urban hotels where she typically met Salter. Those were the places the Agency budget stretched to. Functional, comfortable enough, but not luxurious.

It was likely that, once they realized she'd stayed in the city, they'd do a trawl of all the hotels. But she hoped that this place wouldn't be high on their initial shortlist, and it was large and discreet enough for her not to be exposed too easily.

It was a counter-intuitive decision. Her first thought had been to seek out an anonymous back-street bed and breakfast, but she'd felt that would leave her too exposed. A suspicious landlord might ask questions about a woman travelling on her own, and, if her disappearance had been reported in the media, put two and two together. In this place, she'd be just one of many.

She took a deep breath to steady her nerves and approached the reception. A young man in a neat suit looked up and smiled. 'How can I help you, madam?'

She glanced at her watch. 'I'm a little early, but I've got a reservation for tonight. Wondered if there was a chance of checking in so I could freshen up? Penny Walker.'

The man nodded. 'I'll just check for you, Ms Walker.' He had a trace of an Eastern European accept, though his English seemed flawless. He tapped away rapidly on his keyboard, then frowned. 'You did say Walker?'

'Yes. Penny. Penelope.'

The man tapped again. 'I'm sorry, I can't seem to find it. It wouldn't be under any other name?'

'I booked it through the office. Suppose it could be in the company name.' She gave him the name of a fictitious IT company.

He entered some more data, his frown growing more pronounced. 'Doesn't seem to be there,' he said. 'When did you make the booking?'

'As I said, I didn't.' She allowed a touch of impatience to enter her voice. 'It was done by my secretary, through the agency we use. Must have been a week or so back. You're sure it's not there?'

He was still tapping frantically. 'No, I've tried variations on your name in case someone entered it wrongly. But there's nothing similar. You're sure it was for tonight?'

'Well, I'm sure I asked for it for tonight,' she said. 'Wouldn't be the first time somebody's cocked up, though.' She fumbled in her handbag for one of the inoperative mobile phones. 'Let me check.'

She thumbed the phone's buttons as though accessing an address book and pressed the silent handset to her ear. She allowed a few seconds to pass, then said, 'Gill, hi. It's me, Penny. Yeah, fine. Just arrived at the hotel, though, and they can't seem to find the reservation.' She paused, as though listening. 'Well, that's what I thought. Have you got the confirmation?' Another pause. 'And it definitely says for tonight. Have you got the reservation code?' She gestured silently to the hotel receptionist, who slid a pen and a notepad across to her. She scribbled out a set of numbers in the format used by the booking agency that she'd usually dealt with. 'OK, I'll try them with that. I'll get back to you if I find myself out on the street.' She laughed with an undertone that indicated she wasn't entirely joking. She paused again, as though her imaginary interlocutor had continued the conversation. 'No, no joy, I'm afraid. It's turning into a perfect day so far. Reported it to the police, but I'm not holding my breath. Thanks, Gill. Call you later.'

Switching off the fictitious call, she turned back to the receptionist. 'Well, it was definitely booked. My secretary has the confirmation.' She pushed the scribbled code across the desk.

He drummed on the keyboard for a few more seconds, then said, 'Ah.'

She caught her breath, wondering what he might have found, but realized that his frown had melted to a faint smile. His world was beginning to make sense again. 'Can't find that code exactly. But we've a Mr Welford booked through the same agency,' he said. 'Same initial. I bet the agency mixed up the two records. Happens all the time, I'm afraid.' And it's not our fault, was the unspoken subtext. He straightened, the smile fully operational again. 'Luckily, we're not full. We can fit you in and still find room for Mr Welford, assuming he's actually expecting to stay here.' He made it sound as if he'd taken control of a situation that would otherwise have spiralled dramatically out of control. 'We don't have any standard rooms available. But we can offer you an upgrade to one of our executive rooms. At no extra charge, of course, in the circumstances.'

She managed not to look too overwhelmed at this benefi-cence. 'That's very kind.'

He completed the various administrative niceties and then said, 'If you could just let me have a swipe of your credit card?'

'That's my other problem,' she said. 'That's what I was talking about to my secretary. My purse was snatched on the way up here. Some little bugger in the coffee bar at Euston. I put it down on the table for a minute, and he grabbed it and legged it before I could get near him.'

'I'm sorry,' he said. His regret sounded genuine enough, but it wasn't clear whether it was directed towards her or himself.

'It's a pain in the backside, that's all. Fortunately, there wasn't much cash in there. But I've had to cancel all my cards, and then there was all the stuff like driving licence, member-ship cards. You name it. There must be some special circle of hell reserved for little toerags like him.' She paused, warming to her theme. 'And why does the bank need five working days to send you a replacement, that's what I want to know.'

The receptionist was looking baleful again, the expression of one who'd successfully deflected one major calamity only to find another coming along immediately behind it.

261

'I'm going to have this problem all week,' she said. 'So I went and got cash from the bank. Luckily I didn't lose my passport so I could still prove who I was. Is it OK if I just pay upfront?'

'Well, I know it seems a little untrusting—'

'Don't worry. I spend my professional life chasing up bad debt. It's just business.' She lifted up her handbag and pulled out a small selection of the cash. 'Three nights,' she said. 'So that totals . . .?'

She allowed him to make the simple calculation, giving him the sense that he was taking control again. When she'd paid out the money, he said, 'I'm afraid you'll just have to pay for any extras as you go.'

'Story of my life,' she said. They were both smiling again now.

Upstairs, the door locked behind her, she ran a hot bath, feeling an intense relief as she lowered himself into the scalding water. It was hardly the point to relax, she knew. This was no more than a temporary respite.

Jesus, there was no point in worrying. She'd done what she could. However she'd played it, she'd be fretting about the consequences. She was in a mess and all she could do was try to find the best way out of it.

She was becoming conscious, for the first time, of how difficult it was to stay hidden, even in a large city. She'd spent much of her career working in surveillance, but hadn't truly registered how all-pervasive it was. If she used her credit card, made a call, even just walked down the street, she was giving out clues about her location. They'd soon know, if they didn't already, that she'd withdrawn cash from a bank in the city centre. With time, they might even trace CCTV footage of her walking the surrounding streets, maybe even to the hair

262

salon or the taxi. For the moment, though, they wouldn't know for sure whether she was still in the city, or whether she'd withdrawn the money to fund a move out of town.

Her biggest hope was that the local police wouldn't be giving this the highest priority. Even if he'd managed to keep his record clean, the police would know that Jones was a small-time crook, a legman for the bigger boys. He wouldn't be much missed, and certainly not by the police. They'd most likely assume that his murder was some bit of underworld business that wouldn't merit much more than token resources.

She expected equally that, for the moment at least, Welsby and his bosses would want to keep this under wraps. They wouldn't want the embarrassment of revealing that an undercover officer had gone AWOL. Her guess was that they'd allow the local plods to keep thinking that she was of interest to the Agency as a target, not as one of their own. They might even put some pressure on the locals to back off.

With a bit of luck.

That depended on the motives of whoever was behind this. By now, she had no doubt that somebody was. And that somebody, one or two steps removed, would be Boyle and maybe Kerridge. They knew who she was. Maybe not the whole of her role, but enough. She'd been exposed. Perhaps it really had been Morton. It looked as if he'd known, or guessed, more about her than he'd let on. Perhaps that was why he'd embarked on a relationship with her in the first place. Not her winning personality and cute looks, after all.

More likely, though, it was whoever was leaking from inside the Agency. Undercover roles were kept confidential even within the team, so her role should have been known only to a handful. Welsby, Salter and a sprinkling of others, mostly at senior levels. But it was possible she'd been hung out to dry a long time before, that they'd been playing games with her for months. The thought wasn't comforting.

If so, the set-up had been beautifully engineered. Once she was arrested – perhaps already – her credibility was gone. At best, the Agency would just suppress everything, maybe not even give her the chance to clear her name. She'd be sacked or paid off. Jones would be forgotten. The local police would be blamed for disrupting some unrevealed operation, and would write it off as another instance of the Agency's high-handedness. And the case against Boyle would be quietly dropped.

At worst, they'd leave her twisting in the wind. She'd be cut off from Agency support, charged with murder. Maybe she'd be convicted, maybe she wouldn't. But it wouldn't be in anyone's interest to help her. It might suit everyone for her to take the fall, tie up the loose ends of Jones' death. She could protest, try to get her story heard, but she'd just be dismissed as another rogue copper.

She was getting nowhere, thinking herself deeper into depression. She already knew she was in a mess. Now she had to devote her mind to thinking of a way out of it. She'd considered a direct approach to Kerridge, but couldn't see where it would get her. She had tried to identify some inter-mediary who might help uncover the truth about Jones' murder, but anyone sufficiently close to Kerridge or Boyle to be of use was, well, likely to be much too close.

She pulled the plug on the rapidly cooling water and stepped out, drying herself hurriedly and pulling on the thick towel-ling dressing gown supplied behind the bathroom door. One of the perks of the executive-level room, she presumed. She hadn't noticed many others.

She needed more time to catch her breath. All she could feel was a rising panic, a growing sense that time was running out. There was no one she could risk calling. The police might be monitoring the phones of any of her friends and acquaintances, and would track her back here in minutes. Even assuming, she thought bleakly, that she had any real friends or acquaintances left to call.

There was no one up here. Back home, there was just her family and Liam . . .

Shit, she thought. Liam.

He'd be going spare. She'd tried to call him the previous evening after her return from meeting Jones. There'd been no answer early on, and she hadn't bothered leaving a message on his voicemail, assuming that she'd try again later or – more likely – that he would call her. In the end, exhausted by the previous disrupted night and the trials of the day, she'd fallen asleep in front of the TV. She'd woken at eleven or so, and barely opening her eyes, staggered into the bedroom, sleepily undressed and fallen into bed. She hadn't stirred till she'd been disturbed by Blackwell's unexpected arrival.

Had Liam tried to call her back? It was likely. He didn't allow many evenings to go by without a call. She'd have expected the phone to wake her, but had been so knackered she could easily have slept through it. She hadn't thought to check the voicemail this morning.

Would the Agency have contacted Liam? If so, Christ knew what they'd told him. And no doubt he'd been trying to call her on one of her inoperative mobile numbers ever since.

She couldn't even phone him now. Liam's line would surely be monitored. Shit, she thought. He'd never forgive her for this.

She pulled open the door of the bathroom, rubbing her face with a towel, her mind still wrestling with this latest problem.

It was the sound that made her stop. The sound of a cough and a shuffle of feet. The sound of someone in the room.

She lowered the towel slowly from her face, as a voice said, 'Jesus, Marie. You're one hell of a woman to keep up with.'

23

Her first reaction was fear, then bafflement and finally anger.

'What the fuck are you doing in here, Joe?' A small part of her mind was thanking Christ that the executive room had included provision of a dressing gown. Another part was registering her handbag, open where she'd left it on the bed.

Joe was half-rising, in the manner of someone about to greet a visitor. Seeing the look on her face, he slumped back down into the armchair.

'Sorry. Didn't mean to startle you.'

'Little tip, Joe. If you don't want to startle people, don't let yourself into their fucking hotel rooms.'

'Sorry,' he said again. 'Wasn't really thinking.'

'What are you doing here, Joe?' She paused. 'More to the point, how'd you track me down?'

'I followed you.'

'*Followed* me?' She'd been keeping an eye out all the way, looking for professional pursuit. How could she not have spotted Joe?

'I'm sorry,' he repeated.

'Don't keep apologizing, Joe. Makes me nervous.'

'Police came to the shop, early this morning. Before they

came to you. Six thirty or so. I'd gone in early. Didn't sleep very well last night, and we had the Henshaw job to finish. Darren had messed up—'

'Get to the point, Joe.' Her anger was subsiding now. It was difficult to sustain it in the face of Joe's abject demeanour.

'Yeah, sorry. Anyway, I got in about six. About six thirty, these coppers turned up. Couple of plain clothes, one in a uniform. Looking for you.'

She frowned. 'Why'd they go to the shop?'

'I think they were expecting a domestic address or that you lived above the shop or something.'

'Christ, Joe. Did you give them my home address?'

He shook his head. 'No. Honestly. They realized straight-away you weren't going to be there. And then one of them made a phone call. Spoke to someone who gave him your home address. I didn't say anything.'

That was interesting, she thought, and probably confirmed everything she'd been fearing.

'No, of course, not. Sorry, Joe. I shouldn't take it out on you.'

'What's this all about, Marie?'

'Jesus, Joe, it's a long story. Tell me about this morning.'

Calmer now, she lowered herself on to the bed. Casually, she pulled the handbag towards her and began rooting through it, her eyes still fixed on Joe. The data stick was still there, tucked into a side pocket. To cover her actions, she pulled out a pack of tissues and made as if to blow her nose.

'Well, I tried to call your mobile, but it was turned off. Left you a message.' One of the many messages she'd failed to check this morning. 'Didn't have your home number. So in the end I set off after them. Stupid, really. I had this idea that they might not go straight there, that I might get there first and at least warn you they were coming. But of course they were already there when I arrived. There was a police car parked out front.'

She nodded. 'Go on.'

'I hung about across the street. I had an idea I'd wait till they'd gone, then come across and make sure you were OK.' He paused and lowered his head, as if embarrassed by the concern he was showing.

'And you saw me leave?'

'Well, I was a bit taken aback. I was sitting there and saw you scurrying around the building. Didn't know what to think. Then I saw your car coming out of the car park. In the end, I decided to follow you. I'm not really sure why.' He paused. 'Just a bit worried, I suppose.'

'You followed me all the way?'

He shrugged, reddening. 'Well, yes. Saw you park up. I drove straight past you, parked on the floor above. Nearly lost you after that. Came out into the street just as you were going into the bank—'

'And you hung around while I had my hair done?'

'There was a coffee bar over the road. Read the paper.'

She was staring at him, incredulous. 'But I got a cab to the hotel.'

'Follow that cab,' he mumbled.

'Jesus, Joe, you're fucking incredible. Why didn't you let me know you were there?'

'I don't know, really. You looked . . . focused. I wasn't sure how you'd react.'

It was a fair point. She'd probably have punched his lights out. She nearly had just now.

'You haven't told me how you got in here.'

He was even more red now. 'Didn't know what to do when I saw you coming to the hotel. Nearly turned on my heel and went back. I hung about near the door while you checked in.

Watched you call the lift, and then watched what floor it stopped at.' He paused, as if scarcely able to credit his own ingenuity. 'Then I followed you up. I thought I'd lose you then. But I saw you at the end of the corridor, opening the door just as I came out of the lift.'

'And how'd you get in?'

'I did knock,' he said. 'I kept knocking. But you must have already gone into the bathroom. Then one of the cleaners came by.' He dropped his head, unwilling to look her in the eye. 'Didn't know what else to do. Told her I'd locked my key inside. She opened it for me.'

'You've got hidden depths, Joe. You're wasted in printing.'

'I don't know what I was thinking, really. Just wanted to make sure you were all right.'

She smiled for the first time. 'Very sweet of you, Joe. I'm OK.' She hesitated momentarily, then said, 'Pretty much in the shit, though.'

'What's this all about, Marie?'

She didn't know how to respond. She desperately wanted to share all this with someone. At least have the chance to talk about it. But, even if she could bring herself to trust Joe, she couldn't tell him everything. Not yet.

'Like I said, it's a long story. I've got myself involved in some things I shouldn't have.'

'Can't say I'm entirely surprised by that,' he said.

She raised her head at his unexpected response. 'What do you mean?'

'I keep my head down,' he said. 'But I'm not a total idiot.'

'I don't—'

'I look at the business, the printing stuff. We're doing all right, but the finances don't add up. We'd be struggling if we weren't so well capitalized. So I ask myself, now and again, where the capital comes from. Seems to me it probably doesn't

270

come entirely from reprographics.' He smiled faintly. 'We're good. But we're not that good.'

She shook her head. 'Like I say, you're full of surprises, Joe.'

'Dunno,' he said. 'But I've also seen one or two of the people who come into that place. People who come and talk to you in the office. I was brought up in Cheetham Hill. I know some of those faces.' He smiled faintly. 'They were the ones my mum used to tell me to steer clear of. Can't imagine they come to get their business cards done.'

'You might have a point,' she said.

'Jesus, Marie. Why get mixed up with stuff like that?'

'I'm not some fluffy airhead, Joe. You know that. I understand what I'm involved in.'

'But you're in the shit now,' Joe pointed out.

'These things happen.'

'Christ,' Joe said, suddenly vehement. 'I know these things happen. My younger brother's serving ten because these things happen. Armed fucking robbery in his case. Thought he was smart and was well out of his depth.'

'Should have listened to your mum, eh?' Marie said, though she knew that it wasn't funny.

'Something like that. So what's your story?'

She was learning more all the time, she thought. She'd underestimated Joe, that was clear enough. Who knew whether she'd underestimated anyone else.

'You come across Morgan Jones in your travels?' she asked.

'Jones? Professional Welshman. Bit of a creep? That one?'

'Sounds like the one,' she agreed. 'Thing is, he's now the late Morgan Jones. Shot dead. And I was the last one to see him alive.'

Joe looked up at her. 'You're a suspect?'

'I think, at the moment, I'm *the* suspect.'

271

'Shit.' He was silent for a moment. 'You didn't . . .?'

'Joe. I know we've just spent the last five minutes surprising the hell out of each other, but what do you think?' Before he could reply, she added, just in case, 'No. No, I didn't.'

'Do you know who did?'

'I don't know who actually pulled the trigger, if that's what you mean. But I know who wanted him dead. You know Jeff Kerridge?'

'I know of him,' Joe said. 'Client of ours, isn't he? His company, anyway.'

'One of his companies, yes. We do printing for them.'

'Got his finger in all kinds of pies, from what I've heard,' Joe said. 'Most of them dodgy. You think he was behind Jones' death?'

'Pretty much. Jones was a grass. Kerridge's associate Pete Boyle's in custody at the moment. Jones is probably one of the people who put him there.' It was a précis of the truth, but close enough.

'That would do it,' Joe agreed. 'I'd heard about Boyle. If the rumours are right, Jones wouldn't be the first grass that Kerridge's had taken out.'

Marie said nothing for a moment, wondering quite how much Joe knew about her and Jake. 'I don't know. I just know he's landed me well and truly in the crap.'

Joe shook his head. 'This is crazy, though. Why've you done a runner? It's only a matter of time before they catch up with you. You've just made it look worse.'

'Maybe. I wasn't thinking straight. It felt as if they'd got me bang to rights.'

'Hardly. Just because you were the last to see him. When was this, anyway?'

'Yesterday,' she said. 'When I left the office.'

'Thought that wasn't your style,' he said. 'You looked knack-ered, but you don't usually let that stop you. Why'd you go to see Jones?'

'Reckoned he had a bit of business he could put in my direction.'

'Not printing?'

'No, Joe. Not printing. Anyway, I went up to see him. Something and nothing, as it turned out. But it means my prints are all over the room where he was found.' *Not to mention the murder weapon*, she thought.

'But that doesn't prove anything. I mean, it doesn't prove you killed him.'

'Maybe not,' she said. 'But it's not a bad start. Might discourage the police from looking too hard for any other suspects. I don't suppose they're too fussed about finding Morgan Jones' real killer, so long as they can close the case. Anyway, if they start delving into my life, Christ knows what they'll find.'

'OK,' he said wearily. 'So you're not planning to give yourself up just at the moment. What are you planning?'

'Like I say, I wasn't thinking. Now I'm trying to, but I'm not getting very far.'

'I could do some digging for you.'

'What sort of digging?'

'I don't know exactly. But, like I say, I know Manchester. I know a lot of these people. My brother . . . well, people knew him. They know me. They know I'm straight. They won't tell me everything, but they do trust me and they won't bullshit me. I can maybe find out what people know about Jones' death. What the word is.'

It didn't sound a lot, but it was better than anything else she had. 'Thanks, Joe. That's good of you.'

He regarded her for a moment, clearly wanting to say

something more. 'If you get through this, Marie, you should have a real think, you know? You're too good for this.'

'I've told you, Joe. It's a long story. Sometime I'll tell you.'

'I'd like that,' he said after a pause. 'I care about you, you know.' He stopped again, as if he were gearing up for some more momentous announcement. 'You and me, we could be good for each other, I reckon.'

For a moment, she felt close to tears. It was a long time since anyone had said they cared about her. Not Jake, not in so many words. Not even Liam. She knew Liam did care, but it wasn't anything he'd ever say. And, in any case, Liam suddenly seemed an awfully long way away.

She was suddenly conscious that she was sitting on the bed, clad only in the hotel dressing gown, her body still damp from the bath, alone in a hotel room with an attractive, likeable man. She pulled the dressing gown more tightly around her, briefly tempted to do the opposite, to take advantage of this unexpected intimacy, this brief respite from the isolation and fear that had become her life.

She quashed the impulse as soon as it arose, knowing that her feelings were nothing more than a reaction to everything she had been through. Joe was a nice man. Maybe they could be good for one another. Maybe one day, perhaps even soon, she might find out.

But not yet. Not till she was through all this.

'You might be right, Joe,' she said finally. 'When this is out of the way, we'll have that drink, and we can talk about it.'

He smiled, and it wasn't clear to her whether he'd expected anything more. 'I'll hold you to that,' he said. 'Now, keep your head down. I'll call you here as soon as I've any news.'

24

Welsby had his head almost permanently stuck out of the window, chain-smoking cigarettes before tossing the butts into the street outside. It wasn't a good sign, Salter thought. He closed the door noisily behind him, hoping to prompt the older man to turn around.

Instead, Welsby kept his head facing the street, blowing clouds of smoke into the damp air.

'That can't be comfortable,' Salter said.

'Fucking uncomfortable,' Welsby agreed. 'But better than being smokeless, just at the moment. Where the fuck is she, Hugh?'

'Christ knows. We think she's somewhere in the city still, but even that's not certain.'

'Jesus. We can't lose one of our own officers.'

'That's the trouble, though, isn't it? She knows what she's doing. Better than Beat Bobby Blackwell, anyway.'

Welsby laughed and finally brought his head in from the window, flicking the fag end out behind him. 'Aye, that's true enough. Met that doughball a few times. Pompous arse. Almost worth losing her to imagine the look on his face when he plucked up the courage to kick in the bathroom door.'

'Yeah,' Salter agreed. 'Almost.'

He lowered himself into the chair opposite Welsby. The

older man looked regretfully at the packet of cigarettes on the corner of the desk, then devoted his attention to the issue at hand.

'So where the fuck is she, then?' he said again.

'Like I say, Christ knows. We're not making much progress.'

'Local plods not helping, then?'

'What do you think? We're not exactly being forthcoming, are we?'

'Not my shout. Orders from on high. They're still trying to keep a lid on this. We have to keep schtum about Donovan. Besides, we want to keep a grip on this, you and me. Till we know just what's out there.'

'If you say so. But the locals just think we're being precious. So they're not exactly busting a gut to help. Which in turn means we don't have the resources to track Donovan down.'

'What've you got so far?'

'Bugger all. She used her mobile internet to make that funds transfer. We've been able to pin down her location to an area in the city centre, most likely the Arndale car park. She made the call to you from a few hundred yards away. And she withdrew the cash from a branch in the same area. That's about it. No word since. Her phone seems to be out of use. She's made no attempt to use her bank cards.'

'No need with all that cash,' Welsby said.

'Exactly. What we don't know is whether she withdrew the cash to make a getaway, or whether she's still lying low somewhere. We're speaking to the staff at the various stations to see if anyone recalls her buying a ticket, but I'm not hopeful. Can't imagine they take much notice of who they're selling tickets to.'

'What's your feeling?' Welsby said. 'You reckon she's still around?'

276

'Who knows? We've tried to contact that boyfriend but there's no answer on the home number. Don't know whether that's significant. We've put in a request for the local plods to pay a visit, but the Met don't tend to jump when we ask them to, either. But, yes. I suppose my instinct is that she's stayed put. It's what I'd do. She won't know what resources we've got looking out for her. She'll probably think we've got the stations covered, and that we'll be looking out for her car.'

'If only she fucking knew,' Welsby said, leaning back in his chair. 'She could have been safely away to Marbella by now.'

'You reckon she did it?' Salter said after a pause.

'God knows. But, either way, Boyle's had her neatly stitched up. I don't see her as a killer, do you?'

'Not a stupid one, anyway. Not the kind who leaves fingerprints all over everything including the murder weapon.' Salter paused. 'But also not the kind to get involved with a grass, I'd have thought.'

'Aye, that's the bugger. Even if Boyle's behind them, there's no denying those photographs.'

'There might be. You can do a lot with Photoshop. I don't think we should take any of this at face value."

Welsby shrugged. 'Maybe not. But if Morton really did send her the rest of his evidence, we need to find her. Trouble is, like she said, she doesn't know who to trust.'

'Including us.'

'Especially us.' Welsby was reaching for his cigarettes again, his gaze fixed on Salter. 'Question is, Hughie boy, is she right?'

25

It was a comfortable enough hotel room, as hotel rooms went, but after two hours Marie was already going stir crazy. Her room had a partial view of the city centre, St Peter's Square, the Victorian grandeur of the Town Hall. The city looked lively and bustling in the patchy sunshine, and she found herself longing to be out there.

She hadn't eaten since the previous evening. She thought of ordering room service, but the prospect of having to pay in cash made her uneasy. It would just be something else to draw attention to her, another eccentricity to lodge in the minds of the hotel staff.

On the other hand, she couldn't go out. Apart from the risk of being spotted, Joe had no way of contacting her if she left the room. She assumed that it would take him a while to come up with anything – if there was anything to come up with – but, with time pressing, she didn't want to miss his call when it eventually came. If it came. She knew she was pinning her hopes on the flimsiest of chances. Joe would do his best, but that might not mean very much at all.

She made herself a cup of tea, munched her way through two complimentary shortbread biscuits, and lay down on the bed to wait.

She was woken, what seemed like minutes later, by the

insistent ringing of the bedside phone. She fumbled clumsily for the receiver, her mind momentarily baffled by the lack of light. She finally raised the phone to her ear and mumbled, 'Yes?'

'You OK, Marie? You sound odd.'

Joe. It was Joe. 'Think I fell asleep. Sorry – you woke me. Still half-asleep.'

She rolled over, the phone still pressed to her ear. The window was a paler rectangle in the dark, tinted orange by the street lights below. *Jesus*, she thought. *How long have I been out?*

'You got anything, Joe?' She was reaching for the bedside lamp, fingers groping till she found the switch.

'Might have. I've found one of Kerridge's associates who might be prepared to talk to us.'

The sudden burst of light momentarily dazzled her. She looked at her watch. After seven. How could she sleep so long at a time like this? Because she was dead on her feet, probably.

'One of Kerridge's associates? Who?'

There was a short hesitation at the other end of the line. 'He didn't want me to say. Not yet. I told him something about you – not who you are, but that you're in the frame for Jones' murder. Laid it on a bit thick, probably. But in the end he said he'd tell us what he knew, so long as he didn't have to get involved any further.'

'And does he know anything useful, do you think?'

'Maybe. He was being very cagey, but he wouldn't have offered to talk to us if he didn't have something to say.'

'You think we can trust him?'

'I hope so. He was a friend of my brother's. They worked on some stuff together and it was Greg who ended up taking the fall. He kept quiet and didn't take anyone with him. So this guy owes him one.'

'I'll trust your judgement, Joe. You think he's straight.'

'I don't think straight's the word. But, yeah, in this, I think we can trust him, so long as we don't push him too far. Just listen to what he has to say, and then leave it at that. Don't know whether it'll help you or not, but it's all we've got.'

That was true enough. It was clutching at straws, but at least for the moment there was a straw or two to clutch at.

'What's the arrangement?' she said.

'I said we'd meet up with him. About eight thirty. He wants it to be as discreet as possible. Out on the coast. I'll pick you up, and we can head on up there.'

It was a risk. Joe had no experience in these matters. Whatever his brother might have done, he wasn't used to mixing with the kind of people she'd dealt with. But it was all she had. If it came to it, she could look after herself. With a bit of luck, she could look after Joe as well.

'OK,' she said. 'Let's give it a go.' She paused, conscious of the anxious silence at the other end of the line. 'Thanks, Joe,' she added. 'You've done great.'

Fifteen minutes later, she was standing waiting for Joe on the narrow concourse at the front of the hotel. It was a chilly evening, the rain threatening to return, and there was only a scattering of other pedestrians walking past. Office workers heading home. A gaggle of young men heading for the pub. She stepped back into the shadows, watching for Joe's car.

She felt conscious of every passing vehicle, alert for watching eyes. Behind her, the hotel lobby was as quiet as the street, empty except for a couple of business types chatting over coffee.

Another car passed, not slowing on its way up into St Peter's Square. Then, finally, she heard the distinctive puttering of Joe's clapped-out Ford Escort. He pulled into the bay in front of the hotel and threw open the passenger door.

'Hope I'm not late.'

'Spot on,' she said, climbing into the passenger seat.

'You OK?'

'Well as can be expected. You reckon this will go smoothly?'

'Hope so. Can't promise it's going to tell you anything new, though.'

'Worth a shot. You're sure you want to come with me?'

'Think I'd trust you with my car?' he said. 'I've seen you drive.'

'Fair enough.'

They were travelling through the centre of town, past the rows of brightly lit shops along Deansgate, then out into the gloomier reaches of Salford and on to the motorway, heading west.

From time to time, Marie glanced in the wing mirror. There were cars behind them, but that was no surprise. It was mid-evening. The main commuter traffic had died away, but there was still a steady stream of vehicles leaving the city centre.

Joe fiddled aimlessly with the radio as he drove, flipping from one anonymous pop station to another.

'You were mentioned on the news earlier,' he said. 'Least I presume it was you.'

She caught her breath. 'What did they say?'

'Not a lot. Surprisingly low-key, I thought. Well down the news. Body found in suspicious circumstances. Police treating it as a murder investigation, want to interview a young woman. There was a short description.' He glanced across at her. 'Don't think it would help anyone identify you, though.'

'I can see that "young" might be misleading. Did they say "attractive" as well?'

He smiled. 'Something along those lines.'

'Well, that's me safe, then.'

They were out of the city now, into the suburbs. The houses

281

visible from the motorway were larger and fewer. Trees lined the roads.

'Where are we meeting?' she asked.

'Out on the coast. Near Formby.'

'Formby? Couldn't have picked somewhere less convenient, could he?' She had only a vague idea of where the place was. On the Lancashire coast, somewhere between Liverpool and Southport. Someone had told her it was pleasant, a nice place for a Sunday walk. There were red squirrels, she remembered irrelevantly. Just the place for a clandestine meeting, no doubt.

'He's doing us a favour,' Joe pointed out. 'Lives out in that neck of the woods these days. Think he'd upset a few of the wrong people in Manchester.'

Marie sat in silence as they made their way up the M6 and on to the M58, past Skelmersdale, heading now towards north Liverpool and the coast. At the end of the motorway, they turned north along the bypass. Marie glanced again in the mirror. Now they'd left the motorway, there was just one set of headlights behind them, some distance back. Surveillance distance, she thought. Or just a sensible driver. Moments later, the headlights vanished as the car behind turned off the main road. Further back, she could see another set of lights, another car, gradually gaining on them.

'Much further?'

'No. We turn off soon.'

She didn't know this area well and she'd lost any sense of distance. They'd been travelling for an hour or so. Maybe forty or fifty miles from Manchester. In the darkness, she caught the occasional glimpse of open fields, farms, neat bungalows.

A few minutes later, Joe slowed, peering through the windscreen. 'Turning's somewhere here.' He gestured to their left. 'Yes. Here's the roundabout.'

They turned on to a narrower B-road. Marie glanced in the mirror and saw, with unexpected relief, that the car behind had sped on past. They drove another half-mile or so, past more fields and then rows of smart-looking houses, an occasional convenience store, a pub. Joe turned left at the next junction, along another residential road. Larger houses, half-concealed behind tidy wooden fences. The place was more built-up, more suburban than Marie had expected. Usually, as you approached the coast, there was a sense of the sea, of windswept openness. This felt like a dormitory town; it could have been anywhere.

Gradually, though, the road narrowed and the houses fell away. They were into woodland now. Ahead, beyond the pale beams of their headlights, there was nothing but trees, darkness and, presumably, the sea.

'You know this route well,' she said.

He glanced across at her and laughed. 'Not really. We used to come here as kids sometimes. Place to come on a Sunday afternoon. Get an ice cream, play on the sands. You know. Of course, as kids, we'd rather have gone to Blackpool. Not much here but sea and sand.'

The place felt eerie enough in the darkness. 'Half a mile or so,' Joe said. He had slowed slightly again, his eyes fixed on the road, searching for a turning.

They rounded another bend, and there was a car park ahead of them. Abruptly, Joe hit the brakes and took a sharp right. It was a small parking area, designed for summer visitors. She could envisage lines of parked cars, families munching on sandwiches, preparing for walks along the beach, paddling in the grey-green water. Tonight, the car park was deserted, the place looking bleak and windswept.

'No one here yet?' Marie said.

'I'm quite glad,' Joe smiled. 'This used to be where all the doggers came, apparently. Think the police have cleared them out for the moment.'

'Would be just my luck,' Marie said. 'On the run for murder, and I get arrested for suspected exhibitionism.'

'We'll be OK. Police patrols won't be out till later.'

She couldn't tell whether or not he was being serious. 'What about your contact?'

'He won't come here. He'll park further up the shore, walk up the beach to meet us.'

'The cautious type.'

'He doesn't know you. Probably wants to check this is kosher before he shows himself.' He pushed open the car door. 'Shall we go?'

All her anxieties were returning again, but there was nothing to be done now. She pushed open her own door and climbed out. The wind from the sea caught her unexpectedly, nearly knocking her off balance. Jesus, it was cold. She stood for a moment, tasting the tang of the salty air, looking around. She could imagine that on a sunny day this would be an attractive place to be. In the dark, it just felt bleak and threatening. At the far end of the car park, there was a dilapidated hut, with signs proclaiming that ice creams and cold drinks could be bought there. Perhaps in the summer, though it looked as if the place hadn't been used in a while. Ahead of them, there were ragged dunes and beyond those the beach.

'What now?' She felt her words being whipped away by the wind, but Joe nodded and gestured towards the sea. He pulled a flashlight from his pocket and shone it towards the dunes. There was no sign of life. He looked back at her, shrugged, and began to walk forwards.

'Joe . . .' She had a sense somewhere in the back of her mind that this wasn't right. 'Be careful.' But her voice was lost on the wind.

Joe was still walking forwards, his eyes fixed on where the torchlight illuminated the narrow path over the dunes. He began to climb, the loose sand shifting under his feet.

Marie hurried along behind him. He had stopped, momentarily, at the top of the dunes, shining his torch left and right along the shoreline. She caught up with him just as he began to descend towards the beach, his boots crunching in the damp sand. The sea was yards away, luminous spray and spume flung up on to the beach. Out at sea, she could see a scattering of lights. Off to the left, there was the orange glow of Liverpool.

'Joe, I don't think . . .'

He'd taken a few more steps forwards and was standing, staring into the darkness, the torch beam playing uselessly across the sand. She drew level with him, baffled now.

'Joe, this is . . .'

He turned back towards her. The flashlight was held loosely in his left hand, pointing vaguely in her direction. His right hand held something else, an object that glinted in the wavering light. An object that was also pointed, much more steadily than the flashlight, towards her.

'Jesus, Marie. I'm sorry,' Joe said.

26

Somehow, it was hardly a surprise. She recalled her unease, days before, at Joe's unexpected appearance next to her parked car outside the shop. She remembered her suspicions, vague and unfounded, but still nagging at her. *Trust your instincts,* she thought. *Always trust your fucking instincts.*

'What's going on, Joe?'

He looked down at the pistol, as if surprised by its presence. 'I'm sorry, Marie.'

'I don't understand, Joe.' She had thought she was clutching at straws coming here, but she hadn't realized how desperate she must have been. Joe had turned up out of the blue, and she'd seen him as the only friend she had. Even when he'd been sitting in her hotel room right next to her fucking handbag, her mistrust had melted away because there was no one else to turn to.

He gestured with the gun. 'That way.' He directed her further along the beach, away from the car park, into the darkness. 'Then we can talk.'

'Talk about what, Joe?' She stumbled on the soft ground, her flat shoes sinking into the wet sand. Joe was a few feet behind, the gun barrel pointing steadily towards her. He didn't look like an amateur, she thought. He looked like someone who'd handled a gun before.

He glanced over his shoulder, judging whether they were sufficiently far from the car park, then pointed the gun down towards the sand. 'Kneel down,' he said.

She contemplated whether she could jump him, but knew it was hopeless. By the time she reached him, he could have fired without difficulty. Somehow she knew he wouldn't hesitate. This Joe was different from the shambling, well-intentioned figure she'd known from the print shop. This wasn't some innocent who'd been inveigled into betraying her.

She knelt slowly down on the beach, feeling the cold, wet sand through the thick cloth of her jeans. She could hear the roaring wind, the occasional gentle crunch of Joe's boots. Nothing else.

'I didn't want things to end up like this,' Joe said from above her. There was a note of what sounded like genuine regret in his voice. 'We could've been something.'

'Spare me, Joe. What the fuck is this about?'

'You weren't trusted right from the start. My job was to keep an eye on you.'

So much for deep cover. She'd been exposed from day one, strung along. Was it her own incompetence, or had her presence been leaked?

'And did you?' she asked. 'Find out what I was about?'

'Just another fucking grass, aren't you?' He spat the words out. 'Scrabbling around for information, selling it for your thirty pieces of silver. Birds of a feather, you and Jake fucking Morton.'

Was that what he knew, or thought he knew? He had her pegged as an informant, nothing more. Not that it would help her now.

He'd moved a step or two closer. 'You've got a choice, though. Doesn't have to be this way. We can do a deal,' he said. 'I've got the authority for that.'

'What sort of deal?'

'You've got stuff we want,' he said. 'Hand it over. Tell us what you know. Then everything can be hunky-dory.'

It was bollocks. He was just trying to sweet-talk her into handing over the evidence. He wouldn't let her go, not after this. He'd brought her up here to eliminate her. They'd put her in the frame for Jones' murder, but she'd made life difficult by slipping away. Or maybe they'd even expected that. Either way, Joe had kept tabs on her. He could have just handed her over to the police that afternoon, tipped them off while she was waiting in the hotel. But this was better. He'd shoot her, make it look like suicide, wait for the body to be discovered.

The police would assume, maybe with some encourage-ment, that it was some underworld spat. That she'd killed Jake's murderer, and then killed herself or been bumped off in her turn. They wouldn't care much, especially if they could dismiss her death as suicide. All the loose ends would be neatly tied up.

The Agency would keep quiet to avoid embarrassment. Strings would be pulled, and her deep cover role would be silently forgotten. Deniable.

For a moment, absurdly as she knelt in the wind-buffeted darkness, her mind turned to Darren, slogging away ineptly in the print shop. Poor useless bugger. He'd be out on the street again.

'I don't know what you mean,' she said. 'What have I got?'

'We know Morton sent you some stuff. It's not in your flat, so where is it?'

That answered one question. Her flat had been searched by Kerridge's men, looking for what Morton had sent her.

'I've not got anything,' she said. Her handbag was clutched in her hand, the data stick secreted in the lining. 'You can search me.'

'This can be simple, you know. You can just hand it over, and I can let you go.'

She hesitated. She could try to buy herself a little time, lure him closer. She might have a chance of doing something. Kneeling here, she had no chance at all. 'Fine. It's here,' she said. 'In my handbag.'

'Throw it over. Don't try anything. Just throw the handbag over here.'

Joe was too smart to fall for any half-baked stunts. He wouldn't waste time searching the handbag. Not while she was alive, anyway. He'd try to get her to talk, then he'd pull the trigger.

She had nothing to lose, then. She swung round quickly, throwing the bag as hard as she could at the gun. At the same time, she flung herself sideways, rolling frantically into the darkness, out of range of Joe's flashlight.

A moment later, she was scrabbling on her knees, trying to pull herself upright, urging herself to run, away from the light, down the beach.

It was hopeless. The sand sank under her feet, throwing her off balance, slowing her down. Running was almost impossible. She staggered onwards, aware of Joe's torch beam flickering across the beach, not daring to look back.

When the shot came, it was startlingly loud, even above the pounding rain and wind. She threw herself down again, and the bullet missed her. Joe was already gaining, pounding steadily across the beach, torch and gun held out in front of him.

There was nowhere to run. If she continued along the beach, he'd catch her in seconds. If she tried to get past him, he'd shoot. Out of ideas, she stopped and stood her ground, hoping he'd come closer before he fired again.

He paused, four or five feet away from her, and raised the gun once more.

'You're a stubborn cow, aren't you? Always have to do things the hard way.'

She waited until his hand was steady, watching as he took aim. Then she leaped forwards, hoping to grab his arm and force the gun away from her. It was desperate, hopeless stuff, but it was all she had left. It was the desire to go down fighting, not just to be shot in cold blood. The desire at least to do him some harm before he did the ultimate damage to her.

It almost worked. He was taken by surprise, and she managed to clutch his arm and force it back, sending them both tumbling on to the ground. She thought he was about to drop the gun, but he regained his grip and rolled over violently, forcing her back on to the yielding sand. His hand was on her throat, and, a second later, the barrel of the gun was pressed to her temple.

'Bitch!' he hissed. 'I ought to do more than fucking kill you.'

She could feel the cold metal against her skin, sense the tightening of his finger on the trigger. She closed her eyes, waiting for whatever the end would feel like.

There was a sudden, soft, indescribable thump, scarcely audible above the roaring tide. Joe's fingers loosened on her throat, the pressure of the gunmetal relaxing against her head. Then Joe toppled sideways, falling away from her on to the sand.

She opened her eyes, bewildered. A tall, thin figure was standing over her, a piece of concrete clutched in his hand.

'You know your trouble, sis,' Salter said. 'You mix with the wrong crowd.'

290

27

'You OK?'

She still felt dazed, dream-like, as if none of this was real. 'Guess so. Considering.'

'Sorry,' Salter said. 'That was closer than I'd intended. Too fucking close.'

They were heading back towards the bypass, enclosed in the warmth of Salter's car. His driving was characteristic – precise, cautious, unostentatious. Efficient.

'How come you're here?' Marie said finally, as her mind came to grips with the question that had been troubling her. It was as if her wits had been slowed by her brush with death. Every thought seemed out of reach. She felt like a toddler reaching to grab floating bubbles. When she caught one, it melted in her grasp.

'Hellhound on your trail,' Salter said. 'I was right behind you. Well, almost. Nearly got caught out at the end. Sorry about that.'

'You were right behind? Since when?'

'Since this morning. With a bit of unofficial help from young Hodder. Before then, really. But this morning was when it mattered.'

She pressed her back against the passenger seat, enjoying its solidity beneath her aching spine. 'Christ, I thought I was off and running. Turns out the whole world was following me. I'm beginning to think I'm not cut out for this job.'

'Don't beat yourself up too much, sis. You ran rings around the local plods. You weren't to know that I'd already got you under surveillance.'

She could feel her bafflement mutating into anger as his words sank in. 'I'm not getting this,' she said. 'I'm supposedly in the frame for Jones' murder. You've already got me under surveillance – Christ knows why – and then you allow me to slip away under the noses of the police. What the fuck's going on, Hugh?'

'You didn't kill Jones, sis.' It wasn't a question.

'Of course I didn't kill Jones. I was set up.'

'So that's the question, isn't it? Who set you up?'

'Kerridge and Boyle, I presume. They're the ones who benefit. Boyle, anyway.'

'Yeah,' he said. 'Boyle, anyway.'

'Jesus, Hugh. I'm knackered, confused and I've just come within ten seconds of having my fucking head blown off. Don't play games.'

'Your friend Joe back there,' he said, as if he hadn't heard. 'Take it that was a bit of a surprise?'

'Well, what do you think, Hugh? That I'd commissioned him to blow my own brains out?'

'No, sorry. Stupid question. Out of idle curiosity, I did a bit of digging on Mr Morrissey.'

'Morrissey?' She'd known him as Joe Maybury. 'That his real name?'

'Apparently. Scouser by birth, though he's lived in Manchester most of his adult life. Minor criminal record. Juvenile stuff. Then he disappears off the official radar for a bit. But he pops up again a year or two back. One to keep an eye on.'

'I had him checked out,' she said. 'He came to the shop

from the Job Centre. I got the office to run him through the system.'

'Yeah. Isn't that interesting?'

'Shit. You mean . . .?'

'Reckon someone intercepted your request. Report you got didn't make the connection with Morrissey, so you drew a blank.'

'So what about him, then?'

'Reason he appears on our radar is that he's an associate of Boyle's. Maybe legit, maybe not. Not clear what the nature of his dealings are. But we think he's one of those Boyle hires to do his dirty work.'

'Hitman?'

'Maybe.'

'Christ. And he's been working with me for the last six months.'

Her mind went back to the evenings she'd spent alone with Joe, finishing off some late order. She'd felt comfortable in his presence. She could even recall using the word 'unthreatening' to herself. She'd meant in a sexual way, and maybe that at least had been true. A safe pair of fucking hands. Half an hour earlier, one of those hands had been around her throat.

'Have you tracked down who intercepted my request? There must be something on the record.'

'Maybe,' he said ambiguously. 'Speaking of Morrissey, it's probably time we let someone know he's there. I'd hate anything bad to happen to him.'

Salter had clubbed Morrissey over the head with a piece of concrete he'd found at the edge of the car park. It had been, he'd admitted to Marie, a more improvised solution than he'd planned. He'd followed Joe's car all the way from the hotel – his had been the second set of headlights that she'd glimpsed, Marie presumed – but judged it too risky to follow them immediately off the bypass. He'd continued past the turning up the beach, done a U-turn and pulled into the car park of a pub further down the road to allow them a few minutes to get ahead. But he'd taken a wrong turn in trying to find his way back to the beach in the darkness and had found himself caught up in a warren of residential streets. He'd wasted precious minutes retracing his route, before finally following them down the correct road to the sea.

When he had arrived in the car park, it had taken him a further few anxious minutes to locate Marie and Joe on the beach. He'd finally spotted Joe's flickering flashlight along the shoreline and realized immediately that things weren't right. Up to that point, he said, he hadn't been quite sure what game was being played and by whom. At that moment it has become clear that, whatever the game might be, Marie was definitely losing.

He'd grabbed the piece of concrete – part of a decaying wall along the edge of the car park – in the absence of any other weapon. Even in the last few seconds as he approached the struggling pair, his crunching footsteps drowned by the roar of the wind and the sea, he hadn't been sure what he was going to do. As he drew closer, he'd seen that, whatever it was, he had to do it quickly.

He'd tried not to hit Joe too hard, intending only to stun him. In the event, Joe had collapsed forwards, unconscious or worse. Salter had grasped Joe's shoulder, dragged him back from Marie, turned him over on to his back. Still breathing, thank Christ. Spark out, though. No blood, as far as Salter could see, but he'd have the mother of all headaches in the morning.

Marie had scrambled to her feet, face white with shock. Salter left Joe and went to help her, letting her lean on his shoulder as she recovered her breath.

'Come on,' he'd said. 'We're out of here.'

She'd looked at him blankly. She was still dazed, but she'd assumed that this was it. That Salter would call the police and an ambulance, and she'd have to wait to face the music. In a way, it would have been a relief.

Instead, Salter had left Joe lying unconscious on the sand, and helped Marie stumble back towards his car. He'd hesitated momentarily, wondering what to do about Joe's gun, but then had left it on the beach by Joe's head.

'What about Joe?' she'd said, as they reached Salter's car. 'We can't just leave him there.'

'You care?' Salter had asked, then shrugged. 'I'll put a few miles behind us, then we can call him an ambulance.'

'He'll shop me,' she said. 'He'll say I brought him out here and tried to kill him. He'll tell the police I was here.'

'I doubt it. Because then he'd have to explain why you didn't kill him. Also, I don't think Mr Morrissey will want to spend any more time with the police than he has to. If he wakes up before the ambulance comes, he'll make himself scarce. If he doesn't, he'll concoct some story. Mugged while out dogging or something. Did you know this place used to be the dogging centre of the north-west?'

'So I understand,' she said, wondering quite why it was that everyone seemed to want to share that titbit of information with her.

He waited till they were back on the bypass, then dialled 999. He used a secure phone, untraceable, and gave a false name. Just a tip-off about an unconscious man on the beach. He didn't even bother using the hands-free, Marie noted. Not the usual cautious Hugh Salter.

She'd expected him to head back towards the city, but instead he'd turned north. She was baffled now, wondering what he was up to. For the moment, he didn't seem inclined to enlighten her. They sped on through the night in silence. In spite of everything, Marie found herself beginning to doze, overcome by sheer exhaustion.

She came awake as they turned off the main road. She'd missed the sign and had no idea where they were.

'You must be knackered,' Salter said, in a tone that sounded almost kindly. 'Not far now.'

'Where are we?'

'At the seaside. Edge of Southport. One of your better resorts. What passes for upmarket up here.'

'Can't wait.' She looked at the clock on the dashboard. She'd been asleep half an hour or so.

She could see what Salter meant about the town. Most British seaside resorts were long past their best, but this still retained a Victorian elegance. Wide streets, open spaces. It looked as if there was probably some money about. She could imagine that it would be bustling and attractive in the summer. At this time of year, at this time of the night, though, for all its natural charms, the town still looked a little bleak and drab, with rows of shuttered shopfronts, closed bed and breakfasts, everything waiting to be spruced up for the summer. Salter drove through the town centre, then headed north along the main street. The Irish Sea was off to their left, invisible behind rows of Edwardian buildings.

They left the main town behind and entered a residential area. Salter turned left and then immediately right, and Marie saw that they were in a small estate of neatly serried bungalows. They looked as if they'd been built in the 1960s or 1970s to house aspirational young couples. They'd passed through some more modern, more upmarket-looking housing. These looked slightly more down at heel, though hardly neglected. Marie tried to imagine who might choose to live there. Older couples perhaps, retiring to the coast, or maybe still the youngsters trying to get a foot on the housing ladder. One or two of the houses were boarded up, perhaps awaiting renovation or new owners, but the majority seemed well cared for. There were lights burning inside most of the bungalows.

Salter pulled into the side of the road and cut the engine. 'Here we are,' he said. 'Home from home.' He climbed out into the windy night.

Marie hesitated for a moment, then followed him. 'Any chance of you telling me what the bloody hell's going on, Hugh?'

'Just a few minutes more,' he said. 'This way.' He gestured towards a narrow alleyway between two of the bungalows.

'If you think I'm going into any dark alleys after what's happened tonight, you've got another think coming.'

Salter smiled as if she'd made a joke. 'We're going via the back entrance,' he said. 'Don't want to leave the car too obviously parked outside the place we're staying. Just in case.'

'Staying?' she said. 'Who said anything about staying?'

'Don't think you've a lot of choice, sis. We need to keep you out of circulation for a little while.'

He was already striding away down the alley. After a moment's hesitation, she followed. The alley led to a further passage between the rear gardens of the two parallel rows of bungalows, providing access to their back doors. Salter turned left down this passage then, three or four houses down, unbolted a garden gate and made his way inside.

By the time she'd caught up, he was already at the back door of the bungalow, fumbling with a bunch of keys. In the darkness, the bungalow looked much like all the rest. The garden had apparently been tended, though only in a functional manner – a neat lawn, mowed, some concrete slabs, a few pots currently devoid of plants.

Salter finally succeeded in opening the door and stepped

inside, turning on the light as he did so. She followed him into a clean but basic-looking kitchen. Salter stood looking around the room as if it were new to him also.

'Here we are,' he said. 'All home comforts. Cup of tea?' Without waiting for a response, he picked up an electric kettle which was standing by the sink.

'What is this, Hugh?' she said. 'A safe house?'

'Something like that,' he said, his back turned to her.

She left Salter at the sink, knowing that she'd get nothing more from him till he was ready, and went to explore the rest of the house. It took her no more than a few minutes to check out the remaining rooms, and what she saw largely confirmed her external impressions. Beyond the narrow hallway, there was a small sitting room, a poky bathroom, two double bedrooms. All apparently maintained, newly decorated, but bare and functional. The only gesture towards ornament was a scattering of anonymous pictures on the walls – framed prints of the kind that adorn the walls in budget business hotels. The furniture looked like a job lot from some discount chain store. Nothing offensive, but nothing memorable either.

Salter entered the sitting room bearing a tray laden with a teapot, milk jug, sugar bowl and two mugs. Even a plate of sodding biscuits.

'Very domesticated,' she commented.

'All mod cons,' he said. 'You must be hungry. Shall I get something for us?'

'Jesus. This I've got to see. Hugh Salter, domestic goddess.'

'There's a freezer full of ready meals and a microwave. That's as close as you get to the culinary arts.'

'Fair enough. Yeah, that would be good. In a while. First, though, tell me what the fuck's going on.'

As if he hadn't heard her words, he poured tea for them both, leaving her to add her own milk. He sat down heavily on the sofa, gesturing her to take a seat. She lowered herself on to one of the armchairs.

'So?'

'We've got a leakage problem,' he said. 'The Agency.'

'You said. At our last meeting.'

'It's an occupational hazard. You know that. However careful we are with vetting, you get the odd bad apple who'll take a backhander. But they're usually juniors. The admin staff who get paid three-fifths of fuck all because we think that their sense of national duty will cover their mortgages. They take a few quid, leak a few titbits. Doesn't usually do any serious harm. Every now and then we spot one and give them the bullet. Part of life's rich pattern.'

'And this is more than that?'

'A shitload more than that, yes. This is someone at a senior level who seems to be working hand in glove with the other side.'

'And by the other side, you mean Kerridge and Boyle?'

He stretched himself back on the sofa. 'Ah, now, that's an interesting question.'

'Is it?'

'You're assuming that Kerridge and Boyle are, as it were, one entity.'

'Well, aren't they? As it were? Joined at the hip, from what I've seen.'

'Always been that way, hasn't it? Kerridge the intellectual, the business brains. Boyle doing the dirtier work, but still managing to keep his hands more or less clean. The perfect partnership.'

'You're saying it isn't?'

'Not quite. Not any more. Or so it seems.'

'My heart grieves. Wonder who'll get custody of the kids.'

He smiled, very faintly. 'Impression I get is that Mr Boyle

was perhaps getting a bit too big for his boots. Taking too much for granted. Maybe becoming a wee bit of a threat to the old man. Not so much *Who's Afraid of Virginia Woolf?* as *Oedipus Rex*, you might say.'

'I'll take your word,' she said. 'All that book learning will get you into trouble one day. So what's the upshot of all this?'

'The upshot,' Salter said carefully, 'is that Kerridge shafted Boyle.'

She looked up, surprised for the first time. 'You mean Boyle's arrest?'

'Looks that way. A lot of information came our way. Interesting thing was, most of the evidence implicated Mr Boyle while leaving Mr Kerridge squeaky clean.'

'Maybe Kerridge was just smarter.'

'Could well be. But it was all just a little too neat. We've been pursuing this bunch for years, and then this stuff falls handily into our lap. Very convenient.'

'Where did it come from, this evidence?'

'Various sources, over the last few months. Most recently, quite a lot from your friend Morton.'

'You think Morton was doing this for Kerridge? I can't see it. He wanted to shaft both of them.'

'I don't doubt it. You knew him better than me.' He left the comment hanging in the air for a beat or two. 'I reckon Morton acted in good faith. If you can ever say that about a grass. But I think Kerridge had him sussed.'

'As an informant? Jesus.'

'Well, that's where our leaker comes in. Could be that Kerridge had been tipped off. And was able to use Mr Morton as a nice little conduit to spread more poison about Boyle.'

'Honour among thieves. Still, I imagine you didn't look a gift horse in the mouth.'

'Christ, no. Only too happy to have a bit of internecine

warfare if it helps us do our job. We want to get both of them, of course, but Boyle will do nicely for the moment. The worrying thing is the leak, though. It might have helped us with Boyle, but it leaves everyone exposed.'

'Including me.'

'Including you.' He paused. 'If I'm not mistaken, you provided us with one or two useful titbits on Boyle.'

It was true. The information had been nothing spectacular, just intimations she'd picked up on the grapevine about deals that Boyle had supposedly been involved in. Something and nothing, most of it, but stuff that was worth logging if it added to the sum of intelligence. She couldn't even recall where most of it had come from. Just whispers. But who had been doing the whispering?

'You reckon he might have had me sussed as well?'

'I don't know. But, yes, we think so.'

'Shit,' she said. 'That's scary.'

'Yeah. Potentially means that all our operations could be compromised. And all our agents.'

She could feel a rising tide of anger. How long had Salter known this? How long had he allowed her to stay out there, knowing that her role had been exposed? Had he been happy to leave her at risk, hoping that she might become another nice conduit?

'What about Morton? Who killed him?'

'Boyle's people. They've been systematically shutting down anyone who might provide witness evidence. Couple of grasses just disappeared. Frightened off, I'd guess. Probably couldn't frighten Morton so went to the next step—'

'And me,' she said quietly. 'Framed.'

'Yeah. And you. Framed.'

'That why you think I've been sussed?'

'One reason. But, yes, if Boyle thinks you're worth bothering

301

with, there's a reason for that. I don't know whether he's got you pegged as undercover, but my guess is that he at least thinks you're a grass.'

'That was what Joe— Morrissey said. Christ.' She looked around her at the shabby sitting room. 'So where does all this fit in?'

'Professional Standards.'

'What?'

'I'm working for Professional Standards. Have been for a year or two.'

'But you're not—'

'No, well. Covert. Aren't we all?'

She stared at him, trying to take in the implications. Professional Standards was the internal division charged with ensuring the integrity of the Agency's staff. Watching the watchmen. Policing the police. Investigating corruption, vetting staff. An essential function in an organization like theirs, but nevertheless regarded with suspicion and distaste by their colleagues. Big Brother. The Stasi.

'So who are you working to?' she said.

'The highest. This goes a long way up.'

'Good to know you're above suspicion, anyway.'

'I don't imagine I was to start with. They must have had me checked out pretty thorough. But they need someone on the ground. Top brass doesn't get its hands dirty with stuff like this. They've been aware of the problem for a long time. Just didn't know how to deal with it.'

'Till you came along. Must be very proud, Hugh.'

'God, Marie. It's the job we do, isn't it? No different from what I did before. No different from what you do.'

'Except that you're spying on your own.'

She knew she was being unfair, that Salter was right. He was just doing what he had to, the way they all did. But she was still angry with him, and she was feeling a growing anxiety, as if the ground was continuing to shift beneath her, as if nothing was certain.

'They're not our own, anyway, are they?' he went on. 'Not if they're working for the other side.'

She gazed at him for a moment. 'OK. No. You're right. You're just doing a job. Doesn't mean I have to like the thought of you spying on me, though.'

'Not you,' he said. 'You were never seriously in the frame.'

'Should I be flattered or insulted? Who then? Who is in the frame?'

There was a long silence. Then, without responding, Salter rose and disappeared into the kitchen. She heard the sound of a cupboard being opened, the clink of glass on glass. A moment later, he reappeared bearing two half-filled tumblers alongside a bottle of Laphroaig.

'Fancy a drink?'

'Or three,' she said. 'Thanks.' What she really needed was food, she thought. A good solid meal inside her. But Scotch would do for the moment.

Salter reached over to hand her one of the glasses.

'Welsby,' he said gently.

'What?'

'It's Welsby,' he repeated. 'Our leaker. Welsby. Good old Keith.' He had finished his own Scotch in a single swallow. He poured himself another, and then handed her the bottle. 'What do you think of that?'

She took a large swallow of her own drink. 'This your idea of a joke, Hugh?'

'Wish it was, sis. Looks as if old Keith's been on the Kerridge payroll for quite a little while.'

'You've got evidence for this?'

'I'm not just trying to screw Welsby to advance my career,

if that's what you mean. Look, sis, this was as much of a shock to me as it is to you. And, yes, we've got evidence. Not enough for a court, not yet. But enough for me.'

'Jesus,' she said. She wanted not to believe it, wanted to believe that Salter was lying. That this was just some convoluted, cynical game he was playing.

After all, why should she trust Salter? Because he had saved her life? But the whole situation was increasingly surreal. What were they doing here, late in the evening, drinking Scotch in this glorified holiday home? Even if Salter was telling the truth, she couldn't begin to fathom where he was heading.

She poured herself another drink – just half a glass, but probably a bad idea nonetheless. She could already feel her head beginning to spin. Knackered, no food and too much booze. A terrific combination. Perfect for keeping your wits about you.

'I don't believe Keith's on the take,' she said. 'It's not his style.'

But was that really the case? She wanted it to be, but Salter's claim had the ring of truth. She'd always had the idea, without really articulating it even to herself, that Welsby's character, his bluff cynical manner, was somehow a guarantor of his integrity. That he was above, or perhaps below, all the usual careerist machinations, the politicking, the sordid temptations that went with this territory.

But maybe the opposite was true. She thought back to Winsor's psychometrics. If you were the sort of character who bent the rules, eventually you'd bend them too far. You'd make that almost imperceptible shift from the acceptable to the unacceptable. From good to bad. And, as Marie had seen too many times, once you stepped over that line, it was almost impossible to step back.

'Believe what you like,' Salter said. 'It's true.'

The implications of Salter's words were just beginning to sink in. If he was right about Welsby, it blew the whole deal right open. Her own position would have been compromised right from the start. Morton's death warrant would have been signed the moment they persuaded him to come across. They'd all have been living on borrowed time, or being used for Kerridge's own ends. The whole thing had been a farce.

Salter was already pouring himself another drink. He waved the bottle towards her and she topped up her own glass. Half the bottle gone. No wonder she was feeling woozy.

'So what's your plan now?' she said. 'Why've you brought me here?'

'First thing was to get you somewhere safe. I thought at first that Boyle would be content with the frame-up. That his plan was just to take you out of commission in the short term and bugger your credibility in the long term.'

'So long as that was all. Wouldn't want anything bad to happen to me.'

'No, well. We could have got you out of all that, I'm fairly confident. We'd have pulled a few strings, got it sorted. Might have taken a little while, though. With that and Morton's death, Boyle would have got what he wanted. We'd have had to drop the trial. But then I saw our friend Joe sniffing about your hotel. That was when I did my digging and found the link between Messrs Morrissey and Boyle. Occurred to me that Morrissey's interest might be – well, professional. It was a smart move from Boyle. If Morrissey had managed to top you, even our lot might not think it worthwhile stirring things up just to clear your posthumous name.'

She found herself shivering at Salter's characteristically blunt colloquialisms. 'Nice to be loved.'

'Just being realistic. Anyway, when I realized what Morrissey might be up to, I thought it best to organize a little hideaway for you. Keep you out of harm's way until we can get things sorted. Welsby doesn't know about this place. That's why it's a bit rough and ready. Run by Professional Standards, but they don't have cause to use it that often. Don't seem to get too many agents grassing on each other, oddly enough.'

'Except you and Welsby?'

He shrugged. 'I've grassed no one. This is a big deal. Welsby's potentially buggered a lot of major operations over the last year or so.'

They sat in silence for a few minutes. Salter had knocked back yet another glass of Scotch, but was showing no obvious ill-effects. Marie was sipping gently at hers, enjoying the taste and the burn in her throat, but conscious of a growing haziness in her thinking.

'So what's the plan?' she asked again.

'We can talk about that tomorrow. Get a decent night's sleep first.' He gently patted the sofa cushion next to him. 'Why not come over here? We can relax a bit now.'

Christ, she thought. Is he making a pass at me? Not here, not now, surely. But Salter wouldn't let sensitivities like that stop him from going after something he wanted. Or maybe she was just flattering herself. God, she felt tired.

'Don't think so,' she said. 'If I get up now, I'll probably just fall over.'

'Fair enough.' He was smiling, as if he'd just completed the preliminary step in an extended campaign. He poured himself another Scotch. 'You?'

She shook her head, holding up her nearly full glass. 'Can't keep up. You'll have to go on without me. Don't let me hold you back.'

He leaned back on the sofa and stretched out his legs, his

manner suggesting that he was envisaging a large open fire, rather than the three-bar electric that was actually there.

'What about Morton, anyway?'

'What about him?' She could feel herself enunciating more clearly, as if trying to compensate for the fuzziness that was beginning to afflict her brain.

'We talked the other day, when Welsby was there, about what evidence Morton might have had. Whether he had anything he hadn't handed over.'

Even through her fogged head, she could feel mental alarm bells ringing. 'Yeah, I remember. It's possible, I suppose.'

'He gave you no idea?'

'Why would he? You were his handler. Anyway, I thought you said that he was a conduit for stuff coming from Kerridge.'

'Still useful stuff, wherever it came from. And maybe Morton was cuter than that.'

'You reckon?' She hoped that her words were still clear, but it felt as if her mind was slowly coming adrift of its moorings.

'He was no fool, was he? Maybe he knew he was being used by Kerridge. He'd still be quite happy to pass on whatever Kerridge might want to give him about Boyle. But he might also have been collecting some stuff on his own. Doing a bit of freelancing, as it were.'

'Stuff about Kerridge?' She recalled now that the material on the data stick had seemed almost entirely to focus on Kerridge. There had been very little about Boyle.

'Maybe stuff he could use as an insurance policy, if he knew he was being used. Or maybe he did just want to bring them both down. You get that impression?'

'Might be,' she said. She could feel herself tensing. Salter's tone was as casual as ever, but his questions felt increasingly pressured, probing. Her head was spinning, and she didn't trust herself to say the right thing. Whatever the right thing might be. 'I really don't know, Hugh. You were closer to him towards the end.'

Another thought struck her. If Salter was right about Welsby, that would explain why Welsby had wanted to keep Morton's handling 'in the family'.

Salter gazed at her over the top of the glass as though he were reading her mind. *Well, good luck with that,* she thought. *At the moment, I can barely read my own.* She swallowed the last of the Scotch and looked at her watch. Just gone ten. It felt a lot later.

'I'm going to turn in, Hugh. I'm knackered.'

'Sure you don't want anything to eat?'

She shook her head, and it felt as if her brain was in danger of coming loose. 'Should have had something earlier. Can hardly keep my eyes open now.'

She pushed herself slowly to her feet, finding it harder than she'd expected, the room swaying gently around her. 'Christ. Must be getting old. Can't take my drink.'

Salter rose to take her arm. 'My fault,' he said. 'You're exhausted. Shouldn't have plied you with spirits on an empty stomach. Let's get you to bed.'

She couldn't work out whether there was any intended undertone to the last sentence, but barely had the energy to care. If he tried anything, she'd no doubt summon the will to knee him in the balls.

He led her across the hall and pointed to one of the bedrooms. 'You take that one,' he said. 'Occurred to me that you'd have left your stuff back at the hotel, so I organized you a few bits and pieces. Washbag, dressing gown. Some basic clothes. Hope they're more or less the right size. Guesswork.'

And observation, she thought. Salter wasn't the only colleague who undressed her mentally, but he was probably

308

the only one who'd make a note of her vital statistics in the process.

She paused at the bedroom door, taking in the neat double bed, the slightly garish duvet cover, the magnolia walls and beige carpet. The bed, at least, looked irresistibly inviting. She glanced over her shoulder.

'Goodnight, Hugh,' she said. 'And thanks. Really.'

28

She woke in pitch darkness, with a headache, a mouth that tasted like the wet sand where she'd struggled with Joe hours before, and an unaccountable sense of unease. It took her a moment to recognize where she was. After some blind searching, she found the curved shape of the bedside lamp. It took her another few seconds to find the switch, and then the room was flooded with light.

She lay back, her dazed mind piecing together the sequence of events that had brought her here. The police. The hotel. Joe. The beach. Salter. The sense of unease was mounting as her mind tracked through the incidents of the previous day.

Shit. Her handbag. She'd left it in the sitting room. She'd been too befuddled to think about it before going to bed, but it had been sitting by the side of her chair. With the data stick still tucked away in the lining. Shit.

She dragged herself slowly out of bed, trying to get her brain back into gear. She'd stripped off her clothes before climbing into bed and donned a fairly unflattering nightdress that had been left among a neat pile of clothes on the flat-pack dressing table. Now she caught sight of herself in the dressing table mirror. *Nice taste, Hugh*, she thought. But it could have been worse. She could imagine him contemplating some far more revealing outfit. She pulled the towelling dressing gown on over the top and turned to the door.

She'd been relieved to discover that there was a bolt on the inside. It wasn't exactly that she didn't trust Salter. Whatever she might think of him, she couldn't imagine that he would force his attentions on her against her will. But, after everything she'd been through, she needed the sense of security.

Now, she slid the bolt back, and as silently as she could, opened the door. She hadn't been asleep for long. Across the hallway, a light was still burning in the sitting room.

She took a noiseless step along the hall and peered through the doorway. Salter was still sitting on the sofa, side on to her, head down. Her handbag was open on his knee, and he was systematically sorting through the contents.

She considered walking into the room and challenging him. Instead, she continued silently past the sitting room and into the kitchen. There, she turned on the cold water tap and began searching, deliberately noisy, through the cupboards in search of a glass.

'You OK?'

She turned. Salter was standing in the doorway. 'Just getting some water. Somebody filled my mouth with sawdust while I was asleep.'

'Glasses in there.' Salter gestured towards a cupboard in the corner. 'There's juice in the fridge if you want it.'

'Water's fine.' She busied herself locating a glass, filling it with cold water. 'Don't suppose there're any painkillers around?'

'That drawer, I think. There's a load of first-aid stuff.'

She pulled open the drawer. Sticking plasters. Rolls of bandages. A thermometer. An antiseptic spray. Boxes of paracetamol, ibuprofen, aspirin. She tore open a box of paracetamol and popped out two tablets.

Sipping the water, she made her way back into the sitting room, curling herself up in the corner of the sofa. Salter stood by the door, watching her.

'How are you feeling?'

'Oh, I'll be OK. Just too much of that stuff on an empty stomach.' She gestured towards the Scotch bottle on the table. Its contents hadn't noticeably reduced while she'd been in bed, which was interesting in itself. Salter had a nearly full glass in his hand, but it could have been the same one he'd been drinking when she'd retired. She held up her own glass of water. 'Prevention's better than cure, and all that. If I deal with it now, hope I'll feel less crap in the morning.'

She was still feeling pretty awful. Not just the dry mouth, the headache, the incipient nausea, but something more. An odd light-headedness, a sense that she wasn't fully in control of her thoughts and movements. The feeling that she'd been sedated.

Was it possible? Maybe. Salter could have slipped something into the tea he'd given her earlier. Perhaps he'd hoped that it would combine with the whisky to knock her cold. Get her out of the way so he could check through her things, as he'd apparently been doing with her handbag. Or maybe his aim had just been to relax her, get her disinhibited. Encourage her to talk.

'Jesus, I must have been out of it,' she said.

'How d' you mean?' He was still standing motionless in the doorway.

'When I went to bed. Left my handbag out here.'

'Did you? Well, safe enough, I should think.'

'Yeah, but I'm a woman, Hugh, in case you hadn't noticed. Never like to be more than two feet from my handbag. Makes me feel insecure.' She pushed herself to her feet and picked up the bag. 'I'd better turn in again. What time do you want me up in the morning?'

'Up to you. I've some business first thing.'

'What sort of business?'

'Shaking the cage. I reckon Kerridge is getting a bit rattled. He thought he'd got Boyle out of the way, but Boyle's been more resourceful than he expected. Now Boyle's slipping out of our net, and Morton might've had something up his sleeve that puts Kerridge in the frame. Squeaky bum time.'

'So what are you going to do?'

'Just have a chat with a couple of people. Set some hares running. Increase Kerridge's jitters a bit. If he's rattled, he might start to make mistakes. He might also put a bit of pressure on Welsby to help him out. Maybe they'll get careless and give us some of the harder evidence we need.'

'Sounds a long shot.'

'You know the game, sis. It's all long shots. But you keep going, and once in a while something comes good.'

'If you say so, Hugh. OK, I'll see you when I see you in the morning. Then we can talk.'

'A pleasure in store.' For a moment, he remained unmoving in the doorway, and she thought that he might block her way. Then he eased himself back and gestured her past, with the air of someone holding open an imaginary door. But he remained half across the doorway, close enough to cause her some unease as she passed. Game-playing, she thought. Macho fucking game-playing.

'Sleep well, sis.'

'I plan to.' She didn't look back. 'You do the same, Hugh.'

She closed and bolted the bedroom door behind her, then took the hard-backed chair from the dressing table and wedged it under the door handle. Hardly Fort Knox, but the best she could do.

She climbed back under the duvet and switched off the bedside lamp. The curtains on the bedroom window were cheap and flimsy, but there were no street lights on this side of the house and the darkness was complete. She lay listening to the tiny noises of the night – the click of a contracting radiator, settling woodwork, the faint skittering and cry of some animal outside. She had a sense, probably unfounded, that Salter was still out in the hallway, perhaps even listening at her door.

A word had lodged in her mind during her last exchange with Salter, and now it refused to be dispelled. *Bait*, she thought. That's what I feel like. *Bait in a fucking trap.*

She lay staring blankly into the darkness, and it was a long time before sleep finally overtook her.

In the end, she slept fitfully, disturbed by fragments of dreams that melted into one another without ever gaining coherence – somebody pursuing her, something she had to do, something she'd left undone. Jake in the background, never quite glimpsed. She stirred two or three times in the darkness, each time half-convinced that someone else was in the room. She woke finally as the first grey light began to filter through the thin curtains.

She felt better than she had the previous night, but her body was still telling her it had consumed something more potent than a few glasses of Scotch. There was a dull ache behind her eyes, a sense of dislocation from the world.

She checked the plastic alarm clock on the bedside table. Seven twenty. Outside, there was a flurry of birdsong, some-where the burr of a passing car. She pulled herself upright and listened.

There was movement inside the house, easily audible through the flimsy internal walls. Someone moving about in the kitchen. The thump of a cupboard door, the rumble of a boiling kettle, the metallic twang of a pop-up toaster. Salter preparing for the day, getting ready for whatever business he had planned.

She considered whether to go out and speak to him, but thought it best to wait. She wasn't clear whether he was intending to conduct his business, whatever it might be, from the house or whether he'd be going out. If he went out, she'd have the opportunity to look round the place, look for any clues as to what his game might be. Try to get some idea what the hell was going on.

Her first question was soon answered. She heard the sounds of Salter rinsing a plate in the kitchen sink, footsteps padding along the hallway. She moved quietly across the room and slipped back beneath the duvet.

Salter had paused outside her door, and she heard him gently pressing down on the door handle. She held her breath, wondering if he would try to force his way in but, having silently tried the door, he released the handle. She heard his footsteps retreating down the hall, a brief pause, and then the dull thud as the front door closed. Some distance away, she heard the gentle roar of a car engine starting.

Grabbing a selection of the clothes Salter had provided, she removed the chair and unbolted the bedroom door. As she stepped into the hallway she froze, startled by a murmur of voices from the living room. It took her a moment to realize that it was nothing more than the television news. Did that mean Salter would be returning soon?

There was no way of knowing, and she was pretty much past caring. She took a rapid and tepid shower in the poky bathroom and dressed quickly. The clothes were not a bad fit – testament either to Salter's precision or his over-intent observation of her figure. She ended up in a pair of jeans and a baggy T-shirt that were hardly flattering, but suitably functional.

There was instant coffee in the kitchen cupboard and milk in the fridge. She prepared herself a drink to help clear her head and then, with the steaming mug in her hands, began to explore the bungalow more thoroughly.

It didn't take long. The bungalow comprised nothing more than the five rooms she'd noted the previous evening. The place looked as if it had been recently but cheaply redecorated and refurnished. There was a free-standing cupboard in the sitting room, but it contained only a pile of old newspapers – from about six months before, she noted – and a couple of board games. There was a second cupboard under the television containing a handful of DVDs, most of them freebies from some Sunday newspaper or other.

The kitchen was no more fruitful. There were plenty of cupboards in the kitchen units, but they contained nothing more interesting than the usual range of kitchen utensils, crockery and glasses. Everything bought as a job lot from some discount homeware store. The fridge, freezer and cupboards were well-stocked with food. As Salter had implied, it was all instant meals and staples, most of it tinned, dried or frozen. Stuff designed to have a long shelf life.

Salter had left her a scribbled note on the kitchen table. *Help yourself to whatever you want. Back mid-morning. Stay in the house.*

She soon discovered that the last instruction was unnecessary. She tried the back door, hoping for a breath of air. It was firmly deadlocked, with no sign of a key. She made her way through the hall and tried the front door. Deadlocked too.

It had already begun to occur to her that the building was remarkably secure. Heavy-duty deadlocks on the front and back doors, all the windows similarly secured. As far as she could judge, the windows themselves were toughened glass.

Not so much a safe house, then. More a sodding prison. Superficially, the bungalow resembled a badly appointed holiday home. Below the surface, it was something odder. It wasn't just the locks that were seriously solid. The front and back doors themselves had apparently been reinforced, with metal plating and strengthened hinges.

The Agency's safe houses were anonymous places, normally tucked quietly away in some suburban estate. They had a degree of electronic protection – high quality but discreet alarms, CCTV, links to local police – and reasonable domestic-style security. But not stuff like this – industrial locks, reinforced panels. Nothing that would attract attention.

This felt more like private enterprise. The centre of operations for a big-time dealer, maybe. The sort of place you might need to keep safe, not just from the police, but from your immediate competitors. She couldn't imagine this house being run by the officious busies who populated Professional Standards. Was Salter telling the truth about Welsby? Could she trust Salter at all? The truth was that there was no one she could rely on. Not down here. Not away from Liam.

God. Liam. True to form, she'd managed again to forget all about him. He'd still be wondering what the hell had happened to her. She glanced around, but there was no phone in the bungalow. Her own mobiles were inoperable after she'd destroyed the SIM cards. She couldn't imagine that Salter would have left a mobile handily hanging around for her use.

Shit. There was nothing she could do right now. All she could do was get in touch with him as soon as she got out of this – whatever that might mean. She'd have a lifetime of apologies ahead of her.

Her frustration growing, she returned to the front door,

wondering if there was any possibility that the key might be concealed somewhere in its vicinity. Her eyes wandered upwards and she noticed, for the first time, a small trapdoor set into the ceiling, positioned to provide access to the loft space above.

What would be up there? Probably not much. Some dust and a few spiders. The usual detritus that accumulates in an old house over the years. Bits of discarded junk, old papers, forgotten toys.

There was no rational reason for her to explore it. Except that she had nothing else to do and was being driven slowly crazy by the well-secured walls around her. She hesitated for only a moment longer, and then fetched one of the high-backed chairs from the kitchen.

Standing on the chair, she was able to pull open the trap-door. Like the rest of the bungalow, its initial appearance was deceptive. It was a much more sophisticated affair than it looked, the trapdoor counter-weighted so that it opened smoothly, an aluminium folding ladder tucked neatly behind it. She pulled down the ladder, noting that it seemed well-maintained and lubricated. This was a space that had been used relatively recently.

Intrigued now, she returned the chair to the kitchen and made her way cautiously up the ladder until she was able to peer into the space above. At first sight, it looked unremark-able – just a small area of unused space below the pitch of the roof. Given the quality of the trapdoor, she had half-expected that the loft would have been adapted for regular use. But there was no real floor – just the usual joists with the plasterboard ceiling nailed beneath them. She would have to be careful. If she slipped off the joists, she would most likely just crash through the plasterboard.

She noticed that, although there was no floor, a number

of doubled planks had been positioned across the joists to provide a safer route across the loft. Not just a temporary measure, either. The planks were neatly nailed into place.

There was some light up here – lines of sunlight creeping through gaps below the roofline – but it remained gloomy. She looked around and found a light switch. As she pressed it, the space was flooded with light from two large spots set in the corners of the roof. Again, she thought, not what you'd expect from your average loft. Looking around, she saw that, otherwise, her earlier expectations had been largely fulfilled. There were various items scattered about the attic, most of them nothing more than discarded junk. A rusting child's tricycle, a discarded toaster, an old television. Beyond that, there were a number of cardboard shoe boxes filled with papers. She made her way carefully along the planks towards these, hoping that their contents might be of interest.

But they were simply more rubbish, sheet after sheet of old domestic bank statements, all at least ten years old. She scanned a handful briefly, but the name of the account holder meant nothing to her and the amounts in the account were small. She flicked quickly through the rest of the boxes, but the papers were of a similar type and vintage – old utilities bills, tax returns, bits and pieces of formal correspondence. All of it unremarkable, the kind of thing you might find in any household. Stored up here by some previous occupant in the hope that it might come in useful someday. It clearly never had.

She straightened up, careful to keep her balance on the narrow planks. There didn't seem to be much else. This was another wild goose chase, of no value except to waste another half-hour of the endless morning. If nothing else, she'd enjoy Salter's reaction to the mess she'd made of these new clothes in the small time he'd been out of the house.

There remained one interesting question, though. Why had someone installed that expensive-looking entrance and then taken the trouble to put the planks down? Her eyes followed the path of the planks across the attic. They led to an area at the far gable end, lost in the gloom. Her immediate guess was that the planks led to the house's water tank, although she couldn't see it in the dim light. Still, while she was here, there was no harm in looking.

As she drew closer, she realized that the arrangement was more professionally constructed than was at first apparent. The planks broadened to a reinforced platform. What she had taken to be the gable wall was a neatly made plasterboard screen, painted a dark colour so as to be invisible to anyone taking a casual look into the attic.

Examining the panelling more closely, she saw it was designed to slide back on stainless-steel runners set at ground level and head height. Like the loft entrance, the structure had been well maintained and drew back easily. She opened it to its full extent, and peered to see what lay behind.

At first, she was disappointed. Immediately behind the panel was a steel water tank, pipes leading off to the bungalow's plumbing and central heating. She craned her head to look further around the panel. Behind the tank was something much more interesting.

It was a large industrial safe, a squat cast-iron monstrosity that lurked almost threateningly in the semi-darkness. The platform beneath it had been reinforced to ensure that it would take the weight. Christ knew how it had been brought up there. She could imagine only that it had been lifted by crane and brought in through the roof. Hardly an inconspicuous activity, although maybe the kind of thing you could disguise as part of a rebuilding or renovation exercise.

Why in God's name was it here? Whatever else it might be,

it clearly wasn't a repository for superannuated utilities bills and bank statements. She climbed past the screen and examined the safe more closely. It was the kind of object you might find in a large retail store. Somewhere to keep the day's cash takings.

She tried the handle, with no expectation that it would move. Sure enough, the safe was firmly locked, requiring both keys and a combination number to open. Not much else was likely to provide access, short of maybe a piledriver. So what was in there? It could be anything. Cash. Drugs. Arms. Perhaps all three. Certainly nothing that you'd expect to find in a domestic setting. Or, for that matter, in one of the Agency's safe houses. Which raised the question of what this place really was. And what Salter was up to.

She spent a few more minutes searching the area around the safe for any clues to its contents, but found nothing. But then, her eyes now accustomed to the darkness, she noticed something else. There were wires running alongside the safe, just below the bottom of the roof. In itself, there was nothing remarkable about that. The attic space was strewn with domestic wiring, grey cables snaking across the plasterboard, tacked to the rafters, powering the ceiling lights and electrical points in the rooms below.

But this was different – lighter than domestic wiring, with the air of having been hastily installed. It trailed back to some sort of unit in the far corner. It took her a few moments to work out what she was seeing. Covert recording equipment. Voice activated. One of the Agency's machines. So the question was even more pertinent.

What the fuck was Salter's game?

She was on the point of making her way back towards the entrance to the attic, when she heard a sound from outside.

A car.

She stepped rapidly back along the planks, wondering whether she would have time to make her descent into the hallway before Salter came through the door. She would rather keep Salter in the dark about her discoveries up here. Though, looking down at her dust-covered clothes, she had to admit that this was probably an optimistic goal.

In any case, the question was academic. Already, she could hear a murmur of voices from outside the front of the house. Salter was not alone. Whatever his game might be, it was becoming more convoluted by the minute.

Moving quickly, she leaned down to pull up the ladder and drag the trapdoor back into place. She had expected that the weight might be too much for her, but the counter-weighted design was as easy to operate from above as from below. Even so, she was only just in time. As the trapdoor clicked into place, she heard the fumbling of a key in the front door below.

She quietly straightened up and looked around. On her way into the loft, she'd noticed a small pile of rusting tools left, presumably forgotten, just inside the entrance. She flicked through them and selected an old screwdriver, its shaft rusting, its handle thick with dried paint.

She laid herself carefully down along the length of the planking, her face close to the ceiling boards. Then, as silently as she could, she used the screwdriver to bore a small hole in the plasterboard. She worked away at it for a few moments until it was large enough for her to gain a clear view of the hallway below.

Salter himself entered first, still talking to someone behind him. He sounded nervous, she thought, his voice a little too high, words a little too fast. Well, she knew how he felt. She was already wondering about options for escape. Would it be feasible to break out through the roof itself, push through the tiles? It would still leave her with the problem of how to reach the ground, but that shouldn't be impossible. Not ideal, but better than nothing, if it came to that.

As the second figure came into sight below, she caught her breath.

Kerridge. Jeff fucking Kerridge.

There was no question. She had seen that figure too often – the body running to fat, the greying slicked-back hair, the clothes slightly too expensive for the circles he usually mixed with.

So much for keeping her secure. So much for Professional Standards. So much for this sodding safe house. Her instinct had been right again. She'd walked straight into it. From frying pan to fucking fire, in one not-so-smart move.

Salter had snatched her from Boyle's clutches just to hand her straight over to Kerridge. Now she understood why Salter had been pumping her about what evidence Morton might have against Kerridge. They knew – or thought – she had something. Morton's 'insurance policy', as Salter had called it. They'd probably been afraid that if she'd ended up in the frame for Jones' death or even dead herself, the material might still leak out. So they wanted to get their hands on it. She'd given nothing away to Salter last night. Now they'd come to get the information out of her, no doubt using the same techniques that Boyle's people had used on Jake.

She'd kept her eye fixed on the hallway as the third figure entered. Welsby. So Salter had been telling the truth about that at least. Welsby really was on Kerridge's payroll. Salter had just omitted to mention that Welsby wasn't the only one.

She heard the three men move into the sitting room. Moving as silently as she could, she edged her body slowly forwards along the planks, until she judged that she was above them. Conscious of every creak in the wooden joists, she pressed her ear to the plasterboard ceiling, hoping to hear something of the conversation below.

Their voices carried clearly through the thin boarding, and apart from a few mumbled words, she had no difficulty following their discussion.

'Of course it was Boyle,' Salter was saying. 'Who else would it have been?'

'So how the fuck did he work out who she was?' Kerridge's voice was low and growling, the voice of someone used to getting his own way. She'd never seen this side of him. In his few dealings with her, he'd always displayed an old-fashioned courtesy that, she'd thought, was only just the right side of patronizing sexism. Outside of that, she'd seen him only in unctuous mode, glad-handing the great and good at business and charity events.

'How the hell would I know?' Salter said. 'Maybe he didn't. Maybe he just worked out that she was close to Morton. Maybe he's just flailing in the dark like we all are.'

'Bollocks. Boyle does nothing without thinking. If he thought Donovan was worth putting down, he must have had a good idea who she was.'

Marie felt a chill down her spine. Putting down. Like a fucking dog.

'Someone tipped Boyle off, then.' Welsby's voice.

'Well, what the fuck do you think? Boyle's smart, but he's not a fucking clairvoyant. How the hell else does he know that Donovan's one of yours?' There was silence for a few moments, then Kerridge went on. 'OK, tell your story again and let's see if it sounds any more convincing this time.'

This was clearly addressed to Salter. After another pause, Salter said, 'I don't know what you're trying to insinuate—'

'Oh, fuck off,' Kerridge said. His voice had dropped, and Marie could hardly made out the expletive. He sounded even more intimidating when speaking quietly. 'I'm not *insinuating*. I'm telling you to your fucking face that I don't fucking trust you. Little Boy Scout who's suddenly decided to join the bad guys. That clear enough?'

'Crystal,' Salter said. His voice was icy, but to Marie's ears he still sounded the most nervous of the three of them. Out of his depth, she thought. Well out of his depth. 'I just thought I was doing you a fucking favour.'

'Very generous of you. So tell me again.'

'I've been keeping tabs on her,' Salter said. 'Like we agreed.'

'You didn't tell us she'd been to see Jones.' Welsby's voice again. 'Not till after he was dead.'

'I didn't get the chance,' Salter said. 'I didn't think Jones was significant. I thought he was small fry.'

'He is fucking small fry,' Kerridge said. 'But he's small fry who works for Boyle.'

'Christ, I didn't know—'

'That's your trouble, Hugh. There's a lot you don't know. And you don't even know how much you don't know.' Welsby sounded dismissive, as though he was wearily trying to deal with a student who'd failed to live up to his initial promise.

'I don't know why I fucking bother, that's what I don't know,' Salter said. He was trying to match their aggression, Marie thought, but he succeeded only in sounding petulant. 'I'm not a fucking clairvoyant either, you know.'

'So you kept tabs on her after she slipped out of brother Blackwell's clutches,' Welsby said. 'Why didn't you tell us where she'd hidden herself away? Why wait till now?'

There was another pause. 'I don't know,' Salter said after a moment. 'Just being a bit too smart, like you say. Maybe I just felt a bit sorry for her. I thought I could get whatever she's got without things coming to this. I thought she'd trip up and I'd get it out of her. Then things moved a bit quicker than I expected.'

'Story of your life, Hugh,' Welsby said.

'Don't notice you doing all that much better. Don't notice you having much success in keeping a lid on all this,' Salter said. 'Don't notice you doing much at all. Seems to me that we could all be up shit creek if Boyle gets hold of this stuff and uses it against Kerridge.'

'We don't even know that there is any stuff.' Kerridge. 'Unless you've got your hands on something you've not told us about.'

'Not yet,' Salter admitted. 'But she's got it. Or knows where it is.'

'And you think Morrissey was after the same thing?'

'Sure of it. I stood there listening for a bit. She'd said she'd got something in her handbag. That could have been a bluff, though. She threw it at him. Tried to distract him.'

'Resourceful lady,' Kerridge said. 'Maybe you should have let Morrissey finish the job.'

'Then we'd be even deeper in the shit, wouldn't we? Wouldn't have had any way of getting hold of it.'

'Might have stayed buried,' Welsby pointed out.

'Not if Morrissey had found it. Anyway, Donovan's not stupid. She'd have made some insurance arrangement of her own. She's probably got someone lined up to release the material to the authorities if anything happened to her. That boyfriend of hers, for example.'

If *only*, Marie thought. She'd had no time to organize any backup arrangement. And, for that matter, no one to arrange it with. Even if things had been different, she wouldn't get Liam involved in something like this. Still, she was happy to let them carry on thinking it. She'd also noted what Salter had said about listening to her and Morrissey. So the lateness of his intervention hadn't been entirely accidental.

'Whichever, you went in like some fucking white knight and saved her neck. Hope she was suitably grateful.' Kerridge let out a salacious snort.

'Not grateful enough to hand over the fucking evidence, it seems,' Welsby said. 'So where is she?'

'Must be still in bed,' Salter said. 'I slipped her a couple of pills last night to give myself a chance to go through her stuff.'

'But you didn't find anything?' Kerridge.

'Not yet.'

'I'm ever the optimist,' Welsby said. 'I'd expected a bit better of you. Thought you were a smart lad. One of life's high-flyers even. Imagined you'd be a bit cleverer than this.'

'I don't—'

'You really must think we're a right pair of fuckwits, Hughie. That's what really disappoints me. I expected a bit more respect.' Marie could hear movement from the room below but couldn't work out what was happening. 'Where are they, lad? Where are the fucking microphones? Or is it cameras? Smile, Jeffrey, you're on candid sodding camera.'

'That's not—'

There was a crash.

'Stop fucking us about, lad. This crap about coming across. Doing us a favour. Bit late in the day to change sides, I'd say. We got you sussed, Hughie boy, well and truly sussed.'

There was more noise. The sound of a struggle. Something breaking. Whatever was happening, it was clear that Salter was getting the worst of it.

Short of breath, Welsby said, 'Don't you try it, son. Just don't you fucking try it.'

She could hear some response from Salter but the words were too muffled to make out. Then she heard Kerridge's voice, slightly softer than Welsby's. He sounded relaxed, untroubled.

'Take it easy, Keith. We need to think this through.'

'If you think I'm letting this bastard—'

'We'll deal with him. But we need to get some things straight first. Like who the bastard's working for.'

She heard another sound. The crunching, brutal sound of a boot hitting flesh. An agonized groan from Salter.

'So who is it, Hughie boy? For a bit I thought you were working for those buggers in Standards. That right, Hughie? Those bastards put you up to this?'

Another crunch. More muttered words from Salter. Jesus, she thought, this was almost worse than witnessing it. Her hands were clutched tight to the joists, her head pressed against the ceiling below. Her great fear was that, at any moment, the dust would get into her lungs and she'd explode in a fit of coughing.

'Yeah, and they've got us fucking surrounded. You know what, Hughie? I don't think I believe you. I don't think you're working for fucking Standards at all. Which, the way I see it, leaves only two possibilities.' There was the sound of another blow, another pained yelp from Salter. 'Christ, you're pathetic, Salter. Look at you. At least try to show a bit of dignity.' Welsby laughed. 'So which is it? Either you're on some frolic of your own, or you're working for our friend Peter Boyle. I wonder which you'd rather we believed. Interesting dilemma, that one, Hughie.'

Another blow, seemingly even harder than before. Another cry, shrill now. The sound of someone with not much more to offer.

'Not sure it matters all that much, Hughie. If you're working for Boyle, this should send him a clear enough message, I'd have thought. And if you're not – well, more fool you, boyo. Shouldn't go playing with the big boys.'

Another scream from Salter.

'OK, Keith, he's got the message.' Kerridge again. 'Let him stew for a minute. You reckon Donovan's even here?'

Marie tensed at her own name. She could hear no sound from Salter now.

'I doubt it,' Welsby said. 'Don't know whether our friend here's just lying through his teeth, or whether he's got Donovan tucked away somewhere else. Either way, he wouldn't just leave her here for us to find.' There was a pause and some exchange she couldn't make out. Then Welsby said, 'Yeah, yeah. I'll go check if it'll keep you happy.' More movement. The sound of Welsby tramping through the hall, her bedroom door opening. Some scuffling, more doors being opened. Welsby returning.

'Who'd have thought it? She's been here all right. Look at this.' She heard the sound of something being thrown clatteringly to the ground. Her handbag, she guessed. Her handbag with the data stick still in it. 'All right, Hughie boy. So if she's not here now, then where the fuck is she?'

She could hear Salter saying something, but could make out none of the words. Welsby's response was clear enough, though. 'Don't fuck with me, Hughie. I'm not a happy bunny as it is. You really don't want to antagonize me.' Another blow, louder this time, again the awful sound of a boot on flesh. 'Tit for tat, I'd say, if you really are working for Boyle. I saw what you bastards did to Morton. I've got no problem in doing the same to you. What goes around comes around. You got some bad karma, Hughie.' Another louder sound. Then something falling over.

Marie could sense that, whatever might be in store for Salter, it would be worse even than the kicking he'd received so far. He might be a duplicitous bastard – Christ, they were all duplicitous bastards – but he didn't deserve that. She thought back to Jake and what he must have been through. No human being deserved that.

'Now, if you tell us where Donovan is, we can get this sorted nice and gentle, just like my friend here would prefer,' Welsby went on. 'If you don't – well, then we'll just work on you till you do. Nice and slowly.'

Finally, she heard Salter's voice. 'I'm telling you, Welsby. I don't fucking know. If I knew I'd fucking tell you. She was here. I left her here . . .' His voice sounded cracked, as if they'd done something to his throat.

'And you left her the key to that door, did you?'

'The whole place was fucking secured. There's no way she could have got out. Have you checked . . .?'

'I've checked every inch of this sodding place,' Welsby said. 'She's not here.'

'But that's not . . .' Salter's words collapsed into an inco-herent gurgle as there was yet another crunch. Something harder than a boot this time, Marie thought.

'Where is she, Salter?'

'I don't . . .' That sound again, cutting his words short.

Marie had been hesitating. The smart move, she thought, would be just to lie low. Hang on until they'd finished with Salter, wait till they left, then just get out. Through the bloody roof if necessary. She told herself she owed Salter nothing. He'd lied to her, used her as a pawn in whatever game he'd been trying to play, even risked leaving her to die at Joe Morrissey's hands. She had no doubt that, if he had known where she was, he'd have betrayed her already.

But another thought had already struck her. Whatever they were planning to do with Salter, they wouldn't want any witnesses. They'd already worked out that Salter must have the place wired up with surveillance equipment. They'd assumed Salter was acting alone – it sounded as if his claim to be working for Professional Standards was just so much bullshit – so the equipment would be for recording rather than providing any live feed. But they wouldn't want to leave any possibility of evidence at the end of this. Which would mean they'd scour the house for any recording or intercept devices.

Which in turn would mean they'd find her.

She knew that, if it came to it, they'd treat her the same way they were treating Salter. Sentiment wouldn't count for very much in Welsby's world. And I thought he was a fucking father figure, she thought. The sort of father they wrote misery porn about.

There was another dull thud and a scream from below. Christ, she couldn't just stay here and allow this to happen. Allow them to complete their work on Salter, and then, in due course, start on her. It would suit them to leave Salter and her here, dead or close to death. They'd probably torch the place. Leave not much but a dealing house – this place must be one of Kerridge's after all, a fitting location for Salter's intended double-cross – and two charred corpses. When the corpses had been identified, they'd leave behind only the kind of mystery that doesn't demand much police time. She was already on the run, suspected of murder. Salter would be denounced as corrupt – maybe even as the suspected leaker. No one would know what had brought them up to this neck of the woods, or what their connections were with whoever had run this place, or even whether their deaths were accidental or deliberate. And no one would care. Whatever the story, they'd just be two bent coppers getting their desserts. Worth no one's time of day.

She looked around her for something she might use as a weapon. There was the screwdriver, which might do as a last resort, but the pile of old tools might yield something better. There were a couple of spanners, an old hammer, and, lying beyond the next joist, a rusting Stanley knife. That looked the most promising.

Her body was pressed flat against the planking, her left ear still resting on the ceiling. She reached out carefully to pick up the knife, which was just at the limit of her reach. *Gently now*, she thought, *gently*.

But as she stretched out for the knife, her body shifted slightly, her foot brushing softly against one of the joists behind her. She looked back but it was already too late. An old yoghurt pot, filled with rusting screws and nails, tottered momentarily on the edge of the joist and then tipped sideways, scattering its contents noisily across the ceiling.

Marie held her breath, realizing that the men below had fallen silent. A moment later, she heard Welsby's voice moving beneath her as he made his way into the hall.

'What the fuck . . .?' he was shouting eloquently. 'What the fuck was that?'

29

Marie could hear Welsby stomping through the hallway, his voice echoing around the small building. 'The lying bastard. She's here. She's fucking here.'

Following the sound of his voice, she shuffled on the planks, finding the tiny hole she'd drilled in the ceiling. She could see Welsby's figure framed below, his red face staring up at the ceiling. 'Donovan,' he said, his voice lower than before. 'You up there, girl? No point in hiding yourself away now. Why don't you come down and make it easy for both of us?'

Why did everyone want her to make it easy? She held her breath, perfectly motionless, but knew that it was too late. Welsby had no doubt now that she was up here. She couldn't imagine him dragging his own hefty bulk through the trapdoor, but he'd find a way. It was only a matter of time.

'Don't be smart,' he said, as if reading her mind. 'I'll tear this fucking place apart brick by brick if I have to. You can't get out.'

She was barely even thinking. She'd had enough of all this, that was the truth. Enough of the lying, the game-playing, the deceit. Enough of not knowing who were her friends and who were her enemies. Enough of being out here, on her own, too far from anyone who might care for her and anything that she might still count as home. Whatever happened, she didn't want to carry on this way. And she didn't want to end up caught like a rat in a trap.

Almost without knowing what she was doing, she lifted herself on to her haunches, hearing Welsby's footsteps beneath her. She waited until she was sure he was directly below her. Then she threw herself as hard as she could at the flimsy plasterboard ceiling, the rusting Stanley knife clutched firmly in her hand.

She didn't know quite what she expected to happen, or what the impact would be. In the event, it was better than she could have hoped.

She fell through the ceiling with an ear-splitting crash and a shattering of wood and plaster and dust. She saw Welsby's startled face staring up at her, heard his chopped-off expletive, and then she was on top of him, his bulk perfectly breaking her fall as he collapsed underneath her. She was winded, but, as far as she could tell, otherwise unhurt. She sprawled across Welsby's body, then rolled to her left, trying to regain her equilibrium.

Welsby lay motionless, stunned or worse. She pulled herself round on the floor as he uttered a groan, his eyes flickering.

She didn't, just at that moment, feel too inclined to worry about Welsby's state of health. She was more concerned for her own, conscious that at any moment Kerridge would emerge from the sitting room. She pulled herself forwards and jabbed the blade of the Stanley knife hard against Welsby's neck.

'Your turn, Keith. You try anything smart, and I'll slit your fucking throat. You think I wouldn't?'

Welsby grunted, his eyes still screwed shut. He'd winced slightly as she pressed the blade against his flesh, but otherwise gave no acknowledgement. He looked more than winded. The stark whiteness of his face, the beads of sweat on his brow, the sharp gasping of his breath, all suggested something more serious. Unless it was just play-acting.

She eased herself round, still holding the knife against Welsby's throat, until she was sitting upright. What now? She was still waiting for Kerridge to appear. Her only tactic was to use Welsby as a hostage, hope to keep Kerridge at bay long enough for her to – well, what? Try to get out through the now unlocked front door? How far would she get if Kerridge was determined to stop her? And in any case would Kerridge give a fuck about what happened to Welsby? As far as Kerridge was concerned, Welsby might be little more than another witness, better disposed of.

But she knew she had nothing else.

She was struggling to position herself ready for Kerridge when she heard a scuffling and a mutter of voices from beyond the sitting room door.

Then there was the sound of a gunshot, startlingly loud in the narrow confines of the bungalow. She was facing the doorway, still pressing the blade to Welsby's skin, as ready as she could be for whatever was happening, whatever was about to happen.

The door opened slowly. It was Salter standing there, his white face bruised and bloody, one arm hanging limp. He leaned against the doorframe, barely able to stay upright.

'Jesus, sis,' he said, his voice hardly more than a whisper. 'That was some entrance.'

'What happened?'

'Kerridge's dead.' He said the words matter-of-factly, but there was a blank look in his eyes. 'He had a gun on me. I was on the ground. Think he thought I was unconscious. But your floorshow created enough of a distraction for me to grab his foot and drag him over. He was trying to shoot me, but

335

I forced the gun back. Don't know what happened then, but it went off. Thank Christ it's his brains all over the wallpaper and not mine. Jesus.'

He sounds in shock, she thought. Not quite in touch with reality. Or was she projecting her own feelings? 'Are you OK?'

'Not really. That bastard gave me one hell of a kicking. But I'm not dead yet. How're you?'

'I'm OK, I think. Just getting my breath back.' She looked at the figure next to her. 'I don't know about Welsby, though.'

'I'll try to contain my grief. Just make sure the bastard isn't trying it on. I don't trust him any more than I could throw him. Which, given what a fat bugger he is, would be no distance at all.' Salter pushed himself away from the doorpost. 'Hang on.'

He disappeared back into the sitting room and emerged, a moment later, with a pistol in his hand. 'I'll keep the bastard covered. Here . . .' He tossed his mobile across to her. 'Call the police and an ambulance. Better call back to the ranch, too. They'll want some warning before this all breaks.'

She climbed slowly to her feet and looked at the phone. There was barely any signal. 'I'll have to phone from outside,' she said.

'Be quick. I don't want to give this fat bugger even a ghost of a chance.'

She pulled open the front door and stepped outside. It wasn't a bad day. The sun was peering between a scattering of white clouds. The air felt warmer than for some days. She could taste the sea salt in the air, even fancy she could hear the distant washing of the waves.

She dialled 999, identifying herself as an Agency officer and saying she had urgent need for police backup, an ambulance. Without going into details, she explained she'd been engaged on an operation, that another agent had been hurt and they needed help. The call handler might assume the call was a hoax, even though Marie had tried to give enough detail to authenticate it. But they'd come anyway, eventually.

Her mind was still churning. Something was nagging at her. The gun. Had Kerridge really been carrying a gun? It wasn't his style, she thought. From what she'd heard, he usually left that kind of thing to the juniors, though these were hardly normal circumstances. Maybe the gun had been Welsby's? If so, who'd trained it on Salter? She'd heard Salter being beaten, but no mention of a gun.

An uncomfortable thought had wormed its way into her brain and was refusing to leave. Was it possible that the gun was Salter's? That he'd had it concealed about his person and had used the commotion as an opportunity to shoot Kerridge? That his story about the gun going off accidentally was just bollocks.

Did it matter? However it had happened, if Salter hadn't acted, they'd both be toast by now. Why the hell should she care what might or might not have happened to Kerridge?

She dialled the number for Agency HQ and asked for the Director-General's office. She spoke briefly to his PA, a woman she'd met a few times and been impressed by. She was warm but efficient, with a remarkable capacity for taking everything in her stride. Now, she took in the gist of Marie's incoherent account and said she'd ensure the DG was informed immediately.

'We'll get someone straight on to it,' she said, in the tone of one dealing with a minor domestic crisis. Marie had no doubt that she would. Quite what that would mean was harder to predict.

She stepped back into the house, feeling a momentary anxiety that something might have happened in her brief absence. That

Welsby had been feigning. Or – and with a mild shock, she realized that this felt more likely – that Salter would have found a reason, real or concocted, to shoot Welsby as well.

But everything was as she'd left it. Salter was hanging on to the doorpost, the gun barrel trained unwaveringly on Welsby. Welsby himself was lying motionless, eyes still screwed shut. His leg was bent awkwardly. She found herself hoping that the bastard was suffering.

'Police and ambulance on their way. Spoke to the DG's secretary. She'll make sure the right people are informed.'

'Bet she will,' Salter said. He looked in nearly as much pain as Welsby. Marie held out her hand for the gun. He hesitated, as if unsure why she wanted it, then handed it over. She pointed it at Welsby, still fearing that this was not yet over.

'Sit down,' she said to Salter. 'You look all in.'

Gratefully, he lowered himself to the floor. He sat, his back propped against the doorpost, watching Welsby's motionless body.

'We need to get our stories straight, sis.'

'Do we?'

'Yeah. Wasn't quite true what I said about Professional Standards.'

'Really?'

He shook his head, wincing as if the movement caused him some pain. 'Been chasing this one on my own. Didn't know who to trust. Knew it went high, thought even Standards might have been compromised.'

'They're the incorruptibles,' she said. 'You know that.'

'Yeah, aren't we all? Still don't know who to trust. Don't know if Welsby was acting on his own, or if others were on the Kerridge payroll. But we've got enough now to convict Welsby, even if some of the surveillance stuff here's inadmissible.'

'You set this place up? I saw the wires upstairs.'

'Multi-talented, me. Last couple of days, I let Welsby know I'd sussed his relationship with Kerridge. I tried to persuade them that I was onside. Not exactly on the payroll, but prepared to help them deal with Boyle. Do them a few favours if they'd do a few for me. Thought I had them fooled. Seems I didn't.' His white face looked momentarily rueful, as if he'd been caught out in some technical error. 'This was Kerridge's place. Kerridge likes this neck of the woods. Bit more upmarket than the places he sells his shit to, convenient for the sea, inconspicuous. His people used to deal from up here. But lately they've just used it as an occasional hideaway or stash. Welsby suggested it when I said I was going after you yesterday. He gave me the keys so I could prepare the place – just had time to get the recorder up there. I thought I could get them to come here with you as bait.'

'Nice to be in people's thoughts,' she said.

'Yeah, well. It nearly worked.'

'And even more nearly got us both killed. So what story do we need to get straight? I was planning just to tell the truth. Thought it might make a change.'

'That's fine,' he said. 'Just don't want them to know I was following you. That I let you get away from Blackwell's clutches. Or that I knew where you were all the time the police were searching for you. That might be seen as bending the rules too far. Young Hodder helped me as well. Want to keep him out of it.'

'You're all heart. So what do I say?'

There was a moment's pause. 'I think you should say you'd called me yesterday to give yourself up. You wanted to do it discreetly, rather than just stepping into Blackwell's clutches, so you asked me to meet you at the hotel. I got there just as Morrissey was taking you away – against your will. Once I'd

339

dealt with Morrissey, we decided between us to try to lure Kerridge and Welsby out here, put this thing to bed once and for all. How does that sound?'

'Convoluted as hell, but then so's the truth. Your story puts me more on the side of the angels, too. Panicked and went on the run, but then was going to give myself up. Do the right thing.'

'That's what I thought,' Salter said. He was smiling, now, as if he'd just pulled some confidence trick that no one else had seen.

She looked away from him, uneasy. She had the sense that she'd just taken her own first step into the unknown, had walked over that line. Trivial enough in its own right. But impossible to step back from.

In the far distance, she could hear the sound of approaching sirens.

30

'How are you feeling?'

He was staring up at her, a look in his eyes she hadn't seen before. Something she couldn't quite read. 'Is that a real question? How do you think? I'm feeling like – what is it? – like shit.'

He was lying back in the hospital bed and, for the moment at least, he looked like a shadow of his old self. His left hand was shaking more than ever, she noticed.

'So what happened exactly?'

Liam shook his head. 'Don't know. I was in the studio. I'd been working a bit late. One of the new paintings. Couldn't get it quite right. Kept tweaking. Then realized – probably about nine – that I was feeling pretty awful. Went straight to bed.'

'I'd tried to phone you,' she said, conscious that it sounded as if she were trying to justify herself. 'Couldn't get an answer. Home or mobile.'

'I'd forgotten to charge the mobile. You didn't leave a message.' It wasn't a question.

'I didn't think. I just assumed I'd call you later.'

'Or I'd call you.' Which, they both knew, was more likely to be the truth.

'Yes. So what happened?'

'I didn't wake up, basically. Just slept round the clock. Woke up – I don't know – maybe thirty-six hours later. Feeling like death. They reckon I was badly dehydrated on top of everything else. Could barely move. In the end, I managed to phone Jean.' This was the old lady who lived in the house opposite. They'd given her a spare key some months before so she could water Liam's plants when the two of them were away. 'She came in, took one look at me and called an ambulance.'

'And here you are,' she said, looking around the small hospital ward. Most of the other patients were elderly, she noticed. Much older than Liam, certainly. 'So what do they reckon?'

'They reckon it's the illness,' he said. 'It's just one of the things it can do. The way they talk about it, there doesn't seem much that it can't do. But apparently it can just knock you out like that, especially if you've picked up some other bug alongside it.'

'But if you can shake off whatever that is, you can get back to normal?'

There was a moment's silence. 'That's the thing. They seem to think that it's probably knocked me down a step or two. Increased the decline.'

'But that can't happen overnight?'

'It can, apparently. Maybe not quite literally. But sometimes it happens unexpectedly quickly. It can go for years with nothing or not much, and then – wham.'

'What kind of wham?' she said. 'In your case, I mean.'

'Shit, I don't even know exactly. It's partly my mobility. I can still walk, but it's getting worse. I walk more than a few steps, I'm knackered. I try to walk too fast, I feel like I'm going to fall over. Christ, I do fall over . . .'

She could tell from his expression that this wasn't all of it, or even perhaps the worst of it. 'What else?'

'It's my brain,' he said. 'My mind. I feel like I'm in a fog. I can't think straight. Things that used to make sense don't any more.' He paused, frowning, as if he was trying to get his description exactly right. 'I don't remember things,' he said. 'I don't mean big things, important things. It's the small stuff. Things people said, things I did only a few minutes ago. I can be in the middle of something and not know why I'm doing it.'

'We're all like that,' she said. 'It's called getting older. You're just imagining it. I've see no signs of anything like that.'

'You've not been here,' he pointed out, and for once it sounded like something more than his usual reproach.

'But it doesn't affect your mind – your mental abilities. That's not the way it works.' She thought back to all the material they'd pored through when he'd first been diagnosed.

'It can,' he said. 'It does. In around 10 per cent of cases, it does exactly that.'

'Yes, but that's minor stuff,' she said. 'I remember reading about all that. Stumbling over your words. Being a bit forgetful. Jesus, like I say, that's me already.'

'That's usually the way it works,' he said. 'But they reckon that sometimes – rarely, but sometimes – it can be more. Sometimes it can be much more serious. It all depends on which parts of the brain have been affected. It's the luck of the draw. Fucking Russian roulette. But they're concerned about it. They're going to do tests. You know – what do they call them? Psychometrics.'

'If you can remember a word like psychometrics, you can't be doing too badly.' Her mind went back to Winsor, his batteries of psychological instruments, his relentless game-playing.

'It's not a joke, Marie.'

343

'No, I know it isn't. I'm not making light of it. It's just – well, it doesn't help just to look on the black side, does it? Not before we know there's anything to worry about.'

'I should just cheer up, then? That what you're saying? Jesus, Marie, you weren't here. You didn't see what happened.'

It sounded like a reproach now, she thought. And she couldn't argue with him. He was right. At the moment he'd really needed her, she hadn't been there. She hadn't even been able to come as soon as she'd known. It had taken her three or four days to get everything sorted. They hadn't allowed her to leave, to come back here. They'd wanted her on the spot, while they went through everything. Endlessly, repetitively, exhaustingly. After all, as they'd pointed out, she was still a suspect in a murder enquiry.

She'd been phoning Liam's mobile incessantly over those days, wondering where he was, but it was turned off. She'd left messages at the house, but there was no response. On top of all her own troubles, she'd been climbing the walls with worry about Liam – when push came to shove, her thoughts always went back to Liam. It was only on the fourth day, when they'd finally allowed her to return to her own flat, that she was able to dig out Jean's number and been able to phone the old woman.

'He was rushed into hospital,' Jean had said, in a voice that remained only just this side of condemnatory. She had always made it clear that she neither understood nor approved of the younger couple's long-distance relationship. 'You need to come down.'

Marie had had to clear it with the powers that be in the Agency. In the end, that hadn't proved too difficult, though the inevitable bureaucracy ensured that it wasn't a swift process. No one believed now that she was responsible for Jones' death. The evidence had only ever been circumstantial, and as she'd expected, wasn't supported by the forensics. They had DNA evidence linking Jones to Morton's death, with traces of Morton's blood found on Jones' clothing. The assumption was that Jones had had some secondary involvement in Morton's death, and that he'd been eliminated as a potential weak link in an otherwise highly professional killing.

The line they were now pursuing, largely at Salter's instigation, was that the whole sequence had been designed to remove potential witnesses against Boyle. Morton, as the key prosecution figure, had been killed directly. The murder of Jones and the attempted murder of Marie were attempts to tie up two remaining loose ends. If that was the intention, it hadn't worked perfectly, but it had worked well enough for Boyle's purposes. The exposure of Welsby's corruption and links to Kerridge had been the last straw. What little evidence they had was tainted, and the prosecution case had been dropped. Boyle was a free man, contemplating the possibility of suing for wrongful arrest.

And the worst thing, for Marie, was that she hadn't felt able to share any of this with Liam. The Agency hadn't managed to contact him about Marie's disappearance, just because he'd been in no state to answer the phone. They'd asked the local police to check up on him in case he'd absconded with Marie, but that had been overtaken by events.

So he knew nothing. When she'd discovered how serious things were, how much his condition had deteriorated in the short time since she'd last seen him, she decided that she couldn't burden him with everything she'd been through. She couldn't tell him about Jones, about her near arrest. About what had happened with Joe or at the bungalow. None of it.

'Jesus, Liam. I'm sorry I wasn't there. It's the job. You know that.'

'Yeah,' he said, turning away from her on the bed. 'Yeah, it's always the fucking job. But you could change the job, you know? We've been through this.'

They had, countless times. And that was another thing. She really could change the job. She had the perfect opportunity. She just didn't know what to do about it.

She was on back-room duties for the moment. They'd pulled her out of the field. They'd even offered her counselling, for all the good that that was likely to do. As she'd expected, the business had just been closed down – no warning, no reason given. Not even to Darren. She could imagine the poor little bugger turning up, day after day, wondering why the doors were locked, why the mail was piling up below the letterbox. Only gradually realizing that the place was finished, that she and Joe must have done a runner. They'd got an accountant sorting out the liquidation of the assets. She checked with him to make sure that Darren would at least get the pay that was owed to him, and she'd lobbied hard for him to be given a bit more besides. But she'd no confidence that it would happen. That wasn't the way bureaucracies worked.

So she was back at HQ, doing desk-based intelligence work. For the moment, she was living in what she was relearning to call home, commuting daily into the office in central London. It was a routine. It was calming. It meant she could be close to Liam while he was in hospital. But she knew that the job itself would drive her slowly crazy.

Nobody intended to keep her there, of course. It was a short-term measure, to allow her to regain her equilibrium. They'd want her in an operational role again before long. And that was the thing.

She'd been sitting at her desk that morning, working her way painstakingly through a pile of largely uninformative files, when she'd grown aware of someone standing a few feet away, watching her.

'How you doing, sis?'

'Not so bad, Hugh. Considering. You?'

She hadn't needed to ask. Salter was thriving. His star was definitely in the ascendant. There'd been a formal enquiry into the whole affair, in the light of Kerridge's shooting. But Salter had emerged as a hero – the man who'd single-handedly taken on corruption in the Agency and brought down a major villain in the process. Although Kerridge's wife had tried to kick up a stink about the circumstances of her husband's death, her lawyers could make nothing stick. Everyone had witnessed Salter's injuries, and once Marie had handed over the data stick, the emerging evidence against Kerridge was enough to torpedo any defence. Salter's position was further eased by the fact that, in vainly trying to save some portion of his own backside, Welsby had sought to shift as much blame as possible in Kerridge's direction. No one had challenged Salter's claim that he'd pursued Welsby solo because he hadn't known who else to trust, and Marie had confirmed Salter's version of what had happened over those last few days. All this just made Salter appear more heroic. He'd exposed the bad apple in their midst. Set things right. Because no one wanted to believe that Welsby might not be the only one.

'Yeah, I'm doing all right,' he said. 'You heard about Welsby?'

She shook her head. For all his wriggling, Welsby had been charged with corruption. Bail had been refused and he was being held in custody in Wakefield prison, pending his trial.

'They found him this morning.'

'Jesus.'

'Makes you wonder, doesn't it? Shouldn't happen in prison. Supposed to be on suicide watch. What do you reckon? They just turn a blind eye? Or is it more than that?'

'I don't know, Hugh,' she said coldly. 'Christ, you're a heartless bastard, aren't you?'

He shrugged. 'Didn't notice the fat bastard showing much compassion when he was kicking seven shades of shit out of me.' He paused. 'Just got what was coming, if you ask me.'

There was something about the way he said it that chilled her. It felt, just for a moment, like a threat.

She didn't trust him. She still didn't fucking trust him. She thought back to what Welsby had said in the bungalow, and realized that she didn't know the answer. She didn't know whether Salter was just a ruthless careerist bastard. Or whether there was something more than that.

He'd been the first to urge them to consider what Boyle had gained from Morton's and Jones' deaths. He argued that the case against Boyle shouldn't be dropped, that the CPS should try to gain them more time. He'd insisted that they could still succeed in building a case against Boyle. He'd stormed out in righteous anger when it was confirmed that the case was being dropped.

And the result was that the case was neatly passed into his hands. If you're so smart, they'd said in not quite so many words, you land Boyle.

And maybe that was the way he'd wanted it all along. Maybe he'd wanted to take control of the case. So that, over time, he could quietly bury it. She thought back to what Kerridge had said in the bungalow. Someone had told Boyle who she was. Not Welsby, obviously. So who else?

'Got some good news, sis,' he'd said that morning. There were times when he had the air of an overenthusiastic teenager. Someone not quite house-trained.

'That so, Hugh?'

'Got my promotion. Finally got my own section.'

'Chasing Boyle?'

He'd looked at her for a long time. A few seconds too long. 'Yeah, among other things. I've put in a good word for you.'

'For me?'

'Yeah, sis. Rate you highly. You've got real talent. Want you on board. Part of my team. You could work down here. Be close to that boyfriend of yours. What do you reckon?'

What did she reckon?

That was the question. Salter didn't trust her, that much was clear to her. He wanted to keep her close. For her part, the thought of working alongside Salter repulsed her. Whether or not he was bent, he was an odious bastard. But if he was bent, he was something else as well. If he really was bent, if he really was on Boyle's payroll, then that meant he was the one who'd betrayed Jake Morton. He was the one who, in the end, was responsible for Jake's death.

Shit. She knew then that she couldn't let this go. That she had to stick close to Salter. She had to finish this off.

She told herself that it was about justice. But she knew that, really, it was about revenge.

She told herself that it was about Liam. That, if she took this job, she could carry on living with Liam, looking after him, making sure he was all right. That was what she told herself.

But she knew that, really, it wasn't about Liam.

It was about Jake.

So now, here she sat, in this sterile, depressing ward, with Liam in front of her, his body surrounded by drips, monitoring equipment, piles of paperwork and dressings. Not knowing what the future held. Not knowing what she wanted. Not even knowing what was driving her. Trying to decide.

She reached out and took Liam's quivering hand and held it tightly for a moment. 'You're right,' she said finally. 'I can change the job. I can do that.'

Read on for an exclusive interview from a new star in the crime and thriller arena, Alex Walters

An Interview with Alex Walters

When did you start writing?
I've written fiction for as long as I can remember. I started writing mainly because I've always been an enthusiastic reader – of anything and everything. As a child, my parents thought it was a good thing for me to be reading anything at all – Enid Blyton, comics, science fiction, horror stories, the backs of cereal packets – just so long as I was reading. The result was that I developed a passion for books, and then tried to produce my own versions of the stuff that I most enjoyed. So, as a teenager, I used to fill notebooks with short stories in virtually every genre – all of them awful (I've been back and looked, but only once!). I read English at university, and always carried on writing mainly for my own pleasure, although I did have some non-fiction books and the odd story and poem published. I kept starting novels that never got beyond the first two or three chapters, partly because it took me a long while to find the stories that I really wanted to tell.

Where do you write? And what's your routine?
I have what I rather grandly call a study at the top of the house – a really nice airy room which on a good day (we get a few in Manchester) has the sun streaming in through the skylight. It's an ideal mix because I can see the blue skies and

the tops of the trees, but I can't see the glorious views of the Pennines properly unless I stand up, so most of the time I can avoid being distracted. I do most of my writing there, and I fit it in around the other work that I still do as a management consultant. I've discovered from experience that I'm not very productive at writing in the mornings, so I tend to deal with less interesting work then. But once I get into a rhythm, I tend to lose contact with the world around me and can work as late into the night as I need to.

I'm always slightly astonished by writers who still work in longhand – possibly because my own handwriting is so awful. I love writing on the computer because it means I can make changes as I go – changing wording or dialogue, or moving scenes around to accommodate new ideas or developments. Once I've got an outline plan in place, I tend to just start at the beginning and write till I reach the end of the first draft, but I'll also juggle the content as I go so that I can try to give the story the best shape.

The other advantage of writing on a computer is that I can do it more or less anywhere. I've discovered that, oddly, I can be very productive writing on trains (I spend far too much of my life commuting between Manchester and London), as long as I can shut out the rest of the world with my laptop and iPod. That seems to work well, though I've occasionally noticed other passengers peering worriedly over my shoulder as I tap out a murder scene . . .

What are the pros and cons of being a writer?
When it's going well, it's the best job in the world. And even when it's going badly, it's better than most other things. I really enjoy losing myself in the world I'm creating, and I particularly love it when that world and its characters start to take over. It's a strange but exhilarating feeling when the life that you're

creating starts to seem more real than the life outside. That means that you've got to be comfortable spending a good proportion of your day working on your own, living largely inside your own head. I've occasionally suspected that you have to be at least slightly mad to want to write, but I hope it's an entertaining form of madness.

And of course the writing doesn't always go well. Sometimes you just feel that a story or a scene isn't working, or that you've reached a dead-end or lost your way with the plot. That can be nerve-racking, particularly if you've already invested a lot of time and emotion in what you've produced – but so far, I'm relieved to say, it's generally come good in the end. Usually the dead-end turns out not to be that at all, but just a sign that it's time to change direction and that something even more interesting is waiting up ahead. The worst thing is that, when you hit those difficult patches, it's very difficult to put the work aside, so it ends up dominating your mind for days until it sorts itself out. I suspect I'm probably not the easiest person to live with at those times.

Which writers have inspired you?
Countless writers have inspired me in various different ways. I grew up in Eastwood in Nottinghamshire which is famously D H Lawrence's birthplace, and I went to the same primary and secondary schools that he did. So his work was an indirect inspiration in the sense that it proved that it was possible for someone from a very similar background to my own to become a writer.

As a teenager, my first inspiration was for science fiction – not so much because I wanted to write it myself, but because writers like Samuel R Delany and Philip K Dick showed me just what the imagination was capable of. I came to crime fiction at around the same time, managing somehow to get mildly addicted to both Agatha Christie and Raymond Chandler! I

355

remember also discovering 'literary' writers who happened to be terrific story-tellers, like Stevenson, Dickens and Wilkie Collins. That gradually led me to discover the wealth of great crime writing that's out there. My enthusiasm for crime fiction is now very diverse – including 'golden age' English writers like the extraordinary Margery Allingham, Americans like Donald Westlake and Ross Macdonald, the best British writers such as Reginald Hill and John Harvey, and newer writers like Jo Nesbo.

How important is a sense of place in your writing?
Very important. I almost always have a particular place in mind when I'm describing a scene, even when I might have fictional-ized it to suit my needs. My earlier books had exotic settings – even more exotic than Manchester – so I had to work hard to supplement my own direct experience with research to make sure I got the details right. It's been a pleasure writing about Manchester and its surroundings because I can use the books to explore places that I know and love (or, in a very few cases, know and dislike!). It's also brought home to me the remarkable diversity of the environment and landscape in the area – and I've only just begun to explore some of the more unexpected locations.

Do you spend a lot of time researching your novels?
One way or another, yes. But it's a very varied mixture of activities. My non-writing life as a consultant means that I end up working in countless different types of organizations, both in the UK and overseas, so I often gain very direct experience of how things work. As it happens, I've spent a large part of the last decade working in various parts of the criminal justice sector – police, prisons, probation – so that's given me a very solid grounding in the realities of that world (even where I've chosen to apply some fictional licence).

Beyond that, I'll go and talk to specific individuals about their particular fields of expertise and a lot of that will feed into the books, though often anonymously. And of course I spend a lot of time reading relevant background material and hunting about on the internet for information. One of the great advantages of the web as a research tool is that it's now possible to obtain fairly easily the kind of trivial information (what's the exact road layout in that particular part of the Lancashire coast?) that is irrelevant to most people, but is often critical to getting a fictional setting right.

Do your characters ever surprise you?
All the time. I tend to plot my books fairly carefully in outline, but leave a lot of space for the narrative to change direction or develop as I write. I find that the characters almost invariably take on a life of their own. Sometimes they just take off in a direction I didn't expect – in one of my earlier books, this happened very early on and unexpectedly took the whole plot with it . . . for the better, fortunately! Sometimes apparently minor characters become much more significant as the book proceeds – that happened with at least one character in *Trust No One*. Very often, too, I find that, although the character has taken me by surprise, in fact I've already been working towards the new development without knowing it. One of my books had a major twist part-way through. I hadn't planned the twist before reaching that chapter, but then I realized that I'd been unwittingly setting the scene for it for several chapters before. The subconscious mind is a strange thing – or at least mine is!

How much of your life and the people around you do you put into your books?
I'm always getting asked that, usually by nervous-looking friends. The truth is very little, at least directly. I've never

written a character consciously based on a real person. But of course in creating a character you're likely to draw on elements of people you know or have met. Quite often, I might have someone's physical appearance in mind, but combined with quite a different personality or character. Equally, because I spend a lot of time working in different organizations, my depictions of organizational politics or tensions – how bosses treat their teams, how people try to manipulate others or exercise control – are often loosely based on people or incidents that I've observed – though I'd never say where!

I should say that there's one specific aspect of *Trust No One* which does draw directly on my own life, and I hesitated for a long while before deciding to include it. My late wife, Christine, died tragically young as a result of multiple sclerosis, and I wanted to write about that – partly as a tribute to her courage and partly to help raise awareness of the impact of this illness. But I was concerned about the risk of trivializing the subject if it were to become just another plot-device. In the end, I just tried to write about it as openly and honestly as I could, drawing on our own experiences. No case of MS can be described as 'typical' because the effects of the illness are so varied, and Christine's symptoms were more extreme and aggressive than many. Liam's illness in the book isn't the same as hers, and his relationship with Marie is certainly very different from our marriage, but I hope that I've managed to convey some of the emotions – the fears, the anxieties, the uncertainties – that face those who are diagnosed with MS. Christine's love and support made it possible for me to write in the first place, and I hope that the book does some justice to her memory.

Killer Reads.com

The one-stop shop for the best in crime and thriller fiction

Be the first to get your hands on the **latest releases**, **exclusive interviews** and **sneak previews** from your favourite authors.

Browse the site and sign up to the newsletter for our pick of the **hottest** articles as well as a chance to **win** our monthly competition!

Writing so good it's criminal